THE
IRON
THORN

THE IRON THORN

CAITLIN KITTREDGE

Delacorte Press

Text copyright © 2011 by Caitlin Kittredge
Jacket art copyright © 2011 by Lara Jade
Illustrations copyright © 2011 by Robert Lazzaretti

Visit us on the Web! www.randomhouse.com/teens

Educators and librarians, for a variety of teaching tools, visit us at www.randomhouse.com/teachers

Library of Congress Cataloging-in-Publication Data
Kittredge, Caitlin.
The Iron Thorn / Caitlin Kittredge. — 1st ed.
p. cm.
Summary: In an alternate 1950s, mechanically gifted fifteen-year-old Aoife Grayson, whose family has a history of going mad at sixteen, must leave the totalitarian city of Lovecraft and venture into the world of magic to solve the mystery of her brother's disappearance and the mysteries surrounding her father and the Land of Thorn.
ISBN 978-0-385-73829-3 (hc) — ISBN 978-0-385-90720-0 (glb) — ISBN 978-0-375-89598-2 (ebook) [1. Fantasy.] I. Title.
PZ7.K67163lr 2011
[Fic]—dc22
2010000972

The text of this book is set in 11-point Berling.
Book design by Trish Parcell
Printed in the United States of America
10 9 8 7 6 5 4 3 2 1

First Edition

To Howard Phillips Lovecraft,
who first showed me that strange far place

The moon is dark,
and the gods dance in the night;
there is terror in the sky,
for upon the moon hath sunk an eclipse
foretold in no books of men.

—H. P. LOVECRAFT

Lovecraft

Nephilim Foundry

Boundary Bridge

Erebus River

The Rustworks

Nightfall Market

N

W

E

To Half - Moon Point

The Engineworks

Cristobel Charitable Asylum

Lovecraft Academy

Uptown

St. Oppenheimer's Cathedral

Banishment Square

Old Town

Ravenhouse

Derleth Street

South Lovecraft Station

Jitney Depot

GRAYSTONE

floor one

basement

Music Room

Boiler Room

Aether Pipes

Rear Parlor

Grayson's Portrait

Front Parlor

Formal Dining Room

Grand Foyer

Kitchen

Butler's Pantry

House Controls

Conservatory

Library

floor two

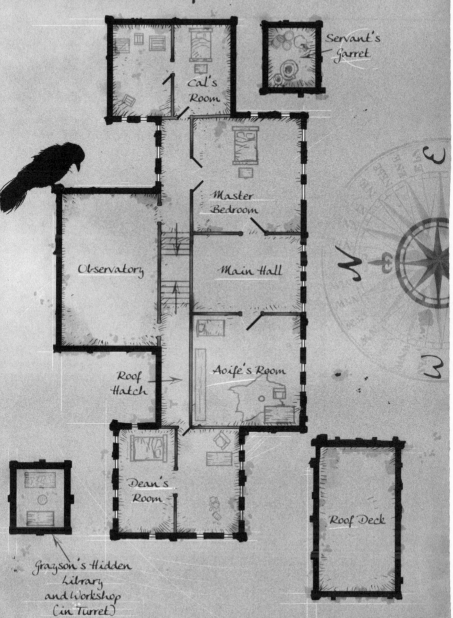

Servant's Garret

Cal's Room

Master Bedroom

Observatory

Main Hall

Roof Hatch

Aoife's Room

Dean's Room

Roof Deck

Grayson's Hidden Library and Workshop (in Turret)

The Ashes of the World

THERE ARE SEVENTEEN madhouses in the city of Love-craft. I've visited all of them.

My mother likes to tell me about her dreams when I visit. She sits in the window of the Cristobel Charitable Asylum and strokes the iron bars covering the glass like they are the strings of a harp. "I went to the lily field last night," she murmurs.

Her dreams are never dreams. They are always journeys, explorations, excavations of her mad mind, or, if her mood is bleak, ominous portents for me to heed.

The smooth brass gears of my chronometer churned past four-thirty and I put it back in my skirt pocket. Soon the asylum would close to visitors and I could go home. The dark came early in October. It's not safe for a girl to be out walking on her own, in Hallows' Eve weather.

I called it that, the sort of days when the sky was the same color as the smoke from the Nephilim Foundry across

1

the river, and you could taste winter on the back of your tongue.

When I didn't immediately reply, my mother picked up her hand mirror and threw it at my head. There was no glass in it—hadn't been for years, at least six madhouses ago. The doctors wrote it into her file, neat and spidery, after she tried to cut her wrists open with the pieces. *No mirrors. No glass. Patient is a danger to herself.*

"I'm talking to you!" she shouted. "You might not think it's important, but I went to the lily field! I saw the dead girls move their hands! Open eyes looking up! Up into the world that they so desperately desire!"

It's a real shame that my mother is mad. She could make a fortune writing sensational novels, those gothics with the cheap covers and breakable spines that Mrs. Fortune, my house marm at the Lovecraft Academy, eats up.

My stomach closed like a fist, but my voice came out soothing. I've had practice being soothing, calming. Too much practice. "Nerissa," I said, because that's her name and we never address each other as mother and daughter but always as Nerissa and Aoife. "I'm listening to you. But you're not making any sense." *Just like usual.* I left the last part off. She'd only find something else to throw.

I picked up the mirror and ran my thumb over the backing. It was silver, and it had been pretty, once. When I was a child I'd played at being beautiful while my mother sat by the window of Our Lady of Rationality, the first madhouse in my memory, run by Rationalist nuns. Their silent black-clad forms fluttered like specters outside my mother's cell while they prayed to the Master Builder, the epitome of human reason, for her recovery. All the medical science and

2

logic in the world couldn't cure my mother, but the nuns tried. And when they failed, she was sent on to another madhouse, where no one prayed for anything.

Nerissa gave a snort, ruffling the ragged fringe above her eyes. "Oh, am I? And what would you know of sense, miss? You and those ironmongers locked away in that dank school, the gears turning and turning to grind your bones . . ."

I stopped listening. Listen to my mother long enough and you started to believe her. And believing Nerissa broke my heart.

My thumb sank into the depression in the mirror frame, left where an unscrupulous orderly had pried out a ruby, or so my mother said. She accused everyone of everything, sooner or later. I'd been a nightjar, come to drink her blood and steal her life, a ghost, a torturer, a spy. When she turned her rage on me, I gathered my books and left, knowing that we wouldn't speak again for weeks. On the days when she talked about her dreams, the visits could stretch for hours.

"I went to the lily field . . . ," my mother whispered, pressing her forehead against the window bars. Her fingers slipped between them to leave ghost marks on the glass.

Time gone by, her dreams fascinated me. The lily field, the dark tower, the maidens fair. She told them over and over, in soft lyrical tones. No other mother told such fanciful bedtime stories. No other mother saw the lands beyond the living, the rational and the iron. Nerissa had been lost in dreams, in one fashion or another, my entire life.

Now each time I visited I hoped she'd wake up from her fog. And each time, I left disappointed. When I graduated from the Lovecraft Academy, I could be too busy to

3

see her at all, with my respectable job and respectable life. Until then, Nerissa needed someone to hear her dreams, and the duty fell to me. I felt the weight of being a dutiful daughter like a stone strapped to my legs.

I picked up my satchel and stood. "I'm going to go home." The air horn hadn't sounded the end of hours yet, but I could see the dark drawing in beyond the panes.

Nerissa was up, cat-quick, and wrapping her fingers around my wrist. Her hand was cold, like always, and her nightgown fluttered around her skin-and-bones body. I had always been taller, sturdier than my slight mother. I'd say I took after my father, if I'd ever met him.

"Don't leave me here," Nerissa hissed. "Don't leave me to look into their eyes alone. The dead girls will dance, Aoife, dance on the ashes of the world. . . ."

She held my wrist, and my gaze, for the longest of breaths. I felt cold creep in around the windowpanes, tickle my exposed skin, run fingers up my spine. A sharp rap came from outside the doors, and we both started. "I know you're not making trouble for your lovely daughter, Nerissa," said Dr. Portnoy, the psychiatrist who had my mother's care.

"No trouble," I said, stepping away from Nerissa. I didn't like doctors, didn't like their hard eyes that dissected a person like my mother, but listening to Portnoy was preferable to listening to my mother shout. I was relieved he'd appeared when he had.

Nerissa's eyes flickered between me and Portnoy when he stepped into the room. Anxious eyes, filled with animal cleverness. Portnoy patted the breast pocket of his white coat, the silver loop-the-loop of a syringe poking out.

4

"I'll kiss you goodbye," my mother whispered, as if it were our secret, and then she grabbed me in a stiff hug. "See, Doctor?" she shouted. "Just a mother's love." She gave a loud laugh, a crow sound, as if it were a colossal joke to be a mother in the first place, and then she backed away from me and sat in the window again, watching the dusk fade to nighttime. I turned my back. I couldn't stand seeing her for another moment.

"I'm very concerned about your mother," Dr. Portnoy said. He'd walked me to the end of the ward and had the mountain of an orderly open the folding security gate. "Her delusions are becoming more pronounced. You know if she continues this behavior we'll have to move her to a secure ward. I can't risk her infecting the other, trustworthy patients if her madness worsens."

I flinched. My mother was undeniably mad, but a secure ward? That meant a windowless room and a bed with straps. The contents of the syringe in Portnoy's pocket. No visitors.

"Now, I know you're a ward of the city," Portnoy continued. "But she's still your mother, and you have a better chance of connecting with her than I. You must impress upon her the urgency of her situation, the need for improvement in her diagnosis."

I put my hand on the big front door of the madhouse. I could feel the cold air seeping in around the cracks. "Dr. Portnoy." I felt the stone again, dragging me back, back to my mother no matter how I struggled. "Nerissa doesn't listen to anyone, least of all me. She's been crazy my entire life."

5

"The preferred term is 'virally decimated,'" he scolded me with a smile. "Those poor souls who lose their mind to the necrovirus can't help it, you know. No one would choose to have viral spores eat her mind away until only delusion is left."

I did know. Too well. Before the necrovirus had appeared and begun its spread across the globe, seventy years before Nerissa was even born, I supposed the mad occasionally got better. But never in my lifetime. Never my mother.

Done talking, I pushed open the door, letting in the roar of Derleth Street at the foot of the granite steps and the smell of cooking from the diner across the sea of jitneys and foot traffic. Steam wafted from exhaust pipes in the pavement and the vents of wheeled vendors' carts alike, making a low mist that hung over the asylum like a cloud of ill omen. Far away, just a whisper under my feet, I could feel the din of the Lovecraft Engine as the great gears in the heart of the city turned and turned. Trapped aether powered the machine that gave the city steam and life.

Portnoy waited for an answer like an unpleasant professor in a class I was already failing. I sighed in defeat. "However you call it, she's mad and I can't help you, Dr. Portnoy."

I stepped out the door, and he caught me. His grip was hard, but not desperate, not like Nerissa's. This grip was hard like the grasp of a foundry automaton lifting a load of new iron. "Miss Grayson, you have a birthday coming up."

I swallowed the millstone in my throat. Panic. "Yes."

"And how are you feeling? Any dreams? Any physical symptoms?"

6

His grip tensed as I did, and I couldn't get away. "No."

Portnoy frowned at me and I looked at my shoes. If he couldn't see my eyes, he couldn't see the lie therein.

At last, Portnoy said, "I suggest you think about your mother's final disposition before your birthday, Aoife. Make arrangements with the city while you are able. It can go badly for charity patients with no one to care for them. Cristobel is an experimentation facility, you know."

Experimentation, a glorious word to most of the students I studied engineering with, sent a spike of nausea straight into my stomach. It didn't mean the sacred tradition of hypothesis, theory and proof here. It meant electricity. Locked rooms. Water tanks and halogen lights. Portnoy didn't fool me—he wanted to be the one to cure viral madness, to find the golden key where all before him had failed. I'd seen some of the creatures he wheeled through the halls. Twitching limbs, shaved heads, empty eyes. Experiments.

My mother tethered me to her madness, but no matter how much I wanted escape, I didn't want it to happen like that.

The bells on St. Oppenheimer's cathedral started tolling five, and I pulled my arm out of Portnoy's grasp. He looked at me, the steam from the outside world fogging the lenses of his spectacles. "I have to go," I said, and tried to still my hammering heart.

"A pleasant evening to you then, Miss Grayson," he said. The sentiment didn't reach his eyes. Portnoy slammed the door behind me with a final bang, a tomb sound. All of the madhouses had the same heavy doors, the kind that let you know they always kept a piece of you, even when you could leave.

7

As I walked, I wrapped my school scarf around my face to keep the cold air out of my lungs. Leaving the madhouse always felt like a temporary stay of execution. I'd just have to go back next week, assuming my mother hadn't lost her visitor privileges again. I hurried, letting the cold burn the torrent of anger and panic out of me, calm me, turn me back into an anonymous girl rushing to catch the jitney. The White Line, back to the Academy and the School of Engines, was three blocks away, on the corner of Derleth and Oakwood, and it only ran once an hour after five bells.

I arrived at the corner just as the jitney pulled away in a roar of gears and a dragon belch of steam. Cursing, I kicked the pavement. A passing pair of Star Sisters glared at me and made the sign of the eye, two fingers to their foreheads. I looked away. The Star Sisters and their Great Old Ones could curse me all they liked—it wouldn't supersede the curse that was already ticking time down in my blood.

I put my scarf up over my head and walked on, since there was nothing to do but walk until I caught up to a jitney that would take me back to Uptown. Dr. Portnoy's words turned in my mind, mingling with Nerissa's dreams. My head hurt, steadily throbbing in time with my heart, and I still had studying to do, an exam in the morning. My day wasn't likely to improve.

When I'd gone a few blocks, my mood worsening with each step, I heard a voice yelling to me from across the traffic stream.

"Aoife? Aoife! Wait!"

A nimble figure darted in front of a pedal jitney pulling a roast-nut cart, and the driver shouted something in

8

German. I'd taken enough courses to know it wasn't the least bit polite, but Calvin Daulton hadn't.

"Made it to you!" he panted, pulling up beside me, his cheeks twin combustions of red in the cold. "Almost didn't. Saw you walking by."

"Why are you all the way in Old Town?" I said, surprise coloring my question. Cal hefted a sack from the stationer's store across the way.

"Nibs and ink. Only store in the city that carries a decent india ink. We've got a schematic due tomorrow—or did you forget again?"

"Of course not. Mine's already finished." Only a small lie. Not like my lie to Dr. Portnoy about my dreams. The sketches for my schematic were finished, but the transcription to good paper, the writing in of technical specifications, the math—all of that was waiting for me back at the girls' dormitory. That bit, I'd forgotten about. Nerissa ate up my thoughts the way the Great Old Ones were said to devour suns on their journey through the spheres.

"Course it is," Cal said, catching his breath. "You missed the jitney too, huh?"

"Only by a little," I said, feeling furious all over again. If Portnoy hadn't kept me in the madhouse . . .

"I guess it's leftovers for us," Cal sighed. Even though Cal was the rough size and shape of a pipe-cleaner boy, he ate like a barbarian at a feast. He'd been my friend since the first day of our time at the Academy, and if he wasn't thinking about comic books or asking me for advice on getting my roommate, Cecelia, to notice him, Cal was thinking about food. Leftovers was a tragedy of the same order as being expelled from the School of Engines and

9

having to transfer to the School of Dramatics. Me, I couldn't care less tonight. My stomach was still in knots.

We were at the foot of Derleth Street, the wide blood-rust expanse of the Erebus River boiling with slow-moving ice before us. To one side lay the river walk, lit up ghost-blue by aether lanterns and packed with late-evening tourists and shoppers. The arcade whistled enticingly, the penny prizes a temptation that I could feel pulling at Cal.

On the other side crouched Dunwich Lane, a completely unlit expanse of cobble street, except for the old-fashioned oil lantern hanging in front of a pub called the Jack & Crow.

Dunwich Lane ran under the feet of the Boundary Bridge, the iron marvel that Joseph Strauss had erected for the city some thirty years before. Cal and I—along with the rest of the sophomore class—had taken a field trip to it at the beginning of the year. It was the model we practiced drawing schematics with, until we were judged competent to design our own. If you couldn't re-create the Boundary Bridge, you had a visit with the Head of the School and a gentle suggestion that perhaps your future was not that of an engineer. There had been three other girls in the School until that exam. Now there was only me.

The bridge looked much different from below, crouched over the river like a beast at rest, its iron lattice black against the dusk. I plucked at Cal's arm. "Come on."

He looked blank. "Come on where?"

I started down Dunwich Lane, the cobbles slick under my feet from the frost. Cal bounded after me. "Are you crazy? Students can't be down here—all of Old Town is off-limits. Mrs. Fortune and Mr. Hesse will have our hides."

10

"And who's going to tell either of them?" I said. "This is the quickest way back to the Academy on foot. There's nothing to be worried about if we're together." I didn't know that for fact. I'd never walked through Old Town after dark. Students, especially charity cases, couldn't afford to bend the rules of the Academy, and like Cal said, Old Town, night or day, was not a place where a nice girl went. Not if she wanted to stay nice.

Still, we were in a city, far from necrovirus outbreaks and the heretics that Rationalists preached against. No storefront fortune-tellers or charlatan witches, or the "virally decimated," were going to leap out and attack us.

At least, I really hoped not.

Cal waffled, looking back at the bright glow of the aether lamps and the arcade.

"Leftovers," I reminded him. That did it—Cal caught up with me and stuck his chest out, shoving his hands deep into the pockets of his buffalo plaid coat like some tough in a comic book.

We walked for a bit, the sounds of Derleth Street fading and new ones creeping in. The faint music from the Jack & Crow. The drip of moisture from the roadbed of the bridge above. The rumble of lorries crossing the span to and from the foundry with their loads of iron.

"This isn't so bad," Cal said, too boldly, too loudly. We passed boarded-up row houses, their windows all broken, diamond panes like insect eyes. Alleys that wound at head-turning angles to nowhere. I felt the damp of the river, and shivered.

No student of the Schools was allowed to come to Dunwich Lane. I'd always thought it was to keep the boys

11

away from the prostitutes and poppy dens that we weren't supposed to know about, but now I wondered if I'd been wrong. The cold worsened. My exposed skin was so chilled it felt crystalline.

"Say," Cal said, making me jump. "Did you listen in to *The Inexplicables* on the aether tubes last night? Really good this week. 'Adventure of the Black Claw.'"

I clenched my fists and resolved that I'd be braver from now on. Dunwich Lane was poor and seedy, but it wasn't going to sneak up on me. "Didn't catch it. I was studying." The only time it was acceptable for us to hear about the way the world used to be—before the virus spread, before the Consortium of Nations built Engines after the first great war, before any of the curfews and government police in every city—was when it was being mocked by cheap, state-sanctioned tube plays.

Cal ate them up. I rather hated them.

"You do too much of that. Studying," Cal said. "You're going to need glasses before long, and you know what they say: boys don't make passes—"

"Cal . . ." I stopped, irritated, in the center of the street. I was all set to lecture him when a scream echoed out of an alley between the next pair of houses. ". . . shut your piehole," I finished.

Cal's mouth twisted down and he froze next to me. We stood in the road, waiting. The scream came again, along with soft sobs. I had a memory, unwanted, of the Cristobel madhouse and the madhouse before that, the ever-present crying on the wards. If my fingers hadn't been balled up, they'd have been shaking like dead leaves.

Cal started forward. "We should go help."

12

"Wait," I said, pulling at his coat. "Just wait." I didn't want to walk ahead, and I sure didn't want Cal leaving me here alone. Why had I taken the shortcut? Why had I tried to be clever?

The sobbing escalated, and Cal jerked his arm out of my grasp, running forward and making a hard turn into the alley. "I'm going to help her!" he yelled at me before he disappeared around the corner.

"Dammit," I swore, because no professors were around to stick a detention hour on me for cursing. "Cal! Cal, don't go down there!"

I followed him into the alley, his straw-colored hair bobbing in the dark like a swamp light. "Cal," I whispered, not out of discretion but purely out of fear. I'm not a boy. I admit when I'm scared, and the screams had done it to me. "It might not be what you think." If Cal got himself hurt, and it was my fault . . . I hurried after him.

From the entrance of the alley, I could spy a pile of rags, a hunched hobo's form in oilskins and overalls. The smell of decay permeated everything, sweet like a rotted flower is sweet. Cal had plowed to a stop, confused.

"That stinks."

I watched as the nightjar lifted its head from its feast of the transient, the few scraps of hair still clinging to its skull fine as cobwebs. My throat constricted, sweet bile creeping onto the back of my tongue. I'd never seen a nightjar up close. Never *smelled* one. It was worse than any warning our professors could give.

"Oh, please help me," it said in a human girl's voice. "I'm so cold . . . so very alone. . . ." It drew back swollen black lips to reveal its set of four fangs.

13

"Oh, shit," Cal said plainly.

The nightjar stirred the rest of its body, pale leathery limbs fighting to free themselves from its camouflage skin. The hobo's clothing and the remains of the man himself slithered away in a heap, and the nightjar expanded desiccated arms with tattered wings growing on the underside. "Come to me," it pleaded, still in that plaintive, soft voice. "Just one kiss, that's all I need."

Staring at the thing was hypnotic, like looking at a study corpse in the School of Hospice, and its smell overpowered me; the voice that drifted to Cal and me was as lulling as a caress on the cheek, or the scent of poppy that caught the wind in the summer, when the air came from Old Town. Cal took a shuffling step forward, reaching out one hand. He and the nightjar were mere feet apart. "Don't . . . ," Cal whispered.

That snapped me awake. The thought of the thing touching Cal, that foul black-nailed hand with its water-logged dead skin on Cal's face, passing the necrovirus into his blood with the contact, so that slowly, day by day, he'd turn to a nightjar as well, made my stomach turn violently and brought me back to the wintry night, in the alley, not the floating summer place the nightjar's voice had shown me.

I plunged a hand into my satchel. There were safety guidelines, drills. The Academy projectionist had shown us a lanternreel about this. *The Necrovirus and You!* How to understand transmission, infection, and lastly, how to deal with a person who was beyond help.

I'd been bored as I always was during those presenta-

14

tions. Everything useful, if there had been anything useful, had flown from my head at the sight of the thing's frozen-pond eyes and rotted skin.

I tried to think. Nightjars hated iron filings. Unfortunately, I didn't generally make a point to carry a handful of those in my bag, next to my lipstick and hairbrush. That strategy was out.

Light. Nightjars hated light, their skin photosensitized by the virus. My scrabbling fingers found my portable aether tube, filled with the blue marvel of Mr. Edison's gas, charged only enough to listen to scratchy music or receive the latest reports on protest activity so I could avoid spots where the Proctors were tangling with rioters in the city. It couldn't even pick up the serial plays Cal loved from the big antennae in New Amsterdam. But it would be enough, I hoped.

"Cal," I said sharply. "You better move." He blinked, but he did as I said. I cocked my arm and threw the aether tube straight at the pavement. The brass housing flew apart and the electric coil sparked. The tube itself exploded, shards of treated glass flying everywhere as the gas inside struggled to escape. I'd watched aether reactions before on lantern-reels, huge ones that the government detonated in the desert, but this close, even a small wisp of gas was like a bomb. "Cover your eyes!" I cried, and threw myself against the alley wall.

The aether let out a *whump* when it made contact with the oxygen in the air and blue flame blossomed, glowing like a lightning strike for a few seconds before the reaction gasped away, leaving the scent of burnt paper.

15

The nightjar began to scream. It wasn't anything like the bell-tone voice from before. This was harsh, guttural and hungry.

Cal got me up, tugged me by the hand. "We should go now." I clung to his bony fingers and let him pull me away. My feet refused to work, my knees wouldn't bend, but somehow I ran.

I looked back once to see the nightjar writhing on the ground, great swaths of skin flaking off into the air as the last bits of the aether danced above it on the breeze.

I didn't need to see any more. I caught up with Cal, and we ran for the Academy.

2

The School of Engines

We reached the head of Dunwich Lane and turned onto Storm Avenue before I realized I was still shaking. The gates of the Academy weren't far, but I stopped and leaned against a lamppost.

Cal tilted his head. "Aoife, you hurt?" He fumbled in his satchel. "I've got my first-aid kit somewhere in here . . . had a valve-fitting lab earlier today."

"I . . . I . . ." I wrapped my arms around myself, even though I had on a peacoat and my uniform jumper beneath it. I was freezing. It felt like death had put a hand on my cheek, put the chill inside me down to my bones, even though the Rationalists taught there was no death, only an end. A period on a sentence, and a blank page.

"I just want to go inside," I said, unable to take Cal's anxious expression. Cal was an advanced worrywart. In the two years I'd known him, he never got any less skittish.

"All right," Cal said. He offered his elbow and I took

17

it, just grateful to hide my shaking legs. I'd never seen a viral creature so close. Madwomen like my mother were one thing, merely infected. A thing fully mutated by the necrovirus from a person with a consciousness and a face into an inhuman nightjar was quite another. The smell of it lingered, like I'd fallen asleep in a nightmare garden.

The gates of the Academy loomed up from the low river fog, and we passed underneath the gear and the rule, the insignia of the Master Builder. The ever-present sign that watched us everywhere, from the stonework of our dormitories and the badges on our uniforms to the arch of the Rationalist chapel at the edge of the grounds. The sign of reason, a ward against the necrovirus and the heretics, that all rational citizens of Lovecraft who followed the Master Builder's tenets adhered to.

Cal looked at the dining hall, still lit, and sighed. "I guess it's useless to try and pretend we're just late."

Mrs. Fortune proved him right by flying out the hall's double doors, her long wool skirt and cape flapping behind her. "Aoife! Aoife Grayson, where on Galileo's round earth have you been?"

Mr. Hesse was hard on her heels. "Daulton, front and center. You know you're past curfew." Mr. Hesse was as sharp as Mrs. Fortune was round, and they stood like an odd couple in the lights of the dining hall.

"Aoife, you're filthy and you stink like a whore's perfume," Mrs. Fortune said. I was still chilled but I felt my cheeks heat in humiliation—and in relief that she hadn't pried at me further. "Go to your room and wash up," she continued. "You'll get no supper as punishment."

No supper might as well have been a warm embrace. If

18

Mrs. Fortune found out I'd been in Old Town and had contact with a viral creature, I could be expelled.

Mr. Hesse cleared his throat loudly, and Fortune favored him with a raised eyebrow. Mrs. Fortune had climbed mountains and trekked Africa as a girl, before she'd landed here. Few crossed her. "What is it, Herbert?" she demanded. I waited. Hesse was notorious for handing out canings and detentions. He was also far more suspicious that we were all misbehaving at all times than Mrs. Fortune. I drew a breath, held it.

"Well?" Mrs. Fortune asked him.

"The girl was wandering the city after six bells, doing stone knows what, and you're merely withholding a meal?" Hesse said. To punctuate his opinion of my punishment he snapped, "Daulton, the quadrangle. Now. Stand at attention until I come for you." Standing in formation on the quad didn't seem unpleasant, on the surface, until you'd be standing at attention, perfectly still, for hours in the cold. Marcos Langostrian had lost a small toe last year from frostbite after he'd been outside all night. He'd deserved it, the little worm, but I felt a pang for Cal as Mr. Hesse glared at him.

Cal heaved a sigh. "See you tomorrow, Aoife. And thank you for . . . er . . . before. You're pretty great." He set off at a jog for the quad. Hesse peered at me through his glasses. The thick Bakelite frames were too big for his face and made him look even mousier.

"What was he thanking *you* for, Grayson? Did you lift your skirt for him on the way home? I know you city wards and how you operate, especially the ones with mothers in a—"

"*Mister* Hesse," Mrs. Fortune said in a voice that could have stripped gears. "Thank you for your assistance. Aoife,

19

go on to your room. Don't you and the unfortunate Mr. Daulton have an exam tomorrow?"

"Yes," I said, glad it was mostly dark and Hesse couldn't see that he'd made me turn colors. I'd learned a long time ago that shouting and fighting over my mother or my reputation just made things worse, and talking sass to a Head of House, well . . . it didn't bear thinking about after the trouble I was already in.

It didn't mean that the thought didn't spring to mind, to wipe Mr. Hesse's superior smirk from his mouth. He thought he knew me. The entire Academy thought they had the blueprint of Aoife Grayson, city ward and madwoman's daughter.

They didn't know a thing.

"Off you go, then. You've been dismissed." Fortune made a shooing motion with her hands. I trudged to the girls' dormitory, mounting the four flights of stairs to the second-year floor, tucked beneath the garrets of the old place. The Lovecraft Academy of Arts and Engines was built from several stately homes and their assorted outbuildings, and the girl's dorm had been a stable. In the summer you could still smell hay and horses up under the eaves. It reminded me of a ghost, a tiny connection to a past that had no necrovirus, no madhouses and no Aoife Grayson, charity student.

My small desk, with its whirlwind of blueprint paper, engineering textbooks and class notes, should have been my destination, but instead I curled up on my bed. Studying wasn't something that would happen tonight, not after what had transpired with my mother, and with Cal. The iron bedsprings groaned, but I ignored them and rolled on my side, facing the low wall where the ceiling joined. My

20

roommate, Cecelia, was at choir practice for the Hallows' Eve recital, and aside from the gentle hiss of the aether lamp I was alone.

I wadded up my jacket and tossed it into the far corner, trying to erase the smell of Dunwich Lane, and then I got out a pencil and an exercise book from under my pillow and started doing math problems for Structural Engineering. Far from busywork, numbers are solid and steady. Numbers keep the mind orderly. An orderly mind can't fall into madness, become consumed by its dreams, get sick on the fantastic and improbable nations that only the mad can visit.

At least, I'd been telling myself that since my mother was committed. Since I was eight years old. Eight years is a long time to lie, even to yourself.

Interrupted by a scratching at the door, I snapped my head up. The chronometer on my desk, with its whirring gears and swinging weights, read half-nine. I'd fallen into a fugue over the page. "Celia, did you forget your key again?" I called. Cecelia was famous for losing everything from sheet music to hairpins.

Instead of an answer, the mellowed corner of a vellum envelope appeared under the door, and a quick clattering of feet ran away down the corridor. I plucked up the letter, saw the address in proper square handwriting:

Miss Aoife Grayson, School of Engines,
Lovecraft, Massachusetts

The envelope was charred at one edge, smeared and shiny with dirt, the ink blotted like a bloodstain. It looked like something that had come a long way.

21

My heart froze. I ripped the door open and looked out into the corridor, my blood roaring.

There was no one. Dusty and dim as always, the dormitory was silent save for snatches of a variety show coming from down the hall. The studio audience laughed over the aether when the host asked, "What's the difference between a nightjar and my girlfriend?"

Just as quickly, I shut the door and bolted it behind me. The letter lay on the bed, poisonous as a widow spider. The handwriting was as unmistakable as it was unremarkable.

Before I could open the envelope, the door rattled again. "Aoife? Aoife, open this door at once."

Mrs. Fortune. Of all the rotten times. I shoved the letter under my pillow. Mrs. Fortune was as kind and understanding as any house head could be, but seeing that letter would stretch even her goodwill.

"Aoife!" The bolt rattled again. "If you're smoking cigarettes or drinking liquor in there . . ."

I quickly shed my school tie, undid a few collar buttons and turned the taps in the corner sink on full. I didn't need to muss my hair—the dark unruly strands stood out and frizzed up on their own. I unbolted the door. "I'm sorry, Mrs. Fortune. I was washing up."

Her face relaxed, and she stepped inside. "That's all right, dear. I'll keep this brief. I was going to tell you at supper, but . . ."

I lowered my head and hoped I looked appropriately guilty. Really, I was just praying *Don't look at the bed.*

"Aoife, there's no easy way to tell you this," Mrs. Fortune said, crossing her broad arms under her equally broad bosom. "The Headmaster requires your presence on Tuesday, after supper, for a meeting about your future here."

I kept my expression blank, though inside everything lurched. If you want a course on keeping your face composed, become a city ward and go through a few strict homes where the nuns smack your hand or mouth for the slightest snicker or frown. "I don't understand," I said, though I did. I was keeping up the order, the routine and sameness that kept truth at bay. Mostly. Not now, with the letter burning a hole in my mattress.

"Aoife, you're not unintelligent," said Mrs. Fortune. "For a girl to be accepted into the School of Engines at all is a feat. Don't disgrace yourself by playing dumb."

"I don't understand," I repeated, softly and innocently. My voice broke and I hated myself for it. "My birthday isn't for another month."

"Yes, and on that day, if we are to look at things historically, certain . . . events may occur," said Mrs. Fortune. "Your mother began to show signs at sixteen, although sadly I understand we don't know when or how she was exposed. Your family carries a latent infection, this has been proven by her doctors. The Headmaster needs to prepare you with certain truths. That's all." Her big face was flushed, red from neck to hair, and she swayed from one side to the other in her hiking boots, like we were on the deck of a ship.

I stayed quiet and listened to my breath hiss in and out through my nostrils. Proven my behind. There was no reliable test for the necrovirus—half the time someone was committed because someone else didn't like their look.

23

That much, I *had* learned from Dr. Portnoy and my dealings with the asylum.

Mrs. Fortune clucked when I was quiet. "Do you have anything to say for yourself, Aoife?"

"I'm not my mother," I snarled, vicious as the nightjar. I was different than Nerissa. I didn't want to wander lost in dreams. I had iron and engines in my blood.

"No, dear, we're not saying anything of the sort, but you must admit that Conrad . . . ," she started. I glared at her, a hard glare made of tempered glass. Mrs. Fortune swallowed her last words.

"I'm not my brother, either," I ground out. "Is that what the Headmaster will say? We're mad because my mother didn't marry our father? Her being easy made us mad? Well, it's *not* true and I'm *not* mad." Heat rose in my cheeks like too much steam in a feed pipe. The pressure was going to make me explode.

Mrs. Fortune, for her part, looked relieved to be back on familiar footing. "You will not speak to a head of house so, young woman. Now finish your schoolwork and get into your nightclothes. Lights out in one hour."

"I'm not going to go mad," I said again, loudly, as she backed out of the room.

"Oh, Aoife." Mrs. Fortune sighed. "How can anyone possibly know that for sure?" She smiled sadly and shut the door.

The aether hissed. I felt tears spill over my cheeks and I didn't wipe them away, just let them grow cold on my skin.

I waited for a good while after Fortune's footsteps moved away, then grabbed the letter from under my pillow

24

and tore it open with my thumbnail. Three other letters had come in the year since my brother Conrad went away, and I kept the envelopes in my footlocker, underneath my blue sweater with the moth hole in the armpit.

The letters in his handwriting always arrived invisibly, never more than a few lines, but they told me that Conrad was still alive. After his escape from the madhouse, where the Proctors sent him after his sixteenth birthday, it was the only sign I had left. Treated with ghost ink, the letters smelled of vinegar and smoke. Ghost ink had been Conrad's favorite trick—treat the paper and the ink with the patented Invisible Ghosting Liquid, and when you held the missive over heat and set it aflame, innocuous poems turned into full-length letters written in smoke that would disappear when the paper finally burned down to ash.

If the Headmaster or the Proctors in Ravenhouse, dedicated to protecting us from the heretics and viral creatures, found out I was getting letters from a condemned madman, I'd be locked up as quickly as Conrad had been. I unfolded the thick paper, feeling the fibers coarse against my fingertips, expecting something like the last letter:

Winter comes with sharp teeth
Wind to polish my bones

Which, burned, read:

Dear Aoife,
Cold here, and snowing, dreary and dark as the Catacombs in Ravenhouse at home . . .

Conrad never sounded mad in his letters. Then again, to anyone who didn't know her, my mother didn't seem particularly mad at first glance. Until she started talking about

25

lily fields and dead girls. You had to look deep, in the cracks and crevices, to see the madness of the infection eating her insides. Once you really looked, though . . . there was no question it was there. Just like Conrad's words in smoke.

This newest letter was crinkled, like it had been shoved in a pocket too quickly, and across the center of the page a single word sprawled.

HELP

I stared at the word, the word in Conrad's hand, the desperate word glaring at me from the page. I stared for a long time, my mind whirling like a winter storm. It was so unlike him, so brief and terrifying. The Conrad I knew could always organize his thoughts, like a professor laying out a lesson plan. He was the man of our house. Conrad never asked me for my help. With anything.

I didn't know that Conrad was in danger. I didn't know that the letter was anything except the deranged mind of a boy driven mad with the necrovirus, spilled on the page.

But I still sat, looking at the letter and wishing I could creep away to burn the real words inside out, until Cecelia came back from her rehearsal and the heads of house dimmed the lamps for sleep.

3

Heresy and Banishment

I FELL ASLEEP with Conrad's letter crumpled in my fist, still unburned, and was little use to anyone the next day, least of all myself during my classes. Fortunately, our only morning engagement was Civic Duty with Professor Swan, something all students in Schools were required to take and, I was fairly certain, none paid any attention to.

Cal leaned across the aisle when I slid into my seat. "This should be good. He's got new pamphlets."

Marcos Langostrian turned around and glared at us. "Show some respect. The Bureau of Proctors print those for a reason."

"Yeah." Cal leaned back in his seat and laced his fingers behind his head. "To make naughty little boys like you afraid of the dark."

"Cal," I sighed. Cal's favorite program on the tubes was *Have Gun, Will Travel* and sometimes he took it entirely too far.

27

"Get bent, Honor Scout," Marcos hissed. Cal flushed. The muscles in his neck tensed and I reached across the aisle and touched him on the elbow.

"He's not worth getting a detention over."

Marcos sneered at me, and I rolled my eyes at him. The Langostrians lived on College Hill. They dined with the Head of the City on Hallows' Eve. I'd prefer to spend the rest of my life with Cal and his flat wrong-side-of-the-track accent than five seconds alone with Marcos.

Professor Swan rapped his podium with a pointer. "That's enough, students. This instruction is your duty to the city, to the country and to the Master Builder." He turned and tacked a new notice, bearing the black border of the Proctors and the signature of Grey Draven, Head of the City, on the board, then glared at each of us in turn.

Cal smirked at me. "Told you," he mouthed. I kept my eyes on the new pamphlet the professor had hung. It looked like a funeral notice, heavy with ink and import.

Conrad's letter, the weight of it in my pocket, reminded me that the Proctors, Draven and the Master Builder were watching. It was hard to smile back at Cal.

"Stand and recite the pledge," Swan ordered. He was thin and sallow, and his collegiate robes flapped around him like a black version of his namesake bird. More than his robe, his beaky nose and his hard black eyes, which picked out any imperfection or deviation from the laws of the Master Builder, reminded me of a crow, not a swan.

I mouthed the pledge while the rest of the class droned. "I pledge to remain rational and faithful to the foundations of science, laid down by my forefathers in defense of reason. . . ." I hadn't spoken the words since Conrad left.

28

They weren't words that held any comfort. You couldn't defend against a virus no one had found a cure for in seventy years. You couldn't fight off a person's delusions with science. Not if they really believed.

My eyes wandered to the twin portraits of the President and Grey Draven above the board. Draven's piercing eyes accused me of all the sins I already knew I was guilty of—lying, communicating with a madman, shirking my duties as a scientist and a citizen. I felt the weight of every one of my transgressions under Draven's eyes, the gimlet stare that had made him the youngest Head of the City Lovecraft had ever seen. He'd promised to clean Lovecraft of heresy, to keep every rational citizen safe in their home. With the might of the Bureau of Proctors behind him, he did what everyone who bought their party line considered a fine job. And he never missed a chance to plaster his picture on every surface.

Head of the City was a dire and powerful position, but there was talk that Draven could be the president of the country before he was through. I hated having him stare at me in every classroom. I looked at the floor until the pledge was through and Swan snapped, "Sit down. No talking."

He rapped his pointer against the new Proctor notice. "There have been reports of viral creatures as far north as Storm Avenue," he said. "The Lovecraft Proctors remind us all, for our own safety, that consorting with those poor souls struck down and changed into inhuman fiends by the necrovirus is a crime punishable by confinement in the Catacombs."

Cal sobered, and I knew he was remembering the nightjar. The Proctors did their best to keep Lovecraft free

29

of viral creatures, but there were old sewers, old train tunnels and the river itself gave birth to some of the worst. No one could keep the horrors from creeping in at the edges of things. We weren't an island, like New Amsterdam, and we weren't walled like the modern marvel of San Francisco. Lovecraft was a previrus city, and it was dangerous.

"Contact with a viral creature can what, students?" Professor Swan fixed us with his pale eyes. His robes made him appear to be bodiless, just a diaphanous mass.

Marcos raised his hand. "Cause madness in a healthy person, Professor. In almost every case."

Cal dropped his Civic Duty text on the floor with a crack like a steam rifle. "Or sometimes just a nasty case of influenza. Isn't that what you had last week, Langostrian? Been kissing ghouls?"

The class tittered, and Professor Swan tinted from pale to flushed like a developing sepia. "Daulton. Two detention hours." The rest of us got another sweep of his lantern eyes. "You think it's a diversion, this talk of protecting our city, the city the Master Builder gave us?" He hit the podium again. "The world is a harsh place, a dark place, made darker by the heretics who would fill your heads with fancy notions like magic spells and fortune-telling. They do this to keep you from your true purpose. The necrovirus is not fancy. It exists, and it eats at each and every one of your reprehensible, superstitious cores. Now each of you will write an essay on the menace of madness infection to Lovecraft and how you suggest we better defend our city."

The class groaned. Marcos muttered, "Thanks a lot, Cal."

30

"You started it, twit," I grumbled back. Marcos gave me a baleful look.

"Don't you have a birthday coming up, Grayson?"

My cleverness died in my throat, replaced by a lump. Was there no one in this damn school who didn't know about that?

Before I could grab him again, Cal started out of his seat. "You need to learn how to speak to a lady, pip-squeak." Someone Cal's size calling anyone a pip-squeak would have been funny, if Marcos hadn't looked ready to pound his face.

"*Sit* down," Swan bellowed. "Two more hours."

"Just leave it," I said to Cal. It was plain truth that I'd always be a city ward, the daughter of a madwoman, to Marcos. It was a fact of life, like uniform stockings itching behind the knees—unpleasant and inevitable. Fighting back just told the Marcoses of the world that their barbs hit home.

Cal glared at the back of Marcos's head, slick with hair oil. "He shouldn't say those things."

"He can say whatever he wants. His brother is a Proctor in their national headquarters and his family could buy and sell me ten times over." Not that it wouldn't give me immense satisfaction to see Marcos take a sock in the jaw, just once. I filled up my pen and pressed it against the ruled paper. A little bit of ink dribbled out and made a dark sunburst on the top line.

"One last announcement before you begin work," Swan said. "The heads of house will be conducting their monthly sweep for heretical contraband tomorrow. Remember, merits will be granted to those who turn in their roommates.

31

Informants are the backbone of the Proctors. All glory to the Master Builder."

The class chorused back raggedly. I didn't join in. Heretics—heretics who practiced magic, at any rate—were a child's story. Those glass-eyed fanatics who threw Molotov cocktails at Proctor squads could no more practice *real* magic than I could fly without a dirigible. Magic couldn't hold a candle to the necrovirus, to the great Lovecraft Engine that turned below the city, to the invisible grace of the aether. There was no magic. Not the way the heretics believed. If there were, why would I be stuck in Civic Duty writing a pointless essay?

The Engine had powered the city for twice as long as my lifetime, a heart made of brass and iron and steam. The Engineworks would be my eventual workplace, my home. Unlike spells and scrying, the Engine was a real place, a real device that managed to keep an entire city warm and lit and free of ghouls. That was real magic, not the ephemeral and heretical conjurations of self-proclaimed witches.

That was what Professor Swan and the Proctors would say, at any rate. My mother would disagree.

Instead of writing the essay Swan wanted, I pulled out Conrad's letter and read it. *HELP*, over and over again.

Things didn't improve during our schematics exam in the afternoon. I watched, my stomach leaden, as each student went forward and placed their folded plans on the professor's table.

Finally, when it was just Cal and me left in the room, I gathered my things and walked out.

Cal caught up with me in the passageway, in between the stone pillars that held up the slate-roofed porch of the main classrooms. The rain was light, just fingers of mist drifting over the peaked gables of Blackwood Hall.

"Hey," Cal said. "You didn't turn in your schematic."

"Hey, you've got eyes," I returned, my anger landing on Cal instead of the one I really wanted to scream at. Cal's mouth twisted downward.

"Aoife, what's the matter?"

"Nothing," I grumbled. The failed exam was just the final nail in the coffin. Nothing had been right since I'd seen my mother. Cal leaned against the opposite pillar, a genial scarecrow after all the crops have gone.

"You know, if you fail exams this year we can't apprentice at the Engineworks together next."

Apprenticeships were far from my mind at that moment. Conrad's letter was a guilty secret barbing me from where it sat in the pocket of my uniform skirt, and Dr. Portnoy's words were its sound track. *An experimentation facility. HELP.* Over and over.

"I have to go," I said, gathering my books and satchel. "Study," I added.

Cal drooped at the shoulders like a sad clockwork man.

"Yeah. I have to get to detention anyway. See you after supper." Cal loped away and I fingered the letter again. I needed to find a quiet place to burn it, to read the real words hidden in the ink. My dorm room was useless, with Cecelia meddling in everything. I'd make up for snapping at Cal later. That was the thing about Cal—you could push him away and he kept coming back. Cal was loyal. He wouldn't hold my mood against me, and because of that I

33

felt doubly guilty for snapping. I didn't think of it as often as I should, but truthfully Cal was the kind of friend a poor girl like me should thank the Master Builder for.

And I would. Once I'd read Conrad's letter.

"Aoife!" Cecelia's bell of a voice cut into my thoughts and made me jump. She grinned at me. "Did you want to come?"

"No, I have to make up my schematics exam . . . ," I started, surprised to see her outside our building. The Lovecraft Conservatory, where she studied, was on the other side of the campus. "Come to what?" I cocked my head at her flushed cheeks.

"It's a burning!" Cecelia exclaimed. "It'll be the last one before Hallows' Eve. Come on!" She tugged me along and I had to follow, or be yanked off my feet.

"I have a lot of work to do . . . ," I tried again, diplomatically hinting I'd rather not go. Students were filtering in and out the front gate, crimson scarves like comet tails in the bright afternoon. The mist-shrouded night before seemed like a year ago.

"Work, shirk." Cecelia giggled. "Get it? Besides, you work too much anyway. Just look at your hair. You'd think you'd never met a brush."

She tugged me along and we walked down Storm Avenue, the leaves from the oaks swirling around our ankles. The rain stopped as we walked and the sky turned bright. The stone in the houses along Storm sparkled diamond hard.

"This is exciting, huh?" Cecelia trilled, squeezing my arm. I managed to pull away, this time. Cecelia was small,

34

every bit of her round and bouncy from her curls to her patent-leather pumps. She could be excited over everything from a concert to a burning. I was less excitable. Mrs. Fortune would say that was why I was an engineer.

"I suppose," I said. I didn't want to be here, out in the cold. I didn't want to see a person burned. The Proctors would say that made me unpatriotic, but dead flesh and screaming reminded me too much of the madhouse.

I had to read Conrad's letter. If he was in trouble, if he needed me . . . The thought that I wouldn't be quick enough to do any good cut at me and I crossed my arms and tucked my chin against the wind.

"Heretics." Cecelia pursed her lips, pink like her nails. "Is there anything more disgusting than trafficking in unnatural arts?"

I watched her wet tongue flick out and take off a patch of lipstick. I could think of a few things. "I suppose you could strip the skin off of corpses and wear it, like the springheel jacks down in Old Town," I said aloud. Cecelia wrinkled up her nose.

"You are so strange, Aoife, I swear. I guess it comes from doing such mannish work in the School of Engines, hmm?"

At least she wouldn't come out and call me trash, like Marcos. Cecelia regarded herself as refined. I regarded her as an idiot.

"Without the Engine, there wouldn't be any burnings," I pointed out. "The Engine creates the steam. The steam is the blood of the city."

"All glory to the Master Builder," Cecelia mumbled

35

automatically, unwinding one of her curls between her fingers.

Banishment Square was half full of people, just normal-looking people, some of whom were eating a late lunch from twists of newspaper. The centerpiece of the square, the castigator, was deserted.

"I hope the scum's accused of something good this time," Cecelia said. "Not just conjuring or selling magic or fortune-telling."

Cecelia had a gram of belief under her parroting of the Proctor's laws. Most of the students did. They wanted to believe that magic could be real, something to be giggled over in secret, like smoking or kissing or wearing a garter belt instead of the ugly, itchy underthings the Academy issued us.

I had learned the day my mother was committed that crimes against the Proctors mattered very little, individually. Belief or disbelief in heretical topics mattered even less. Some of us were just unfortunate. I was supposed to be afraid of the man about to be burned, but I was more afraid of being next.

Two Proctors, their midnight black cowls around their faces, led a skinny man in iron shackles up the steps of the castigator. The brass fixings hissed as escaping steam met the biting air. A third Proctor, his cowl thrown back so that I could see he was just a young, dark-complected man in a black uniform with brass buttons on the chest, followed with a key. The pair of them, Proctor and heretic, could have been anyone. They could have been my brother.

Cecelia sneered. "Heretic looks like a deviant. What do you suppose he did?"

36

"I'm sure they'll tell us," I muttered. I knotted my hands together for warmth, and tried not to look, but it was impossible. It was like watching a person being hit by a jitney. You freeze, and you can't even blink.

The Proctor with the key inserted it into the castigator, a contraption that resembled a brass coffin with three holes in the front and a gear assembly in the back. I knew from Mechanics in first year that a pipe connected it directly to the Engine, far below.

Heretic or not, the man in the shackles looked terrified. He sagged, gray, a puppet of a man held up by the Proctors. Cecelia sniffed. "It's so cold. I hope they get on with this."

"The charges are as follows," said one of the Proctors holding the heretic. "Consorting with dark forces."

That was a given. Anything not explained by the necrovirus could be nothing in a Proctor's eyes but heretics attempting magic.

"Corruption of human flesh, desecration of the dead and performance of pseudo-magic rites, outlawed under the Ramsay Convention of 1914," the Proctor rang out. His voice reverberated off the black stone of Ravenhouse and washed over the crowd. The murmur settled and for a moment the scream of the wind and the hum of the Engine were the only sounds.

Then the heretic began to sob. It was a droning sound. I'd heard it in the madhouse, the helpless sobbing of a mind whose gears have fouled into slag. My chest clenched for the man. I'd heard that same fear the day they took my mother.

"Human flesh." Cecelia's tongue flicked out. Another wedge of pink. "Decadent. For once."

"At this time," the Proctor said, "for rejecting the great

truths of the Master Builder, the truth of aether and of steam, for rejecting the twin foundations of reality and science"—he looked over the crowd, the no-face beneath the cowl rippling black—"burning of the hands is penalty."

I curled up my own hands inside my gloves. They were numb, slow to respond.

"Just the hands?" Cecelia echoed the grumble from the crowd. "I say hands and face, for that sort of thing. Human flesh. Honestly."

The heretic struggled only a little as the Proctors put his hands into the two lower holes in the castigator. The third Proctor turned the key one, twice, thrice.

Steam rushed into the October air. The heretic screamed. I couldn't blink.

Suddenly, my stomach lost its tolerance for my lunch and I felt turkey casserole lurch up my throat. I turned and staggered to the gutter at the edge of the square. Cecelia bolted after me.

"Poor thing." She pulled my hair away and rubbed my back. "I know you don't like to think about what that disgusting man must have done, but it's all right. He's being punished now."

I shoved Cecelia off me.

"*Honestly*, Aoife!" she cried. "I'm trying to *help*!"

I stared at her for a moment, her moon face blocking out the platform and the castigator. I'd seen burnings in lanternreels, but this was different. A little more fighting back, a little less sympathy from the Proctors, and my mother could have been there. My brother.

Me.

38

"I need to go home," I gasped. I ran out of Banishment Square. I pelted down Storm Avenue, but I swore I could still smell the bubbling flesh of the heretic in the castigator. Hear his screams borne on the winter wind.

All I could see, in my head, was Conrad.

4

The Secret in the Ink

AFTER A NIGHT of sleepless tossing and chills, I begged off my morning classes and spent an hour pacing the sophomore common room, waiting until the chronometer above the fireplace told me the library would be deserted. I didn't try to find Cal. Cal only knew what the other students knew about Conrad. That he'd gone mad from the necrovirus, attacked his sister. Escaped the Proctors and the madhouse and Lovecraft itself. Cal didn't know Conrad, my brother, who'd taken care of me when our mother was committed. The boy who'd taught me how to strip and repair a simple chronometer and later an entire clockwork device, put bandages on my fingers when the gears cut me, told me forbidden stories about witches, fairies and the gruesome king of imaginary monsters, Yog-Sothoth.

Cal could take me straight to the Proctors for harboring a madman and he'd be within his rights. Memory didn't matter, only the madness.

Mrs. Fortune was coming toward me along the walk, and I remembered the meeting with the Headmaster after supper. I took a hard left through the passage to the library, avoiding her sight line.

The Academy's library was a silent place, a morgue for books and papers, lined up on their little-disturbed shelves like stacks of corpses.

Passing through the dank, musty stacks, my footsteps muted on carpet soft with rot, I spied Miss Cornell, the librarian. She glared at me from under her wispy red bun before she turned back to stamping overdue textbooks.

I climbed the iron spiral stairs to the turret room, deserted but for books, oil lamps and shadow. I took an oil lamp off its wall hook and put it on the reading table. Closing my fingers around the wrinkled paper, I held Conrad's letter up to the light.

As much as I loved numbers, my big brother loved puzzles. Mazes, logic, anything that required him to spend hours with his head bent. I wondered if that was his way of keeping his mind orderly, like math was mine. And I shuddered at the knowledge it hadn't worked for him, just like music hadn't worked for our mother.

Conrad had showed me tricks, before our mother got taken away and we went to the charity orphanage. He showed me tricks of the eye and tricks of the mind. The ghost ink was his favorite, and had the added benefit of destroying his letters. My brother looked out for me.

I held the vellum over the oil lamp, and the paper browned and curled at the edges like a dead oak leaf. I chewed my lip, praying the whole thing wouldn't disappear before my eyes. Ghost ink was a tricky substance—

41

soak a letter too long or give it too much heat and you could singe your eyebrows off and lose your fingertips in the bargain.

"Foul the gears, anyway," I hissed as my hand got too close to the lamp's globe and pain crawled over my hand like a spider. Hands are the engineer's fortune.

The letter curled up and smoke began to puff from the center of the page. The vellum crumpled in on itself, turning to ash as the smoke grew denser and darker, a chemical smell billowing from it that made my eyes water. Miss Cornell's footsteps approached. "What's going on up there, missy?"

"Nothing, ma'am!" I called. "Just . . . making up a test."

"Don't think you can hide up there all afternoon when you have classes! This is not a common hall!" Miss Cornell barked, and then the bone-cracking clack of her cheap heels retreated down the steps.

I exhaled. That had been closer than I liked to play things. When you were a charity case, it behooved you to give all outward appearances of decorum and class. My rebellions, unlike Cal's, were nearly always in my head or scribbled in the margins of my workbooks. The five-pointed mark of the witch, a fanciful sketch of a fairy hiding among the gears of my practice schematics. Always burned or studiously forgotten before a professor or a Proctor saw. I didn't believe in magic, but the rules the Proctors preached were against more than that. They were against ideas. And science without ideas was useless. That, I believed.

People in Lovecraft had been sent to the Catacombs or to a burning for far less than idle drawing. Proctors didn't delineate between a rational person having a fancy and a heretic stirring dissension. I knew that the Proctors were doing their best to protect us from ghouls and from the encroachment of the necrovirus. Viral creatures and infected people swarming in the streets were a true nightmare, more than the specter of witches or their craft. If it weren't for the Proctors, Lovecraft would become another Seattle, just a ghost town overrun with madness and horrors like the nightjar.

The shame of my family was the price we paid to keep ourselves safe. Professor Swan hammered the facts home time and time again, but I couldn't seem to stop dreaming.

Perhaps if the professor were less of a toad about his Proctor-mandated lectures, I'd be inclined to listen.

Heat warned me that the ghost ink was close to combusting, and with a small pop of displaced air the entire letter disintegrated, the ash swirling around me like darkling snow. The ink of the *HELP* lifted off the page, suspended in the smoke, corpse-pale. As the smoke dissipated, the ink stretched and re-formed, spelling a new phrase in its ghostly hand, the encoded message the ghost ink had kept hidden.

Go to Graystone
Find the witch's alphabet
Save yourself

A string of numbers followed, and I grabbed a fountain pen from my pocket and scrawled the entire message on my hand before it blew away on the draft.

31-10-13

The ink bled into my skin, like a scar.

Cal was waiting for me outside the library. "Knew you'd be here," he said. "You always hole up in that worm factory when you're sour."

"It's not a worm factory, it's a library," I sighed. "And what business of yours, exactly, is my mood? Worried I'm going to lose my marbles before my birthday and embarrass you in front of Marcos and his pals?" I ducked around Cal and started for the dormitories. Conrad, and the words in the smoke, dominated my thoughts.

Cal stopped me with a hand. "All right. What's wrong? This spitfire act isn't like you."

"Can I trust you?" I questioned Cal. I wanted to trust him. He was the only one I *could* trust.

He blinked and ran a hand through his hair. A bit fell into his eyes.

"Of course, Aoife. Is it something with your mother? She acting up?" His thin eyebrows drew together and his face tried to form a frown. Cal couldn't look dour to save his life, but at least he was trying.

"Not my mother," I said, walking. "Conrad." The words whispered to me. I felt as if I'd crack open if I didn't give them voice.

"Conrad?" Cal's eyes widened. "You can't just leave me hanging with that, Aoife. Can't just drop your crazy brother's name . . ." He paused, and swallowed. "Sorry."

"Like I haven't heard worse." I showed him the writing on my skin. Cal frowned.

"I don't get it."

"Conrad sent that to me," I said. "In a letter. He needs my help."

I didn't expect Cal to grab me by the wrist, sliding his big bony palm to cover the writing on mine. "Are you *trying* to get sent to the madhouse, Aoife? Is what everyone's saying true?"

My wrist burned under his grasp, flesh heating, while my face matched it at his words. Out of all students in the Academy, I'd hoped Cal wouldn't buy into the rumor. I squirmed, but Cal didn't let go. "What are they saying this time?"

Cal's jaw worked. "That the Grayson line has bad blood. From the first infected on down. They say that you all go mad sometime around sixteen . . . that you're dangerous."

Tears burned behind my eyes, but I shut them, so the tears wouldn't betray me by falling. "Cal, I thought you were my friend."

"I am," he said. "I'm your only friend right now, Aoife. I don't believe any of it, but you know what they say. You know what Conrad did."

My throat went tight. I remembered the point of the knife warmed to the temperature of skin, Conrad's tears wetting my hair as he held me close. *"I don't want to, Aoife, but they whisper and watch and they lap up the blood. I don't want to listen, but they won't stop, until there's blood on the stone. . . ."*

"Conrad didn't mean to hurt me," I told Cal. "Dammit, Cal, you know that." I pulled away then. If Cal thought that

45

I carried the necrovirus in me, then I'd never be more than a thing to be pitied in his eyes.

My school scarf covered up the crooked scar most days, unless it was getting near the end of the year, when the wet breath of summer on my skin made wool unbearable.

"He went mad on his birthday, Aoife, and he tried to cut your throat. Your birthday is coming and now you're talking about helping him. Like it or not, that *sounds* mad."

"Conrad was your friend too," I whispered. My only friends: Conrad and Cal. Cal and Conrad. I had thought nothing could change that.

Cal grimaced. "Yeah, and when he snapped, how stupid do you think I felt for believing he'd fight off the madness? This—this gibberish he's feeding you—is just a delusion. Same as the fairies and demons that your mother sees."

I didn't think, I just lashed out and slapped Cal across the cheek with my free hand. He recoiled, hissing in pain. "I'm sorry," I said instantly, though my blood still pounded through my ears and I didn't feel sorry. At all.

"Dammit, Aoife, you really clocked me." He wiggled his jaw.

"Conrad *isn't* like my mother," I insisted. Conrad had never showed any signs of madness. He never told me his dreams. My brother had to be different. Because if he wasn't, then there was no hope for me. "He needs my help," I told Cal, "and I thought you just said I could trust you."

Cal sighed and scratched at the top of his ear, a habitual gesture that meant his nature was warring with the rules of the Academy and the Proctors. "What do you want from me, Aoife?"

"Read it," I said, putting my palm under his nose. Cal frowned.

"What's Graystone? What are these numbers?"

"Graystone is my father's house. It's upstate, in Arkham," I said. "At least, that's what my mother told me." I sighed. "The numbers . . . I don't have the faintest idea."

Truthfully, I hadn't the faintest idea about my father, either. I had his name—Archibald Grayson—and my mother's rambling about his strong hands and moss-green eyes. They were my eyes, and they caused Nerissa by turns to be doting and furious toward me. Most days, I wished the bastard had kept his eyes to himself.

But if Conrad had evaded the Proctors long enough, if he'd made it to Arkham . . . he could have found our father. A man who'd fall for and get a woman with the necrovirus in a family way, twice, unafraid of madness. A man who might help him.

"Please, Cal," I said when he hesitated. "I just need someone to believe that this might not all be madness."

"I can't believe I'm helping him again—*or* you," Cal sighed. "The Proctors could have me in the Catacombs in a heartbeat."

I nudged his shoulder. "Not if you don't run up to Ravenhouse and confess to them." Relief lightened me and stopped my heart from thudding. Cal wasn't going to turn me in. He was still the boy I'd met on Induction Day.

"Ravens are wise, Aoife," Cal said. The rain was coming down in earnest now, and I dug my collapsible umbrella out of my satchel while we walked back to the common house. "The Proctors use them for a reason."

"Ravens are too busy chasing real live heretics and

47

Crimson Guard spies down in the Rustworks," I said, hoisting the umbrella over Cal's much taller head. I left out the rumor that Conrad had told me, that the Crimson Guard were witches who could do impossible things. Cal was sensitive enough. "Ravens have bigger worries than a couple of Academy students."

"If you say so," Cal muttered darkly, looking over his shoulder as if a Proctor were closing in on us.

"I do say so," I told him as we climbed the steps and shook off the rain inside the common-house door. I patted Cal on his damp shoulder. "Nothing is going to happen to you."

"So what are you going to do?" Cal asked, looking longingly at the other boys sitting around the aether tube listening to the baseball game. "Maybe you could send him a letter back, or something. You can write it and I can get the score."

The truth that had been circling my thoughts since I read the letter solidified. Writing wasn't going to help Conrad. "I'm going to Graystone," I said. "Like Conrad asked."

Cal choked. "What? Right now?"

Mrs. Fortune loomed in my head, and the meeting with the Headmaster. "Tonight."

I thought Cal was going to faint on the floor of the common house. "You really are mad, Aoife."

"Stop saying that," I warned. I unwound my scarf and passed my fingers over the scar that Conrad's knife had left. Conrad wasn't like our mother. Conrad fixed our meals. Conrad braided my hair for school.

But no one cared about the Conrad before. They just saw him standing over me, his knife crimson on the tip,

48

madness burning in his eyes. They didn't see the torture he went through, how hard he tried to hold it back.

If Conrad needed my help, he'd get it, for all the years before he came into my room on his birthday, holding the knife.

They won't be silent until I do it, Aoife. I'm so sorry.

"How are you proposing to just . . . take flight from the Academy with nothing except this wild notion to go to Arkham?" Cal demanded, when I stood silent for too long.

"Will you speak up?" I said, jolted to attention as the group of boys turned toward us. "I don't think *everyone* on Academy grounds heard that."

Cal pulled me down onto one of the threadbare sofas and leaned close, as close as we'd ever been. "This isn't a simple thing, Aoife. Even if we made it out of the school— which is impossible, by the way—there's still the city lock-down at dusk. We'd never make it over the bridges before they close the roads and the sewers against the ghouls. We're underage. We could never convince the Proctors we had passage papers."

"I'm aware of the variables," I said. Lovecraft was a fortress against the necrovirus, and its citizens; at night, when the viral creatures were most active, the same citizens became prisoners within the city blocks.

Cal shook his head. "Math isn't going to give us one lick of help this time, Aoife."

I chewed on my bottom lip, a habit Mrs. Fortune deplored as unladylike. " 'Us'?" I said after a time, casting a sidelong glance at Cal to test his expression. He heaved a sigh too large for his skinny chest.

49

"If you think I'm letting you run off from school on the word of some madman on your own? Then you're not mad, Aoife . . . you're just nuts."

As quickly as I'd slapped him before, I threw my arms around Cal. He let out a small grunt. "Thank you," I whispered fiercely. He returned my grasp, tentative.

"All right, Miss Engineer . . . how are we hauling out of Lovecraft?"

"Well . . . I . . ." My reasoning hadn't led me much beyond "help Conrad." Cecelia, her sharp eyes and sharp words during the burning, came back to me. "The Nightfall Market."

Cal let out a groan. "Great. We barely get clear of Dunwich Lane, and you want to go someplace twice as dangerous."

"Oh, listen to you. You're worse than an old woman. When have I ever lead you into danger?"

"Yesterday," Cal said. "That bloodsucker in the alley."

"And I got you back out again, didn't I? Don't go to supper," I said, the plan forming and gaining momentum in my mind. I felt the same when I sketched new machines, things that could fly or burrow or glide under the river like fish. "That'll be our chance." Supper was the one time all of the students and heads of house gathered in one place. "Play sick if you have to. Meet me behind the autogarage once the dining bell rings."

Cal nodded grimly. "Be careful, Aoife. I'd hate to see you . . . taken away. Before your time." He squeezed my hand and went and joined the boys listening to the tubes.

50

5

Nightfall

Running away had never crossed my mind before. Certainly, I was an orphan for all intents and purposes, but I'd been accepted into the School and I had at least a journeywoman's career ahead of me at the Engineworks. I wasn't a cinder-girl from a storybook. A prince didn't need to ride up on his clockwork steed and take me away.

When I was small, my mother told me that before the spread of the necrovirus and the madness it inflicted, before the Proctors had burned every book that even smacked of heresy, fairy tales had been different. They'd contained actual fairies, for one thing.

I didn't take any memories of her when I packed my things, just a change of clothes, a toothbrush and hairbrush, all the money I'd received from the city when they auctioned Nerissa's effects—a paltry fifty dollars—and my toolkit, the leather pouch of engineer's equipment that every student was issued upon their acceptance into the

51

School of Engines. I withheld one uniform shirt and unscrewed my last bottle of ink, splashing it down the front in a violent pattern.

As soon as everything was secreted in my satchel, I went to the first floor and knocked at Mrs. Fortune's pin-neat room. She cracked the door and sighed at the sight of me. "I'm very busy, Aoife."

"I'm sorry, ma'am, but there's a bit of an emergency," I said, holding up the shirt. "I was drawing my schematic, and—" I had the lie planned to the last word, but Fortune cut me short.

"Oh, stars, Aoife." She shook her head. "You're clumsy as a fawn. It'll be comportment classes next year if you don't pull yourself together and learn how to be a lady."

I chewed my lip in remorse and dropped my head. "I'm ever so sorry, ma'am. But if you could have the security officer let me out, I could run up Cornish Lane to the China Laundry before they shut," I said. "I only have two shirts, as you know"—I moved my toe across the crack in the floor—"being a ward, and all." People like Mrs. Fortune— wealthy and well-meaning—were conditioned from birth to be charitable to the less fortunate. Even when the less fortunate were lying to their faces.

Fortune patted her own cheek in sympathy, but stayed firm. "You are most certainly not running about the city after curfew on your own. What would the Headmaster say?"

"Oh, it's not a problem," I said, prepared for this variable. "Cal will go with me. And I'll be back before I have to meet the Headmaster about me going mad and killing people on my birthday. I swear."

Mrs. Fortune raised her eyes heavenward. "The mouth

52

on you, Aoife Grayson, could fell a Proctor. Master Builder forgive me the blasphemy." She waved the edge of her tartan shawl at me. "Go on. I'll have the man at the side gate let you out."

"Thank you, ma'am," I said, keeping my eyes on the floor so my victory wouldn't live in my gaze. I struggled to keep my shoulders drooping and my expression contrite. "It should take me no time at all."

Waiting by the autogarage in the cold, doubt swooped down on me like the Proctor's clockwork ravens on their black silken wings. Conrad could be sitting contentedly in some pub, whispering to his invisible friends while he wrote fanciful letters that put me in danger.

Or Conrad could really *be* in danger, as he'd never lied to me, not even on his birthday.

He picked up the knife from his toolkit, the same toolkit I'd receive at the start of term, and ran his thumb along the blade. "Have you ever seen your own blood, Aoife?" he murmured. "Seen it under starlight, when it's black as ink?"

They said the virus was in our blood, an infection passed from mother to child until time immemorial. Dormant, until a signal from within our biology woke it up, brought on the madness. No one could tell me how far back it went, as my mother refused to speak of her parents at all. I'd wormed my father's name out of her before she dipped too deep into the pool of illusion and fancy. I'd verified that Archibald existed in the city records at the Academy library, that he was real and not cut from the whole cloth of her madness. I'd also discovered that he didn't appear to be mad. But he'd been with Nerissa, so there must have been something cockeyed in the man's schematic.

My fingers were cold inside my gloves and I stamped my feet, expelling steam breath into the night. A hand on my shoulder made me shriek in alarm and slam my palms over my mouth. I tasted lanolin and soap.

"It's me!" Cal hissed. "It's only me."

"Don't *do* that," I cried, rasping. "That sneaking. That's for ghouls and thieves."

He grinned at me halfway in the dim light of the auto yard, his crooked teeth and blond hair standing out stark like a negative photoplate. "Sorry. I'm quiet enough to be either, I guess."

I pressed my hands together to regain my composure and smiled to hide the shaking. "Not funny, Cal."

He chuckled softly. "You know, for a girl taking me to the Nightfall Market you're as jumpy as if you're juggling aether tubes."

"You're not?" I said, incredulous, as we started for the gates. "Scared, I mean." The Academy was brick banded in iron fencing to keep out viral creatures, and spiked with finials along the fence's top to keep students bent on mischief in. The iron spikes' jagged shadows breathed out cold when we approached.

"I'm a young man set out on a great adventure," Cal said. "The way I see it, the least that can happen is I have a story to tell the guys when I get back."

"*When.* Aren't you the optimist," I teased.

"You did save me from the nightjar," Cal said with a smile. "I feel my chances of coming back to school with all of my fingers and toes are better than average."

54

I knew that fighting off viral creatures was unladylike at best, but to have Cal's praise warmed me a bit, even though my extremities and nose were still numb. It made me feel that maybe this wasn't a doomed idea, that we could find the Nightfall Market, find Conrad and manage to come back again. Never mind that I'd never heard anything but thirdhand rumors of how to find the place, and the Proctors were eager to deny its existence at every turn. Something they couldn't shut down and couldn't even find was a grave embarrassment to law and order.

When we reached the gate, a plump ex-Proctor sat in the security officer's hut, and he stepped out to stop us. Before he could shout at us for being out of doors without permission, I held up the shirt. "Mrs. Fortune said I might be let out to go to the China Laundry." I practiced my poor-ward-of-the-city look again.

The guard examined us. "Just you," he said. "You, boy—stay in."

"Oh no," I said, couching the protest as alarm. A regular girl would be terrified to leave the safety of the Academy after dark. "She was very firm that I have an escort."

"Old Fussbudget Fortune ain't his head of house," said the guard. "He stays."

"But—" Cal started. The guard rattled his nightstick against the post.

"You deaf, kid? Get back to supper and leave me be."

The old lump was clearly immune to my charms, so I switched to the other sort of false face I knew—the snooty Academy student with no time for the help. "Could you just open the gate and let me launder my *only* blouse?" I snapped, trying to adopt the tone of Marcos Langostrian

55

or Cecelia. The guard grunted, but he took the keys off his belt and walked over to the bars.

"Get ready," I murmured to Cal, slipping my gloved palm into his. His hand was cool and thin, and when I squeezed I could feel all his small bones.

The gate opened, and I started walking, Cal pulled with me. The officer gawped. "You there! Student out of bounds!"

"Dammit to the deep, anyway," Cal said. He just stood there, and I jerked him with me.

"Run, idiot!"

We made an odd pair fleeing down Cornish Lane, past closed-up shops and slumbering vendor carts. Cal loped along, stumbling over his own feet. I put my head down and ran as if all the ghouls of Lovecraft's sewers were on my heels.

At the intersection of Cornish and Occidental, I could still hear the shriek of the officer's whistle, and I ran harder. Cal gasped like the faulty bellows in the machine shop. "Maybe . . . we . . . should . . . go . . . back."

"And then what?" I shouted as we took a hard left, pelting past the colorful Romany shacks of Troubadour Road, toward the train tracks and the bridge.

"I don't"—Cal sucked in a lungful of the night air—"I don't know, but this is a terrible . . . terrible . . . idea!"

We crossed the tracks, like a frontier border in their cold iron gleam under the moonlight. I twisted my ankle in the gravel as we stumbled down the other side of the embankment, and then Joseph Strauss's marvelous bridge was in front of us, leading across the river and into the maze of the foundry complex.

56

We were in the train yard, among rusted boxcars and Pullman carriages waiting for engines that would never arrive. I could see the pedestrian walkway of the bridge beyond the fence, and I watched it while Cal and I leaned against a United Atlantic car to catch our breath.

Two Proctors in black hoods stood at the crossing, silent, their long coats fluttering around their legs in the wind off the river. One hid a yawn behind his fist, but the other's eyes traveled into all the dark corners of the train yard. Searching, watching for movement in the shadows.

"Come on," I said, tugging on Cal's arm when he just stared at the Proctors, licking his lips. "We can cut through the yard and take the old coal paths down to the Rustworks." Cal still didn't move, so I tugged harder and he grunted.

"You're not very gentle. Girls are supposed to be gentle," he grumbled, finally creeping after me.

"You should know me better by now," I teased softly. I stuffed my ruined blouse into a dustbin as we crept by the South Lovecraft Station, its brick spires reaching up into the night, and we threaded between rolling stock sleeping on the rail, leaving the lights of Uptown behind. As they faded, my breath-stealing fear of being spotted diminished a little. Even Proctors hesitated to go into the Rustworks. The wreckage was dangerous and there were supposed to be old entrances to the sewers hidden among them, leaving the ghouls easy access to aboveground.

Of course, those facts brought their own set of fears.

At last, the train yard ended at a ditch, and the terrain grew more turbulent, treacherous under my slick school shoes. A fence loomed above me, the border between

57

Lovecraft and the Rustworks. For a gateway between worlds, it wasn't much. Just corrugated steel eaten away into lace by exposure to salt air and rain. Beyond, I saw indistinct piles of slag and metal—small mountains, really, of everything from jitneys stacked high as a house like domino tiles to disused antisubmarine rigs, with their great steam-powered harpoons blunted, which had been brought back from the defense lines on Cape Cod and Cape Hatteras after the war. So many machines, all of them dead. It was like happening upon the world's largest open grave, silent and devoid of ghosts. If I'd believed in ghosts.

I slipped through a gap in the fence, and the last of the aether lamps of Uptown winked out behind me, eclipsed by the wreckage. As Cal and I were enclosed by the bulk of the Rustworks, I felt a curious lightness in my step. I never walked out of bounds at the Academy. Storybook orphans were always meek, well-behaved, mousy things who discovered they possessed rich uncles who'd find them good husbands. Not the sort with mad brothers and mothers, who would rather stick their hands into a gearbox than into a sewing basket.

Now I was as far out of bounds as one could go, and it felt like a crisp wind in my face or jumping from a high place. I looked to Cal's comforting height, and smiled at him as we walked.

I'd heard whispers from older students that you could buy anything at the Nightfall Market—outlawed magic artifacts, illegal clockworks and engine parts, women, liquor.

Most importantly, I'd heard from Burt Schusterman, who'd been expelled during my first year for hiding a still in his dormitory room, that you could buy a guide in and out of the city after lockdown and before sunrise. A guide who wouldn't necessarily need passage papers to cross the bridges out of Lovecraft.

I just hoped he didn't want more than fifty dollars, or strike his bargains in blood, or dream fragments, or sanity. I didn't know that I had anything of the sort to give.

I chided myself as we walked through the silent, frost-bitten lanes of the Rustworks, enormous mounds and heaps of junk threatening to topple their aging bones onto our heads. "Grow up, Aoife." I was so lost in staring at the dead machinery in the junk piles that I didn't realize I'd voiced the thought. Burt Schusterman could have been the most enormous liar. Rotgut was supposed to fiddle with your brain, wasn't it?

"Huh?" Cal said at my outburst.

My flush warmed my cheeks. "Nothing." I walked a bit faster. The light wasn't here, and the shadows were long, with fingers and teeth. On a night like this, with a scythe-shaped moon overhead, it was easy to believe, as the Proctors did, in heretics and their so-called magic.

It crossed my mind, only for a second, to suggest we turn back, but the thought of Conrad somewhere just as dark and cold, and by himself, kept me climbing over half-rusted clockworks, through the hull of a burnt-out dirigible and past all the wreckage of Lovecraft's prewar age, before the Proctors, when heretics had run rampant and viral creatures waited in every shadow to devour the unwary.

59

Finding the market was a bit like seeing a ghost—I didn't truly believe it was real until we happened on it, and I saw shadows in the corner of my eyes and smelled the dankness of an eldritch thing, its breath misting on my face.

The Nightfall Market crept up on Cal and me in shadows and song—I saw a low lump of tent, and heard a snatch of pipes, and slowly, slowly, like a shy cat coming from under a porch, the Nightfall Market unfolded in front of our eyes.

Tucked into the dark places of the Rustworks, below the crowns of old gears and the empty staring heads of antique automatons, the Nightfall Market pulsed with movement, with sound and laughter. I hadn't expected laughter. Heretics were meant to be grim, weren't they? Concerned only with the trickery they called sorcery and the overthrow of reason?

I put aside my nerves. I didn't belong here, that much was obvious, in my plain wool uniform skirt and with Uptown manners, but if I showed that I was terrified of ending up an example to next year's frosh—"Did you hear about Grayson? The crazy one who got taken by heretics?"—the citizens of the Nightfall Market would never help me find Conrad.

Cal and I wound among the tents and stalls, made up of oddities and things that regular people would cast aside—fabric and metal and leather, stitched or riveted into a riot of color and odd shapes. The strange bit was, that haphazard as it first appeared, there was a sense of permanence to the place.

A pretty redheaded girl smiled and winked at Cal, her eyes an invitation into a big candy-striped tent that smelled

60

like overripe oranges and orchids. "You looking for a port, sailor?" she called.

"Keep walking, partner," I told Cal when his head swiveled toward the girl. He gave me a lopsided smile.

"You're not the type to let a guy have any fun, are you?"

"When we're safe in Arkham and we've found Conrad you can have all the fun your immune system can stomach," I said, with an eye on the girl and her cosmetic-caked face. She reminded me of a cheaper, brassier version of Cecelia.

Cal made cat noises, and I didn't hesitate to punch him on the shoulder, though not too hard.

"If you wanted a date, Aoife, you should have passed me a note or two during Mechanical Engineering," Cal teased. "There were plenty of school dances we missed our chance for."

I snorted. The idea of a respectable boy like Cal with a girl like me was as ridiculous as the idea of him with the girl from the tent. She'd probably be more acceptable to the professors and his parents. Boys were allowed to go wild once or twice.

"Believe me, Cal, nothing is further from my mind than a date right now," I told him as I tossed the girl a glare. She waggled her fingers at me before sticking out her tongue. I returned the gesture. I suppose I often don't leave well enough alone, but Cal was *my* companion on this little adventure. She could go and find her own.

We turned a bend in the market's alleyways and came to a square thronged with people. I paused. I had expected the girls of questionable reputations, accompanied by bandits and vagrants of the type popular with sensational

61

writers. But in actuality, an old pipe fire from a house long ago made wreckage was open to the air, and vendors had set up grills and kettles over the flame. The smell was oaky, earthy, a good cut of meat rubbed with spices. My stomach burbled at the scent, and I was reminded that I'd had to miss supper to come here.

"Books!" A boy in a checkered cap and an outdated newsie coat, half again as old as I was, shoved himself into my path, chest puffed like a bullfrog's. "Spell books! Charmed paper! Never needs erasin'! Tinctures! Good for what ails you!" He squinted into my face. "Not much, by the look of it. Face like an angel on you, girlie."

"I don't have any money," I returned. "You can save your pitch for some superstitious twit who does."

"Ain't no superstitions for sale here, miss," he chimed back. "All of my charms 'er one hundred percent gen-nu-wine. I've got magics in my pen and a witch in my kitchen."

"Magic's not real," I said. "If you're so smart, you should know that." I was trying to seem like someone who wasn't easily conned, but my voice sounded small against the chatter of the market.

"Sure, an' if you really believe that you'd be home in bed." The kid wrinkled up his nose at me. "I could tell you where to buy a hairbrush instead, maybe. You need it."

"Say," Cal intervened, before I could make a move to strangle the little brat. "Where's a guy find a guide around here?"

The boy spat in the dirt near Cal's feet. "Piss off, townie. I look like I give out help to Proctor-lovers?"

Cal swiped at him. "You don't know anything, you little rat. . . ."

62

I fished in my pocket for a half-dollar and held it up. The boy's eyes gleamed to match. "What's your name?" I said.

"Tavis. Thought you said you didn't have any scratch?"

I made a second half-dollar join the first. Conrad had liked sleight of hand, though the Proctors frowned on something so close to what heretics considered magic. Tavis was practically panting. "We need a guide out of Lovecraft," I said. "All the way to Arkham. I have money for that, and you seem like you know how things work around here. Or do you have a big mouth and nothing else?"

The first thing you learned in the School of Engines— if you want to understand how something works, ask the one who does the dirty job. Gear scrubbers and steam ventors and their foreman were in the pits. They knew their Engine intimately.

"I do, at that," Tavis said. He pointed past the pipe fire to a blue tent. "You want old Dorlock back there. He's a guide, best damn guide in the Rustworks. He could guide steam back into water. He could—"

I held up a hand, and dropped the two coins into his. I wondered what a pair of silvers bought in the Nightfall Market, besides bad manners from a shyster kid. "That's fine. And for the record, I like my hair this way." Truly, I hated it and toyed with chopping it into a modern style daily, but like I said, sometimes I don't know when to leave it. Besides, I had a feeling Dorlock wasn't as easily put in his place, and it might well be my last chance to feel in control of things tonight—or ever. Once I found Conrad, I'd have to face running off. I might be expelled. I didn't think beyond that, because beyond expulsion was a cell in the

63

Catacombs, shock therapy to burn the madness out of me and finally, a place next to my mother. If I lived.

"Sure there isn't," Tavis snorted, brandishing his worn wares again. "And hey, townie," he said to Cal as we started into the crowd. "You watch your girl. She's got an edge of the pale on her, that one, and it's like honey in a beehive down here."

I shuddered, feeling like something rotten had touched me. Cal rolled his eyes. "Stupid little runt."

"You mean, you don't feel the urge to be my white knight?" I teased, nudging him in the ribs. "Thought that was your dream job." This was my idea, and I wasn't about to let Cal see that second thoughts had started the moment we left the Academy. A good engineer stood behind her plans as sound until they'd been tested and proved otherwise.

"Like you said, Aoife," Cal grumbled, sounding for all the world like Professor Swan, "grow up."

An edge of the pale. If I'd had more coins to spare, I'd have asked Tavis what he meant. But my mother's money was precious, and I needed every penny of it for this man Dorlock.

We skirted the fire and approached where Tavis said the guide lived, my feet slower with each step. Still, I grasped the tent flap firmly and pulled it aside. "Hello?" I peered into the tent, which smelled like a barbershop mixed with cheap liquor. "M-Mr. Dorlock, sir?"

"Hello!" The voice boomed back, sonorous and clearly used to the stage. Dorlock was entirely bald and sported a handlebar mustache, like a circus strongman. Somehow

64

I had expected our guide to be thin and shady, dark as the shadows he slunk through. But Dorlock would stand out at a Hallows' Eve carnival.

"Why look at you, young lady!" he exclaimed. "Aren't you ripe as a peach!"

If I were to treat him mathematically, take his measurements, he'd be extraordinarily large—a rolling tub of a man boiling over with cheer. I didn't see what was so funny.

"We need a guide," I said. "We need to leave Lovecraft. Tonight."

Dorlock laughed, his kettledrum stomach trembling. "Doesn't waste any time! Going to grow into one of those modern women, I fear, always in a rush!" He reached out to pinch my cheek, and I ducked. I'd grown an aversion to being touched a long time ago. Nuns will do that to a person.

"Please, sir," I protested, trying to keep myself stiff and ladylike, like Mrs. Fortune. "Can you help us, or not?"

"Of course," Dorlock boomed. "Of course, of course." He crossed his bare arms over his leather vest and matted chest hair. I tried to look only at his face. "It's all a question of payment, lassie."

I looked back at Cal. "I have fifty dollars," I said. Cal's eyes went wide at the mention of the sum. Dorlock's eyes, by turn, narrowed.

"Fifty United States American dollars, eh? Well, missy, it won't buy much Uptown way but down here in the rat hole of the Rustworks, you just might have yourself a deal."

I felt crestfallen, realizing at the gleam in Dorlock's gaze why Cal had looked so alarmed. It was all my money.

65

I should have struck a harder bargain. A boy would have bargained. Conrad probably would have *made* money on the deal.

"We'll leave in an hour or so, to beat the sunrise," said Dorlock. "Up and down and all around we'll go. It'll be a grand adventure for you two kids."

"I care less about the adventure than the Proctors," I said, trying to stay firm.

"Yeah, and we're fifteen," Cal interjected. "We're not *kids.*"

"Of course not, you're a strapping young lad, aren't you?" Dorlock chuckled. "Going to feed you up and get you big. Why don't you go get something from the fires for your lady friend, strapping lad? It's a long walk down under the ground."

I frowned at that. "Ghouls live underground," I said. Not even Proctors went into the old sewers and railway tunnels, the only "underground" I knew of. The new sanitation system ran on clockwork and didn't need tending. Nobody went underground. Nobody alive, anyway.

Dorlock shook his head, brows drawing in like a bank of thunderheads. "You just have a head stuffed full of learning, don't you, young lady? Worry less. You'll get wrinkles before your time." He laughed like he was the chief audience for his own joke.

I opened my mouth, knowing there was murder in my eyes, but Cal touched me on the arm. "I'll get you a weenie with chili. If these people even know what one is." He gave me a small nod before he walked away. I knew that nod—it was the *please don't get us into trouble* nod. If Dorlock was

66

responsible for us not getting arrested, mouthing off would just be stupid.

As it turned out, the Nightfall Market didn't possess any weenies or any chili to put on them, and Cal ended up standing in line to buy us two newspaper cones full of fish-and-chips. I sat on the fender of a Nash jitney that had rusted to chrome and bones next to Dorlock's tent, where I could keep Cal in sight. Dorlock grinned at the white of my knees, and I pulled my skirt down over them.

"You do look sweet," Dorlock said, reaching to push the hair out of my face. "Beauty soon fades, down here. You're a rare treat."

I glared up at him, knowing the knot in my throat that had started when he grabbed for me wasn't going to go away anytime soon. "Don't. We hired you to guide, and that's all."

"I'm just being friendly," Dorlock said. "Loosen up, lassie." He laid a hand on my shoulder and I shrunk, but it was like trying to pull myself out of a bear trap. "It's a long time out of the city, and we might as well get along."

Maybe that was the single blessing Nerissa's madness had given me—I'd never had a mother to teach me smiles and manners, to do what a nice girl would do. I reached up and knocked Dorlock's hand off my shoulder, hard. "Perhaps I don't want to get along that way."

Dorlock's pouchy face fell in on itself, anger stealing into his small eyes. Hidden anger, like a snake. The most dangerous type.

"You don't have any weight to throw around, lassie. I'm the one watching your hide underground, and it'd behoove you to treat me sweet."

67

Before I could snap back at him, the Nash creaked as someone sat down next to me. "You know, Dorlock, I'm impressed. *Behoove* is a big word for you."

I turned to stare at the stranger and met his eyes. They were silver. His smile was crooked, and his hair was long, swept back with a rash of comb tracks. The stranger's hand was firm and ridged when he took mine and shook it. "Dean. Dean Harrison. And you might be?"

I opened my mouth, shut it. I didn't quite know what to make of the stranger, except that he didn't seem to care for Dorlock any more than I did, and his hand was warm.

"I might—" I started.

"She *might* be with me." Cal reappeared, irritably juggling his camp duffel and two helpings of takeaway. I watched Dean tilt his head back and look up to Cal's considerable knobby-kneed height.

"Sorry, brother. I didn't know she was spoken for."

"Oh, for the sake of all His gears," I huffed at Cal. Of all the times for Cal's tough act, this was the absolute worst. I shook Dean's hand in return. "I apologize for my friend's manners. I'm Aoife Grayson."

Dean's eyes and smile were both slow, but there was nothing dumb about them. He took the seconds to memorize everything about my face. I'd seen the same look on master engineers, contemplating a new device or problem. Dean took me in, and he smiled. "Pleasure to make your acquaintance, Miss Aoife."

I returned the smile, writ much smaller. Boys—men—weren't in the habit of smiling at me. I was odd, and I knew it. The few smiles before Dean's had lead to pranks, but when I looked Dean in the eye, his pupils just grew wider.

68

Cal grumbled, his face turning colors. "Aoife. We need to go with Mr. Dorlock."

Dorlock himself had turned a plummy shade of purple, huge hands clenching and unclenching like they wanted for a neck. "Harrison, you little ratlick, what are you doing yakking to my clients? They hired me fair and square—go poach somebody else's hire, vulture."

"Like I was about to bend your girl's ear on," Dean said. "You don't want Dorlock, miss. He pays the barter boys down here to talk him a good game, and he poses the part, but it's all fancy. Man will have you chumming a ghoul nest inside an hour if you go with him."

"Guttersnipe!" Dorlock roared, raising his fist to Dean. "They chose *me*. Market rule says free hires to all. The sweetheart here and her companion want to go underground, and underground they'll go." He didn't have the false face of a kind old uncle any longer. Rage had turned him crimson.

"Never knows when to shut his yap, either," Dean muttered, standing up. His full height was a head shorter than Cal, but Dean was broad and solid where Cal was still disappearing inside his school clothes. Dean's face wasn't but a year or two older than mine, but it held a spark of wickedness, a blade-edge of worldly knowledge that a person could only light by seeing too much, too soon. Conrad had the same look. I didn't trust Dean, but I was starting to like him.

"Listen, Dorlock," Dean said. "I'm being a pal and giving you a chance to walk away dignified-like."

Dorlock's nostrils flared. "Or?"

This time, Dean's smile wasn't slow and it wasn't warm.

69

"Or," Dean said, "I can show your shame to these nice Uptown folk. You choose."

I stepped back to stand by Cal in anticipation of a blow or a knife between the two. Dean had to be crazy, mouthing off to someone the size of Dorlock.

"You runt," Dorlock panted, a vein in his temple throbbing like a swollen river. "What do you mean, poaching on this sweet little thing?" He reached for me again, my hair, my cheek, and I swatted at him again. It was like fending off an ungainly octopus.

"She's a little young for you, don't you think?" Dean drawled. "By decades or so?"

I took another step back, this one involuntary.

Dorlock let out a yell and pulled a length of pipe with a wrapped handle from his belt. Dean reached into the pocket of his leather coat and brought out a palm-sized black lacquer tube. "You know that saying about bringing a knife to a gunfight?" he asked Dorlock. "Same principle applies, old man. Don't think I won't show steel just because we're in market grounds."

"They hired *me*," Dorlock rumbled. "You're just a huckster, kiddo, not worth my time to spit on." He turned to me with a smile revealing one missing front tooth. "Come on, lassie. Come away from that trash now and we'll go down under and on to the country like you wanted."

Dean moved just a bit, so that his body was between Dorlock and me. It was an artful move, executed like a dance. "All right, hard road is your road, old man." He gestured, his leather jacket creaking. "Show her your arm, Dorlock. Show off a little for us here."

Dorlock fell silent. "You," he said to me. "Come on *now*."

70

"No," I said, shrinking away from his grasp. "If I'm paying you fifty dollars, you can show your arm."

Dorlock sneered. "I don't need the whingeing of a spoiled schoolgirl," he said. "Or a deadbeat doper boy who doesn't know his north from his south."

"North," Dean said, pointing over Dorlock's shoulder. "True iron in my blood. What's in yours?"

"I think you better show us your arm, mister," Cal said. "See what this guy's on about."

Dorlock balled up his fist, but Dean caught it and turned Dorlock's great fleshy slab outward. Three straight lines were burned into the skin, puckered and red with trapped infection. Cal grimaced. I didn't want to move closer, but at the same time I couldn't resist staring at the pus-filled wounds. They were wide as my wrist, weeping and hideous.

"What *are* those?" I asked.

"Those, boys and girls, are ghoul kisses," Dean said. "Comes from the acid on their tongues, when they lay them against you to claim ownership. This fat bastard has a deal with one of the dens downside in the sewer, to deliver fresh meat when he's able." He released Dorlock and folded his arms. "Ain't that right, tubby?"

I stared at Dorlock, feeling sour creep up the back of my tongue. I'd been ready to hand over my money to a man who'd sell us for meat. Conrad would have seen this. All I'd done was nearly gotten Cal and myself eaten.

Dorlock's stomach jiggled with fury, and he let out a roar. Dean stuck his fingers in his mouth and whistled. "Spare me! Free hires within market bounds, Dorlock, you said it yourself. You want to debate the law, we can take it

71

to the old spider-lady who keeps the books." He winked at me. "Nice old gal. Bites the head off of you if the verdict don't come down on your side. Figuratively speaking."

There was a long, razor-sharp moment between the four of us, and then Dorlock swore. "It's your funeral, stupid girl. Next time you trust a pretty face I hope it's a springheel jack waiting underneath."

He stomped back to his tent, and Dean flipped the black cylinder one last time before he shoved it back into his pocket. "So, it seems you folks are in need of a guide."

"Y-yes," I managed. I sounded like a child who'd been caught out of bed, and I cleared my throat. "I mean, we are. Still."

Cal scoffed. "And let me guess—you're the answer to our plight?"

Dean passed a hand over his hair, putting the slick strands that Dorlock had mussed back in place. "I'm a bit of a tradejack, and guiding is one of my trades. I don't need to advertise because I'm good. And I sure won't charge you any fifty dollars."

"Was Dorlock really going to feed us to ghouls?" I asked him, the blue tent now crouched like a poison mushroom. It seemed like the sort of thing you'd read in a Proctor manual, something that was supposed to scare us into behaving.

"Sweetheart, your white flesh would be their filet mignon," said Dean. I flinched. Cal glared.

"Watch your language, fella. That's a young lady you're talking to."

"Word of advice, kid," said Dean. "This may be the Wild West down here, but you ain't a cowboy. You're not even a boy in a cowboy suit."

"Cal," I said sharply when a lean, angry look came over his face. "Why don't you make sure we have all of our supplies before we head out?" It was for his own good—Dean was twice his heft and carrying a knife, but Cal wasn't the type to consider mathematical odds.

"I'm not leaving you alone with *him*," he told me, pointing at Dean.

"She's snug as a bug with me, brother." Dean flashed me a smile that promised rule breaking and breathlessness. I decided to be interested in the laces on my shoes rather than risk turning red.

"I'm not your brother," Cal grumbled, but he found a space to open his duffel and check out his supplies. I did the same with my book bag.

"So, Miss Aoife," said Dean. "I guess now's a decent time to tell me what's on the other end of this skedaddle."

Oh, nothing much. Just a plan to find my mad brother and rescue him from a danger he may or may not actually be in. I settled for the abbreviated version.

"My father's house. In Arkham." I counted the number of pens and pencils in my satchel, refolded all of my spare clothes and tried to look like I knew what I was doing.

"Woman of few words," Dean said. "I like that. Here's the deal, pretty one: I get half when we're clear of the city and half when I deliver you safe and sound and without any Proctors crawling all over you. Dig?"

"How much?" I said, bracing myself for a price even worse than Dorlock's. I'd learned one thing at least in the Nightfall Market, and that was nothing came free or easy.

Dean lifted his shoulder. His leathers and grease-spotted denim were as far from my idea of a guide as I probably

73

was from Dean's idea of an adventurer, but in an odd way we fit. Neither what the other thought we should be. I rather thought we complemented each other.

"Bargains are different for everyone," Dean said. "From some I take a lot and some nothing they'll miss at all. You'll know when it's time to pay up."

I thought of Dorlock's hand on me, and shivered. But Dean had intervened, and he hadn't tried to con me out of my money, either.

Conrad would be decisive, show that he wasn't worried. I gave a nod. "All right."

"Good," Dean agreed. "For now, we gotta shake a leg if we want to be out of raven's sight by sunrise." He whistled to Cal. "Saddle up, cowboy! The Night Bridge is waitin' for us and the earth is turning fast."

6

Across the Night Bridge

W E FOLLOWED DEAN away from the pipe fire, away from the music and the light. I never thought I'd regret leaving the Nightfall Market, but as the noise faded, my apprehension swelled.

The groan and creak of the ice on the Erebus River grew loud as we approached the embankment, like two giants shouting at each other.

"What kind of backwards way are you taking us?" Cal demanded. I wondered too—there was nothing on the other side of the river but the foundry, and the road was patrolled by Proctors.

Dean stopped at a set of steps slick with ice and river water. The river rushed below our feet, beneath a walkway bolted to the bulwark with flimsy rivets oozing rust. I could look down through the gaps and see black, freezing nothing waiting to swallow me whole.

"I'm taking you out," Dean said. "What you wanted, ain't

75

it?" His engineer's boots, leather over steel toes and hobnail soles, clanked on the metal as he descended the stairs.

Cal grabbed my arm and slowed my steps, so we fell paces behind Dean. "I don't trust him, Aoife. He could be leading us right into a trap."

I concentrated on placing my feet on the icy steps. The water whispered to me as it swept along the ancient embankment and the old sewer lines that emptied out at the base of Derleth Street. A ghoul could practically reach up and touch the sole of my foot, we were so far down.

"If I wanted to trap you," Dean yelled back, "I would have turned right instead of left back at the Rustworks fence." His roughened voice was loud enough to echo from the opposite bank of the river.

Even in the cold, my face flushed. I gave Cal a censuring glance. This wasn't one of his adventures—if he made Dean cross, we'd be at the mercy of the Proctors. Or something worse.

I fell into step behind Dean, careful not to slip and pitch myself over the walkway into the water. "Why? What's right instead of left?"

"Right is the old submersible launch. Ran the Hunleys and the diesel subs down to Cape Cod during the war. Nowadays, the mill workers come from Lowell and snatch pretty little girls like yourself to work your fingers to the bone on the assembly lines and in the mills." He tilted his head to Cal. "Him, they'd just put a shank in his skinny gut and leave him to freeze to death on the riverbank."

"I didn't know that," I said quietly.

Dean shrugged. "Now you do, miss."

76

"I can handle myself," Cal huffed. "And you're going to find out if you keep up the lip."

"How much farther?" I said, attempting to keep things peaceable.

"Not far now," Dean said. "The Night Bridge is just up and around the bend. It's always waiting for travelers who need it, and for those who don't . . . well." He jerked his thumb over the rail, toward the black and rushing river.

"That sounds like something my brother would say," I murmured without thinking. Dean cocked his head.

"Oh? He a heretic too?"

A stone dropped into my stomach, cold and smooth as the ice churning below my feet. As the walkway creaked and shuddered, I shuddered with it.

Dean swiveled his head toward my silence, his bright eyes searching my face. "I say something wrong, Miss Aoife?"

"Forget it," I gritted, concentrating on where I stepped. Conrad wasn't any of Dean Harrison's business. Dean was a criminal, who smuggled other criminals for cash. What did I care if he thought my family was strange or common? We *were* strange. No power in science or the stars could change that. To all Rationalist folk, Conrad *was* a heretic—a boy who'd rejected reality and substituted the fantastical lie of magic and conjuring for science and logic. Heretics were, by their very definition, liars. Dean and Conrad would probably get along famously.

"Forgotten as yesterday's funny papers," Dean said easily, and then let out a low whistle. "Night Bridge ahead. In the shadows. This isn't something many from Uptown get to see."

Like one of Conrad's hidden picture puzzles, the Night

77

Bridge revealed itself to me by degrees. I saw the struts, the dark iron towers reaching for the bleak velvet sky, piercing it with sharp finials. The scrollwork railings crawled into focus, the cables knitting themselves into cohesion as my eye pierced the darkness. I felt something sharp catch in my chest as I beheld the antique span, dark and skeletal, drifting through the night air.

"Well?" Dean spoke close to my ear. I could feel his breath.

"I've seen this before," I said. The Gothic bridge arched a spiny back, cables rattling in the harsh wind blowing up the channel from the Atlantic.

"Reckon you have," Dean agreed. "In history books at whatever fancy school that uniform of yours belongs to."

The bridge before me was as familiar as the ceiling of my own room at the Academy, a span that dominated my structural engineering texts. The Babbage Bridge, a marvel of design, erected by Charles Babbage in 1891.

"This isn't possible," I said out loud. "The Babbage collapsed in 'twenty-nine."

"That's what they said," Dean agreed. "But you tell me, Miss Aoife—what are you seeing now?"

The Babbage Bridge, known to the citizens of Lovecraft as the Bouncing Baby, was a marvel in every way except one—its thin spiky towers and ultralight span were ill-equipped for the nor'easters and winter ice that bound up New England during the cold months, and on a particularly breezy January morning, the Babbage had given up the ghost, plunging twenty-one to their deaths in the Erebus. Condemned by the city, the usable pig iron had been salvaged and turned into the bones of Joseph Strauss's newer, stronger, more practical bridge.

78

Of course, people said you could still hear the screams of the twenty-one the Babbage claimed moaning through the cables of the new span, if the wind was from the east.

But this was impossible—I was not seeing the bridge that had broken its back against a gale nearly thirty years earlier. That bridge was gone.

"I'm not seeing things," I told Dean. "That is not the real Babbage."

"Let me ask you something," Dean said, walking again. I was forced to follow or be left behind. "You think just because the Head of the City or the Proctors down in Washington say a thing doesn't exist, all memory up and fades away? You think twenty-one deaths don't resonate in the aether to this day, on this spot?"

"I don't . . . I . . . Cal, are you seeing this?" I looked to him in confusion. Tales of phantoms were one thing. A phantom bridge was another, entirely.

He grunted. "Uh-huh." Cal couldn't take his eyes from the span either, stumbling over his own feet as he approached it with the same reverence he used when opening the newest issue of *Weird Tales*. But this was beyond anything the Proctors used to make heretics seem like either fearful phantoms or a joke with the stories they paid people like Cal's favorite pulp writer, Matt Edison, to pen. This looked *real*, in the way my own hand was real.

"The Babbage became the Night Bridge," Dean said. "Don't ask me to explain all that existential beatnik stuff, about memory and manifest will, 'cause I can't, but what I know is that the Night Bridge is here when I need it, because I can find it."

"If you expect me to believe that we're crossing out of

Lovecraft on some *ghost bridge*," I started, drawing myself up severely like Mrs. Fortune, "you're patently crazy."

"Boss design," Cal said. "But is it sound?"

"Don't be ridiculous," I said. "It wasn't sound in 'twenty-nine, was it? Babbage didn't account for the wind drag and . . . I can't believe I'm even explaining this. That is *not* the Babbage. It's a trick."

It had to be. According to the laws of the Rationalists, the bridge was impossible.

"No trick," Dean said. "And it's sound enough for your footsteps, Miss Aoife. I promise you." He beckoned when he reached another set of steps, spiraling upward toward the span. "Come on. Now that we've seen it, we can't very well not cross it."

"Let me guess—I'll be cursed by the ghost of faulty engineering?" I said as we started up, to the bridge bed. Sarcasm wasn't befitting a young lady, but I had to say something or I'd be too terrified to go another step. I couldn't be seeing what I was seeing. And yet I was walking it, feeling the frozen iron of the span under my hand, crossing a bridge that existed only in memory.

"Now the Night Bridge has seen you, too," Dean said, "and if you turned back, it could keep your soul forever."

I shivered, tucking my hand back into my pocket.

"People don't have souls," Cal interjected. "That's blasphemy."

"Do us a favor, cowboy," Dean said. "If you have the urge to call blasphemy again on this trip . . . don't."

Cal's lip curled back, but I grabbed his hand. "It's not worth it. We need his help." I didn't believe in souls the way the Rationalists explained them, but something was

80

keeping this bridge hidden—keeping it *in existence*—and it wasn't engineering.

Cal growled in his throat. "I don't like him, Aoife. He's a heretic, and he's common besides."

I stopped in my tracks, shoving a finger into Cal's chest. "Why is he common, Cal?" I demanded. "Because he's poor? Because he doesn't have a family? Because he's not like you?"

He backed away from my prodding. "Aoife, I didn't mean . . ."

I dropped my hand and placed myself equidistant between Cal and Dean, in the orbit of neither. "Leave it. I don't want to talk about it. With either of you," I added when Dean's ears pricked. I put my attention on the bridge. It could still be a trick. Mirrors, or a modification to Mr. Edison's light-lantern.

The stairs ended at a dilapidated tollbooth at the beginning of the span. Through cracks and holes the size of my body in the roadbed, I could see down to the water. My stomach flipped. I had no fear of heights, but a healthy one of drowning.

From where I stood, I watched the span sway in the light wind, groaning and shuddering down to its base deep below the riverbed. I looked upward, at the towers moving. Bony fingers clawing at a cloud-streaked sky, trying to peel back the vapor to the stars. I shook my head at Dean. "This is unsafe. We need to turn back." I didn't care any longer if it was a trick or . . . something not a trick. I simply didn't want to step foot on it.

Dean lifted his shoulders. "Told you already, Miss Aoife—too late."

With a creak, the tollbooth window swung open. I jumped inside my coat. A brass face topped by a ragged cap and a brass arm encased in the tatters of a city worker's uniform swung forth, nearly nose to nose with me. "Toll, pleassssse."

Dean reached inside his white T-shirt and pulled out a worn iron key on a chain. "Just a traveler, friend."

The automaton's eyes flashed with a blue spark and it cranked its hand backward to pull aside the tatty blue uniform jacket hiding the rusted ribs beneath. A keyhole sat in place of a heart.

"Pleasssse insert youuuur passsss . . . key," the automaton creaked. The voice box wound slow, and every syllable dragged forth from the dented throat.

I watched with fascination. Automatons were the purview of graduate students, those who passed their apprenticeships and were recommended to be master engineers. Powered by aether or clockwork, they worked in the foundries or in stately homes like the Langostrians'. This was likely the closest a common engineer like me would ever get to one.

Dean inserted his key and turned it. Something whirred to life inside the automaton, its clockwork innards firing with a click-clack of gears wanting oil. Its eyes lit, small blue aether flames that stared at me. This wasn't usual—automatons couldn't see, couldn't hear or feel. They were just metal laborers, doing tasks too punishing or delicate for human labor. Someone had modified this one, made it look and act like a man. It was wrong, like a springheel jack taking on the face of a trusted friend, until it could show its true, monstrous face and gobble you up. I didn't want to

82

look into its blue-flame eyes, any more than I wanted to look into the heart of the Engine without shielding goggles.

The automaton croaked at me. "The traveler walkssss the Night Bridge freely. The ssssstranger paysss the toll."

"Does it want money?" I asked Dean, reaching into my skirt pocket. "How much?"

"Easy," he said, removing the key and tucking it back under his shirt. "Your money's no good on the Night Bridge."

Cal shifted behind me. "I don't like the look of this."

"What does it cost?" I demanded of Dean. "I'm not doing anything inappropriate."

"And I wouldn't ask you to, Miss Aoife—least, not while you're paying me as a guide. That's a sacred, serious bond between guide and traveler and breaking it isn't something I do." His frown drew a line between his dark eyes, and he swiped a loose strand of hair off his forehead.

"Fine," I said. "What is it I have to pay?"

Dean pointed with his chin at the slot below the tollbooth window, while the automaton looked on. "From an Academy girl like you, only blood will do."

My eyes must have gone wide even as I felt the color drain out of my cheeks, said blood coursing hard through my heart. I could be forgiven for going to the Rustworks, even the market. In the eyes of the Proctors, I was only a girl, and I couldn't be expected to display the sense of a boy. A week's suspension, a lecture or two from Mrs. Fortune and Professor Swan, and I could go on with my life at the School.

But this was real, heretical dealings I'd be a part of.

Giving blood in oath was a grievous offense, something the Proctors would have your hands in the castigator for. Blood was too much like the old ways, the old superstitions the Rationalists had burned out of the world when the necrovirus came.

Dean tilted his head to the side. "That's the toll, Miss Aoife. Prick your finger on the spindle and tumble on into dreamland, or go back to those safe stone walls and those cold metal gears before you're a heretic and a criminal besides."

Cal gripped the straps of his pack so hard the buckle creaked. "We should turn back, Aoife. This was a terrible idea."

Over the roar of blood in my ears, borne on the rush of fear, I heard myself say, "I can't. Conrad—"

"Conrad's cast his lot, Aoife! Don't be stupid!"

"Why don't you let the girl make up her own mind?" Dean snapped. "She has got one, you know."

"Why don't you mind your own business before I put my knuckles through your heretic teeth?" Cal snarled.

"Both of you be quiet!" My voice echoed off the suspension cables. The automaton turned its blank slate of a face to me.

"Blood on the iron. Blood . . . isss the toll," it droned.

I flexed my hands. How did you choose which one went into the mouth of the iron beast? I was left-handed— another mark against me as far as the Proctors and the Academy were concerned—but I needed both for any task I might encounter in the Engineworks.

If I graduated the School of Engines.

84

If I came back from Arkham.

"Just prick your finger, Aoife," Dean said softly. He dipped his head, so his words tickled my ear. "It doesn't hurt. I promise you."

"I'm not worried about the pain," I said. Madhouses, the Catacombs, no one left to watch out for my mother, Conrad desperate and alone . . . but not the pain. Pain was something I could choose to acknowledge, or not. That, at least, I'd learned long ago.

"If you want to get out of Lovecraft before the sun goes up, this is the way to do it," Dean said. "Now, I know no Uptown princess is going to come down to the Rustworks looking for yours truly. No girl who can't pay the toll would come this far." Dean grinned at me. "You're no princess."

I swallowed hard. My throat felt like it was lined with sandpaper. "And you're no white knight," I told Dean, and before my nerve failed me, stuck my hand into the gap an acetylene torch had cut in the tollbooth's side. My fingers brushed a thin iron spike set where the coin slot should be.

I placed it against my index finger and pressed down. My blood dribbled into the crevice of my knuckle, warming the skin. The spike was cold where it bit into my flesh.

No Proctors swooped down on me and no fanciful black magic swarmed up to turn me into the wanton heretic that Professor Swan and his newsreels warned about. My finger started to ache, and I pulled my hand away, sucking on it and getting an aftertaste of iron.

The automaton regarded me with its flame eyes and then withdrew its arm into the booth. "Proceed, travelersssss."

"There," Dean said. "Not so bad, is it?"

Cal stepped up. "What about me? What do I do?"

"Nothing," Dean said. "You didn't hire me, she did." He tilted his head toward me. "You're awful quiet, Miss Aoife. You all right?"

I tried not to think about the warm throbbing brass of the castigator where it waited in Banishment Square. Dean pulled a stained red bandanna from his back pocket and held it out. "Here. A little more blood won't matter to this old rag."

"What, and risk an infection?" Cal fumbled in his knapsack. "Hold it, Aoife. I've got a plaster."

"Cal," I sighed. "You remind me of Mrs. Fortune sometimes."

Dean's mouth curled up at that. He stepped past the tollbooth, onto the bridge. The wire grating beneath our feet bounced and creaked as we advanced, and I unwillingly flashed on the images of the twisted span after the collapse, suspension cables flapping in the wind like tangled hair.

As we walked, the holes grew wider, until finally we were just walking on the mesh used by Babbage to undersling the roadbed, a thin half-inch of wire keeping us out of the river. I looked back at Cal and saw that his face had gone sheet white with an undertone that matched his thatch of hair.

"Come on," I said, holding out my hand. "I'm sure it's perfectly safe. We don't weigh that much."

He looked at me, looked at Dean, and then stepped forward, his jaw twitching. He ignored my hand and shoved his own into the pockets of his car coat. "Let's just get across, okay?"

I pulled my hand back to my side, a small pain with it.

86

Cal had never refused my help before. At least my bleeding had stopped and I didn't appear to be branded a heretic for it. Not like the five-pointed stars and crosses and sutra wheels the Proctors told us to watch out for, because a mark like that was the first sign. Heretics believed in gods, in magic, and carried their marks. A rational person knew there was no need of such decoration.

Dean walked with me, Cal a little behind, and together we crept across the span, over dark water and cracking ice. When we'd passed under the halfway mark, the Gothic arch that Babbage had proudly declared the gateway to New England, Dean spoke. "So, Miss Aoife. Arkham. What's a city girl want with that worm-eaten little town?"

I didn't answer for a moment that stretched long and thin, listening to our feet clang against the span.

"Something that's none of my business?" Dean guessed. "That's usually the way. But the more I know, the quicker I can get you to your Point B."

"I have a brother," I said. "His name is Conrad." I glanced back at Cal, trudging a few paces behind with his eyes glued to his feet. "He needs my help," I told Dean. "In Arkham."

"Answer me straight, Miss Aoife, and I won't bother you again," Dean said. "Are you in trouble?" He held up a hand, long knobby fingers spreading like spider legs. "I'm not talking sneaking out of school, lifting a pack of cigarettes, and going out to the jitney races. I'm talking bad trouble. Bloody trouble."

"I don't smoke," I said.

"You want to tell me the truth on this one, Miss Aoife. If it's trouble that can get me beat up or buried six feet

87

under, and you don't fess up, your guide might be disinclined to pull your fat out of said trouble. Catch my meaning?" Dean's face looked like it had when he'd confronted Dorlock—perfectly pleasant, except in his eyes. They were hard like stone and my chest went tight in response. I didn't want Dean looking at me like that.

"There's no trouble," I said, and even managed a smile. Up until Conrad's birthday, I'd never made a habit of lying. My mother babbled endlessly about things that weren't there and couldn't exist. I preferred to keep on solid ground. After Conrad came at me with the knife, I lied out of necessity, to keep the eyes of the school and the Proctors turned away from me.

Those had all been small lies, more voids of truth than falsehoods. I looked Dean in the eye. "I'm not in trouble," I repeated. "Not yet, anyway."

He loosed a small chuckle. "All right, miss. That's all I wanted to know."

"Now I should get to ask you something," I said. Dean shoved his hands into his pockets.

"I don't know about that, sweetness. I think you're much smarter than I am."

Behind us, Cal gave a snort. "Isn't that the truth."

"Why do you do this sort of thing?" I said, before Cal could get a nose full of Dean's fist. "Smuggling people in and out of Lovecraft, I mean. It seems, well . . . dangerous, for starters."

"About the only thing I'm suited for," Dean said. "My old man wore out his bones as a gear monkey in the Rustworks, and my brother got himself killed in Korea a few years back. Got no money, got no family. Nothing but this

88

talent of mine to get folks where they need to be. It's a rambling life, but it's mine."

"What about your mother?" Cal said. "Surely even you have one."

Dean fixed Cal with his hard stare. "Don't bring up my mother unless you want me to talk some crap about yours."

There was a sentiment I could take to heart, and shame over interrogating Dean heated my cheeks. "I didn't mean to pry," I told him. "I just wanted to know a little bit about you, seeing as you're taking us so far and—"

His head whipped skyward. "Button your lip, Miss Aoife."

I followed the finger he touched to his mouth, up and up through the black bones of the Night Bridge. We were in the darkness between the embankments of Lovecraft and the glow and burn of the foundry beyond. Wind whipped my hair into a fury of knots; over the wind, the whirr of wings carried on frozen air.

"Raven patrol," Dean said. "Flying out from Ravenhouse."

"They'll see us," Cal hissed, instantly panicked. "The Proctors will take us into custody and lock us up in the Catacombs and—"

"Is there any shelter on the bridge?" I demanded in the loudest whisper I could manage. The hum grew louder, filled the air and drowned out the ice.

"Not unless you're gonna swing down among the pilings like a river rat," Dean murmured.

"What are we supposed to do?" Cal shoved his hands through his hair. "We're sitting ducks. We're totally exposed!"

I started when Dean grabbed my hand. "We hoof it." He tugged and I stumbled. "Run!" he elaborated when Cal stood, wavering between us and the way back to Lovecraft.

"Move it, Cal!" I shouted, silence forgotten. Avoiding capture mattered more than detection. Besides, nothing escaped the notice of the ravens.

Dean's loping stride easily outmatched mine, and sharp pain shot up my arm as he dragged me along, our feet pounding on the span.

They could not drown out the sound of wings.

I knew that I shouldn't look back, that I should tuck in and run like my life depended on it, because it did, but I couldn't help turning my head to see what was coming.

The raven's feathers gleamed liquid black in the cold starlight. Their eyes blazed with yellow aether, burning up the night sky like a flock of sparks. Their beaks were glass and their talons were sets of tiny gears and rods that clacked and grasped as they swooped in a low V over the river. Their feathers were hammered aluminum, painted black, and their innards were marvels of clockwork that printed everything their burning eyes saw onto tiny lantern-reels.

A raven, unlike an automaton, *could* see, and if it marked a heretic, it could fly back to Ravenhouse and croak to its masters from its metal throat. The whirr of their gears and the hiss of their aether flames drowned out everything, even my own heartbeat.

"Not but a hundred steps," Dean panted. "Then we'll be in the foundry. Those spy birds can't spy through steel."

I dug down, my feet clanging against the grate, my school bag slapping my hip, breath scissoring its way in and out of my lungs. Cal trailed us, his limbs flying in every direction as panic caught his feet and took him to ground.

90

"Cal!" I whirled, and my wrist wrenched in Dean's grasp. He stumbled in turn, cursing.

"What in the blue hell are you doing, kid?"

I covered the two steps back to Cal, as the faint ghostly lamps atop the span of the Night Bridge winked out, one by one, covered by dusky wings.

"My ankle," Cal moaned. "I think I broke it."

"Aoife, we need to *go*," Dean snapped, his panic creeping up to his eyes. "If I get caught and dragged to Ravenhouse, it's curtains for the whole trio, you get me?"

Cal's eyes were wide, his nostrils flaring in pain. I slung his arm over my shoulder. "Up. Put your weight on your good leg."

"Just leave me," he groaned. "Just leave me here . . . I swear I won't give you up. . . ."

"Cal Daulton, *I* swear that if you don't shut your trap, get up and run, I am going to sock you in the jaw and give you to the Proctors myself." I had passed the point of my usual nervy fear, the kind that made my hands shake and my voice go soft. Now I was afraid on a much more basic level. I wasn't going to the Catacombs. I wasn't leaving Conrad on his own.

I'd come this far. I wasn't turning around.

I stood, heaving Cal along with me. He was much heavier than his frame belied and I felt the rush of air along my face as the raven's wings stirred the air.

Cal's weight lifted all at once, and Dean was next to me, taking Cal's other arm. "It's a good thing I took a shine to you, Miss Aoife," he said. "Because this is above and beyond."

Dean muttered a swear as we dragged Cal between us.

91

"Hard left. Head for the automaton sheds inside the foundry fence."

The gates of the Nephilim Foundry were shut for the night, but Dean found a gap in the fence and I helped Cal through. In the shadow of the outbuildings and the loaders—the sleds that ferried the slag, the by-product of the foundry—we stumbled through a patchwork world of glow and shadow, iron and frozen ground.

I could barely breathe from our dash and Cal's weight, but I forced myself on, staying close to Dean.

He rattled the doors of the nearest building, a machine shed with the phantom shapes of automatons waiting for repair beyond the dirt-coated glass panes. "In here," he rasped. "Put yourself on the floor—those things are still coming."

Spurred by the ever-present sound of wings, I skip-hopped across the open space with Cal and we ducked through the doors just as the ravens swooped over the towers and tin roofs of the foundry and banked, turning back toward Lovecraft in the same rigid pattern that mimicked life but was as cold and precise as a surgeon's tool.

I let Cal down gently, and slumped next to him. My heart was beating on my ribs like a fist on a madhouse door.

Dean exhaled and leaned his head back against the corrugated wall. "That was entirely too near for my taste." He pulled a flattened packet from his back pocket and a silver lighter from his jacket. "Care for one?" he said as he bit off a Lucky Strike from the pack.

"Girls with good breeding don't smoke." I quoted Mrs. Fortune without even realizing it, and then blushed. Dean wasn't the kind of person who'd care what a school matron thought. He wasn't the kind of person who put stock

92

in girls who did, either, and the last thing we needed now was for him to think me silly. Which I was, to be worrying about comportment at a time like this.

"All right, then," Dean said, touching the flame to the tip. "Lemme know if you decide not to be good, miss."

I gave him what I could of a thankful smile before I crouched next to Cal, taking in his flushed face and shallow breaths. He looked like poor Ned Connors had, after Ned chopped off his little finger in a drill press during Machine Shop. I moved Cal's hair, soaked with freezing sweat, off his forehead. "How's the ankle?"

"Awful," he said. He kicked off his boxy school shoe and pulled down his argyle sock. I winced at the sight of the swelling around the joint. I had barely passed our first-aid course—to treat the burns, breaks and slashes associated with work in the Engine—but I gingerly prodded Cal's foot, and he yelped.

"Quiet!" Dean commanded. "You think the foundry doesn't have its own bits of mean metal rolling around after dark?"

I considered being stuck here overnight, and our chances of escape in the light of day. Even with the raven patrols, the night was our only friend right now. I bit my lip, looking at Cal. "We're just going to have to wait until we get to Arkham," I told him. "I'll find you a surgeon or a hospice there, I promise. Can you walk at all?"

Cal pressed his lips together. "I can try, if you help me."

"I'm sorry," I said again. "But we have to keep moving." I reached for him, tried to lever us into some kind of duet.

"I'm your guide, full stop," Dean said quickly. "Don't expect me to get in on that dance."

93

"Nobody asked you to dance with anyone," I snapped, helping Cal up. My shoulders protested the weight, but I let him lean on me. "Just do what I'm paying you for." Dean Harrison might not be a heretic in the sense the Proctors understood the word, but he was certainly no gentleman.

Dean dropped his Lucky Strike and ground it under his boot. "Aye, aye, Miss Aoife." He rolled the door back without another word and stuck his head out. "All clear."

The narrow avenue between the long steel sheds before us rippled with fog, the aether lamps nailed to poles on each building face spitting in the moisture. In the distance I heard the whine of gears and saw a pair of blue lamplike eyes riding through the fog. I shivered, not just because of the wind on my sweat-scrimmed skin. The automatons of the foundry reminded me too much right now of everything I'd left in Lovecraft—nightjars, madmen, the looming turn of the year since Conrad had gone away. The feeling hadn't left me that this journey into the wilds of Arkham was all a terrible mistake, and we weren't even off the foundry grounds. There were worse things waiting for me outside the city gates than madness. Ghouls, roadside bandits, and the specter of heresy that my brother represented. If I came back from Arkham alive, I wouldn't just be a potential infected—I'd be condemned as a heretic.

If I left the city, I might never be able to come back. Conrad had to have known when he sent the letter. He needed my help enough for me to risk it.

Or he was mad, and I was following him, the infection dropping my guard, making me take risks. Follow criminals. Act irrationally.

I rubbed the scar under my jaw with my free hand. My

other was around Cal's waist, fingers pressed between his ribs. "Thanks, Aoife," he whispered. "But maybe we can just forget this bit when I tell the guys about our trip?"

He smiled at me, and I managed to smile back through my effort of supporting half his weight. "Whatever you say, Cal. You're the hero of that story."

Dean whistled low from up ahead. "Back gate," he said. "Locked, though." He extended his palm to me. "Got a hairpin you can spare, miss?"

I pulled the bobby pin out of the left side of my regulation bun and handed it to him. Dean bent it open with his teeth and worked on the padlock. It popped with an irritable creak. I wished misbehavior came as easily to me, with as few compunctions. The nervous knot in my guts wouldn't be nearly choking me now.

"Nice work," I said. He shrugged and tucked the pin inside his pack of cigarettes.

"Easy trick. If you like, I'll teach you sometime."

"You'll do no such thing," Cal said. "Aoife's a nice girl."

"You don't spend a lot of time around the fair sex, do you?" Dean teased, that insufferable grin coming into play.

"It's fine," I told Cal when he tensed. Cal was easy to tease—the Master Builder knew that for a fact—but he was hurt and Dean wasn't playing fair. I cast Dean a sharp look. "It's not such a far journey upstate. It'll be over before you know it."

"Not soon enough," Cal huffed, but he let me help him through the foundry gate all the same.

95

7

The Berkshire Belle

I DEVELOPED A discordant rhythm walking with Cal, down from the county road outside the foundry, through a ditch that soaked my feet to the ankles with freezing brackish water, up the other side and across a frozen field patchy with forgotten cornstalks. Dean stayed a few feet ahead, his back and body tense, hands shoved in his dungaree pockets like a gunfighter waiting to draw. I knew better than to ask him where we were going, but it didn't mean I wasn't wondering. As an Academy student, I was rarely permitted to leave the grounds, never mind the city. The last in recent memory was a field trip to a quarry. Even by engineering standards, not exciting.

The pulse of the lighthouse on Half-Moon Point winked through the trees as our footsteps disappeared into a carpet of early snow and pine needles, the field ending at a broken stone wall.

96

"How much farther?" I whispered to Dean, as Cal's soft pants of pain warmed my right ear.

"Not far," Dean said. "Other side of the woods, on the point. That's where the airship lands."

"Airship?" I almost lost my grip on Cal from surprise.

"Sure thing." Dean grinned. "You want to get to Arkham—the *Berkshire Belle* and her crew are the quickest route."

The trees thinned as the ground became rock and I could hear the rush of the ocean and feel the tinge of salt on my skin. We were much farther away from the city than I'd realized.

Directly beyond was the Lovecraft lighthouse, the white spire with its black band standing guard at the mouth of the river. Moored beyond, where the water met the rock, was an airship.

I'd seen airships before, small skimmers that flew from Lovecraft to New Amsterdam, or out to Cape Cod and Nantucket when the weather was fair. This craft was different from all of them—the silvery hide of the rigid balloon was patched and the passenger cabin was battered, windowless and military gray, not sleek and welcoming like the Pan Am and TWA zeppelins that took off from Logan Airfield. The fans clicked as they rocked back and forth against their tie-downs in the wind. It was beautiful, in its own way, scarred and slippery—a shark built for air.

"Now, you let me do the talking," Dean said. "Captain Harry's here every night, and passage is included in your fee, but if he doesn't like your look . . ." Dean drew a thumb across his throat. My scar itched in response.

97

"This Captain Harry sounds like a real pirate," Cal said. Cal *would* bring up pirates. As if we hadn't had a year's supply of excitement just getting here.

I looked at the *Berkshire Belle*'s hulk and listened to the moan of its moorings as we came closer, the sound like the murmuring of the madhouse after lights out, or the whispering of a ghost, if I believed in such things. Which I emphatically did not, but seeing the Babbage appear from nowhere, the ghostly dirigible, the moonlight and the frost called up echoes of a spectral world. The Proctors abhorred unsanctioned tales of witchcraft and fairies, angels or demons, but I'd never been chastised for listening to a ghost story. Now I wished that the girls in my hall hadn't delighted in passing them around quite so much. Tonight, I could almost believe.

"Harry's a card," Dean said. "Came out of Louisiana, swamp folk. He'd cut your tongue out soon as look at you, but the *Belle* ain't never been stopped by the ravens."

"Never?" I said. The ravens saw everything—nothing lifted more than a foot off the ground under its own power in Lovecraft without Proctor approval.

"Never," Dean said. "Harry's too fast for ravens."

"Yeah, well," Cal groused. "Fast, slow . . . he better have someplace for me to sit, with this bum ankle."

Dean banged on the hull. After a moment the hatch wheel spun and it opened with a creak and a rumble of abused gears. Captain Harry might be stealthy in the sky, but he needed to learn his way around an oilcan.

"Evening," Dean said to the figure in the hatch, a massive man in a greatcoat, profile shielded in shadow. "Got two with me looking to take passage up Arkham way. The usual fee."

98

There was silence for a long time, and even though I only caught the gleam of lenses and brass where the man's eyes should be, I could feel him staring. I shifted under the silence and the stare, letting out a small cough. "Hello, sir. Captain, I mean."

"*Bonsoir*, mam'selle," he said, finally. "And Dean Harrison. I think I not see you again for some time after that trouble up Lovecraft way."

"Trouble?" Cal perked like a poodle sniffing hamburger meat. "What trouble?"

I admit I wondered the same, but I had the sense to keep quiet about it in front of Dean and Captain Harry.

"Nothing you need to get excited about, kid," Dean snapped. "Got no time for gossip, Harry. I've charged this young lady fair and square and I'm her guide."

"*Mais oui*," Captain Harry said. His accent was slow as syrup on a cold morning, but his voice was gravel, hardened and crushed by years of smoke and wind. "She's a different class of traveler, no? Young." He stepped out of the hatch, his big steam-ventor boots—bigger, thicker, brassbound versions of the boots Dean wore—crushing the rock beneath the airship with a grating like bone on bone. In the light, Harry was about Professor Swan's age, massive and unkempt, sporting red hair shot with white through the left temple, like he'd been struck by lightning. Bug-eyed ruby glass flying goggles covered his eyes and crimson stubble his face, which was split by a wide grin. He fit with the *Berkshire Belle*—scarred and rough, but in fine working order.

Harry stuck out a large hand and said, "Who might you be, mademoiselle?" I didn't take it. His paw could have

99

crushed both of my hands with room to spare, and I'd abused them enough crossing the bridge.

"I might be Aoife Grayson, and I might be in a hurry," I said, tightening my grip on Cal. I wasn't going to be the pretty, delicate thing who needed men to do her talking. Harry didn't seem hostile, but Dorlock hadn't either.

"Pretty, *hein*," Captain Harry hooted. "But even less manners than you, eh, Dean?"

"We almost got peeped by some ravens on the bridge," Dean said. "If it's all the same to you, I'd like to see the Lovecraft in my taillights just as much as the young lady."

"*Oui*, course you would." Captain Harry gestured with a sweep of his greatcoat. The material was deep blue, and hid a red silk vest and oil-streaked gray trousers. It *was* a navy uniform, I realized on a second glance, from the war before the last one. Harry did look like he'd be at home manning the furnace on a war zeppelin, or pulling his weight as an antiaircraft gunner on a destroyer.

"Come on, then," Harry told me. "The night, she ain't getting longer. *Allez*." He pulled himself into the ship without another word, leaving us alone. I let out my breath, at long last. He hadn't challenged me on being young, or female, or dragging along a friend with a bad ankle. Maybe this would end all right.

Once I'd managed to wrest myself and Cal through the hatch, Dean followed and spun it closed. "We're right and tight back here, Harry!" he hollered.

The hold of the *Berkshire Belle* was one large convex room, hard benches bolted to the arched rib cage of the inner hull, and cargo netting swaying back and forth overhead like Spanish moss. I settled Cal on a bench in easy

100

reach of a tie-down, should we hit rough weather, and tried to give him a reassuring smile. I think I managed one that made me seem only slightly nauseated. "I'm just going to look around, all right? Try to keep your ankle up so it doesn't swell any more." In truth, I was dying to get a look at the *Belle*, to examine her engines and her clockworks, see how she flew. It would calm me down, and give me something to think of besides *I'm a runaway madwoman and the Proctors are coming.*

"Be careful," Cal murmured. "I don't trust these miscreants."

"You don't trust your own mother, Cal." I gave his good foot a nudge. "I'll be fine."

Dean was slouched on a bench opposite Cal, and no one else in the crew seemed to be paying attention to me, so I poked at the various supplies slung into cargo nets, and when I'd determined there wasn't anything more interesting than spare parts and hardtack, went looking for the cockpit. I might never be on an airship—a real airship—again, and I wanted to soak up as much as I could. Girls weren't allowed to attend the School of Aeronautics. Our changeable nature made us unsuitable for flying or the precision work needed to maintain a machine that was really just a steel box slung under a balloon full of deadly explosive gas.

I didn't particularly think that a twitchy idiot like Marcos Langostrian and his ilk would be suited either, but no one had asked me my opinion.

I went forward first, and peeped into the fore compartment, trying to stay out of the crew's way. For all her outward plainness, the *Belle*'s cockpit was a thing of beauty.

101

The windscreen was divided into four parts like rose petals, each a bubble of solid glass. The flight controls, worked in brass, shimmered under the aether lamps laid into the swooping brass walls, and the knobs and switches for the PA system and pitch controls were ebony inlaid with ivory chevrons, like a V of spirit birds.

Or ravens. I chased the thought away. The ravens hadn't seen me. As far as the Proctors knew, the worst I was guilty of was being out of bounds after Academy curfew.

Captain Harry came up behind me. "Welcome aboard," he boomed. "Making yourself right at home, I see." His voice made me start. I could tell myself we'd escaped the city cleanly all I wanted, but my nerves believed differently.

"I was just looking at the cockpit," I offered. "I'm sorry—"

"No sorries!" Harry exclaimed. "She's a magnificent flying machine, *ma Belle.*" He gestured to the twin pilot's chairs, crimson thread stitched into oxblood hide, and the two pilots occupying them. "This here's Jean-Marc and Alouette, the two finest *canailles* ever to sail the stormy skies."

Jean-Marc was thin and unremarkable, rather like Mr. Hesse, while Alouette wasn't much older than Dean, with a round face and blond ringlets like a lanternreel starlet. She had the same cold, calculating look in her blue eyes as one of the femme fatales in the serials Cal loved—that icy cut-glass beauty that belonged to my mother, before sedatives and too much time locked up with her madness dulled it.

"Hello there," I said. Alouette jerked her chin over my head.

102

"What did your boyfriend do to his ankle?"

"He's not . . . ," I started with a sigh, but she climbed out of her seat, brushed past me and knelt in front of Cal.

"Boy," she told him crisply, "we don't take cripples on this boat. You'll be the first one the Proctors snatch up, we get shot down."

"I fell," Cal said. "It's nothing really. Doesn't even hurt anymore." The veins in his neck pulsed as Alouette prodded his ankle. He did a good enough job of hiding his wince when she poked the swollen joint, but I saw it and so did Dean, who gave a snort.

Alouette's frosty expression changed to a smile as she inspected Cal. "Guess you did bang it up, at that. Once we're airborne, I'll dress it. I was a nurse down in Shreveport before I took up flying."

Dean rolled his eyes behind Alouette's back, and pulled a harness around himself. "Best to sit down, Miss Aoife," he told me. "Don't want you knocking your noggin, and the way these cats drive, you will."

"*Oui*, sit," Captain Harry commanded. "On board this ship, you are citizens of the air, and the air, she has a streak of mischief and malice. You disobey an order, you be over the deck rail. Otherwise, you keep quiet and you arrive up Arkham in one piece, *oui*?"

Cal and I nodded that we understood. There was nothing angry about Harry, but he had an air of command that brooked no argument.

Dean leaned his head back against the hull and shut his eyes, like this was all painfully everyday. I fleetingly wished I were calm. How many times had Dean made this trip? More than I ever would in my life.

103

"Lift, you bastards!" Captain Harry bellowed. "And if a storm do swallow us, may she spit us back up again!"

There was a jolt as the mooring lines retracted and then, with a dip in my stomach, the *Belle* sailed aloft, borne on the winter wind.

Once the excitement of liftoff abated, I found myself leaning my head against the hull, feeling the vibration of the wind and the turbines against my skull. Lulled, I felt my eyelids dip and exhaustion wind like wire through every bit of me, twisting and tugging and coaxing me toward sleep.

I decided that sleeping in a shipful of heretics and criminals might not be in my best interest. To keep awake, I focused on Dean. I'd never met a heretic who wasn't strapped to the castigator or locked in a madhouse, and I wanted to memorize him, because soon enough he'd be gone and I'd be . . .

I didn't know. Alone? Searching for Conrad, certainly. Wandering through another person's delusions, the way I had been since I was a child.

Dean reached up and smoothed back his hair, shiny and black as his leather jacket in the aether glow. He plucked the cigarette from behind his ear and stuck it in his mouth, shutting his eyes and rubbing the back of his neck. I was wondering what the short hairs at the base of his skull would feel like under my hand when Alouette spun around in her pilot's chair, her eyes wide through the small slice of open hatch I could see. She leaped up, closed the distance across the hold like a swift golden cat, ripped the cigarette

104

away from Dean and threw it across the cabin. I jumped at her sudden movement, and her shouting. "Are you crazy, boy?" she demanded. "We're floating underneath tons of hydrogen and you want to light up?"

Dean's lips twitched and his entire body stiffened, like a valve with too much pressure on it. "I'm not an idiot, Allie, but I am bored. Being in this sardine can ain't my idea of a fun Friday night."

"You're welcome to step out any old time," Alouette flared, flicking her long fall of golden hair in Dean's face. Dean dropped his eyes and chuckled, taking the Lucky Strikes from his pocket and sticking another cigarette between his lips.

"Don't tempt me, Allie. You'd drive any sane guy off a ledge." I watched the two of them stare at each other for a moment, until Dean crossed his ankles and leaned back against the hull, stretching himself out to his full height. "Go back to playing nursemaid. I'll behave, I promise."

Alouette threw up her hands and went to Cal, brushing me aside as if I were inconvenient baggage. "Let's see about that ankle now that we're up." She pulled off his oxford and his sock, her mouth quirking at the hole in the toe, and slid his school pants up to the knee, her pale hands brushing his skin. "My, my," Alouette said, gently wiggling the swollen joint. Cal hissed, his cheeks caving in and his teeth showing. He looked like he wanted to bite Alouette, but he pulled himself together, covering his mouth to hide the feral grimace. I wanted to sit by him and let him squeeze my hand, like I had when he burned himself during our fabricating class, but I had the feeling Alouette might bite *me* if I did.

105

"Like I said, miss," Cal told her. "It's worse than it looks."

Alouette fluttered at his words. "Listen to you, 'miss' this and 'miss' that. It's Alouette, or Allie."

Cal swallowed and took his hand away from his face, and he was easygoing Cal again. "All right, mi—Alouette. Sorry I'm not in better humor—it does smart a bit."

"You did a number on yourself," Alouette agreed. "Looks like a real war wound."

"It was my fault he fell," I said, rather more loudly than I had to. Her hands were still on his leg. "He was trying to help me," I explained.

Alouette spread a slow smile. "What a gentleman you are." She whipped his ankle to the left, and Cal let out a yell, going stark white in the face. Alouette giggled at his expression.

"Well, it's not broken if you felt that. We'll bandage you up, but no slaying dragons or chasing damsels for a week or so, all right?"

Dean snorted. "Watch yourself, cowboy. I think the pirate wench has taken a shine to you." He stood and twirled a small hatch open, one that I saw led to an outside deck. Cold air rushed in, lifting my hair and dappling my skin with moisture.

"Close her up!" Captain Harry shouted from the cockpit, to my relief. "We none of us arctic creatures!"

"Same Dean," Alouette tsked when the hatch clanked shut behind him. "Still a child at heart."

I didn't think Dean not wanting to be in the same space as Alouette was very childish. I wanted to get away from her cheap bottle-blond hair and tinny laugh just as much as he seemed to.

"I'll be happy when we're rid of him," Cal told her. "He's just some freak Aoife hired to get us out of the city, but I'll take care of her from there. Dean's not an upright moral person like you."

"I'm upright, but honey, I'm far from moral," Alouette said, giving him a practiced smile. "Hold still now and let me bandage this."

I felt irritation swell in me, and it expelled itself with a huff of air. Cal would still be collecting baseball cards and building model airships, hiding in his dormitory, if it weren't for me. I was the one who'd taken us on the hour-long jitney ride to the machine shop where they milled gears for the Engine, who found the best pastries on Derleth Street, who coaxed Cal out into the wide city. I'd swear he was allergic to light before I'd dragged us outside the walls of the Academy. How dare he get to play the adventurer to Alouette while she treated me like a dumb kid? And why'd she have to keep rubbing his leg?

"You look very moral to me," Cal said, in a comically deep tone he no doubt adopted from some lanternreel actor. "And you've got a soft touch. . . ." He hissed. "But your hands are cold."

Alouette simpered at his attention. "I'll have to see if I can do something about that. I like my patients comfortable."

I stood up and grabbed the hatch release Dean had used, yanking at it with force that I really wanted to put into slapping that too-innocent smile off of Alouette. A girl—a woman—like her wouldn't give Cal the time of day if we were in Lovecraft. But if he couldn't see through her act, then it was his own fault. I stepped out. The wind grabbed my breath and sucked it away into the void.

107

A narrow ribbon of walkway ran the length of the *Belle*, leading to a small lip of deck underneath the turbines at the rear, in a dead spot for wind and drag. Dean stood hunched inside his coat at the aft, smoke trailing behind the airship like a banner. I let the hatch fall shut behind me with a coffin clang.

"Airsick?" Dean's breath joined his exhaled smoke, a ghost floating next to him before it blew away.

"Something like that," I said over the roar of wind and turbine. "Alouette certainly is . . . friendly."

"She's a piece of work." Dean shook his head. "Hellcat in a fight. Could drink an Irish sailor under the table."

"You'd know." My words came out tinged with acid, for reasons I couldn't entirely identify. "You and she have all the history."

Dean chuffed. "Can't put much past you, Miss Aoife."

I shook my head. "I didn't have to work very hard on that one. She's been staring a hole through you since we got on board."

"Like I said," Dean muttered. "Hellcat."

"How much farther?" I crossed my arms and pouted, as if I were six years old. I felt like stamping my feet and demanding that Alouette keep away from *my* friends. Felt out of control. Spinning, spiraling, dancing . . .

No. I began to recite a Fibonacci sequence in my head and clung to Dean's voice and to the cold fingers of the wind against my cheeks. Keeping order. Keeping calm. Shutting the door on the madness that made my blood boil.

"To Arkham? Two hours, maybe three." Dean flicked his glowing cigarette over the rail and I watched it sail into the darkness.

108

I shivered. "The sooner, the better. I don't think I like being this far off the ground after all." Truly, I didn't like being shown as the scared schoolgirl next to Alouette and her crew. I already had enough presumptions to deal with back home. To be looked down on by heretics and shoved aside by Cal at the slightest hint of attention was entirely too much.

"I like it." Dean shoved his hands into his armpits for warmth. "It's free air up here. Nobody pointing and saying who's a heretic and who's a Rationalist. No Proctors. Just flying."

I turned to go inside. "I'd better go check on Cal. Make sure he hasn't agreed to run off and marry Alouette."

"She has that effect on a man, sure." Dean whistled. "Poor old Cal has no chance."

"He's never even had the opportunity before now," I grumbled. Dean searched out a comb in his pockets and fixed his hair against the wind.

"I deduced." He followed me through the hatch and shut it behind him. "Come on. You want to see the rest of the *Belle*? Take your mind off Cal?"

I nodded. If Cal was going to behave like a dolt, I didn't need to concern myself. And who knew when I'd be on an airship again? I should make it count. "Very much so."

Dean led me back inside, through the hold and down a narrow corridor to the aft, where the whirring of the turbine blades vibrated my back teeth. "Bunk room." He pointed out a chrome door with an empty brass nameplate, the slot for a card held in the talons of a rigid-winged eagle.

I ran my hand down the chevron wings stamped under the nameplate, the scarred spot where a ship's name and operating number had been burned off with a torch. "This ship was someone else before it was the *Belle*?"

Dean nodded. "She was an enemy rig in the war," he offered. "Officer transport, from what Harry told me. He and his navy boys crashed outside of Bern in 'forty-four and hijacked it from a squad of enemy officers and their necrodemons."

I jerked my hand back to my side.

Dean examined me, leaning in a bit. "You look a little green, kiddo," he said. "Sure you're not airsick?"

"Necrodemons . . . ," I murmured. "Not very pleasant . . ."

"Yep," Dean said, shaking his head. "But they're long gone, miss. Not going to jump out and bite you." He twisted the eagle insignia upside down and chuckled.

"It's not that," I whispered. "I mean, I'm not afraid of necrodemons." I could *become* a necrodemon, if the virus took hold of me. I could be worse than anything that had flown over Europe in the ship that would become the *Belle*. "It's just a bit close to home," I told Dean, and cut him off by pointing at a shut hatch. "Show me something else. I don't want to talk about the necrovirus any longer."

Dean opened his mouth like he wanted to pry, but then shut it again and flipped a hand. "That's the aether room. Where they do communications and nav and the like. Just a bunch of tubes and instruments. Snoresville."

I bit my lip. Anything to take my mind off thoughts of my infection. "I'd still like to see."

"Suit yourself." Dean shrugged. He opened the hatch to a much smaller space, and I gasped at the tangle of wires and shattered aether tubes, the burnt-parchment scent rolling out to smother my senses.

"Is it . . ." I coughed and pulled out my handkerchief to hold over my face as noxious blue-white smoke blanketed us. "Is it supposed to . . ." The aethervox that Harry no doubt used for ship-to-ship was smashed beyond repair, just a slag heap of no use to anyone. Wires and char marks were flung to the four corners of the room, and the recorder roll, the drum covered in thin brass coating that recorded messages sent across the aether, had rolled away and bumped against my feet as the *Belle* banked. "This can't be an accident."

Dean spun away from the hatch and ran for the cockpit. "Sure isn't. That's sabotage."

Jean-Marc let the shredded wires from the vox run through his fingers as if he were holding the last scraps of a broken treasure. "Fire ax, *capitaine*. They chewed it up and spat it out. Wondered why I wasn't picking up no chatter from the aether broadcasts."

Captain Harry punched his fist into the bulkhead. A dent blossomed. "*Merde*. You see anything, boy?"

Dean shook his head. "We were outside. I was showing Miss Aoife the ship when we found it. She's never flown."

Harry turned his ruby goggles on me and I focused on the zigzag scar across his chin instead. "What about you, mademoiselle? You eyeball any black rat bastards taking steel to *my ship*?" His bellow made everyone, including Dean, flinch.

111

"No, sir," I whispered, not able to even look at his face.

"You got enemies, girl?" Harry demanded. "You got a reason to go *aliénée* on my poor *Belle*?"

My cheeks heated to boiling as his accusations crept too close to truth. "No, sir! I didn't do this."

After a long stare, Captain Harry snorted. "Aye. Get back to the hold and stay put," he ordered. "You too, Harrison."

I marched in lockstep with Dean back to the benches, relief warring with worry for a spot in my head. Alouette watched us through the sliver of open hatch to the cockpit, her fingers moving over the controls with their own will. Altitude and windspeed tilted and righted, and my insides with them. But the *Belle* couldn't land at night without a ping from the radio tower in Arkham, could she? Couldn't call for help. We'd had our eyes put out. In daytime, an airship could fly without a radio, but at night in the wind . . . I shuddered.

Cal tugged on my sleeve. "What's going on?"

"Someone destroyed the aethervox," I murmured. "Dean said it was sabotage."

"Well, it wasn't me or Alouette," he said. "She was right here talking with me about the city life until you two started hollering for the captain."

"I didn't say your precious Alouette had anything to do with this," I growled. Cal darted a glance at Dean and then leaned in so that only I could hear.

"Are we in danger, Aoife?"

We were. I had the same certainty I got when I knew Professor Swan was springing a surprise quiz. "We're fugitives from the Proctors, Cal," I said aloud. "What do you think?"

At that moment, Jean-Marc and Captain Harry stepped

112

into the hold and I stood again. Jean-Marc held the recorder drum between his palms. Small clusters of nail taps paraded over the surface, the groupings in Mr. Morse's code spelled out for posterity in the paper-thin brass. If we went down, someone would know what happened.

Jean-Marc's spider-fingers caressed the drum like a blind man searches for meaning on the surfaces of the world. "I got the last transmission, *Capitaine*."

Captain Harry's lips tightened until they nearly disappeared. "Tell me."

"'Fugitives on board. Bearing north-northwest, destination Arkham. Send reinforcements.'" Jean-Marc held the drum out to Harry. "Sent after we flew this night, boss. Someone on board, still on board."

I shot a look at Cal, but he was rapt, his eyes on the captain. He didn't seem to share my alarm.

Captain Harry's massive hands changed to fists, so tight that his leather airman's gloves popped their hand-stitched seams. "Thrice-damned Proctors. Voxed from *my* ship."

Dean stood up. "Are the Proctors wise to this flight?"

I had the same question. If the Proctors knew where we were going, I might as well give myself up now. They'd be waiting when we landed in Arkham, and I'd be going somewhere that the Academy threatened us with when we got out of line.

It didn't seem real.

"*Harry*," Dean snapped. "Answer me—Proctors, or no?"

Before Captain Harry could respond, a sound reverberated from the cockpit—the sound of a body striking glass. Alouette let out a shriek and her nails left a constellation of half-moons in the oxblood hide of her chair.

We turned to the cockpit as one and met the glaring gaze of a raven, its mangled gears and brass-boned wings spread across a cobweb of broken glass.

Beyond it, in the wind-tossed night sky, a dozen more sets of eyes sprang to life. I stared, unable for a moment to move, as if my heart and blood had turned to glass.

"Ravens!" Jean-Marc squeaked. "Boss—"

"It ain't the ravens we got to worry about." Captain Harry slotted himself into the pilot seat and pushed the throttles to full. "It's their masters."

A whine cut the low growling of the *Belle*'s fans, the sound of gears brought to life by coiled inertia. A winding engine, used by some jitneys, sleek British beetles that hugged the road, and warplanes.

Cal grabbed for me, but I evaded his hands deliberately and cycled the deck hatch, leaning over the rail to look toward the *Belle*'s six o'clock. Bouncing in the wake of the big ship like pilot fish, twin chrome gliders swooped like owls in the moonlight, matching the *Belle*'s speed.

"Buggies!" I shouted at Dean as the wind stole my breath. We were speeding so fast it felt like all of my skin was being stripped away by the wind and cold. "P-51 Mustangs!" The snub-nosed shape and the fixed wing were unmistakable.

The moon showed its face, gibbous as the eye of a Great Old One, and revealed to me twin black wings stamped on the Mustang's noses.

I froze, caught out in the moonlight. I could even see the pilots, black leather caps and black goggles shielding their faces from the punishing air. I could see the long guns swiveling, coming to bear on the corpulent bulk of the *Belle*'s gas balloon.

114

Dean yanked me back through the hatch by my collar as the first line of lead cut loose from the Mustang's guns. I fell against him, boneless for a moment, shock rendering me deadweight.

"Your buddy got one thing right," Dean said, righting me. "To Proctors, these cats are pirates. And pirates get shot down."

The *Belle* shook. Harry bellowed orders in French. Cal clutched his tie-down harness and squeezed his eyes shut.

"What do we do, Dean?" I grabbed the nearest rail as another volley ripped through the night, bouncing the *Belle* as if it were a toy.

"Ride it out. Or ride it down." Dean grabbed my arm and dropped me into the seat next to Cal. "Strap in, miss."

The *Belle* dipped and swayed, dancing with the air. I grabbed for Dean's hand. It was the only solid thing I could reach, and just then I needed something solid very badly.

Cal shuddered as another burst from the Mustang's guns rattled past the hull like knucklebones. "We shouldn't be here," he blurted. "We should land. We should land and turn ourselves in and beg for mercy. They won't burn me if I give myself up . . . they won't . . ."

I wanted to comfort him, but before I could say anything, Alouette was in front of us, clutching the cargo net. I saw the fury in her face first and then the pistol in her hand.

"The *Belle* lands for no Proctor." Her voice was as cold as her eyes.

"Allie"—Dean held up a hand—"put that away. The kid's just scared."

"That better be all, or I'll throw him out the hatch for the Proctors myself. I swear by the gears of this boat."

"Leave Cal alone!" I snarled. "Maybe if you didn't hire traitors we wouldn't be in this mess!"

The pistol bounced toward me, and my next stream of invective died on my lips. *Never knew when to leave well enough alone* . . .

"Alouette! Bluebird! I can't fly this bastard ship alone!" Captain Harry bellowed, and saved us.

Alouette lowered her pistol, spun as if she were dancing ballet on the tilting deck and made her way forward, hand over hand on the cargo nets.

All I could concentrate on was not throwing up all over Dean as we lurched from side to side, shaken like dice in a cup.

The Mustangs rolled in concert and pulled up in front of the *Belle*'s bow, visible through the cockpit glass. The pilots were good, but one miscalculated his turn, and I saw him close enough to pick out the name stitched into his airman's leathers. *Bowman*. The pilot turned his head, agonizingly slow, and stared right into the *Belle*'s cockpit as we rushed up at his plane.

Absurdly, I wanted to scream a warning to him.

Then time righted itself. The silver sky became a garden of orange fire-flowers, tangled in vines of smoke. The sound of screaming metal stabbed my ears as the prow of the *Belle* cut the Mustang in half and threw me against my harness, against Dean. His arms closed around me, kept me from falling or snapping my spine. I dug my fingers into his leather and held on.

Fire crowned the *Belle* now, and the night before us looked like Dresden rather than Arkham.

We fell. Like a bird with a lead shot in its heart, we fell

116

into the jaws of the waiting earth. Alouette, not strapped down or sitting, conversely flew to the ceiling, lips peeled back, her scream lost in the cacophony of everything else, human and mechanical, on board the *Belle*.

We fell, and the cruel mistress of the air took sight and sound from me, until all I could feel were Dean's arms.

I woke hanging in space, my tie-down slicing my shoulders. The groan of rivets and the gentle hiss of hydrogen came in, and then, more slowly, the weight of my own body. It felt as if a giant had picked me up and thrown me far as he could, and I'd landed badly.

"Cal?" I croaked. Talking started a fire under my ribs. "Dean?"

"Cripes." Dean groaned, swiping blood from his face. "That was a rough reentry, for sure."

So he was all right. My chest loosened a bit. I swiveled as well as I could, and looked for Cal. He wasn't there. "Cal! Cal, call out if you can hear me!"

"That . . ." Cal raised his head from a diaphanous blob of cargo netting and broken tie-down at the top of the cabin, which was now the bottom. He struggled to his feet, jaw muscles jumping when he put weight on his ankle. "That was a lot more . . . exciting than I expected. Can we please never do it again?"

"Are you all right?" I called to him. He nodded, after a moment of consideration.

"Alive. What matters, right?"

I examined my position. "That and getting out of this blasted harness."

"No help for it," Dean said, craning his neck at the wall of the hull. The *Belle* had shifted onto her side, and we were now strapped to the ceiling. "Gonna have to drop." He jerked free of his harness and fell, landing and rolling. "Come on, Miss Aoife." He beckoned. "The gasbag's ruptured. One spark is going to light us up like Atlantic City."

The inversion was beginning to dizzy me, squashing the fear I'd otherwise be feeling, and Dean's face swam in front of my eyes. "If I land on my head, it's going to be all your fault," I told him, trying to shake my eyes back into focus.

He smirked, even as he stood on the wall of the crazily tilting *Belle*. "I'll take that chance, miss."

I shut my eyes against vertigo and then jerked on my straps. I didn't fall straight down, like the graceful swans we girls were supposed to be in Academy dance classes. I tumbled, as Mrs. Fortune would have put it, arse over teakettle.

When I opened my eyes after the inglorious *thump* of my landing on the cargo nets, I found that I was staring into Alouette's face.

"All His gears!" I gasped, scrambling away from her.

Alouette was entombed in an avalanche of boxes and netting, the veins in her skin like a road map on old paper. I tugged at her shoulders to free her, to no avail. Getting to my feet and gaining purchase, I yanked again, only to have the hot brand in my chest stab me again. I fell back, panting. "We have to get her out of there." A few minutes ago I'd wanted to slug Alouette, and now the same impulse caused a fervor in me that made me yank uselessly at her body until my own gave out, bruised and battered as it was. Alouette hadn't been polite, but no one deserved that plunging, screaming death.

118

Cal reached down, unzipped Alouette's high leather collar and pressed his fingers against her neck. "She doesn't have a pulse."

"And you're a surgeon now?" I demanded.

"I never thought I'd be saying this, but the kid's right," Dean said. He kicked at the exterior hatch, bowed badly on impact. "You ain't strapped down, you don't survive a handshake with the ground."

"Say." Cal exhaled a whistle. "She's got a stigma."

"What?" Surprised, I leaned over his shoulder and beheld the small white scar on Alouette's breastbone. Stamped by a hot iron that left an indelible kiss, the puckered spot on her skin made me think of the heretic in Banishment Square.

"I thought only sailors and delinquents got these," Cal said. He reached out to brush his fingers over the twin wings etched into the scar tissue, and I slapped his hand away.

"Cal, that's disgusting. She'd dead!"

"They're bird wings," said Cal, his fingers traveling back to the spot like it was magnetized. He licked his lips. "You know, pirates used to get swallows tattooed on their skin. To help them find land again. Birds find land."

"That's no swallow's wing," Dean said, his expression darkening like thunderheads. "Now, she's shuffled loose this here mortal coil and I don't love the plan of getting roasted when the hydrogen blows, so let's get into gear." He kicked the hatch free at last. "We hoof it, we can still make Arkham by dawn. Proctors probably think we all died in this bang-up."

Cal still crouched by Alouette. "Raven's wings," he said. "Only Proctors can wear a raven's mark. . . ."

119

Professor Swan's bleating about us turning in fellow students with contraband books and things like tarot cards or Ouija boards—heretical items—unspooled again in my head, along with one of his interminable lanternreels. *How We Fight! Joining the Bureau of Proctors.*

"She's a spy." The word tasted sour. All of the heretics I'd seen burned and hauled away to Ravenhouse, all of the eyes of the clockwork ravens watching, and there were still people who sold out neighbors and friends and even family to the Proctors.

Evil, that was heretics if you listened to the Proctors. Wanton carriers of necrovirus. Breeders of things like the nightjar.

My mother.

"You think she spied on witches?" Cal frowned.

"Open your eyes, Calvin. She was spying on *us*. She probably radioed her pals at Ravenhouse the minute we came on board."

Finding the hold of the *Belle* very small and hot, all at once, I clambered over wreckage to the hatch.

"But"—Cal panted after me—"Proctors only go undercover to spy on traitors. Foreigners and stuff."

I lashed my head around. "You don't get it, do you, Cal? You ran away with a heretic and with me. We *are* traitors to the Proctors, and the Proctors keep their eyes inward. Nobody cares about some far-off country. They watch *us*. They burn *us*. They spy and they kill and they stamp on lives with those horrible shiny jackboots they wear."

Cal just stared at me, fiddling with the buckles on his camp bag. "You know what they tell us, Aoife. We'd all be dead if it weren't for the Proctors. Professor Swan says—"

120

"Oh, grow up, Cal! Think a thought that the Proctors didn't give you for once!" I snapped and took off at a march. We'd landed in a field, the grass and its frost veil knee high. I struggled on, school shoes and school stockings woeful against the frigid gloom.

Dean ran and caught up with me. "Whoa, there. Pump your brakes, kiddo."

"I'm sorry." I was already shamefaced, burning with humiliation. Young ladies didn't lecture and they certainly didn't shout. "That was rude."

"Don't care if the kid riled you," Dean said. "Hell, he'd rile most anyone spent more than a hot minute with him. I can't have you running off, is all. This isn't the city. No Proctors keeping the critters out."

"I don't care," I hissed, fierce as a wounded cat. "Let them digest me." I was practically mad anyway. What harm would it do the world if I wasn't in it?

Dean looked at the dark ground rippling with cold mist, to the high moon slashed with clouds, the bleak barren humps of the Berkshire Mountains beyond, and the ink stain of forest between us and them. "If it's all the same, Miss Aoife, I'd rather keep you alive."

I let a stanza of footsteps pass without speaking, my shoes breaking through the frost with a sound like grinding teeth.

"How far to Arkham?" I said at length. It seemed the most inoffensive topic at the moment.

"Four hours walking. Maybe a little more. We'll set eyes on your old man's house by dawn." Dean yawned and stretched, popping his back like a cat. "Stay awake. Don't let the cold get its teeth into you."

121

"The Proctors will send out dogs and men to the crash site," Cal piped up. "To be sure." He was hopping along, and I slowed and offered him my arm. Cal didn't know how cruel he could be sometimes, with his parroting of the Proctors and by listening to their crowing about the necrovirus, his tacit agreement with them that I would inevitably go mad.

Cal took my arm with a part-smile, and his dogged recitation of propaganda didn't matter as much. That was Cal's way—calm and reliable, bumbling and normal. If only he knew *how* normal he was compared with me.

"We can't be caught," I told Dean. "Not after what that wretched Alouette must have told them." Behind us I saw Jean-Marc and Harry emerge from the wreckage, battered but intact. I hoped they'd make it to wherever they called home without any further trouble.

"Don't worry your pretty brunette head, miss," Dean said. He lit a cigarette as we marched, and puffed a smoke ring. "They haven't managed to catch me yet."

8

The Shoggoth's Dream

Hours of chilled cheeks and aching feet later, a sign on the mud-spattered, ice-pocked road, snugged against the Berkshire foothills, pointed to Arkham. Its wooden limbs stood akimbo, tattered from buckshot.

"Off the road now," Dean said. "Arkham's village police run to mean and bored, and they'll call down the ravens on us if we go through town."

The winding lane sat as a ribbon of darker against dark, overhung with the winter skeletons of oak trees and bound by stone. Dean hopped the low mossy wall and I helped Cal over.

The predawn field rolled and dipped, low curls of ground fog like tongues and tentacles rising from the frosted stubble of grass. The sky made a lid on the earth, a dome of silk dove clouds, and on the horizon the faintest line of blue-white fire sparked the dawn.

The ground was soft and thick as a coverlet, and

I slipped in the freezing mud and fell against Dean. He caught me around the waist.

"Sorry!" I whispered. "I'm clumsy. Always have been."

"I don't see the downside." His smile matched the ghostly glow of sunrise. "Care for a dance, while you're here?"

I pulled myself free too fast and nearly fell again. Dean Harrison wasn't my kind. He was wild-raised, no one I needed to form attachments with. If I let Dean get close, we wouldn't go on a proper date, where I'd smile and laugh behind my hand while I lowered my eyes demurely like a city-bred young lady. Dean was trouble, and I'd be in an even worse stripe if I acquiesced to his charms. "No, that's not happening," I said, and felt myself flush even in the cool damp air of dawn.

Cal grumbled until Dean and I parted, and ignored my offered hand even though he was reduced to hopping on one leg with his bound-up ankle swinging.

We walked through the mist in silence, and it closed in on us like it could see and taste our presence.

"There's a path cut in the rock," said Dean. "Far side of this field." He pointed at the raw gray granite climbing out of the earth. "I'm guessing that honking mansion up on the cliff is your pop's place, since there's not one Grayson inside the village walls that I've ever met."

I had never seen Graystone, except for a curl-cornered picture my mother kept in a shoebox. The house of my father was all angles and turrets and the rough, body-sized granite blocks that gave the estate its name. Singularly unwelcoming, like an asylum or a heretic prison. Much like, I'd always assumed, the man who called it home.

124

Would I see my father? I could ask him how he and Nerissa had come together, what her madness first showed itself as. Cleverness, like Conrad, or her fancies about fairies and witches? Or just that sad, miles-gone stare that looked through me as if I were window glass?

Alternately, I could say nothing, and just savor my first look at the man who was half of me. There were no pictures of my father except the clues in my own face. I wanted to memorize him if I could, because the one thing you learned as a ward was never to assume the same face would open the door when you came home again. It wasn't something to be maudlin about, just a truth, like second-hand shoes or being the last to eat at supper.

"You quit talking, Miss Aoife. You five by five?" Dean said. The mist held us in, kept our secrets close to our skin.

"Squared away," I said, sneaking a phrase from Cal's lexicon.

Dean slowed so we walked abreast. "Ain't thrilled about seeing your old man?"

"You're assuming he wants to see me." That was the other half of the orbit of possibilities. Archibald Grayson could deny his bastard child, shut the door and send me on my way. As would be his right, as a man of breeding and good standing.

Dean winced. "I'm with you there, kid. All the way down the line."

An owl hooted in the trees at the field's edge, concealed by the morning twilight. Nerissa hated owls, shrieked about them watching her, *lantern eyes and iron claws.*

Owls carried the necrovirus, if you minded the lantern-reels. I'd seen pictures of their wings, aerodynamics lessons

125

drawn in fine, careful ink. The rounded tips of the feathers that let them fly silent. What I'd give to fly silent as an owl, unwatched by the Proctors or anyone else. Sometimes I thought that if I made my clothes colorless enough, my shoulders narrow enough, that I could round off all my edges and disappear into the air like the lantern-eyed harbingers of the night. I hadn't managed it yet.

I watched my feet squelch into the mud instead. The mist and the morning called for silence, and even Cal had given up the challenge of talking. I was almost enjoying the quiet, haunted walk until the sweet stench of meat left in a warm place clapped me across the nose, thick and wet as a wool blanket.

Cal pressed his handkerchief over the lower half of his face like a bandit. "Stones . . . what's rotted on the vine?"

The mist parted on a humped black hide with a watery sheen, and a great lidless eye that swam up from the depths of the thing's boneless mass, bilious green and cloudy with cataract.

"Shoggoth," I breathed, stumbling to a halt. "It's an actual shoggoth."

The shoggoth exhaled with a sound of pipes belching steam. Its eye roved over its hide in no particular pattern, floating like a lamprey below the surface of a dark sea.

"They swallow us whole." Cal's whisper came as a shout in the absolute stillness. "Digested by degrees inside that mass. You can stay alive for days, becoming a part of it. Listening to it whisper in your brain. Filthy damn thing." He picked up a stone and flipped it in his palm.

"Cal, no . . . ," I started, but Cal cocked his arm and threw.

126

A fingerlet of skin and muscle snapped out of the creature's mass, sprouting a mouth, round and rimmed with teeth. The rock disappeared into the shoggoth's maw with a snap of gravel.

Dean worried the Lucky Strike behind his ear as the shoggoth shuddered all over like a bear waking up from a long hibernation. "Fine job, cowboy. You work to be this stupid, or is it innate?"

"It doesn't have a brain!" Cal argued. "It's just a dumb, deaf ball of necrovirus. Wasn't even human once. Grew up out of the mud, like a living infection."

I watched in fascination as the creeper of boneless, waterlogged flesh writhed over the ground where the rock had come from, seeking and searching. More eyes opened on the shoggoth's hide, filmy and infected as the first.

"It's blind," I realized.

"And ancient, to get that big," Dean said. "I've seen them from the air, and I've seen the carcasses they leave behind. You want my expert guide's opinion, we need to stoke fires and get outta here."

"We'll have to find another way up to Graystone," Cal sighed. "I knew I should have packed my road atlas. I could practice my navigation."

"Or we could knock off pelting Ol' Stinky here with rocks and just tiptoe on around," Dean suggested. "If that meets with your approval, Scout Leader."

"You know, I've had just about enough of you," Cal snapped. "So far, all you've guided us to is a heap of trouble, and kept Aoife out in the cold and the wet."

"Cal"—I scratched at my scar, underneath the damp wool of my school scarf—"leave me out of this."

127

"We can't just *go around*," Cal growled at Dean, ignoring me completely. "Shoggoth can travel fast over ground, and then we'll be dead, as well as trapped out here in stinking manure."

"Here's an idea," Dean retorted. "Unknot your bloomers and admit that your lily-white city-boy ass doesn't know everything."

Behind Cal, I saw black in the corner of my vision, windy-twisty black that sought warm skin and bone with a sharp, hungry mouth.

"Cal." I raised my numb finger and pointed.

"Aoife, I won't be shouted down this time," he snapped. "You're smart for a girl, but this was a rash idea and I'm sorry I let you talk me into it. Now I'm leaving this shyster, going into Arkham and catching a jitney for home, and you're coming with me. I have a responsibility."

The tentacle from the mass of rotting muscle reared as it caught Cal's scent, and bore down on him. I lunged, planting my hands against the rough wool of his coat and shoving with my whole weight. "Cal, *watch out!*"

In the instant Cal and I touched, the shoggoth struck.

I felt the freeze and smelled the stench of dead orchids rotting in hothouse dirt. The teeth bit into my skin, straight through my clothes, and pain slashed my sight and breath to ribbons.

I fell, hitting hard on frozen ground, and scrabbled for purchase as the shoggoth dragged me backward. I kicked at it, but that did all the good of kicking a pile of vulcanized raincoats—the thing was rubbery and solid, inexorable and hungry.

I felt my skin burning as the shoggoth's mouths ate

128

through the layers of my clothes, heard a low sizzle like slow-frying bacon. I kicked and scratched at it, sloughing off chunks of rotted hide under my nails. I caught a frozen furrow in the ground and held on for dear life as the shoggoth dragged me toward its mass, all its eyes clustered together now and staring at me sightlessly. Blood from under my nails sank into the earth, and I'm sure I screamed.

Through the pain came a buzzing, a humming of locusts or bird's hearts, speaking to me inside the deep, secret place of dreams.

So sweet so sweet meat so sweet blood blood condemned blood hot fresh meat . . .

My eyes flew open. Not my eyes. The shoggoth's eyes. I saw the shoggoth's visions. I *was* the shoggoth.

I saw everything at once, a screaming void of black, a field of starry flowers whiter than snow on a dead man's skin. A great Engine of black iron that ground gears and belched smoke into a sky stained red by a double sunset. I heard the crack of a whip and I shuddered and mewled, forced across barren earth while ice clawed at my soft underbelly. The world was white, entombed in ice, and my brothers built a great stone city on the bones of brick and steel. I knew this skyline. I knew the river that churned red, naked fleshy corpses bobbing on the tide. The spires of Lovecraft lay reduced to blood-colored ash, and all around me tall white figures held whips, glaring at me from solid blue and silver eyes. . . .

I was floating in a void; no, a sea; no, a great birthing tank, watched by men in black uniforms, jagged silver lightning bolts on their collars, skull pins on their peaked caps.

I slithered through grasses the color of bruises and decay

129

while the white figures loosed their great hounds with fire for eyes to hunt me.

I writhed on sand as sailors sank harpoons into me and a pair of men in black coats watched the carnage of my brothers and sisters, the red tide that pushed us onto this foreign shore, where everything tasted like ash and smoke.

My own voice rolled over the tableau of slaughter, and the sailors grabbed their heads, twitching and losing their minds from the very sound.

Help me help me see us see the lost see the forgotten spill the sweet blood set us free send us home . . .

The shoggoth howled and my eyes flew open to find Dean standing above me, wreathed in a halo of mist. He lifted his fist and brought it down. His knife flashed, again and again, hacking at the shoggoth's creeper. Black-green blood the consistency of motor oil watered the ground, eating away the topsoil, sending foul sulfuric smoke into the air.

"Get off her," Dean growled. He locked his long artful fingers around my good arm and pulled, hefting me easily and hauling me over the stone wall, away from the moaning, rippling shoggoth. It was thrashing in a fit, eyes rolling and blinking all over its hide, masses of creepers growing and retreating in every direction as it bled ichor into the field.

Dean gathered me against him. "I've got you, Aoife." His smell of leather and tobacco made my head spin. Dean whispered against my ear. "I've got you."

"It—it talked to me," I jittered. My skirt and jumper were soaked with melted frost, and trickles of my own blood painted a road map down my arm and over my palm

130

where my blouse had torn away. "The shoggoth. Talked to me . . ."

Dean snapped his fingers at Cal. "Kid. You got a clean bandanna in that scout pack?"

Cal just stared at the darkening wool of my jumper, his hands slack at his sides, tongue creeping out to catch between his front teeth.

"*Doorstop.*" Dean's voice could have drawn blood. "She needs help, double-quick time. You want to gawk, buy a ticket."

Cal came back to life and dug into his kit bag, drawing out a pristine red bandanna, still with the paper band from the department store around it. He tossed it underhand at Dean, who snatched it out of the air, a cotton bird interrupted in flight.

"Don't you worry, Miss Aoife," Dean said as he slid his hand under my jumper, under my blouse, and pressed the cloth against my torn skin. "I'm thinking only the purest of thoughts."

The pressure of his hand triggered a fresh wave of pain-fueled giddiness. I danced on air, the world a painting that melted off its canvas before my eyes. Looking through the shoggoth's eyes had been real, too real and too visceral to escape, but this felt like a dream, the kind I lied to Dr. Portnoy about, and I panicked, thrashing against Dean's touch. I just wanted the pain to stop.

"Hey." Dean snapped his fingers in front of my face. "Stay with me, Aoife. Still and steady, and you'll be right as rain."

"Is she . . ." Cal's words twisted down a long and

131

cavernous passage to my ears. "Is she . . . viral? If she changes . . ."

"I'm not . . ." My tongue was thick, and speaking made my head pound, but I found the swirling, twirling giddiness of the necrovirus waited for me whenever I shut my eyes, so I forced them open. "I'm not . . ." *I'm not infected. I'm not mad.*

"She's in a bad way." Dean peeled back my eyelid and brushed his fingers down my neck to where my carotid pulse throbbed. "It took a piece of her. This bleeding ain't stopping on its own."

"Wh-what do I do?" Cal was a pale column of blond and khaki uniform at the edge of my vision.

Dean's hand slid under my shoulders and his opposite arm wrapped around my knees. The ground fell away and I turned my face into his T-shirt to avoid the waterfall of nausea that swamped me.

"What do I *do*?" Cal's shout cracked through the still air.

"Keep up," Dean said, and started to run. Our route pitched upward, and I felt cold wind on my face cut with low, hot throbs from my shoulder as Dean carried me. I tried not to cry, unsuccessfully. The tears just turned me colder as we climbed higher and higher up the mountainside, and I shivered, my teeth grating. There were things roaming in the night, glass-girls with fingers of ice and teeth of gales that stole your blood and breath and made it so you were never warm again.

I felt them pulling icicle fingers through my hair and heard them whispering their poetry of cold, eternal sleep until I mercifully lost consciousness.

9

Poison Blood

WHEN I CAME awake again, I was lying on something lumpy and not altogether soft, while the crisp air teased my bare skin from neck to . . . I flushed, trying to yank the tatters of my blouse together. The last thing I wanted was to be like Stephanie Falacci, the girl Cecelia and her friends had teased mercilessly for still wearing camisoles and long underwear. My brassiere, washed so many times it had gone gray, wasn't any better.

"Easy!" Dean's voice came in as I thrashed. "Easy, kiddo! You have to stay still while I clean this wound."

Everything was out of focus—I felt like I still had a hundred eyes, was still connected to the shoggoth.

Cal's voice piped in, like I was scanning channels in the aether. "Is she going to die?"

"Not if you shut up so I can stop this poison from pumping all through her," Dean snapped. His jacket creaked, and I saw him draw out a flat silver bottle.

133

Dean unscrewed the cap, took a quick swig and then poised the flask over me. "You *have* to stay still, Aoife. No matter how much it hurts. You receiving me?"

"You smoke. . . ." Talking, I sounded as drugged as any of the violent patients in Nerissa's ward. I *felt* twice as looped. My words bled together, and my tongue was too fat for my mouth. "You drink. . . . Is there anything you don't do, Mr. Harrison?" I heard giggling, and realized it was me.

"I was never much good in a beauty contest," Dean said shortly. "Cal, hold her shoulders."

"I'm not getting that close," Cal said. The gold streak of his head shook vigorously. "If her blood gets on me—"

"Listen up." Dean's voice had gone low and hard as the grinding gears of the Proctor's ravens. "Either she's your friend and you're gonna help her survive long enough to get help, or you really are a yellow little bug-eyed worm and you can walk away right now."

"You don't understand!" Cal cried. "The blood . . . it's just so—"

He let out a yelp as Dean yanked him down. Cal's impact didn't make any sound, and I identified the substance under us as moldy hay, the patchwork of sky and dark above as a rotting roof.

"Hold her," Dean said again. "If she thrashes, she's just gonna bleed more."

With that, he tipped the flask over the shoggoth's bite. The pain that came was so fast and hot, I thought for a moment that I was back in Lovecraft, that I'd been caught on the way to Arkham, and that my bare body was strapped into the castigator.

I shrieked and bucked against Cal's grip. "All right," Dean said. "All right, it's sterilizing your wound. Stopping the poison from spreading any further into you."

I didn't care if I was on fire and it was water, I just wanted the pain to stop. I'd had wounds cauterized before, during machine shop classes, but this was worse. It was worse than anything, it was like ice had frozen my veins, was killing me by inches as it reached fingers to my heart. . . .

"Is she going to go viral?" Cal demanded again, as I collapsed back onto the hay. "Is she going to change?"

My sight and hearing faded in and out, and more than anything I wanted to plunge back into that dreamlike floating world that the shoggoth's venom had shown me. At least there, I didn't hurt.

"I look like a damn surgeon to you, cowboy?" Dean snarled. "I don't friggin' know."

Cal let go of me and backed away. "I just thought . . . you seem like you have experience with virals. Creatures and stuff."

Dean snorted. "I steer clear of 'em same as any starched-up Academy boy would. I do want to live until I'm twenty."

Cal started to say something else, but I lurched to the side as I felt my last meal come up. There wasn't much, just some bile, but I retched until I felt the muscles in my back spasm.

Dean tucked my hair back under my collar until I collapsed into a sweating, shivering heap on the hay once more. "There," he said. "Yakking's a good sign. That's your body trying to get the virus out."

I didn't tell him it was already far too late—that a

135

dormant strain of necrovirus had lain in my blood since I was born, and that in a few weeks it would give birth itself, with merciless swiftness, and eat my sanity alive. In a lucid state, I could lie to myself, but not now.

Dean's arms went around me and I was lifted again. This time vertigo caused a giddy drop in my empty stomach, and my head echoed as he pulled me tight against his chest.

"If she's sicking up she might have a chance," Dean told Cal. "We gotta get her up to that house. Get the bleeding stopped. She can sweat it out if we give her proper care."

"You sure know a lot about the necrovirus." Cal's voice made me cold again, even as Dean's proximity sent fingers of heat lighting across my skin, like when you go outside in a snowstorm without gloves. Dean felt like frostbite.

As he carried me up the path to the mansion, I lost myself again in the sensations the venom brought over me, my skin sensitive enough that even the scratch of my uniform stockings was a small agony.

"Make it stop," I begged Dean. He pressed me against his chest as his footsteps bounced us up a steep trail. Bare trees laced their branches over our heads, forming a bony canopy that blurred under my sight until it became actual bones, an army of fingers and hands covered in weeping flesh and a tattered shroud reaching for me.

I moaned and pressed my face against Dean's chest. The nearer to him I stayed, the less it hurt.

"Hang on, Aoife," Cal said. His voice was like needles through Dean's comfort. "Hang on, we're almost there."

"No . . . ," I moaned, and clutched at Dean's shirt. I had fire in my blood, poison burning me inside like oil on the Erebus. "No more, I can't do it. . . ."

136

"Yes, you can," Dean panted. "You can, Aoife. Just a few minutes more."

He squeezed me tighter, and in that way I managed to keep myself from crying out again as we climbed, slowly, through the mist and toward the dawn.

10

Graystone

I SAW GRAYSTONE for the first time through a dream haze, that gray drifting place between dreaming and waking.

Mist parted, running fingers down the pitted bars of a pair of iron gates. Rock walls crawling with moss closed the estate off from the outside world, and a crow atop a copper finial stained green with corrosion opened its beak and let out a dry *caw*.

The house itself sat at the edge of a cliff overlooking the Miskatonic Valley and the huddled, sleeping village of Arkham. The glowering mansion gave the impression of digging claws into the granite skin of the mountain, eyes of thick blue leaded glass staring down from pitch gables and finger-thin twin turrets, unblinking.

Graystone was a house of bones. Its black spires reached skyward from a swaybacked slate roof. Garrets and warrens of rooms spilled away from the four-chambered brick heart, the cross-shaped center of the house crawling with

138

moss and vines that spelled out sigils and signs before my feverish eyes. Aluminum flashing and guttering gleamed like mercury veins in the dawn.

I moaned. Looking at Graystone was to look on something old and sleeping, and when it woke I feared it would be monstrously hungry.

"Get the door open," Dean ordered, and I heard Cal's limping walk on the gravel of the front drive.

"We shouldn't just be breaking in like this," he murmured. "Mr. Grayson would be within his rights to shoot us."

"Listen, cowboy. I ain't lost a customer yet and I'm not gonna start with one as pretty as Miss Aoife here. She needs a bed, bandages, and maybe a shot of whiskey, since I'm dry. Now can you gimp yourself up those steps and open me a door, or can you just flap your gums?"

"You know, I might be more of a pal if you'd quit ordering me around like we're in some war serial," Cal grumbled. "For a criminal, you're real bossy."

"What I am is her guide and my guiding ain't done until I deliver my clients to their threshold," Dean said. "And since Miss Aoife is the one paying me, I'll order anyone else I damn well please."

The crow followed us, landing on the brass Moorish lamp over the massive front doors. It hopped on skinny bird legs and its throat pulsed. *Caw caw caw.*

"Door's open." Cal's voice went faint with shock. "Shouldn't it . . . not be open?"

I watched the crow. I could see every feather on its body, every reflection in its black bead of an eye. The fever in me racked my bones with a violent cough as the bird stared.

139

"Let your clutch out, then, and go find Aoife a bed," Dean said. "She needs to sweat out this foulness."

Cal caught sight of the crow and shuddered. "Grim thing. I hate those nasty carrion birds." He snatched stone from the iron planters flanking the front door, but Dean's free hand shot out and knocked the stone back to the ground. "Bad, bad luck to harm a crow. He'll run back to his witch and tell her all about you, you throw that stone."

"They eat the dead," Cal said. "It just wants Aoife."

I tried to tell him I wasn't dead yet, but I was shivering too violently. Dean's fingers flexed, leaving deep marks in my flesh as he struggled to hold me. "That old boy's just curious," he told Cal. He tipped his head at the black bird above us. "Howdy, battle singer. We don't mean any harm."

The crow stretched its wings, lava-glass beak snapping. It regarded Dean for a moment, then shifted its gaze to me, and to Cal, who sneered at it, making a shooing motion with his hands.

Fluffing its wings in what I'd call irritation, the crow took flight, gliding over the iron-strapped walls and dipping into the valley like a spot of living ink on a vast misty page.

My memory went soft then, like a needle slipping off a phonograph groove. Next I knew, I'd left the hard surety of Dean's arms for a feather bed that smelled like lavender and must, and I wandered through hell and ice as the fever wrung itself out of my flesh and my dreams. The dreams were black, twisting, and tasted of metal. I touched what Nerissa touched—diamond-edged shrieking clarity that let me see everything too bright, too sharp. The madness that let me see the magic she imagined wreathed our ordinary world.

In the fever dream, Dean was a blur, like a smudge of soot against clean skin. Cal floated bloodred and gold around the edges of my sight. The house, Graystone, whispered to me with a voice made of dry rot and dust, in the language of houses, all pops and creaks.

At last, it lulled me into the sleep beyond dreaming, the sleep in a dead space where there's nothing but weary emptiness. I anchored myself there and would have gladly stayed for centuries.

When I woke again, I was disoriented. Night had thrown a velvet mask over the windows of the bedroom. Dean dozed in an overstuffed chair next to the bed, a pinup magazine much worn at the edges folded open on his chest.

"Cal?" I whispered. He was nowhere to be seen. Dean's breath hitched, but he didn't wake.

I swung my feet over the edge of the high bed, carved with animal heads for each post. The heads had enormous ears, bulbous eyes, fangs. Nothing from a natural history book.

Setting my feet on the itchy Persian carpet, I tested my balance. Every bit of me ached, as if I'd turned all the gears of the Lovecraft Engine by hand, but I was solid as the rock we'd climbed to reach Graystone, no longer plagued by dizzying illusion.

"Dean?" He shifted in his sleep, laying his head against the chair. A lock of hair escaped its comb tracks and snaked into his eye. I reached out to brush it away, got close enough to feel the warmth of his skin, and then pulled back. He'd just wake up, and I'd have to explain why I was out of bed. And thank him for saving my life, and admit that now I owed him something more than a fee. I hadn't owed anyone except Conrad a thing in my life, and I wasn't sure I liked it.

From below, a great ticking like a heartbeat echoed. I was thirsty and still half asleep, but I was sure the sound hadn't been there a moment ago. My mind wasn't playing tricks on me any longer—I was myself, clear and focused. The sound was real.

This was my father's home, even if he hadn't yet made an appearance. I was uninvited. Wandering about was for sneak-thieves and vagabonds, not respectable girls. Not for daughters.

I chewed on my lip, thinking, then picked up the oil lamp guttering by the bedside, its small flame throwing spook shadows across the velvet damask curtains and the water-spotted wall panels. At second glance, everything about the room was rotten at the edges, from the moth-chewed carpet to the notes uttered by the warped floorboards under my feet.

Glancing back once to make sure Dean hadn't come awake after all to stop my exploration, I slipped out the high narrow door into a high narrow hall and followed the sonorous heartbeat of Graystone toward its source.

142

11

A Clockwork Heart

MY CREEPING FOOTSTEPS kept time with the invisible pendulum. The lamp in my hand gave off a buttery glow, older and more secretive than the crisp blue of aether globes.

Graystone sprawled like a spiderweb, and the hallway twisted and turned back on itself. Soon enough, I was walking an unfamiliar hall and could only go forward until I reached a landing. The sound came from below me, in the empty space where the stairs and their threadbare carpet vanished into shadow.

Nobody showed themselves. The dust floated in the lamplight like ghostly fireflies, and my only companion was the sound.

I descended the stairs and found myself in a back hallway, which in turn lead to a back parlor. All of Graystone's furniture sat swathed in dust catchers, lion feet peeking out from under their white skirts. The only uncovered thing in the room was an old-style wireless box, its aether tubes cloudy and dim with disuse.

I left the parlor and found another faceless hallway, where portraits of Graysons past watched me with dour frowns, cobwebs trailing from their frames. I stopped and raised the lamp, gazing at each face in turn, trying to find some clue to myself. There were precious few who looked anything like me among the starched clothes and serious eyes. The mossy green color of those eyes, though, was the same as mine. I turned away and tried a few doors, iron handles cold to my touch. Each was locked, and I left them that way. I wasn't a sneak, but my father didn't know that. I could only imagine being caught breaking into Graystone and snooping around. I wanted him to meet me on good terms, and approve of me, and nod in acknowledgment that I was his daughter. My heart sank, though, as I wandered farther and farther afield, each turn of the hall yielding nothing but dust and desolation. And the sound, always. Graystone was dead, hollowed out like the carcass of a beast. My father—or anyone, for that matter—hadn't been here in a long time.

I turned into what I recognized from my fevered state as the front entry hall, and the marble chilled my stockinged feet. I'd been re-dressed in my bloodied sweater and ripped blouse, but they weren't much good for keeping out the cold.

Across from the grand staircase to the second floor, I confronted a pair of pocket doors carved with a peculiar forest scene. Creatures cavorted under fruit-heavy trees, but they weren't creatures I'd ever encountered. These were half men, half goat. I reached out a hand and touched them. They felt delicate under my fingers, wrought by an artist who had the finest touch with his chisel. They were beautiful. Strange. Certainly forbidden by the Proctors, I felt sure.

I pulled my hand away. From behind the doors, springs wound and weights swung. *Tick. Thock. Tick. Tick. Thock.* I hadn't managed to find Conrad or my father, but at least I'd found the source of the sound.

I tugged at the brass pulls, made in the shapes of the north and east wind, great billowy brass clouds for hair and sharp lightning-bolt noses, rings caught in their teeth.

I stuck my finger in the east wind's mouth, then yanked it back again like the thing might really bite me. I let out a nervous giggle.

Tick. Thock. The sound was louder, or perhaps I was just nervy from the dark house and the knowledge that even if my father had locked the place up and gone somewhere less dank and forbidding, I was trespassing here.

When I at last tugged on the handles, the doors were locked and I virtually collapsed from relief. I didn't need to be the lone adventurer any longer. I could creep back upstairs and be in bed before Dean realized I'd ever been out of it.

Still, I wished I'd seen what kind of clock could reverberate its gears through brick and wood, to the ears of sleepers rooms away. I touched the doors once more and gave them a last, experimental tug.

To my surprise, a heavy clacking arose, and the locks

145

opened. The doors themselves slid backward on some kind of self-propelled mechanism, and a puff of stale air kissed my face as they settled open with a clank.

Spinning, I looked behind me to see what might have triggered the doors. My thoughts didn't jump to viral creatures, but rather to an angry Archibald Grayson discovering a thief or my mad brother playing one of his tricks. Shadows leaped with the jostling of my lamp, painting the shadow of man and phantom on the walls of the entryway.

I was alone, though, and when I realized the fact, a little fear got in with it. The walls of the Academy and of Lovecraft were behind me. Here, there was nothing between me and things lurking in the dark, feasting on blood and sanity.

Deciding that I was safer in a closed room than out in the open, I hurried through the doors, which rolled shut behind me. I jumped at the sound, but what was before me was mesmerizing. My lamp showed gold-stamped spines in jolting shadow, mellowed wood and well-used leather chairs. A closer inspection revealed I was in Graystone's library, and my feet sank into rich carpet with a whisper of welcome.

It was truly a glorious library, twice the size of the Academy's. Impressive, I'd wager, by even New Amsterdam's standards. The shelves ascended to the ceiling, and the volumes went on for what looked like miles.

I spun in a slow circle, like another sort of girl might do in a dress shop full of the latest confections for the sort of girls who got asked on dates and to dances. The library was not dusty or dead like the rest of Graystone. It looked loved and lived-in and used. A writing desk sat shoved to one side near a pair of worn leather armchairs. There was nothing on the walls, none of the ornate accoutrements the rest of the house boasted. This was a library, and my father clearly wanted all of the attention on his books.

But, in the golden light of my lamp, I saw there was one object in the room besides the copious volumes.

On the opposite side of the long narrow room was a leviathan clock—a full-bodied, intricate machine, much different than a pocket chronometer. As I watched, the hands swung in a parabolic arc, their wicked spiked finials grinding to a halt at twelve midnight. The chimes let out a discordant, muffled *bong*.

The hands swung again, and I stepped closer, watching them trail across the clock face like compass needles that had lost north, the unearthly ticking echoing loud enough to vibrate my skull. Each numeral was actually a tiny painting, wrought in delicate ink. A naked girl lying sleeping on a stone. A great goat with the body of a man sitting on a throne. A circle of figures in a dark forest who wore the sign of Hastur, the heretical Yellow King, whom cultists worshipped before the necrovirus. According to Professor Swan, and who knew where he got his stories from?

Looking at the clock for too long, at the silver gears beneath the face that spun like saw blades in the bloodred cherrywood case, made me dizzy around the edges. The shoggoth's bite began to throb, sending needles up and down my arm, and I put out a hand to steady myself against the shelves. Brushing the leather and the wood settled my head, but only a bit. Friendly as the library was, the clock was a monstrous thing, a machine of bloody teeth. It

147

didn't scare me—it was a clock, after all—but it transfixed me, started a tremor of unease. I felt the urge to bolt, clear back to my bedroom.

I had to stop thinking of it as *my* bedroom. My father had made it clear by his fifteen-year silence—Conrad and I were Nerissa's children. We had only a mother.

The hands of the clock reached midnight again and another *bong* vibrated my skull. The chimes were dulled, as if stuffed with cotton wool.

As if something was inside the case, muffling them.

I hesitated a moment, the aura of the clock pulsating around me, and then decided I was being a silly child. I tugged at the case until it sprang open, varnish coming off sticky under my hand. Touching the clock made me dizzy again, but I peered into the whirling gears and swinging weights and caught the edge of a vellum scrap stuffed between the black glass chimes. Whoever had broken the clock had left a note.

My small hands, the bane of my mechanical engineering instructor, Professor Dubbins, fit neatly into the thin space. I touched the paper and pulled it free, but I was careless. A gear bit into my thumb and a fat blood droplet welled on the pad.

I hissed, and sucked at the digit. The bleeding didn't stop—the puncture was deeper than I first thought—and when I examined the spot, my blood soaked the corner of the vellum. I let it drop by my feet and wrapped my thumb up in the tail of my ruined blouse, tightening the linen around it for pressure. A little more blood wouldn't matter.

The clock whirred faster, the hands only a blur as they

spun. A rattlebone chorus of ticking grew inside my skull, and I scrubbed at my forehead with my free hand. The shoggoth's poison was undoubtedly still in me. I shouldn't have slipped out of bed. It was the poison, I told myself, not anything else. Not what had been in my blood to start.

I grabbed up the vellum scrap and retreated to the far side of the library, hoping that distance would take away some of the looming malignancy that the clock had set in my mind.

Near the doors, I stopped and unfolded the scrap, holding it close to the lamp globe. What I expected, I can't say. A coded message from a Crimson Guard spy, perhaps, or a warrant issued by the Proctors. A love letter from my mother.

Instead, Conrad's handwriting grabbed me like fingers around the throat.

AOIFE

More ghost ink. More secrets for only my eyes. Conrad had put a note here. He'd made it to Arkham after all. Conrad might still be alive.

Conrad might still be sane.

My hand shaking so hard the paper looked like moth wings in the oily light, I held the vellum over the flame. It curled, crackled, and my fingers singed because the scrap was much, much smaller than my brother's last letter, but I held on.

The ink burned, turned, twisted and, with a huff of smoke, gave up its secret.

149

Fix it.

"Fix what?" I demanded of the acrid cloud. "What, Conrad?"

Sharp needles of heat in my fingertips warned me, and I dropped the paper on the carpet just as it burst into flames and gave a whip-crack *snap* of yellow powder as the chemical of the ghost ink combusted. I stomped on the flames until they went out, leaving a burn hole in the carpet.

That was simply terrific. If my father did return to Graystone, he was going to tan my hide.

A floorboard croaked in the hallway and I froze, mind and muscle. I'd watched a lanternreel about feudal Japan in history during my first year. The emperors of centuries past had fabulous peak-roofed palaces, and in the palaces, nightingale floors. Wood that sang, and announced the presence of the enemy, that warned the feudal lords when assassins were close.

My heart became a stone. My hand itched for Dean's switchblade.

A long thin shadow crawled through the open doors of the library, echoes of long thin footsteps following.

I blew out the lamp and inched back against the books, their soft spines flexing under my weight.

The figure in the door was long-legged and loping, and tangled its feet in the carpet. One pale hand with pale wormy fingers reached out and felt its way along the books, coming close. The shoggoth's bite throbbed in time with my heart, and I shrank back, but too slowly. The fingers brushed my hand, leaving contrails of cold.

150

Terror fired me, and I struck, balling up my fist with my thumb tucked outside and under like Conrad taught me and carrying my blow with the weight of my shoulder behind it. My knuckles glanced off jawbone and it felt like broken glass had buried itself in my hand. The long shadow and I both yelped.

"*Cal?*" My heart could have outpaced a jitney.

"Eyes of the Old Ones!" Gears chattered from an unseen device and then a thin, wavering line of blue lit up the space between me and Cal. Cal carried an aether lantern with a crank handle, the bubbly glass filmed over from age.

"I'm sorry . . ." I tried to touch the rising welt on his jaw, but he jerked his head away. "I thought you were something else."

"What else would I be?" Cal cranked the lantern again, to little effect. The aether inside the globe was ancient and nearly white.

"I thought . . ." *A living shadow, a cold thing from the primordial pool of the necrovirus, something from under the ground looking for a feast.* "I guess I don't know," I finished, looking at my hands—anywhere but Cal's face.

Cal put a finger under my chin and lifted my gaze to his own. "Are you seeing things, Aoife? We can go home right now, petition the city for quarantine. You're a girl. They won't send you to the Catacombs. Probably won't," he amended. "You *are* a runaway."

"I *saw* something in the dark and I didn't want to get digested by a nasty, slobbering viral creature for the second time today." The knuckles on my left hand were skinned and turning purple. Cal always assumed the worst. He didn't realize that sometimes a girl just got irritable.

151

"We could still go back, you know," Cal said, taking my injured hand in his and producing his handkerchief. He wrapped my hand once, twice. My blood made small blooms on the snowy fabric and he stared at them, his throat working. "You'd have to be in quarantine for six months, but there's always a chance they'd let you out if you didn't . . . you know."

I yanked my hand out of his. The handkerchief fluttered to the ground and he snatched it up. "You're so sure I'm going mad, Cal, then why are you still here? I'm sure if you ran home now and licked the headmaster's boots he'd be overjoyed to readmit you." It was bad enough thinking that madness was encroaching. I didn't need my best friend accusing me as well.

Cal's lips disappeared into a thin line. "That was cruel, Aoife."

"Well," I blustered, "you want me in quarantine." Quarantine meant a hospital on the river, outside the city limits. A place full of sterile white halls and sterile aether lamps burning night and day. Far from the madhouse, where the doctors had given up on the patients. In quarantine, the doctors tried to beat the advance of the necrovirus. To shock, burn and drown the heresy out of a human body.

When a court officer suggested quarantine for Nerissa, she grabbed the man's pen and jammed it into the back of his hand, screaming that he was a Crimson Guard witch come to remove her memories and replace them with birdsong.

They decided to skip quarantine after that.

"Sometimes, madness isn't the worst of life," Conrad told me afterward. We sat on the steps even though it was

152

raining, looking down from the courthouse at the dense brick-lined veins of Lovecraft, where normal, usual, uninfected people lived. "Sometimes, it's the belief that madness has a cure."

Every time I passed the Danvers State Viral Hospital after Nerissa's commitment hearing, fingers of ice played notes up and down my spine.

"I'm just trying to help you," Cal said. "Cram it, Aoife, can't you see that?"

I held out my hand again, offering it to his ministrations. "I suppose. I'm sorry."

Cal rewrapped my hand. "Me too." He looked gamely at the books. "This isn't so bad. Kind of stuffy. You know, I hear that you can still go to school in quarantine . . . maybe not to be an engineer, but a teacher or a personal secretary for sure. You're bright enough—"

"*Cal.* Don't try to *help* me, like I'm some dame in one of your dumb aether plays," I said. "Don't try to be my hero. Just be Cal." I stood on tiptoe so I could move the straw stalks of hair away from his eyes. "I like just Cal."

Cal shuffled his feet in the dust coating the broad boards of the library floor, but at least he'd stopped talking about quarantine for the time being. I looked at my feet, too. The spectral glow of the lantern made everything sharp, the tear in my stocking and my footprints in the dust. Beneath them, I discerned an older set, smaller than my feet, heel and toe, period and question mark.

"Look." The footprints crossed the library in a careful, unhurried line and disappeared at the bookshelves on the far wall. I grabbed Cal's arm. "Somebody else was here."

153

Cal's arm went rigid under my grip, and I watched his throat twitch painfully as he swallowed. "Your father must have had a lady visitor."

"A lady visitor who can evaporate through the walls?" I started for the spot and Cal attempted to pull me back.

"Aoife, you don't know what's going on here."

I shrugged free of his bony grip. "The dust is settled over her prints. She's long gone. And since my father never married, I'm doubting she has any business in this house."

"Never *re*married," Cal corrected me, holding up the lantern for a pale imitation of light as I ran my fingers over the shelf. A hidden door would be simple enough, and a fine carpenter could make a hinge invisible with ease.

"No," I said, brushing over the spines. Emerson, Thoreau, Kant. Not heretical texts, but not the sort of thing upstanding rational folk read on Sunday afternoon, certainly. The old ways of superstition and belief, the search for a human soul, were like Nancy Granger. Nancy Granger snuck off to the Rustworks and met a boy at the jitney track. Nancy Granger had gotten in the family way. No one at the Academy talked about Nancy Granger after she went back to Minnesota.

"No?" Cal frowned. "What d'you mean, 'no'?"

"I mean he never *married*," I said. "Not my mother or anyone else."

Cal's mouth opened, and then he shut it again. I knew his thoughts by heart even though he avoided my eyes. *Nice girls aren't bastards. Nice girls have fathers who come home and take off their ties and have a cocktail with the evening paper.*

154

At least Cal knew me well enough to keep his thoughts as thoughts. The only fight I'd ever seen Conrad lose was to a bully over nearly the same words.

It mattered very little. I was already an orphan, a potential madwoman and possibly a heretic. What difference would Archibald and Nerissa having rings on their fingers when I was born really make?

It had bothered Conrad more. He felt like Archibald had denied him and set him up to fail. Without a recommendation from his father, a boy couldn't hope to pluck a prime job as a Maintainer in the Engineworks. He might as well be stuck in the pit next to the steam ventors or doing menial tasks like sweeping or greasing.

Had Conrad and Archibald finally spoken? Or had Conrad found the same deserted corpse of a house I had? For that matter, where was he if not at Graystone?

Too many problems. My mind was starting to become disorderly again, like during the one memorable and horrific occasion when I'd tried to take Fanciful Maths. Numbers outside of engineering work were messy, imprecise, theoretical as fairy stories. Only mechanics made sense.

I turned to the single problem I could solve—the footprints. The shelves were solid, and the books were books, not disguised springs and levers that would show me Graystone's secret places.

I chewed on my lip. "There's got to be something behind this wall. People don't just disappear."

"*People*," Cal agreed. I quirked an eyebrow.

"Surely Cal Daulton, most rational of all the Master Builder's faithful, doesn't cotton with spirits and vapors."

155

Cal huffed through his nose. "Yeah. Rational as the day is long, me."

I got down on my knees, dust tickling my nostrils, and ran my hands over the aged, rippled boards. The floor was solid and heavy with wax, but my fingers picked out an impression the size of my foot.

I put my hand over the spot and pressed down.

The door in the wall opened bereft of any trappings. No shrieking hinges, no breath of tombstone air chill on my face, not even a solitary cobweb. The section of the bookshelves rolled back on soundless hinges, a brass wheel-and-arm assembly pulling the philosopher's books into a hidden pocket of wall. I nudged Cal until he raised the lamp, and peered cautiously into the space.

Within sat a passage made of raw boards and beams, and a warped staircase leading down. I beckoned to Cal. "Come on."

"Are you nuts?" He backed up. "You don't know what's down there. This whole gear-forsaken mountain is overrun with viral critters and you want to go down some hidey-hole?"

With two years of our friendship at my back, I knew how to work on Cal. I put my hands on my hips. "Why, I'd say you're scared."

His forehead furrowed. "I'm not."

"Fearless adventurer Cal, scared of a little dark and dank. What will the guys at the School ever say about this?" Without another word, I turned and walked ahead, leaving him to follow or be left alone in the library, with the eerie, intermittent heartbeat of that awful clock.

After three steps, Cal rushed after me, sticking to my

shoulder like a burr. "And who would be there to look after you if I stayed behind?"

"Dean?" I suggested. Cal made a rude noise.

"The less said about that greaser, the better. He's no kind of gentleman."

"That's all right," I said. "I'm no kind of lady." We came to the bottom of the stairs and another inconspicuous door. This door wasn't hidden or locked, and opened at my approach, like the doors of the library. I theorized about the mechanism that allowed such a slick illusion—some kind of weight-sensitive plate, rigged to a pulley system, or a motion-sensing system that triggered when our shadows passed in front of the pinhole in the wall.

We stood in the doorway, an invitation into yet another expanse of blackness. As before, I stepped forward into the dark, and someone screamed.

"Cal!" I thumped him on the arm in reflexive alarm. "Shine the lantern!"

"You're trespassers!" the voice shrieked. A projectile from the darkness—a woman's shoe—narrowly missed Cal's head. "I'm not infected! Get out!"

"Whoa there, miss!" he shouted. "There's no call to get violent!"

The other shoe flew and I ducked. "Hey!" I snapped at the voice. "Cut that out!"

Silence while the ghostly lantern beam swept the dark room beyond the door. The aether glow picked up stone floors, a vast porcelain sink and pump, an icebox of polished mahogany.

157

"What's your name?" I said to the shadows. I felt confident doing so, sure that viral creatures most likely wouldn't resort to throwing scuffed-up leather pumps at us.

"None of your beeswax!"

Considering it was my father's house, I privately thought it *was* very much my beeswax, but I wasn't about to argue with a stranger hiding in a kitchen, pelting me with footwear.

I gave the rest of the room a cursory glance while trying to discern the voice's source. A dead fire gave its last gasp in the grate, shooting embers to leave black streaks on the hearth. A single chair sat before it, a book draped over the arm. *Alice's Adventures in Wonderland*. A banned text. A text on the Bonfire List, the compilation of all books the Proctors thought rated burning. I'd choked on the smoke as a little girl, while Conrad held my hand to keep us well clear of the mob standing around the conflagration in Banishment Square.

"Is that your book?" I said. There was a shuffle and a sniffle. I fixed on the sound—beyond the sink and before the icebox.

"You can't pin nothing on me. That there was in the library when I came. I never read a word of it. Just like the pictures."

I picked up my first real live heretical book and turned it over. A crocheted bookmark, the kind of thing I'd had to waste hours on in Home Life classes, nestled thick in the pages.

The book looked very ordinary—it was a cheap edition, bound in scratchy paper, and a little ink came away on my fingers when I traced the first line of the page. "'The Hatter opened his eyes very wide on hearing this; but all he said was, "Why is a raven like a writing-desk?"'"

"Why *is* a raven like a writing-desk?" I asked the shadow voice.

"It's a mad tea party," said the shadow. "Riddles without answer, 'less you're a mad one too." A pause, and the voice dipped, like it was shy of quoting the text. "The Cheshire Cat says it—'We're all mad here.'"

While she rambled, I let her voice guide me, and locked my fingers around the plump arm of the voice's owner. The girl in my grip squealed. She didn't sound a day over graduation age at the Academy, and terrified.

"Take your hands off! That ain't ladylike!"

I gave her a shake. "That's quite enough of that. Who are you?"

Copper-pot curls bounced and her chubby face flushed. "The nerve of you, playing handsy with me! Think you'd never had a lesson in manners in all your life!"

"Okay, okay," Cal said, training the lantern on us. "Settle down, the both of you."

"Who are you?" I ignored Cal. "Why are you in my father's house?" My words came out with more ice coating them than I'd intended. Perhaps it was the shadows, or the book, or my throbbing shoulder. Perhaps I was simply wrung out of patience for foolish girls and their foolish games.

"I work here, don't I!" the girl snapped. "I'm the chambermaid. Who in blue heaven are *you*?"

That stopped my indignation cold. Of course such a great house would have servants. Of course I seemed like a trespasser to this girl.

159

"Aoife Grayson," I managed. My own flush crept up my face. "I'm Mr. Grayson's daughter."

The chambermaid screwed up a frown. "Well, *I've* never heard of you."

I let go of her arm and stepped away. Of course she hadn't. My father had no use for me.

"Where has everyone gone?" Cal said. "The other servants? Mr. Grayson?"

"They . . ." The chambermaid shuddered. Her round face went paler than dead under Cal's lantern. "They . . ."

"What's your name?" I amended, as shivers racked her frame.

"Bethina," she quavered. "Bethina Constance Perivale."

"I'm Aoife," I said again. "This is Cal, and we and our friend are searching for my brother, Conrad. He'd be a bit older than me, and taller. Black hair and blue eyes. He was here . . . have you seen him?"

Bethina's eyes, the shade of a Coca-Cola bottle shot through with sun, went wide. "Mr. Conrad? You're *his* sister?"

"Yes. And I desperately need to find him, Bethina. Can you help me?"

Bethina's face crumbled, moisture shine rising like dew on her cheeks as her eyes filled. "It were a terrible thing. Terrible, terrible thing what happened to Mr. Conrad."

Even though my throat tightened with dread, I felt through my pockets for a handkerchief and held it out. The small dingy flag dangled limply between us before Bethina snatched it and gave a great heaving snort into its folds.

160

"Bethina," I said gently. "Don't cry." That only made her louder. "Bethina!" I said, trying to sound like Marcos Langostrian, entitled to boss her. "Is that any way to behave in front of your, er, your betters?"

"I'm . . . I'm . . . s-sorry, miss," she gulped. "I just . . . I've been here for days. Days, alone in the cold. When it gets dark . . ." She dissolved again and soaked my handkerchief with a fresh flood of tears.

A shuffling came from the darkness, the click of flint, and a small flame sprang to life. "You two could wake up a dead thing and get it dancing," Dean said, hiding a yawn. "What's the racket?"

Bethina gasped. "Who is *that*?"

"Dean," I said. "This is Bethina. She worked . . . works for my father."

"Pleasure's all mine, darlin'," Dean said. He lofted his lighter and illuminated an oil lamp hanging over the butcher block in the middle of the kitchen. Dean blew on the flame and after a breath the lamp sprang to life in sympathy, without the aid of the flame.

"Old Ones return!" Bethina gibbered. "You didn't touch that lamp! That's regular witchcraft!"

"Witches aren't real," I said automatically. "They're stories for fools." Conrad's words. He always knew the right ones.

"Stories usually start true, Miss Aoife," Dean said. "A touch of truth makes a lie worth believing." He sat himself at the battered kitchen table and looked about. "Got any food in this dump, Bethina? I'd murder something for a sandwich."

161

"I don't want you here," Bethina blubbered. "Any of you! You'll let them in. The cold things and the creeping shadows. They'll steal me away. . . ."

I glanced at Dean. "Can't you do something?"

Dean grimaced. "Waterworks ain't really my department, Miss Aoife."

"Conrad was here," I grated, feeling control slip. "She saw him. Talked to him." My own tears, hot and thin and angry as Bethina's were fat and hysteria-laden, threatened to boil over and betray me. "She *has* to tell me where he went. What she saw." I took Bethina by the shoulders and gave her a shake. "Stop that infernal noise and tell me where my brother is!"

"Aoife, calm down," Cal said. "You're getting shrill."

"You're damn right I'm shrill!" I shouted. "My brother is missing and my father is gone and my shoulder aches, so *forgive* me if I'm not dropping a curtsy!"

Dean clapped his hands sharply. "Everybody simmer down." He got up, moved me to the side and lifted Bethina's chin with one finger. "Now you listen, Miss Bethina. You're gonna leave off the fussing and talk with Miss Aoife, and I'm going to make you up something hot for your nerves. You got any coffee?"

Bethina swallowed and shook her head, her poodle cut bobbing like soap bubbles on air. "Just hot chocolate. In the cabinet by the basin. Milk in the icebox, if it hasn't turned. Milkman hasn't come since . . . well. Not in weeks."

Dean pulled down a tin of Ovaltine and a saucepan, while Cal helped Bethina to her chair by the fire. In the warm hearth glow of the oil lamp, I saw empty tins and boxes of food stacked on the drain board, dirty plates and

162

mud-spattered petticoats laid across every surface of the kitchen.

"How long have you been living like this?" I said.

Bethina looked at her hands, twisted my handkerchief in a stranglehold. "Since they took your brother away."

I felt the fear crawl back into my chest. "'They,'" I said heavily. "Proctors? The Bureau of Heresy?"

Bethina looked at me mournfully. "Worse," she said. "So much worse."

12

The Chambermaid's Tale

Even as Cal worked to rekindle the kitchen fire, Bethina shivered. "This place . . . it was never a good place, miss, even before Mr. Conrad went missing."

I paced from the table to the basin and back. I couldn't seem to sit still. Bethina had seen my brother, spoken with him, held a rational-enough conversation to learn his name. His letter to me hadn't been a fancy. "If you're expecting me to believe in some far-fetched curse on this place, or some ridiculous heretic story . . ."

Bethina shook her head. "No, miss! It's the Master Builder's own truth. Graystone is built on burying ground, and that's a fact. Puritans, I think Mr. Grayson said. The first Grayson here dug up the gravestones and planted them out in the oak grove, but they didn't find all of the bodies. I know I ain't supposed to believe in Spiritualism and things like that, but it's a foul business. And during the heretic troubles some-odd decades ago, bootleggers dug

164

passages in the cellars. There's limestone caves about a mile on, down at the river. They left casks of money and liquor down there when the Revenue chased them out. And Mr. Grayson said the folks in Arkham have seen nightjars in the tunnels, too, and revenants—those glowing ghostish things that lead you off the path to drown in the underground pools."

"What does this have to do with my brother?" I demanded. "Did he try to go into the caves?" The thought of Conrad trapped underground in some damp stony place, unable to call for help, seized me right about the heart.

Dean poured Ovaltine into a pair of chipped mugs with the flourish of a soda jerk. "Bethina." He handed her a mug covered in ducks wearing glasses and smoking cigars. "Miss Aoife." My mug was plain and blue, and Dean's fingers whispered against mine.

Cal's mouth turned down. "Where's mine?"

"Only enough for two, and I think the girls need something to calm their nerves more than you do, cowboy." Dean settled himself at the table again and lit a Lucky Strike, looking for all the world like he belonged in my father's kitchen.

Cal stole Bethina's chair by the fire and put his foot on the hob, grumbling. His ankle was returning to its normal size. At least that deceitful Alouette had been good for something.

Bethina blew on her mug. "Mr. Archibald hired my mother on when I was just a kid. I used to play in the front hall 'cause it had the slickest floors and I loved rollerskating. He was a nice man. Not cruel, but he had . . . strange habits."

165

"I suppose wealthy folk often do," I said curtly. I didn't know why the urge to defend Archibald rushed words to my lips, but it felt right.

She puffed up like a banty hen. "I wouldn't dream of questioning him. But all the same, miss, there was something not right about this house. I'd wake up from bad dreams and I'd have the most awful feeling that something was watching me, from the back gardens, staring up at my window." She sipped her Ovaltine and made a face. "This milk is gone."

"Working with what I have." Dean waved his flask. "I think there's a sip or two left, if you'd care to sweeten that."

"Certainly not," Bethina said primly, setting the mug down with a *clack*, as if the very idea of liquor were offensive.

"Someone watching you," I prompted her to continue. I kept my irritation in check by tapping my bare foot against the tile floor. "Who was it?"

"I'd get out of bed to check that the window was locked up in the garret," Bethina said. "And . . . I'd see them, out in the moonlight."

"The mysterious Them. I got chills." Dean had already polished off his cigarette and was up digging in cabinets. All he unearthed was an ancient packet of TreacleTarts, the pudding inside the pastry shell gone rock-hard from age.

"I call them the tall men," Bethina said, her voice no bigger than the child with nightmares she described. "They were pale, too. Cold eyes. They came from the woods, single file. Every full moon, they came. I heard Mr. Grayson on those nights, pacing in the library." She reached out and clapped her hand over mine and I started. Her palm was

166

hot from the Ovaltine, while I'd gone cold. "I didn't mean to snoop," Bethina whispered. "I didn't mean to be trouble."

I wriggled my hand free. Hers was slick. "Bethina, what did the tall men want with my father?"

"I didn't never want to find that out, miss," she whispered. "They were awful, the pale men. Their pale fingers and their pale eyes . . . one looked up at my window, and I swear he stole the thoughts from my head. So bright to look on, in that full moonlight. So beautiful . . ." A tear slipped down her cheek, dangled unnoticed on her flower-petal skin. "I could have looked at him forever, even though I had the most awful nervous flutter in my chest when he caught my eye. I wanted to hide but I couldn't. . . ." She stopped, and knotted her fingers together. "I fear I'm not making any sense, miss."

"Trust me, you're making more sense than a number of folks I know," I told her. Even though she was scared and didn't appear overly bright, I couldn't help feeling sorry for Bethina. She'd been trapped alone in the house, and obviously whatever had visited my father had spooked the tar out of her. I gestured Cal out of her chair. "Let's get you settled and then you can tell me the rest of the story," I suggested, trying to be kind like the endlessly patient and immeasurably patronizing nurses at Nerissa's madhouse.

Like the patients with their sedative-addled senses, Bethina didn't cotton to the fact the entire act was for her benefit. "Thank you, miss. You're not such a hooligan as you first seemed," she said, dabbing at her cheek with the edge of her cuff once she'd sat. "Talking about the tall men . . . it does set me off sometimes, like a silly thing."

"Forgive me, Bethina," Cal said, "but could you have

167

maybe seen a real man, flesh and blood, wearing an illusion cloak like in the *Phantasm* comics?"

"Of course not." Bethina sniffed. "*That* Phantasm ain't real."

Cal flushed. Dean shoved a handful of stale TreacleTart into his mouth to muffle what would surely be a sound of derision.

"Did Conrad meet the tall men?" I asked. "Did they do something to my brother?" Conrad wasn't like me. He was fearless, and he'd charge into something strange without a thought. I was the one who worried, who weighed logic before she did anything larger than pick out a new pencil from the box.

Bethina bobbed her head, but I couldn't tell if she was acquiescing or trying to hide embarrassment. "One day Mr. Grayson was gone. Dismissed the staff in a note left in his gentleman's parlor. Some clothes and favorite books, his sturdy boots and his shaving kit . . . all gone. He left his bedroom and dressing room in such a mess it took me all day to straighten up on my own. Even left his diary behind, tossed on the floor like trash." She fiddled with her curls.

"And?" I prompted. "Conrad?"

"Mr. Conrad came a few weeks later. After your father had gone. A wild-eyed type, that's for certain. Mr. Grayson would have been none too happy with his manners. Mr. Conrad wanted to poke about. He kept talking about some birthday and wanting to ask Mr. Grayson about his mother, which I didn't understand none of, because Mr. Grayson's not seen her in near fifteen years. But I still made up a bed and put on some supper. He was a decent

168

sort, if you could get past his comportment." Bethina's voice dipped to a whisper, nearly lost in the crackle of the fire. "They came that night."

"The pale men?" My tongue tasted of chalk.

"No, miss. It weren't the pale men, it was something else altogether. Shadow things. Things I ain't never seen the like of in all of my sixteen years on this earth." She rubbed her hands together, looking to the darkness beyond the kitchen windows. "They didn't whisper or laugh like the pale men. These creatures poured in, miss. They covered every inch of the place, and I shut my eyes tight so they wouldn't see me. They took your brother out, toward the apple orchard, and poor Mr. Conrad didn't even have time to call out. He left everything. Even his letters. Didn't have stamps on 'em, so I did it, and dropped 'em in the post. I figured it was the least I could do. Then I holed up here 'fore dark in case those things came back again at night and I haven't been out since. That was a week ago."

So Conrad's note had reached me under Bethina's auspices. Conrad himself was vanished yet again. We'd been connected for so many months by strings of words, by only the smell of ink and smoke that I ached to see him, put my arms around him and hear his gentle rumbling voice telling gentle jokes at my expense. My wise brother, who'd know exactly how to handle the place I found myself in.

But Conrad wasn't here, and it fell to me to be clever and worldly, to shoulder the load. I felt a bit like crying, but if I started having hysterics in front of Dean I'd never let myself live it down.

"Why didn't you report this to the Proctors?" Cal asked

169

Bethina. "It's a kidnapping, and viral creatures are involved besides."

Bethina shrilled a laugh. "What, and have the same Proctors believe I'm bound for the rubber house? 'Living shadows kidnapped a heretic boy from under my nose!' No *thank* you. I like my freedom if it's all the same to you."

I rose and set my mug into the wash basin, Ovaltine untasted. "That's all? That's all you know?"

Bethina flushed. "I'm sorry, miss, but yes. The shadows stole your brother, and that's the whole of it. No one here except me and the mice."

I wrapped my fingers around the edge of the porcelain drain board and stared at the stained tile of the countertop until the spots of water and mildew spun in front of my eyes. I started multiplying numbers, trying to keep my mind on an even keel, to hold my hopelessly jumbled thoughts at bay.

Conrad kidnapped by viral creatures. Conrad vanished without so much as a scream. Only time to pen the note. Conrad asking *me*, of all people, to rescue him. The vertiginous, swirling pool of madness rushed up at me and I shut my eyes, willing the images from my dreams to retreat. Order. I needed order. I opened my eyes again, started to count tiles, my lips moving.

"I suppose it was cowardly to shut myself up in the kitchen," Bethina admitted. "But I wasn't keen on swanning about with those things running loose. They might take *me*."

"No one's going to hurt you, darlin'," Dean said. His words were directed at Bethina, but his eyes were on me. By the time I'd reached my eightieth tile, the swimming behind my eyes had retreated and I slowly unlocked my aching hands from the edge of the drain board. I hoped that Cal, Bethina and Dean would put my episode down to worry over Conrad. I wished that I could.

"I thank you for your kindness, even if you are a heretic," Bethina told Dean. Dean's eyebrow quirked.

"Keep a razor blade under that tongue of yours, eh?"

"I see what I see, sir." Bethina crossed her ankles primly. In keeping with Graystone's crumbling surroundings, her stockings had a run in them.

"That's it, then," Cal said. "End of the line. Conrad's gone and so is your pop. We'd best be hoofing it back to Lovecraft and praying that we don't get expelled."

Conrad's shaky handwriting floated through my vision, and his admonishment to me:

Save yourself.

"Bethina," I said. "Did my father or Conrad ever mention anything about a book? A specific book, or perhaps a ledger?" I swallowed a lump "The . . . a . . . 'witch's alphabet'?"

Dean's head came up, as if he wanted to interject, but he kept quiet.

Bethina frowned. "No, miss. I never heard them mention no witches. They seemed upright men, the both."

The fire sighed in the draft, and that was the end of Bethina's story.

While Cal escorted Bethina to her garret, Dean walked me back to the room where I'd recovered from the shoggoth bite. He shivered outside my door, and I didn't think it was entirely from the winter air against his bare arms.

171

"Are you all right, Dean?" I hoped the question wouldn't wound his pride too much.

Dean's mouth quirked down. "I suppose, but I gotta say it—this is Weirdsville, kid. Your old man's a spooky cat."

Privately, I was beginning to agree with Dean. Aloud I said, "I expect you want to get back to Lovecraft and the Rustworks. Your life." I reached for the roll of bills I'd secreted in the top of my stocking. "How much do I owe you for being our guide?"

Dean sucked his teeth. "This job's a complicated bargain, true enough. More to it than blood or money."

"What else is there?" I rolled my stocking back over my thigh and watched Dean's fingers curl as they followed the movement.

"You're a pistol, Miss Aoife. You sure you don't belong with us down in the Rustworks instead of at that stuffy School?"

"Oh, keep your remarks to yourself," I said, but only half cross. He returned my small smile.

"I figure that I brought heat on myself during that little airship adventure. Proctors might have my mug now, maybe even my name. Maybe I need some country air, until things cool off and I don't end up down Catacombs way." He shrugged. "Figured you might need a few more dragons slain before we settle up, princess."

"There are no dragons," I said, although a part of me felt immense relief that he wasn't leaving yet. "And no princesses."

Dean rolled his pack of Luckies free of his sleeve and tapped one out. "Not in this dusty old pile of bones, that's for sure. But there's you and there's me, Miss Aoife. I'm calling that good enough."

He tucked a strand of wild hair behind my ear with his long fingers. Dean Harrison smelled of cigarettes and embers, and I breathed him in like he was all the air there was. No, Dean couldn't leave yet. I'd never had this reaction to anyone in my life. He couldn't go. I was beginning to realize I needed him.

"Aoife." Cal appeared from the direction of the landing. "Is he bothering you?"

I took a large, guilty step in one direction and Dean backpedaled in another.

"Not in the least. We were discussing his fee," I said. My heartbeat was louder than thunder at the thought Cal might have been standing there for longer than a few seconds. "For being the guide."

"Well, I sure hope it wasn't for his wit and charm," Cal said. "Listen, I'm going to sack out and you should, too. We need an early start if we're going to make the city tomorrow."

I felt my mouth take on its stubborn set, which usually heralded a detention or an extra essay on something like etiquette. "I'm not going back, Cal. Conrad needs me."

"Aoife . . . ," he sighed. "We've decided this."

"No." I jabbed my finger at Cal. "*You* decided. My brother is kidnapped, and I'm going to help him. If you don't want to help save *your friend*, then by all means, go beg the Proctors to forgive you."

Dean touched the back of my hand, light as a kiss. "I'm out of this conversation. Sweet dreams, kids."

"Please, Cal," I said after Dean disappeared into another bedchamber. "Just sleep on it. If you still want to leave in the morning, then go, but I've made up my mind." I reached for him, but he backed away. "I could use my best friend," I whispered.

"Aoife, you're not being rational," Cal said. "Conrad's gone Builder knows where. You need to go home before your whole future is slag, and mine too. If *you* cared you'd listen to me."

"Why?" I demanded. I'd been holding my tongue all day, playing at politeness, and my frustration boiled over like a crucible left too long on a burner. "Because you're the boy and so I must be hysterical to disagree with you? Because I'm going mad? Or"—I drew close to Cal, realizing for the first time how tall he'd become in the summer between last year and this one—"is it because you're scared?" I demanded. "That's it, isn't it—you're scared that we might find Conrad and he really will be everything they say he is in Lovecraft. That the perfect, clever Cal Daulton made a mistake in befriending him."

Cal's jaw twitched, and I thrust my chin at him, daring him to yell or slap me or do anything except stand there like a boneless scarecrow.

"You need to rest, Aoife," he said finally. "Clearly, the events of the day have gotten your head in a muddle. You're saying things nice girls have no business talking about."

"Oh, go strip your own gears!" I shouted. "I'm afraid too, Cal. I don't want to think that Conrad is mad, but he might be! Or he might be dead, or consorting with real heretics, but I'm not turning tail!"

174

"Well, forgive me if I don't want to toss away my entire life for a guy who may or may not be leading his naive sister on the road to ruin!" Cal growled. "And *forgive* me for watching out for my friend!"

"If you believe that Conrad would hurt me on purpose," I said, matching his snarl, "then we are *not* friends."

With that, I stepped into my room and slammed the door in Cal's startled face. I curled up on the musty bed and lay wretched and sleepless until dawn.

13

The Sinister Clock

MY MOTHER USED to help us find shapes in the clouds while we lay in Von Braun Park, pointing out unicorns and knights and the unfurling, scaly hides of dragons.

It wasn't until much later that I learned you could be burned for suggesting such things existed, independent of their creation from steel, gear and steam in the laboratories of engineers. The Bureau of Heresy in Washington would accept no fantasy, no magic. Nothing that did not spring from viral infection or pure science.

I tried to find the same shapes in the stained plaster of my bedroom ceiling while dawn light spread fingers through the blood-colored velvet drapes.

"Coffee." Dean kicked open my door and backed in, holding a tray made of silver and stamped in roses. In his big, rough hands it was rather ridiculous. "Found some hidden in that rat hole your pop calls a pantry. Old as the hills but brewed up strong."

I pulled the duvet up to my chin, as I'd taken off my filthy, destroyed uniform and not-slept in my petticoat and brassiere. "This is my room, Dean." I didn't want him to see me disheveled and sleep-tossed. Cal seeing me wouldn't matter, but I had a notion it would be different with Dean.

"And I do apologize for barging in, but I figured you'd forgive me." He stepped over the threshold and kicked the door again to shut it.

I felt under my pillow for my jumper and slipped it back on even though it stank to high heaven, and then rolled the coverlet down. I fluttered my hands uselessly at the tray. "Why did you bring me this . . . stuff?"

Dean stared hard at me. "You skittish over something, Miss Aoife? Bad dreams? Starchy sheets?"

"I . . ." I forced myself to look at Dean and not blush. "I'm not usually alone with a boy. Besides Cal. And just when we're cramming for exams."

Dean spit out a laugh. "Relax, princess. It's just coffee."

"I'm quite relaxed," I said in a tone that was anything but, glancing at the lamp on the nightstand. It was a heavy Tiffany number, all glass and iron. I could bean someone with it if I had to. I didn't *think* Dean would try anything, but nothing in this world was certain, and the plain truth was I barely knew him and he was close enough to embrace. "I'd hate to have to scream when you acted improperly," I added.

"You wouldn't scream." Dean poured the coffee out of the silver service into a china cup, a small and frilly porcelain bird in his hand. "You're thinking you'd hit me with that lamp you were just eyeballing and make tracks, because you don't need any kind of rescuing."

"I need it more than you could ever know." The words slipped out and I didn't stop them, wasn't even aware until Dean paused, a little coffee splashing onto the leg of his dungarees.

"Dammit." He sat down on the foot of my bed, his bulk bowing the ancient mattress. "What's that deep-down secret giving you sad eyes and sleepless nights, kid? You can say it's nothing, and Cal will believe you, but not me."

"I . . ." I wrapped my fingers around the cup he handed me, suddenly chilled with the knowledge I'd said too much. "That stays a secret." I liked Dean, probably more than I should, but I was determined to have no one visit me in bleach-scrubbed halls that smelled of antiseptic, echoing with the screams of patients whose medication couldn't stave off their nightmares. I'd rot my days away under the eye of no one but the shadow companions birthed from my viral mind. I wouldn't ensnare sane victims, like Nerissa had. I'd decided it the day my mother was committed permanently.

"All right, it's your secret. For now," Dean said. "But we still need to settle up my payment."

I huddled deeper under the blankets. "I probably can't afford your payment, Dean. I barely have any money and certainly nothing else someone . . . like you . . . would want."

"You've got that secret," Dean said. "Someday, you'll tell it to me. And when you do, I'll take your secret and then it will be mine to keep instead of yours."

Faintly, I remembered one of Nerissa's stories, the poor weaver girl who makes straw into gold and trades with a witch for secrets.

178

"Miss Aoife?" Dean's mouth turned down at the corners. "That secret's my price. We got ourselves a bargain, sure and sealed?"

Nerissa wasn't here, and if she were she'd say nothing to help me. I was just a girl who came and listened to her stories. She no more cared if I ended up indebted to a so-called witch than if I dropped out of the Lovecraft Academy and joined a troubadour caravan.

Though I had the sense that I was stepping over some threshold, and that by promising my secret to a boy like Dean Harrison I could never return, I stuck out my hand and pumped Dean's once. "Yes. It's a bargain."

After Dean left, I ripped back my coverlet and went rooting in the wardrobe for something to wear that wasn't mud-encrusted and days old.

The wardrobe stood taller than me by a head and a cloudy mirror reflected a stained and damaged Aoife back at me. Forget a new wardrobe—I needed new skin with the amount of dirt and blood I was wearing.

Poking behind the various narrow doors of the bedroom yielded me a wash closet with a steam hob circulating heated water in the corner. It hissed like an amiable snake when I spun the tap, and delivered a helping of rusty red water into the basin.

I found a washrag and scrubbed myself clean as I could while minding the bandage Dean had put on my shoggoth bite. He'd done a fair job, fair as I'd receive at the Academy's infirmary, and the bite hardly hurt at all except when I pressed on it. The skin around the bandage carried

179

a pallor, but there was no blue-veined, green-fleshed infection crawling its way through my system from the spot where the shoggoth's kiss had landed. Dean's skills as a field surgeon could have probably netted him legitimate work in Lovecraft, tending to victims of ghoul attacks and Proctors who fell to heretics during rioting. But imagining someone like Dean forced to march lockstep with the severe nurses and surgeons of the Black Cross, the Proctor's medical arm, didn't end well—he'd probably be expelled for his smoking alone before he was a week in.

The worst of the grime fell away with the washrag when I tossed it into the now-empty basin to dry out, and I padded back to the wardrobe. Most of the clothes were for a boy, old-fashioned short trousers, a waistcoat, shirts made for celluloid collars and high leather riding boots. However, at the rear of the cabinet I found a drop-waist silk dress, and a search of its cubbies yielded a comb to twist up my hair. It still looked like a nest for Graystone's crows, but at least it was out of my eyes. The dress gleamed ruby-wet and the comb was mother-of-pearl, glistening bone against the dark of my hair. I tried on the riding boots and found that the long-ago boy who'd inhabited the room had exceedingly small feet. The boots hugged my calves like hands.

When the wardrobe swung shut and the mirror revealed me once again, I caught my breath.

I looked like my mother.

Turning from the mirror so quickly I almost fell over my own feet, I ventured into the hallway. Graystone was vast and deserted in the daylight, muted with emptiness. I wandered back along the route I'd taken to the library and the kitchen, though it was devoid of all its menace in the daytime. The sour portraits of Grayson patriarchs still glared at me from under their layer of finely aged dust in the rear parlor. I paused to read their nameplates, stern as their visages. HORNTON. BRUCE. EDMUND.

The newest portrait's placard read ARCHIBALD GRAYSON. I stopped. I was finally going to get to see what my father looked like. If there was anything of him in me. I stepped close, eager to take in every last brushstroke in the light.

My father was dapper and besuited in the painting, streaks of white in otherwise dark hair at his temples and a piercing set of eyes bookended by lines the only hint he wasn't still a young man. Spectacles on a chain marred an otherwise pristine green silk cravat and his angular cheek-bones gave him a disapproving edge, rather like one of my professors. Though, unlike any of my professors, my father was handsome, albeit in a bookish way. Conrad favored him in feature if not in coloring, and after a bit looking at Archibald became too much like looking at the much older, sterner version of my brother. I moved away, back to Thornton, back down the line into the safety of the past.

I didn't look anything like Archibald. Our eyes were the same, but there the resemblance ended. It put a weight on me, one that I felt like I couldn't shake off. I wanted so badly to ask Archibald about Nerissa, and everything that had happened. I wanted him so badly to come back and answer me. But he wouldn't, because wishes didn't come true, because fairy godmothers weren't real.

Hurrying toward the foyer, I nearly smacked into

Bethina. She shied, and the tray she held spilled oatmeal and toast onto the worn carpet runner.

"Stone and star. Forgive me, miss." She knelt and began to scrub up the oats and tea with her apron corner.

"My fault, really," I said, crouching to pick up the toast. It was all heels and felt rough and stale. "You came out of the kitchen," I observed.

"Can't very well leave the young miss of the house without her breakfast, can I?" Bethina sniffed. "There's still a few things in the icebox and the root cellar. 'Sides, it's daylight and with you three here, I figger the shadows might not find a way in, to . . . well, you know what I'm saying, miss."

She shuddered, and scrubbed harder at the rug.

"That's very kind of you," I said, standing and smoothing down my new dress. Silk felt like what I imagined wearing a nightjar's skin would, slick and cold. "Do you think you could bring my breakfast to the library?"

Bethina wrinkled her nose. "I surely couldn't, miss. That room gives me the creeping spooks, all up and down my back. I'll leave it in the warming oven, should you take a notion to eat." She pinched the back of my knee from her vantage. "And you should eat, miss. You haven't got anything up top or on the stern for a future husband to admire. Like Mr. Harrison, for instance?"

I sputtered at how matter-of-fact she was about the whole thing, jerking from her reach. "I . . . my . . . That's really none of your business, Bethina."

"Just so, miss."

In the entry, I found my schoolbag where Cal had flung it when we made our frantic entry into Graystone.

182

I dug through my possessions—now largely mildewed and mud-spattered—and found my toolkit. Straightening my spine, I went to the library again and, just as before, the double doors slid open at my approach. Ice danced up my skin, into my blood like electricity and aether.

Hearing a curse from the rear parlor, I backed away gratefully and retraced my steps down the portrait hall. I wasn't ready to brave the library again just yet.

In the parlor, Cal was poking a desultory fire. I watched him for a moment, his long limbs bunched up like a new foal's, cursing and red-faced as the twists of paper under the worm-eaten wood sputtered and refused to light.

"Thought you'd be halfway home by now," I said at last. Cal leaped up.

"Aoife." He eyed the full length of my body, for a good few seconds, eyes darkening. "You look . . . different. Those aren't your clothes."

"My uniform is a lost cause," I said. "This was in the wardrobe."

"Do you think it's a good idea?" Cal worried the poker. "I've heard it's bad luck to wear other people's clothes."

I touched the comb in my hair. "What would your professors say, they heard you taking stock in superstition like that? Besides, I like these and that's a stupid rumor."

"It's, well. The dress is very bright. Red, like a Crimson Guard flag." Cal struck another match and cursed when the flame came too close to his fingers.

"I'll be in the library," I sighed. "And for future reference, girls might not be flattered to have you compare their attire to the symbol of a national enemy."

"Aoife, I wanted to say I'm sorry . . . ," Cal rushed, and

183

then sighed, composing his face and standing. "I'm sorry about what I said to you last night. I don't believe that you're naive."

"But you do think I'm wrong about Conrad?" I should simply accept Cal's apology and let things be right between us. The space where I'd kept Cal's friendship was bruised and smarting this morning, after the shouting match we'd endured, but I wouldn't abandon my brother either. Not even in words.

"I don't want us to fight," Cal said. "Can't we just agree that we'll go home tomorrow? He's not here, Aoife."

I drew myself up, the dress falling about my legs making me feel older, taller. "Then I suppose I'll just have to find where he's gone."

"Aoife, be reasonable . . . ," Cal started, but I walked away from his words. Cal and I had been friends ever since we'd both been without a partner for our first tour of the School of Engines, but lately we sat at odds over everything, our conversations going in unfamiliar directions that twisted them into something angry with jagged edges.

Losing my only friend over my family sat poorly, like something rotten and too large in my gut. If I had no Cal, then right now I'd have no one.

To distract myself from my thoughts, which were swirling off in a black direction indeed, I went back to the library, brushing past the doors like I had nothing to worry over.

Conrad had told me to fix the clock, and I would use machines and math to soothe my troubles.

The clock waited at the far end of the long high room,

pendulum twitching at random like a rat's tail. I knelt before it and opened the case, staring into the wicked, sharpened gears.

"I'll fix you," I said. "If you'll let me."

For a moment, nothing happened and then the gears turned faster, pendulum lashing like the shoggoth's tentacles.

"I'm not going to break anything," I promised the clock. "Please. I *have* to fix you." Was this the first sign of madness? Talking to inanimate machines? Perhaps I was only mad if I got a reply.

I reached slowly toward the clock's case, even though sticking my hand inside the whirl of gears with the way they spun would result in me losing a crop of fingers. "Conrad told me," I whispered. "I have to fix it. I have to fix you."

My fingertips tingled, and my head echoed as the clock began to chime; I felt as if a pipe fire had sparked to life in my chest. My entire body ran fever-hot, and dampness broke out under the silk of my dress. The dancing snare of static spread up my arm, all through me, and the tolling of the clock became a single reverberation, splitting my skull in half.

I shrieked. *"Stop!"*

Quickly as it had ramped up at my appearance, every gear within the clockwork ground to a halt, fine metal shavings raining to the bottom of the case as gears fouled themselves against one another's filed teeth.

I waited for a moment, the idea that the clock had stopped on my command ludicrous even to my mind, but the mechanism was still. As if it were waiting.

185

I reached into the case, mindful of my cut thumb and bruised knuckles. Every sharp edge of the clock's innards was hungry, and I exhaled shakily as I felt edges and ridges catch on my skin. If the clock started again it would take my fingers off, but Conrad had told me to fix it, and I didn't see another way to do it.

Trying to recall what I knew about clockwork from our basic class in gearworking the previous year, I loosened and reset each gear that had slipped out of sync, and tugged on the clock's weight to start it ticking again. It groaned in protest and still ticked out of time.

Dean stopped in the double doorway, shrugging into his leather jacket. "I'm going out for a smoke, miss. You want to tag along, or . . ." He came closer, crouching to unzip my toolkit and examine it. "Looks like you're busy."

"The ticking," I lied. "It keeps me awake at night."

"I dunno, princess," Dean said as I tugged at a stuck gear. "Can you really fix this old thing?"

"The timing is fouled," I said, finding a useless lump where the master gears should be. "It looks like I need to strip and recalibrate the entire assembly to get it working properly."

Dean grinned. "Need any help?"

I laid out the first gear and its bolt on the carpet, and noted its position in the clock case. "What happened to your smoke?"

Dean handed me a wrench as I fumbled for it, body half in the clock case. "Smoke'll keep."

The job of recalibrating a large and complex assembly like the one in the library would be a thing even for a skilled clockmaker, and Dean and I were both cursing and

186

had ended. At least it didn't make my head spin anymore. "I know my way around a jitney engine, but this . . ." He smiled. "You're a bright penny, kid."

I wiped the grease from my hands with my toolkit's supply of rags, watching in satisfaction as the clock spun on with nary a hitch. "You can call me Aoife, you know." Not that I minded very much being called princess.

Before Dean replied, a great rumbling like a waking beast began under our feet. Dean's eyes snapped wide. "What on scorched earth is that?"

The books on the shelves vibrated, as if they were itching to shed their covers and fly away. I grabbed hold of a shelf to keep my footing, and Dean reached for me as well. "I don't know," I shouted over the rumbling. From far off, I heard crockery falling and Bethina give a scream. What had I done now?

"Aoife?" Cal stumbled into the library on the bucking floorboards. "What's going on?"

"I don't know!" I didn't, truly, and my panic rose along with the rumbling from under the floor, as if we were standing in the bowels of the Lovecraft Engine, chambers turning at full capacity and pressure building without a relief valve.

Then, abruptly as it had come upon us, the rumbling ceased and a section of wall above my father's writing desk rolled back, soundless as the servant's passage to the kitchen. But this was smaller and older, clearly built into the house at conception. It hid a brass panel, half as tall as I was and twice as wide. Dials and switches, valves and an antique static board using glass breakers filled the tiny recess in the library wall.

I approached it, wondering at the artfulness of the

189

construction even as I felt trepidation build. Hidden rooms and hidden panels that controlled hidden things never boded well.

Dean let out a breath, his fists uncurling. "That's a new one. What d'you suppose it's for?"

"I have no idea," I said. The panel reminded me of the controls on the *Berkshire Belle*, except these were older, more archaic, and there were a lot more switches and keys than a simple airship flight board.

"Don't touch it!" Cal cried when I took a step toward it. I cast a glare back at him.

"Cal, it's brass and wood. It's not going to grow teeth." I was cautious, but not scared. Machines were what I was good at.

I approached the hidden panel with its rows of switches labeled with painfully neat, handwritten placards: *Library, Front Hall* and *Cellar Traps* among at least a dozen others, all in an orderly, masculine hand on yellowed vellum squares.

Conrad had told me to fix the clock and in doing so I'd revealed Graystone's secret heart. Conrad had vanished before he could perform whatever task he needed this panel for himself. But he'd had the forethought to send me the letter, to hide the note. He knew I'd come if he asked.

What I knew ever since that awful day in my dormitory room a year ago came true when I realized that Conrad had been planning for me to come here, to carry on where he couldn't.

My brother wasn't mad.

And if he wasn't mad, then he was in a world of trouble.

190

14

The Iron Bones

DEAN JOINED ME at the panel, examining the controls. "Slick setup. Dare you to press one of those switches." He reached for the closest lever, marked *Kitchen*.

"Don't," I said. For some reason I couldn't define, I wanted to be first. It was my father's house, my father's device, and I wanted to be the one to discover how it worked.

Bethina peered around the library door. "Miss, what was that awful racket? Are we safe?"

"For the time being," I murmured, touching each dial. Every facet of Graystone somehow connected to these antique controls.

"Awful shaking and shivering," Bethina continued. "Like the Great Old Ones returned from the stars. My mum was raised in a Star Convent, and she told me—"

"That's all mumbo jumbo," Cal told her. "This is engineering."

"Flash work, too," Dean said. "I don't think Bethina's that

191

far off, cowboy. This thing Miss Aoife woke up ain't just cold metal and gears. Houses have blood and gristle and bone, just like a person. Houses have souls."

Cal jerked a thumb at me, at Dean. "Aoife, are you going to let him just babble heresy all day long?"

I rather liked Dean's heresy. Graystone *was* like a living thing, old and dessicated, but alive still.

"Give it up," I told Cal. "Let's see if we can piece these controls together."

At the top of the row of knobs, there was a dial marked *Front Hall.* "For what it's worth, Dean," I continued, "I don't think you're just speaking heresy." Because Graystone did talk. It had warned me away like a wounded animal; when I'd fixed the clock, it had come into the open and showed me its face. Graystone wasn't like any house I'd ever stepped foot in, and I knew that it had more secrets to give up, secrets that would lead me to my brother.

I put my hand on the dial. "I'm just going to turn it on and see what happens. If anything harmful was in the workings, it would have gone off when I fixed the clock." Giving what I hoped was a reassuring nod—because in reality, I had no idea what would happen—I ran my fingers over the row of knobs, then settled back on *Front Hall.* If something in Graystone's bones *was* malicious, the front entry was far enough away that we'd probably be safe.

"So you said, miss. I'm having no business with that thing," Bethina said, scuttling away. Cal backed off too. Dean stayed where he was, hands in his pockets. His pale storm-sky eyes were implacable as thunderheads.

The *Front Hall* dial was inlaid with tiny darts of onyx,

"The whole house is alive," I whispered. "Rods for nerves and gears for bones and an iron skin to hide it."

I went to the panel and clicked the dial back to *Lock*. The metal plates retreated with irritable clanking and rumbling, opening Graystone to the world once again.

Cal whistled. "You could lock somebody up like Attica in this place."

"Or lock something out," Dean muttered. "I don't much care for locks, tell you the truth. We in the Rustworks spend a lot of time thinking about cold iron on our legs and stripes on our shoulders in some Proctor work camp."

Entranced as I was, I waved him off. "The whole house is clockwork. The whole house is knitted together with these gears, and this is where one can make Graystone do whatever it likes." The feat of constructing a clockwork house was something that a student at the School of Clockworks could only dream about. The assembly to cobble an entire structure together, to calibrate and time it so that it ran smooth and soundlessly, and then to bring it all into the central mechanism of the clock and the controls . . . the amount of time and care the clockmaker who built the house must have invested boggled my conception of mechanics.

My father hadn't built it—it was much older, Victorian in style—but he must have known about it. He lived in this clockwork marvel.

And it was mine to learn and to control, and only mine. My father had left and in doing so left me the iron bones of Graystone, sleeping and waiting for me to wake them. Until he came back. If he did.

"Well," Cal said. "We should test it out. See what it can

195

really do. I mean, for our own safety." His eyes were bright and I could see that his fingers were twitching, itching to touch the controls of the clockwork as much as my own were.

"Sure," I said, giving him a small smile. "How about you stay here and try out the dials? Dean and I can explore." There would be no more talk of leaving once Cal got his hands on the panel. And I could show him I didn't begrudge him wanting to go home by letting him play with the house's mechanics.

Cal's jaw jumped once at the mention of Dean, but only once. "Watch out for the traps," he said. "All these switches have the setting."

"She's in good hands," Dean told him, ushering me from the library.

I removed my elbow from his grasp. "I'm not in anyone's hands at the moment."

Dean's back stiffened for a heartbeat, but then he gave me a nod. "My mistake."

"It's not a . . ." But I stopped myself before I became an even bigger fool. I wasn't shying away from Dean because I wanted to. I was staying away from him because he was dangerous to me in the same way as an aether flame—bright, hypnotizing and hot enough to burn. I was here to find Conrad, get him out of danger and then go home. Not to let a boy fill my head with dreams and ideas that I could have *if* I didn't go mad, *if* I had been born to a different family. No matter how much I wanted to see how he was different from the boys I knew. And I did want to, but I resigned myself to only wanting.

"Hey." Dean called me into the back parlor. "Think now

196

we can get the wireless working?" He pointed to the old-fashioned console, its tubes set into ruby and emerald glass, the gas inside them drifting lazily back and forth.

"I don't know," I said. "This thing is museum quality. Cal!" I shouted. "Turn the aether switch on!"

After a moment, the crystals that passed heat through the aether and made it active began to glow, and when I turned the glass needle along the spectrum dial, a voice scraped out of the ancient phono horn.

"You're listening to WKPS, Pittsfield, Massachusetts, and this is Dirk DeVille with the news. The President issued a statement today regarding the ongoing necrovirus research purportedly conducted in secret Crimson Guard laboratories, calling it blatant heretical aggression against the United States—"

Dean spun the needle along the spectrum. "Sorry. Listening to that guy's voice is like putting a rivet into my own head." The studio audience for *The Larry Lovett Show* laughed back at Dean.

I spun the dial again. Music crackled faintly, a phonograph that was half static.

Dean's mouth quirked. "Finally, something we can both agree on."

"Aoife, are you going to hang around in there all day?" Cal called. "I want to see what this thing can do!"

"All right, Cal," I shouted back, reaching to turn off the wireless. Dean stopped me.

"Leave it. I like a little music when I'm alone with a pretty girl."

I'm sure the blush I felt showed in my face. Dean kept sending me hurtling off balance. I'd never met someone

197

who spoke as freely as he did. Especially about me. "You're not alone with me, Dean, and I'm hardly the sort of girl someone like you finds pretty."

Dean pushed a piece of hair away from my eyes. "Why don't you let me decide that?"

I ducked away from his touch. I knew damn well I was a smart girl, not a pretty one. Boys at home told Cecelia she was pretty constantly, and she let them take advantage constantly. Not me.

"I should go check the rest of the house," I murmured. "Make sure there's nothing dangerous in here."

Getting to my feet, I stumbled over my own boots as I backed away from Dean, but he just smiled. "You check the upstairs," I said. "I'll go to the cellar and make sure the boiler isn't . . . er . . ."

"Overheating?" Dean prompted.

Could I make this moment any worse?

"Yes," I replied meekly.

"Sure thing," Dean said, standing and brushing the dust from his dungarees. "I'll call out if I see anything."

His easy smile told me that he didn't take offense at my awkwardness, but I felt restless as I walked from room to room. Windows and doors opened and shut by themselves at the merest touch of my foot on the threshold. Iron grates rolled over the windows to protect Graystone's residents from the outside world, but at the flick of a switch, the ceiling of the front parlor rolled back to reveal a rotating display of the night sky, wrought in silver, brass and glass against deep blue velveteen clouds. There were spikes that rose out of the fence around the outer edge of the drive

198

and front gardens, and a phonopiano in the conservatory that played itself while a pair of brass dancers turned atop its keys to a Brahms waltz.

Finally, Graystone had exhausted its wonders and all that remained was the mundane task of checking the newly reinstated boiler for leaks.

"Cal, I'm going to the cellar," I shouted. "I'll be up in a moment."

"Be careful!" he shouted back. "The cellar is the last of the switches on the board, and then I'd say this place is ready for action!"

I found the cellar door off the kitchen and Bethina watched me skeptically when I grasped the handle to go down. "You be careful, miss. Those bootleggers left weak spots and covered holes all over the place down there."

"Bethina, I'm not a child," I told her. Cal had already fussed over me. One surrogate parent per day was my limit.

"All right, then," she grumbled. "But if you fall down a hole and get devoured by a nightjar, it will be no fault of mine."

"Thank you for that, Bethina," I said, and descended the creaking, winding stairs. Graystone's cellars were damp and shadowed, but a row of aether globes strung along the ceiling with wire lit a path to the ancient boiler. The foundations of the house were far older than the stately stone and brick above, rough-hewn rocks set into the bowl of the earth. The floor was dirt, packed by what had to be centuries of footsteps.

I checked the boiler, an ancient but sound Potsdam

model, imported from Europe. The pressure was normal and hot water was flowing through a nest of pipes, hissing in the dark of the cellar. It sounded like the shoggoth's voice in my mind, and I drew back quickly, knocking my head against one of the low-hanging aether globes.

In the swinging blue light, I saw the edge of a bricked-up hole in the foundation. Bethina hadn't been telling tales about bootleggers, after all.

The hiss of the boiler grew louder, more insistent, and my shoulder began to throb as I stared at the dip in the wall. Conrad had read me a story once, from one of Nerissa's few, dog-eared books. The story was called "The Cask of Amontillado." A man was walled up in a cellar, lured with the promise of the sweetest wine he had ever tasted.

The boiler clanked and shuddered as Bethina opened the steam tap in the kitchen, and I retreated up the stairs, a bit quicker than my pride would have liked.

I found Cal at the switch panel and smoothed my hands down my dress to stop their quivering. My momentary scare in the cellar had retreated, and now I just felt silly. Graystone wasn't my house, but I felt at home here, more than I had anywhere else so far in my life. Graystone wasn't going to hurt me. Gears and clockwork didn't have life or a mind of its own.

"You look a little pale, Aoife," Cal said. "You feeling all right?"

"I . . . yes. Perfectly fine." I went about returning all of the dials on the panel to their original positions. "Everything seems to be in order."

"Not quite," Cal said. "The Library dial is stuck."

"I'm sure it just wants a little greasing," I said. "I'll see if Bethina knows where the autogarage is on the grounds."

"Maybe if we tried turning it together," Cal said. "I mean, who knows how long this thing has been shut away? It could have rusted."

"All right." I put my hand on the dial and tried to turn it, to no avail. It was, as Cal said, stuck fast.

Cal slid his hand over mine, his long fingers closing down. They were cold. "Together," he said. "One, two . . . *three.*"

We twisted, and Cal's fingers grated against mine hard enough to force a cry from my lips. Just as quickly, the pressure eased and the dial snapped over hard, a clank of mechanisms speaking to the neglect that Graystone had suffered since my father had gone missing.

But nothing happened. No more miracles of engineering and clockwork revealed themselves. The library stayed stubbornly the same.

"Guess it's busted," Cal grumbled. Dean came tromping down the front stairs, his boots leaving scuffs on the white marble of the entry hall.

"You gotta peep the upstairs of this place when the clockwork's turned on," he said. "There's a map of the world that moves and has a nautical compass, up there in the gentleman's parlor, and a stenotype that types by itself when you say words into a phono-phone." He caught sight of Cal's and my hands, intertwined. "Somewhere else I should be, maybe?"

"It's not that," I said quickly. "We're just trying to get this silly library control unstuck." I twisted again and only

201

succeeded in straining my wrist. It wasn't much compared with Cal and Dean trading glares.

"Forget it, Aoife," Cal said. "If I can't get it working, then you certainly can't. I'm much stronger."

After the thick tension of the day so far, I balked. Of course I was used to being tolerated as an oddity in the School of Engines. Of course I bore it with good breeding and grace. In Lovecraft. But here, in my father's house, a house built with the same vision that made gears dance behind my eyes and steam whisper in my dreams where other girls saw designer pumps and lanternreel stars, I was thrice-damned if I would bear it any longer.

I grabbed the dial with both hands and wrenched, putting my back into it and ignoring the pain. As before, a spark of static flew from the panel and shocked my fingers with enough voltage to make my small hairs stand on end. My forehead began to throb, and then the dial assembly gave, quickly as the clock had stopped for me before.

An abrupt grinding emanated from the ceiling, along with a long plume of dust. I jerked my head up, half expecting to see the cracked plaster ceiling caving in on us. Instead, a telescoping ladder of wood and brass unfolded, spider legs feeling delicately for purchase against the floor. A small trapdoor slid ajar in the smooth plaster of the library ceiling, nearly twenty feet above my head.

"Place has more holes than an anthill," Cal said. "What do you suppose is up there?"

I was already on the third rung of the ladder, the hidden room a draw I couldn't ignore. "I don't know, but I aim to find out."

"No . . . ," Cal started, but then he sighed and held up

202

his hands. "Just don't get yourself lost in some dark hole where we can't find you again."

"Don't you worry." I flashed him a smile from above. "Escaping from dark holes is my specialty of late." I'd been everywhere else in the house, and while it was remarkable, it also told me nothing useful. This had to be the spot where I'd find a clue to Conrad's whereabouts, and Archibald's. Deep down, I somehow knew this hidden room would hold the solution to how I'd find and free my brother and my father. It came on me quick as fear, but it was certainty instead. I had to figure out a way to find them. Because otherwise, I was out of brilliant ideas.

"Aoife, wait." Dean fumbled in his jacket.

"You're not talking me out of this," I told him.

Dean found his lighter and tossed it to me. "Not trying to. Just, I wouldn't want you all alone in the dark up there."

I thanked him by tucking the lighter into the top of my boot for easy reach when I needed it. Then I grabbed the slender ladder and climbed higher.

15

The Forsaken Tomes

I CLIMBED INTO the dark, passing the trapdoor and feeling along on my hands and knees, across boards covered in a half-inch of dust and grime. This attic space was warm and close, cobwebbed by time and neglect, and I tried to touch as little as possible.

Fumbling the lighter from my boot, I clicked the spark wheel once, twice, and a flame shot into the shadow, warning the dark back with a hiss.

The hidden room at the top of the library was small and A-shaped, tucked where the gables of Graystone met the roof. A four-pane leaded window blacked out with oiled paper cast weak light into the space, which showed me the silhouette of an oil lamp. I removed the sooty globe and touched Dean's lighter to the wick. The flame guttered for a moment and then caught, and I lifted the lamp to more carefully examine the room.

Books surrounded me, crowded in, piled on shelves, on the floor, on the single scarred table in the center of the space like miniature ruins. The volumes were nothing like the pristine texts in the library below—these were older, in disrepair, spines cracked where there were still spines to break, water stained and page-rumpled. Books with miles of use. Mrs. Fortune would call them "well loved."

I'd completed one circular survey of the tiny room when the trapdoor snapped closed again and a pair of locks engaged.

"Aoife!" Cal's shout penetrated the floor as I scrambled over to the door, nearly smashing the lamp and setting the entire room ablaze. I scrabbled at the edges of the door, but the seal was tight and the locks were brass, with only a smooth face on my side.

My heart started to pound, and the close warmth of the room became oppressive as I started throwing books onto the floor searching for a release amid the shelves and the thousands of battered tomes. Nothing. I was locked in. I stood and flashed the light frantically along the walls.

Finally the lamp's flame caught a shine and I saw a dial set into the wall at chest height, behind a stack of almanacs from the previous century.

"Aoife!" The ladder clanked as someone heavy—Dean— mounted it and rattled the door. "Aoife, we can't get it open!"

"It's all right!" I shouted. "There's a switch up here!" The switch was a simple two-position job, but to my immense relief, one of them was *Door Open*. The thought of being trapped up here made me light-headed. I undid the collar

205

button of my dress and fanned myself with a battered copy of an almanac until my heart ceased to pound.

Retrieving the lamp, I moved it away from the piles of books on the floor and set it back on the writing table. This surface was crackle-varnished and scarred, covered in ink stains and crumpled vellum scraps, as different from the ornate desk in the library as the School of Engines was from the Lovecraft Conservatory. It was clear to my eyes that my father—or some bygone Grayson—had spent hours here, high in the house's aerie. And judging from the papered window and the frozen lock, they had spent their hours locked away in secrecy, with no one from the house or the outside world able to see in or gain entry.

They may have been content to stay in the dark, but I didn't like the secrets that the long shadows implied. I tore down the oil paper from the window, letting in the weak autumn sunlight and illuminating decades of untidiness.

The eaves hung lower than I'd first imagined, and the space was so crammed with books and oddities I couldn't take more than six small steps in any direction.

There were not just books—although books were most plentiful. In the watchful eye of the sun I spotted specimen boxes, a map cabinet for charts and blueprints, and a naturalist's kit sitting atop it, complete with forgotten specimens in jars of formaldehyde. A globe dotted with the shapes of uncharted countries sat high on a shelf, along with a scattering of empty ink pots. Something crunched under my boot and I looked down to find a massacre of broken pen nibs littering the floor.

I saw on closer examination of the sagging shelves that

206

none of the books had a title on the spine. Many were just diaries stitched together with heavy thread, even the covers filled up with the same square and precise handwriting that had labeled the clockwork that controlled Graystone.

"Aoife, are you coming down?" Cal shouted. "What did you find up there?"

I opened the trapdoor and leaned my head out, still holding the closest handwritten tome. "I'm looking around. I think I'll stay up here for a little while."

Cal waved his hand in front of his face to direct away the cloud of grit that opening the door had dislodged. "You can't be serious."

"You should come up," I said. "There's all sorts of specimens and gadgets in here."

Cal resolutely shook his head. "I can't believe you'd rather bother with a bunch of ancient scratch paper than explore the house."

"The house will be here when I'm done," I told him. "Just come up, Cal."

"No, thank you," he said quickly. "I'm not keen on being that far off the ground." I saw him nudge Dean's shoulder. "Come on, I'll have Bethina make us lunch. Aoife finds a book, she can have her nose in it for hours."

"It seems to have done well for her." Dean looked up and winked at me, but he followed Cal through the hidden servant's passage to the kitchen. I dialed the trapdoor shut again. At least Cal and Dean had stopped sniping at each other for a moment, united by the common boy's love of a hot meal.

That left me with at least an hour to search the room.

207

I was sure that Conrad had meant for me to find it, but what he'd wanted me to see, I didn't know.

I tried the map cabinet first. There were a wealth of charts, all misfolded and crammed together as if their owner had been in a terrible hurry to tidy up. Or hide something.

Yanking the clot of paper free, I was rewarded with nothing but dirt and beetle skeletons. I spread out the maps, finding a star chart like the one we used at the Academy. This one was older, covered in handwritten notations and numbers, and contained far more stars than I remembered from my one course of astronomy. Professor Faroul had been arrested for heresy just after I started my freshman year, for preaching at the class that the Great Old Ones would some day return to earth and attain mastery over human beings. Professor Faroul had been no one's favorite, but he was a hapless and gentle man. That was the first time I'd seen a Proctor up close, other than at the court where my mother was committed. The rasp of their rough black uniforms and the slam of their steel-toed jackboots against the observatory floor stuck with me, like the imprint of a cold hand on the back of my neck.

The next chart was a map of Massachusetts, the kind of thing you could buy in any cartographer's boutique for half a dollar. It, too, was scribbled on, with a heavy concentration of nonsensical ink scratching around the borders and township of Arkham, symbols and stars and glyphs that reminded me of nothing so much as the defiant sketching in the margins of my notebooks.

The last and worse-faring chart was hand-drawn on heavy paper that felt more like dry and ancient skin than pulp or linen. It was heavy enough to smooth out its own wrinkles, but some of the ink was irreversibly blurred and erased.

For a moment all I could make out was a mess of lines and engineer's notations. Then, with a gasp, I realized the shape was familiar, a cross with three radiating wings surrounded by a wall and a garden peppered with outbuildings. The queer paper was a plan of Graystone, and judging by the slapdash nature of the notes on the clockwork schematics, it was the engineer's original blueprint. The date sitting in the corner, nearly rubbed out from dozens of thumbs rolling and unrolling the sheet, was 1871.

I set the chart down carefully and rooted around in the clutter until I found a leather map tube with a strap for carrying the maps of your trade, whether you were an engineer, a clockmaker or simply a naturalism enthusiast trekking in the woods. Carefully rolling up the blueprint, I put it in the tube and laid it against the writing table. I wasn't letting something so valuable out of my sight until I discovered what, precisely, Graystone was still hiding.

And diverting as the schematic was, it wasn't getting me any nearer to finding Conrad. I turned my attention back to the tangle of books and journals, pulling them from their spots at random and dislodging enough dust to choke a ghoul.

The books were largely of the fantastic and heretical variety—potboilers featuring tough-guy detectives on the trail of a treacherous dame, stories of men voyaging to the bottom of the sea inside a living biomechanical submersible, and a fat book with a worn-off spine written entirely in German. All books that had escaped the Proctor's bonfires during the war and after.

We learned German, because it was pertinent to learn the language of a conquered nation, but we were never allowed to read it out of class, or while in the confines of the Academy. The verbs gave me terrible trouble, but I was able to pick out a few easy headings in the battered book. "Snow White and Rose Red." "Rapunzel." "The Robber Bridegroom."

I set the volume with the map carrier for later study. Now it was simply diverting, and I didn't need diversion. I needed my brother. Some Grayson, at some point, must have left a clue to the strange happenings in this house, to the reasons Conrad had come and then vanished.

Paging through the handwritten journals, I tried to scry for any clue. The first few volumes were gibberish, written in code piled onto atrocious handwriting, and I shoved them out of the way, digging deeper into the stack on the bottommost shelf, under the window. Outside, the crows had returned and sat conversing with one another on the sill. "If you're going to hang about, you might at least give me peace and quiet to work," I grumbled. It only seemed to make them louder.

Tugging at a recalcitrant volume, I loosed an avalanche of journals that buried me in bound and loose sheafs up to the shin. I said something unladylike and started to restack them, when I noticed that many of the journals held a notation on the cover or the first page. The notation was numerical and, from what I could decipher, organized after a fashion.

I went through at least twenty journals, and found the same variation of three-digit groupings: *45–6–12, 7–77–8.*

They ranged from cheap cloth-bound ledgers to fine leather volumes overflowing with pages, but the number sets remained. I opened a numbered journal at random, and an ancient collection of loose sheets showed me great, spreading, spindled wings attached to bodies with dog's heads and lion's feet. The next page was a sketch of a flying machine with rigid wings and the body of a great bird. The pages were labeled simply *Machina,* and there were at least a hundred of them, machines that had to have been designed by a fanciful madman. A rolling jitney that belched fire rather than steam. A difference engine small enough to be carried in a knapsack.

I set the volume aside. I loved aerodynamics and calculation science, even though a woman could never spend months aboard a flying fortress, refueling war buggies and chasing storms, or buried beneath the desert at Los Alamos working the difference engine for the Air Corps. It was men's work. Women kept their feet on the earth and their head above it, no exceptions. Like my life—no matter how much I wanted things to be different, reality remained.

The lamp sputtered, and I reached out to turn up the wick, catching the shadow of Conrad's note on my hand. It had nearly faded since my frantic escape from Lovecraft, but the numbers were still there. A triple sequence of double digits.

Save yourself

31–10–13

I dove back into the pile as the connection lit up in my mind, flinging books and papers aside as I discarded one

211

journal after another, the pages flapping like bird's wings as I tossed them over my shoulder one by one.

Until I reached the dozenth journal and finally found what I was looking for. I let out a small breath. I'd found, in this battered little book, what Conrad had called the witch's alphabet.

16

The Witch's Alphabet

CLUTCHING THE LEATHER-BOUND volume marked *31–10–13*, I sank cross-legged onto the floor of the hidden library, my spine meeting the spines of the forgotten books.

Fingers trembling, I opened the journal to the first page. Ink blotting and age had mostly obscured the name of the journal's owner, but not the line below: *Set down at Graystone, Arkham Valley, Massachusetts.*

I touched the page and the handwriting moved and slithered, alive under my touch.

I gasped and dropped the journal. The rearing snakes and spines of pigment settled immediately. They hissed at me, their two-dimensional mouths flickering against vellum aged to slick and shine.

"Witchcraft." I echoed Bethina without meaning to. I didn't believe in such things. Hadn't believed. I didn't know anymore.

I leaned toward the page, my palm hovering above the

213

ink, and then quickly, like passing my hand through a candle flame before I lost the nerve, I pressed down.

The paper pulsed warmly under my hand, alive as an animal, and though I wanted to bolt down the trapdoor and down the ladder and as far away as I could from this unnatural situation that could not possibly be happening, I stayed seated. I knew it was as real as the shoggoth bite that flared and throbbed when I touched the paper.

The ink continued to hiss and writhe. It lifted from the page, wrapping my hand in midnight ribbons. I flinched, waiting for the blot of infection upon my mind, the sting of madness that would finally swallow me like it had swallowed my mother.

Instead, a curious warmth began in the center of my palm, as the ink pressed itself into my skin. A scratchy tingle, like I'd put my hand too quickly in hot water.

The sensation grew painful and I tried to pull away, but the ink held fast. I was immobilized by the very illusion that I was denying even as I watched it happen.

The madness had spared Conrad. Perhaps this wasn't the necrovirus, this pain traveling steadily up my arm like fingernails raking over my skin. I was the prisoner of this strange bewitched ink from a strange bewitched book, and its enchantment held me fast, surely as the thorn maze held the sleeping princess in Nerissa's tale.

I cried out as the ice-hot pain of a burn imprinted itself on my hand. In that moment, I couldn't even struggle. I simply froze, whorls of vertigo overwhelming my vision, and willed my body not to faint from the sensation.

This was not the necrovirus. It was not the dreams that

stalked me through all my nights in the School. Not the looming ghost of my mother, not the bite of the shoggoth.

The feeling causing my vision to black and my body to throb was nothing I had ever known, and nothing I could explain with any of the Proctor's laws or the Master Builder's tenets of rational science.

The closest word I could use was, after all, *witchcraft*.

I didn't care that it made me a heretic. I didn't even care that in the eyes of everyone I knew, it confirmed my madness. Sorcery was the only explanation for what was happening to me, for the pain that was chewing through me from the inside out.

Then, as abruptly as it had stolen my senses from me, the ink's enchantment released. The serpents on the page curled, tongues tasting the air, hissing with satisfaction. I fell back against the books, cradling my palm against my stomach and fighting both tears and panic. My hands were my fortune. I could never be an engineer with a crippled hand. I couldn't even be a stenographer. I'd be less than useless, a ward of the city until I died.

When at last I had the courage to examine my burn, I saw a stigma on the spot where heretic palmists would tell me that my life and heart lines intersected. The mark sat in the shape of a wheel with pointed spokes and sharpened treads—not a wheel, I saw, but a gear, a gear which shimmered just under my skin—not a brand like the Proctors' stigmas, but inky, like a navy boy's tattoo. The spot was rimmed with pink and slightly warm, but I was otherwise whole, with no hint of the agony I'd just endured. My mind, however, was still telling me that my palm was on fire, that I was going to lose my hand, the one thing I couldn't lose and still be an engineer. . . .

"Breathe, Aoife," I ordered myself in a whisper. "Breathe."

I stared at my palm for a long time, feeling the crow wings of my heartbeat flutter and finally still as my panic faded. My hand was still there. It wasn't lost, along with any future hope.

Something had touched me. I could fall back on what they taught us at the School all I wanted, but there was no denying that the ink—the entire journey since Lovecraft— was inexplicable with pure science.

I sat for a long time, turning my hand over, waiting for the stigma to vanish. It didn't. At last, I remembered that the journal was still lying at my feet.

Gingerly, I picked it up. It was only paper once again, good paper bound in good leather, innocuous as my own notebooks from the School. On the page, the ink was no longer twisting and obscured with age. Handwriting clear and sharp as a razor blade stared back at me.

Property of Archibald Robert Grayson
14th Gateminder
Arkham, Massachusetts

My father's hand sat square and precise on the page, and the book was no longer the least aged and mouse-eaten, but whole as any of the volumes in the library below.

There was ghost ink, simple chemicals and trickery. There was Conrad, making a half-dollar appear from under his tongue and disappear again behind my ear.

216

This book was something different.

I was faithful to the science that gave us the Engine and protected our cities from the necrovirus, but in the small attic room I was beginning to feel the enchantment sending slow, hot pinpricks from my palm to my heart.

I was a rational girl, but in that second I admitted this might be magic.

The belief only lasted for a moment. There could be a dozen explanations for what I'd seen.

It didn't have to be magic. Magic was an obfuscation used by the Crimson Guard to frighten their citizens.

But I couldn't change what my father's handwriting had set down, and as far as I knew Archibald was as rational as I. I read.

Witch's Alphabet

My breath stopped. This was what I'd hoped for. The book that would tell me how to find Conrad. I read on.

Set down according to the wisdom of the Iron Codex and those who came before.

Documenting the days of the 14th Gateminder and his encounters with the Land of Thorn herewith.

I'd followed Conrad's cryptic words and I'd found the thing he'd begged me to find. My elation was muted by the fact that the book seemed in no way useful to the cause of helping Conrad. More witches, more magic. More things that would only get me into more trouble. Clearly my

217

father had no such worries, which surprised me a little. He'd seemed like such an upstanding sort from my mother's few stories.

His journal was certainly a treasure in my search for clues about him, but for another time, when I had the leisure to peruse it.

"Conrad, why?" I demanded. "Why did you send me to find this dusty old book?"

I'd seen things since Cal and I had fled Lovecraft that made believing Conrad to be insane impossible. I may not have believed in magic spells, but there had been a time when aether and steam power were myths, as well. Before the spread of the virus, and before the Great War. The burning in my palm alone overturned the notion that I could explain away everything in Graystone. But Conrad hadn't ceased to be cryptic, and I could have smacked him on the head for it.

I gripped the book between my two hands and pressed it against my forehead. "Why?" I whispered. "What do you need to tell me, Conrad?"

I flipped open the journal and let it fall to the first full page. The heading read *7 January, 1933*.

"I'm listening," I said quietly, staring at the plain line of text.

As if something in the library above had heard my exhortation, my vision slid sideways all at once. It was much like the plunge we'd taken in the belly of the *Berkshire Belle*—more and more pressure on my head until I simply couldn't see or sense anything.

This sensation was familiar, though—the hot tickle of the enchanted ink rushed over me again, and when nothing burned or otherwise injured me, I cautiously cracked my eyes open. I wanted to see—the fear was gone, and a slow-churning excitement had replaced it.

Across the room, a gray figure, a bit out of focus, sat at the writing desk, scribbling feverishly in a journal identical to the one I held.

I let out a soft shriek and dropped the volume I held. Immediately, the figure vanished and I saw nothing except the familiar dusty attic.

The chair at the writing table was empty. It had always been empty. I was skittish and excitable from the events of the afternoon, and I was behaving irrationally. I had not just seen a translucent man sitting in the attic with me.

But I didn't leave the attic and go fetch Dean and Cal as my panic dictated. More than I wanted to run, I wanted what I was seeing to be real. I wanted such a thing to be possible because it might mean that I could escape my family's viral fate. I knew I was still sane, and if I was seeing a vision—there had to be another explanation.

Hesitantly, I picked up the diary again, riffling the pages. Each one was choked with script, margins rife with notes in different colored ink. There were drawings, too—diagrams of bones, of bird wings, a symbol like the one on my palm, which I compared side by side. Gears and workings of machines that dizzied me with their complexity, even more so than the portfolio of *Machina*.

Flipping the pages back to the beginning, I began to read.

My father's voice floated out of the past. *7 January, 1933.* The corners of the room flickered again, lanternreel memories wrought in silver and gray.

219

This time, I let them come.

I endeavor to set down in the pages of this book a true and accurate account of my tenure as Gateminder, my father wrote.

My forerunner and father, Robert Randall Grayson, gifted me with this book on the turning of the New Year. It is my duty now, sworn and sealed, as I have reached the age. My Weird has presented itself and I can no longer shirk my duties, among them a true record of the same. I have placed a geas on this volume so that future Minders might withdraw my memories, revisit the events leading to the end of my tenure as speaker and learn from them, but no others may read or see my writings.

My geas is still elementary and the recorded memories pale, anemic things, but I suppose it will have to do. I confess that, in the advanced year of eighteen, I had doubted that any Weird had passed to me from the Minder before. My brother, Ian, with his skill over the air, and our father with his mastery of stone, had caused me to question my place in the brotherhood more than once.

I had an uncle, somewhere, I realized with a swell of excitement. First a father, now a family. Every orphan's dream—the bosom of a family, with money and influence, to take her in, buy her pretty dresses and make life easy.

My imagination was starting to run away with me, until reality inevitably seeped back in. Families like that didn't have hidden rooms full of books, talking about magic as if it truly existed, lived and breathed in their bloodline.

I turned a page and the gray figure returned in a dazzle of light. I didn't drop the book this time. My hand twitched where the ink had marked me, but I stayed resolute and watched the memories born from my father's journal play out.

I watched as the boy, who had to be Archibald, scribbled, pausing only to push his half-glasses up his nose.

"Archie!" A voice, equally phantom, from the library below. *"It's time now. Get your coat and boots and bring your nerves!"*

I watched as my father sighed, licked his pen, wrote faster.

l will take my oaths on the full moon, the blood oaths that lan is so eager to engage in and that l dread so very deeply.

No one but myself will bend the spine of this codex until l am long dead, and therefore l may set down my true and honest feelings: l abhor the blood rites, the meeting with the Kindly Folk, the trappings of the Weird. l dread the Folk's all-seeing eyes and their touch on my innermost secrets. l do not fear the pain that comes with the initiation, but l do fear the stripping bare of my mind, the opening of a vast well within, the free flow of the Weird through my veins.

l fear it may burn me up from the inside, and that l may become ash, nothing, borne on the wind.

I flipped the page and was surprised to see that the next entry was dated nearly two months later.

28 February, 1933.

221

I am the 14th Gateminder now. I bear the wisdom of the Iron Codex and my blood has spilled on the Winnowing Stone.

My father hadn't been writing this for me, that much was clear. I had only the vaguest idea about what he was up to, and none of it sounded like it would keep him or anyone who knew what he was doing out of the Catacombs back home.

The full moon rises tomorrow and it brings the Folk under its withering gaze. I must, for the first time, accept their aid as Gateminder.

The gray figure of my father stood in the library above, much tidier than it was now, where I sat. He rubbed his glasses up and down on his vest, checking his pocket watch. He was wearing a suit instead of a rumpled shirt and trousers. It didn't fit him well, and he kept fidgeting with his tie as if he were about to meet a girl for a date.

The great clock in the library below chimed midnight, and my father went to the garret window. I followed his flickering, transparent form, watched the shadow of the garden discharge three pale figures with faces cloaked by white robes. They looked like members of the Druid cults we'd studied in Professor Swan's class. The thought of the Academy and my professors was startlingly foreign. They'd told me my entire life none of this could be real, but I was seeing my father conjured out of a book clear as day. How could what he was writing about then not be at least partially real?

A girl has disappeared from Arkham,

my father continued on the page.

She is the third, as two more have vanished over the span of months before the year turned. They vanished from locked bedrooms, their windowpanes covered with soot and sulfur. All of the wisdom of the Codex has failed me and I must consult the Folk. I must pay the sacrifice for their wisdom if I am to save the women. The girls, rather, for they are but children.

The scene flickered and I saw a slice of the gardens behind Graystone. My father bowed to the pale figures, and they stared implacably. He held out a photograph, and a pale hand reached from under a cloak to accept it.

As I confess to the page, more and more often, I do not know what I face when I make these bargains. I have seen the terror that lurks in the Land of Thorn. It has teeth that grind bones and voices that knife dreams. It pads on velvet paws tipped with iron claws, and it hungers. I fear, in my dark hours, that it hungers for me and that it is only a matter of time before it eats its fill of my sanity.

The next page contained a drawing as precise and painstaking as the diary entries. My father and I might not share looks, but we did share a meticulous eye for detail. That cheered me a bit. The thing made of ink was familiar, a shandy-man, straw hair and burlap skin, the impossible mouth stitched shut with coarse thread so the shandy-man

223

could only drink down life force as one slept. However, the precise lettering below the thing's clawed feet contained actual information, as opposed to a brightly lettered slogan alleging the horrors of the necrovirus and how a person could become one of these eldritch things.

The shandy-man: a creature from the Land of Thorn, drawn to the life force of young maidens. It steals their virtue and their life as one, consuming the raw magic energy for its own ends. Dies in fire. My Weird was well used this night. One girl is safe. For two, l came too late.

I had lost track of the hours I'd been sitting on the attic floor, the dozens of snapshots of my father that appeared and disappeared as the geas on his journal took hold of my eyes. Him aging, my legs cramping. I should stir myself and let Cal and Dean know I was still alive, but the book continued to give up secrets, and I hadn't found the one I needed yet.

1 May, 1939.
My father died this morning.

No new dusty, jostling reel of memory accompanied the entry, oddly. Only words marked the death of my grandfather.

l set that line down and watched the ink dry on it.
Tomorrow, l will stand with the grave digger and the undertaker while they measure my father for his coffin and the ground for his grave.
Tonight, l am kept by my vigil.
l did not understand when l began this record, why

224

every Gateminder bears witness to the horrors of their calling and the toll of their Weird in these strange, grim little books. I found recounting the heat of battle and laboring on drawings of glaistig, kelpie and bean sidhe onerous. I yearned to escape the duty of my blood and go east to Lovecraft or west to San Francisco, to forge a life under the iron bridges of a city. To pretend the preaching of the Proctors is the rational truth.

Much as I despise their methods, I see the appeal of the Rationalists. Reason over madness. Visible over invisible. Truth over heartbreak.

I understand now why we keep these accounts. I understand that Minders expect to die in the field, brought low by the creatures that move in the shadow of the Weird.

Or like my father, they drop in their tracks returning from a walk to the post office. They leave nothing behind but children or merely an empty house. The next in the line has no recourse.

Yes. I understand now.

Tomorrow, I bury my father. Tonight, I await the Kindly Folk. For it is still the first of May, the ancient rite of the goat gods and their minions. A night when mortal flesh tastes sweet and mortal blood calls the Wild Hunt. The Folk and I have work to do, and when I leave this world the only way my son will understand why his father was silent, distant and hard is this volume.

No mention of a daughter. I did the math. Nerissa wasn't even pregnant with me yet.

We fight and we bleed for this hidden world, and the world eats us alive.

225

The Folk say this is the way of generations past: lone-liness and hate. Witch trials, Rationalists and now the Bureau of Heresy.

So I put pen to paper, voraciously. My life is this Weird, this unnatural duty to this unnatural world, and this alchemy of words. My witch's alphabet, as they call these volumes in the Iron Codex.

I pray to any of the old gods with ears still turned to a mortal man that it is enough.

The Fiery Stars

I CLIMBED DOWN from the attic with the dusk, exhausted. The library was dim, but aether light gleamed from the back parlor and I heard laughter.

Dean, Cal and Bethina sat around a low coal fire, Bethina's round face alight.

"You're a card, Dean!" she exclaimed. "The way you tell those stories I'd take them for true."

"They are true." Dean spun the poker between his palms. "Every word."

Bethina hooted again, but I'd spent enough days with Dean now to know his face when he wasn't teasing.

"We have aether. And light," I said, to announce my presence. It was surprising to see Graystone in the real light of the aether lamps. Cal got up and hobbled over to me.

"We thought you'd died in that dusty attic."

"Well, the kid thought so," Dean drawled. "Bethina and I thought that was a tad dramatic."

"Aether pump had a loose valve," Cal babbled. "But I fixed it up. Routes into the house and runs a real nice little generation globe for heat and light." He jerked his thumb at the hi-fi in the corner. "And I guess Dean got that antique working, not that we get any reception up here."

"I'd die for some dance music," Bethina cried. "The aether hasn't been working since . . . well, since the unpleasantness with your da."

"Cal," I said, ignoring her. She hadn't spent the afternoon seeing what I'd seen. "Cal, I have something to tell you."

He cocked his head. "Spill."

"Alone," I elaborated. Cal was my confidant and he should be first to know what I'd found. I didn't think Dean would call me crazy, but I didn't know him as anything except a criminal guide who wanted me to tell him secrets. With Cal, I knew, there would be no price attached.

"All right," Cal said, his grin vanishing.

"The hallway," I told him, stepping out beyond the door, where we'd be out of earshot.

Behind me, music filled up the parlor, scratchy and antique across the tenuous connection of the aether.

Cal folded his arms. "I don't like the way you just let him act as familiar as he pleases, Aoife. He's basically a member of the help, you know."

I slid the pocket doors shut on Dean and Bethina dancing awkwardly. Dean was liquid-graceful. Bethina was stumpy, her face red and her curls loose. I hoped I'd never looked like that in dance class.

Cal sighed. "Aoife, I'm serious. It's not right to let someone like that run away at the reins."

228

"Cal, I'm not one of those spoiled Uptown girls," I said. "And even if I was, it doesn't mean people who work for their living are less than human. You sound like Marcos." I mimicked his stern gesture.

"You're better than Dean Harrison," Cal grumbled. "At least *I* know that."

"This is emphatically not what I wanted to say to you," I said, trying to steer the conversation back on track. "Cal, listen . . . I found something in the attic."

Cal's face lit like a lucifer match. "Bootlegger's stash? A secret chamber, like for a blood cult? I read about one in *Black Mask* once—"

"I found a . . . a book," I said, trying to pluck up the courage to tell him the exact nature of said book. Cal sighed.

"Oh. Just like school, then."

"Not exactly," I said, my voice going soft and shivery of its own accord. Cal was my friend, but I was about to ask him to believe a whole lot. "Cal, I found it. I found the book Conrad wanted me to use. It's a . . . journal, I guess you'd call it." *Journal* was a poor descriptor of the grimoire I'd found, but it was the one that would placate Cal. "My father kept it since he was eighteen or so."

Cal spread his hands. "So?" I'd never noticed how pale his hands were. They were long and knobby and soft—gentleman's hands. By comparison, my scar-traced knuckles and calloused fingers were rough and unwieldy. But Cal had always excelled at being delicate and careful during classes, while I nicked and cut myself on metal and hot soldering lead every time we did shop.

"*So.*" I stepped closer, going up on tiptoe to get close to

229

his ear. "The ink in the book, I touched it and it . . . marked me. It touched me like it was alive." I extended my palm. "Look."

Cal's eyes dipped, then came back to mine. A frown made a black line between his eyebrows. "Oh, Aoife. It's started, hasn't it?"

I glanced at my own palm. Bare, it stared back at me. The mark had vanished.

"N-no . . . ," I stuttered, confusion making my voice hitch. "The ink . . . it tattooed me. An enchantment, and my father did a geas on the journal, so I could see memories that he'd wrapped up in the words. . . ." I trailed off, my hand dropping as I realized what—who—I sounded like.

"I don't know what you think you saw." Cal put his hand on my cheek. "But there's nothing on your hand, and no enchanted book in the attic." His skin was cold against my flushed cheek, and damp like the fog that surrounded Graystone. "Magic isn't real, Aoife. It's placebo for fools."

I should believe the same thing, but I couldn't explain away the diary that easily.

Cal swiped a hand through his unruly nest of hair. "I knew reading all of those books wouldn't lead you anywhere but fancy. Aoife, you have to stay rational. You saw what happened to your mother. You know that believing in magic opens the door for the necrovirus."

My fingers curled, nails cutting my palms, and tears I'd been holding down stung the corners of my eyes. Cal was supposed to believe me. Out of everyone from my old life, he was supposed to trust me. "It was there, Cal. It was."

"It wasn't, Aoife," he returned. "This is a dusty old house

230

full of dusty old things, and with your father gone it's making you a little hysterical."

I slapped Cal's hand away. "*Hysterical? That's* what you think of me?"

Cal's jaw jumped, and then he grabbed my shoulders tight, his fingers like wire. "This is for *you*, Aoife," he whispered. "If you go back to the city saying these things, you'll be all done. But if you say your head's a little light and you got overexcited, no Proctor will lock you up as a madwoman." He ducked his chin. "Your birthday is in two weeks, Aoife. The infection—"

"You think I forgot?" My voice echoed off the scarred oak paneling around us, and I wriggled free of Cal again.

"That's not . . ." Cal pressed his hands together, drew in a shaky breath as anger warred with calm on his face. "Talking to you is like tap-dancing on claymore mines, I swear."

"I don't care," I said, hot prickles of anger overriding my natural inclination to hold my tongue. "I don't care what you meant. It was an awful thing to say. Stay far away from me, Cal Daulton, because if I do go mad, you'll be the first person I turn on."

The heels of my borrowed boots echoed like a rifle shot as I left Cal and ran to my room, where I locked the door and let myself cry. Half because I wanted Cal to believe me, and half because I didn't know if I believed myself.

After I'd spent an hour by the mantel clock alternately sniffling and silently cursing Cal and his fumbling, ill-thought comments, a knock came at the door.

231

"You in there, Aoife?" Dean's low voice was welcome. If Cal had come and tried to apologize, I probably would have socked him in the mouth.

"I suppose," I sighed, crumpling my handkerchief and throwing it in the general direction of my school clothes, which still occupied the floor by the wardrobe.

"Let me in?" he cajoled.

I snapped. "Don't you and Bethina have more dancing to do?" Passed over for a servant girl. It really was a fairy tale.

"Aoife . . ." The name held sweet resonance through the oak of the door. Then Dean sighed. "I can take a hint. Sweet dreams, princess."

After a few ticks of the clock I realized I didn't want Dean to go away. I jumped off the bed and unlocked the door, opening it just an inch.

Dean was still there. His smile crept to the surface, and I felt marginally less wretched. "That's more like it. What's got those teardrops of yours flowing, kiddo?"

"I wasn't crying." The words were my reflex against teasing. Engineers didn't cry. Especially girl engineers.

"Then I take your word for it." Dean winked at me and offered his bandanna. "For your complexion."

"Thank you," I said softly, taking the kerchief and scrubbing at my eyes. They were gritty, as if I'd looked into the maw of a sandstorm.

"You want to talk about it?" Dean moved closer, so that he filled up my slice of doorway, not as a shadow would but solidly, something I could grab hold of.

"Not here," I said, glancing back at my room, contained by the iron nerves of the house. Dean cocked his head in

232

confusion. "The walls have ears," I explained. Bethina could be around any corner, and I didn't believe that the house itself wasn't echoing my words down into its bones, storing them for its own eldritch uses.

Dean lifted himself away from the jamb. "Grab yourself a wrap and come with me."

"I . . . all right." I shrugged into a wool cape I'd discovered with the dress and wrapped my school scarf around my neck. As Dean led us away from the landing, into the warren of hallways that made up the north wing of Graystone, I finally had to ask, "Where are we going?"

"I'm still your guide, I'll have you know," Dean said. "Trust me." He stopped at a thin door at the very end of the corridor, too small to be anything but a closet. "You weren't the only one who found a hidden surprise today, princess." He popped open the door and gestured toward the open space. "After you."

It was indeed a closet, the only contents a ship's ladder leading up into darkness. A draft caught me and prickled my exposed skin. "Up?" I said, peering into the darkness. The way was black and fathomless, cold as space.

"Up," Dean agreed. "I'll catch you."

I mounted the first rung and looked back at him. "I'm not afraid of falling."

His mouth curled. "That's my Aoife."

I jostled as Dean put his hands on my waist and gave me a boost. Cal had told me to reprimand him for being familiar, but if I was honest I enjoyed that Dean didn't treat me like I was something that might break. And I wanted to see what was up there.

233

I climbed, and even with Dean's added weight the ladder was solid under my grasp, wood polished by decades of hands and feet. Gradually the cold grew sharper, a blade rather than a pinprick.

At last, we crested a platform, rotted wood on a rotating base with a skeleton of iron. The widow's walk rode the ridgeline of Graystone like a ship in choppy seas, wind humming through the railing bars like water under the prow.

Dean swung his legs up and shut the hatch. We were alone on top of the world, moonlight and mist creating a landscape unearthly as the surface of Mars. I should have been scared to be up so high on an ancient, unstable structure, but the view was too eerie, and beautiful, for fear to reach me.

"Pretty boss view," Dean said, lighting the cigarette he kept behind his ear. "Nothing like it in the city, that's for sure." He offered the Lucky to me after a quick drag. I shook my head.

"Told you, I don't."

"Figured I'd tempt you once more," he said, and exhaled. The smoke formed shapes in the air, crow wings and creeping vines.

"Cal thinks I'm insane," I blurted, folding my arms around myself to keep warm. Below the mist curled back on itself, a flock of dragons eating their own tails.

Dean looked askance at me.

"You're about as far from cracked as they make 'em, Aoife. I've known brass statues that were crazier'n you."

I grabbed the railing, letting the dead chill of the iron steel me. "My family has a . . . reputation. Back in Lovecraft."

234

Dean shrugged. I knew because I heard the creak of his jacket. " 'Loony' is just a title they slap on people who don't fit the gray flannel life we're all supposed to chase after. Lots of cats back in the Rustworks got the diagnosis, before they ditched out of the middle class and went downside."

"Cal thinks I'm bound to lose my mind," I said. Dean wouldn't get my secret, not yet, but I had to let some of the pressure off before I burst like a faulty boiler, and the fact that he hadn't just dismissed me as hysterical went a long way to that end. "My brother left me a letter, you know, that told me to find the witch's alphabet. Well, I found it. It's my father's. It's real as you and I standing here and Cal, he"—I shuddered a breath in and out—"he told me in so many words I was mad, that what I *know* I saw didn't matter in the least because what he thinks counts more. Because he's a boy or because . . . I don't know. It's horrid."

My hands burned from deadened nerve endings in the cold, and it reminded me of the ink's toothsome grasp, which only made things worse. I glanced at my palm. It was still bare. "Just because I can't prove to Cal I saw an . . . an enchantment on the book doesn't make me a liar. Cal should have trusted me." That was the real pain of it—I trusted Cal, faithful and absolute. And all he could do in return was wring his hands over my maybe madness.

Dean came to stand next to me and slid his hand over mine. "You ain't crazy, Aoife. I don't care if you said you saw the Great Old Ones themselves returning from the stars, no one has the right to sling that at you."

I looked down over the spires of Arkham, silent. Dean hadn't heard what Cal had. He hadn't read the book and

235

learned about what the Graysons carried. What had my father called it? His Weird. His writings had casually unfolded a world utterly alien from my own, a world where a heretical legend pulsed through my blood surely as his.

Could he be right? I was his daughter, after all.

The village lay silent as a tomb in the night, the moon above a broach on a velvet brocade of stars. Ground fog spun over the valley, the top of Arkham's church steeple and the twin towers of Miskatonic University thrusting upward like a desperate, drowning hand. Rooftops and chimney pots within Arkham's outer wall vanished and reappeared, a ghostly town revealed only by moonlight's gleam.

As I watched, a flame sprang to life at the outskirts of the village, and another. A great clanking borne on the wind echoed off the mountain, back to our ears.

The borderlands of Arkham blossomed with flame, one after the other. Green as a forest, the fire wasn't oil or tar, but something else that sent acrid smoke up the valley toward my nose.

"What *is* that?" I said, waving it away. Dean flicked his cigarette end off the roof. It joined the constellation of fire for just a moment before winking out.

"Ghoul traps," he said. "Keeping the beasties out at moonrise. That two-faced ghoul goddess of theirs hunts with the tide. Least, that's what I heard around the Nightfall Market."

I shuddered. I'd seen the low humps of ambulance jitneys rumbling through the streets the morning after a full moon, when even the Proctors' nightly lockdown and extra patrols couldn't keep the creatures from slipping in

236

through the underground. Cal said if you turned the right way, you could hear the screams from Old Town as the disused sewer system opened and spewed forth its bloodthirsty citizens.

Cal. Cal and his look of pity when I'd shown him my palm. My heart tightened again, painful against my ribs.

"Burning aether tainted with sulfur," Dean explained. "What I hear, the stench and the green light keeps them underground."

"Cal called me crazy because I told him I found an enchantment on that book," I said. Dean opened his mouth, but I held up my finger. "I need you to listen."

"Right. Consider my trap shut," Dean said, settling himself against the rail.

"I know I should say that magic isn't real," I said. That was what everyone I was supposed to trust in my life had told me.

Except Conrad. And I trusted him more than anyone. I swallowed the lump in my throat and continued. "But the ink in the book—it marked me, like a living thing leaves its tooth mark behind. And an enchantment let me see my father's memories. I'm a rational person. I believe in science and I abjure heresy." I sucked in a breath, the faint taste of sulfur parching my tongue. "But to hear my father tell it in his writings, it's not heresy—nothing born of the necrovirus. Nor are all of the inhuman things in the world, the shandy-men and nightjars and the abominations . . . they don't come from a person being infected. They aren't people at all . . . they came from the . . . the Land of Thorn. Wherever that is."

Below, Arkham was ringed in fire. The mist took on an

237

unearthly glow, living and boiling in the cauldron of the valley. "He calls it the Weird," I said softly. "My father. And his father. A Grayson has had it, for fourteen generations. I . . ."

I might not be mad after all. The thought was wishful, but I hadn't been able to get rid of it since I'd read my father's diary.

"Ever since I came here," I tried again, "I've had a feeling that something was awake in me. That there's something not right in this house. And now I don't think it's the house; I think it's me." I ran out of thoughts, because this was as far as I'd ever allowed my speculation—my hope—to go.

Waiting, in the cold and the moonlight, for Dean to speak was agonizing.

"Won't lie to you," he said at length. "I've been up and down the highways once or twice, princess. I've seen some sights that weren't born from the necrovirus." He nodded, as if he'd decided something final. "I'd believe in an enchanted book, I think. I'd believe in magic."

Dean believed me. He made one person, one person in the entire world. Which frankly didn't comfort me much. "What can I *do*?" I cried. "I can't very well tell anyone besides you. I don't know if I have this . . . this Weird or if Conrad does or if we're all just . . . unnatural."

"Here's what you do, see," Dean said. "Before you go fretting about measuring up to the old man, you gotta be sure."

I blew on my hands to warm them, then tucked them into my pockets. I was growing used to the cold. Dean not running as far as he could when I'd brought up enchantments helped a bit. And his not recoiling from me and

238

throwing out that hateful word: *mad*. "I'm sure," I told him. "I can feel it whispering to me when I'm in Graystone. It's like having an aethervox in my head, and you can just hear something coming across the spectrum. . . ."

"Then I suggest you find out what your game is," Dean said. "Way I dig it, sorcerers are supposed to have some kind of affinity, right?"

"I'm not a sorcerer!" I snapped. "It's not even a real thing."

"Fine, fine," Dean said. "But I'm telling you now— 'Weird' don't sound any better." He tapped his chin. "What was your old man's?"

"Fire, I think." I recalled the passage about the shandyman and its burning. "He was vague."

Dean cocked an eyebrow. "Think you could be fire? Make you real handy at bonfire parties."

I had to shake my head, and at once the prospect of embracing the wild, untested truth of my possessing a Weird didn't seem so outlandish. "No, it's not that. I can't even get the thrice-damned coal grates in this place to go." Now that I was thinking about the subject, it was vexing me.

"You'll figure it out," Dean said, hunching inside his leather against the stiff breeze that had come up. "The one thing you aren't, besides crazy, is dumb."

I took Dean's hand this time and squeezed it hard, hoping my gesture telegraphed the waterfall of words that I couldn't get out, except one sentence. "Thank you."

His hand stiffened in surprise under my grasp. "What's the thanks for, princess? I didn't do anything."

"You believe me," I said. "No one has ever done that, just believed me. Without any questions."

239

Dean brushed his thumb under my chin. "You're all right, Aoife Grayson. Don't let anyone tell you different."

I turned back to the vista over the valley, watching the aether fires burn. Dean stayed next to me and we watched for a long time, the only sound between us the wind and the faraway howling of ghouls.

18

The Dark Place of Dreaming

IN MY ROOM, I changed into nightclothes and turned the flow down on the aether globes, crawling into bed with the aid of moonlight. The sheets were new and scented with lavender instead of must—Bethina must have crept in when I was in the hidden library and cleaned up after me. Another first.

I turned on my side and watched clouds skate across the moon through the crack in my drapery. Wherever Conrad was, he saw the same moon. That comforted me, a little.

It wasn't, however, enough comfort to dull my thoughts about my Weird. I'd wished for so long not to be mad, to keep the necrovirus in my blood at bay, that what I'd found in the journal seemed like a wish fulfilled rather than a hope. A wispy, intangible thing, a theory rather than a proof. The Weird might be fiction, a product of my father's teenage fancy as easily as it might be the solution to all of my troubles.

In spite of my mind whirling, the day of discovery proved stronger, and sleep was a fast and true partner.

The madness dream was always the same. I walked through the empty streets of Lovecraft, empty except for the creatures that skulked in the shadows of my real city, my home. Nightjars walked in broad daylight. Springheel jacks shed their human skin and let their long-jawed animal snouts scent the air. The deep-sea aquanoids that swam in the waters off Innsmouth and Nantucket stared at me with glassy, gibbous eyes.

In this Lovecraft, I was alone. In this Lovecraft, only the necrovirus shadowed my footsteps.

I'd had the dream a dozen times, a hundred times. It wasn't even a dream, because dreams come from a person's brain and I knew deep down that this one came directly from my madness.

It had no meaning, except that I was indeed doomed to Nerissa and Conrad's fate. Nerissa saw things. Conrad heard voices. Neither of them had a strange magic in their blood. Just a virus. I wanted to believe my father, but what if he was just as insane?

I dreamed. And I would lie to everyone about the dream, until the day came that I couldn't lie anymore.

As I dreamed I walked, through Uptown and down Derleth Street to the river, watching the red water bubble and hiss, the ghouls came out of their holes to urge me onward, hunched and hissing like a nightmare honor guard.

Every time I reached the riverbank in the dream—and I always reached it—I tried to throw myself in, to swim and escape or drown and forget. I was never certain which. But every time, the ghouls closed in on me before I could do it, their clammy paws holding me back and their rubbery tongues making my bare skin slick.

Only this time, when I reached the riverwalk where Dunwich Lane and the arcade separated, a figure waited for me.

I'd have recognized the tall stooped body, the raven hair straight as my own was messy, the nervous tapping of finger on leg anywhere. My throat constricted, and the ghouls around me hissed and snarled to fill the silence. They ranged in size from child to full-grown wolf, some hunched on four legs and others walking upright like men. Any of them could have torn me asunder, but they stayed far clear of the figure at the river.

I found a whisper, little more than an aquanoid's croak from cold and terror. "Conrad?"

My brother didn't face me, just tilted his head so that the silver sun, eternally blinded by cloud cataracts in this dark dreaming world, caught his profile.

"It's really me, Aoife."

I stopped a few feet from him. At my heels, the ghouls closed in, but I ignored them. They weren't as important as this new turn the dream had taken. They could eat me in their good time, as long as I spoke to Conrad.

"Conrad, I found it. I found the witch's alphabet like you asked me. Tell me how to—"

"Wake up, Aoife." His voice was flat and far away, like it was coming from an aethervox rather than his throat.

243

"Conrad, you have to tell me what to do," I begged. "I don't know what's happening to me. I don't know how to find you."

"Wake up, Aoife," Conrad repeated. "It's not real. Wake up."

"I know it's the necrovirus—" I started.

"It's not real, Aoife," Conrad snarled. "I was wrong. Stop trying to find me."

I drew back, feeling as if he'd slapped me. Even if this *was* a dream, just my brain dancing with the pathogen in my blood, it was a horrid thing for my memory to serve up.

"I left the city," I said. "For you. Conrad, just tell me—"

"Listen." His outline shimmered, and in the refraction of light on water Conrad was only a black shadow, a shimmering insubstantial dream figure just like everything else about this gray, dream-place Lovecraft. "I put you in terrible danger, Aoife, and I didn't know it. I haven't any time and all I can say is stop looking for me. Stop looking for answers. Go home and never, never look back."

I could see through him now, through his outline and into the ruins of the foundry across the river. Above its crumbled chimneys, a flight of wild ravens swooped, their clockwork claws catching and carrying off a shandy-man for torture. The Proctors might not exist in my dream, but the price of heresy still ran strong.

"Conrad . . . ," I begged. I couldn't lose him, couldn't let him slip away again. The thought of waking up alone was more than I could bear, a weight on my chest that wouldn't let me breathe.

244

"I got away, Aoife, but you won't," he whispered. "That's why you have to go back. It's not real. None of it is. . . ."

Conrad's outline curled up at the edges, burned away like a piece of celluloid, and he grew transparent.

I screamed as he vanished, went to my knees and buried my face in my hands. I could endure any torment from my fellow students, any punishment of a care-parent or professor. I could take my mother's fits and Cal's well-meaning scorn with my head held up. But to see Conrad vanish before my eyes a second time was more than I was prepared to withstand. I broke, sorrow and rage ripping themselves from my throat. I screamed into the rank, tainted air of my dream-city until the ghouls closed in on me and smothered me with the scent of the dank underground and the caress of their drowned-corpse hands.

"Miss Aoife!"

I bolted awake, lashing out at the thing holding me down. Bethina shrieked as I cracked her in the nose. "All His gears, miss! You were screaming to wake the dead in your sleep!"

I clapped my hand over my mouth, realizing that the air-raid wailing was emanating from me. Sweat worked its way down my body and I saw that I'd kicked all of my bedding to the floor.

"I'm so very sorry," I said, jumping up and grabbing a handkerchief from the clothespress for Bethina's bleeding nose.

"'S not really your fault, miss," she said around the cloth. "I ran to shake you awake, and that was foolish. You sounded like you was being tortured—are you all right?"

245

"I'm fine," I lied, one I'd repeated innumerably. I twitched back the curtains and was startled to see it was light. I'd dreamed away the darkness, and the morning was silver and woven with mist.

"Didn't sound fine," Bethina said. She examined the blood-spotted handkerchief and made a face.

"I'm sorry I hit you, Bethina, really I am," I told her, wrapping my arms around myself as my sweat went cold in the unheated room. "It was just a silly nightmare."

19

The Mist-Wrought Ring

In the dawn, I decided to go walking. I needed to leave the confines of Graystone and shake off the lingering touch of the dream.

The wardrobe yielded a wool skirt and jumper, as old and out of fashion as the red dress, but I added them to my boots and cape to ward against the morning chill.

No one else was awake, except Bethina cooking breakfast in the kitchen, so I left by the main door and walked around the foundation of the house.

Graystone's estate was larger than I'd imagined, the stone walls of the borderlands disappearing to the vanishing point in every direction as I left the house behind and started down the long slope of the back garden. Oak trees bent over the path, their twisted limbs black against the dove-wing sky.

Mist was my constant companion. It wandered among

the trees, slithered over the ground, wrapped the day in solitude and silence.

The path ended a few hundred yards from the rear of the house, at one of the swaybacked stone walls that veined the landscape. I climbed over the boundary of a forgotten farm field, a ley line traced in moss and rock.

An abandoned orchard crouched beyond the wall, hunched shapes of apple trees writhing in the light wind sweeping up from the valley.

Late fruit crunched under my feet as I walked, putting the scent of cider in the air. Crows flew overhead, their wings and my footsteps the only sounds.

Here, I could forget about the dream, about Conrad telling me to go home and stop looking for him.

Dream-Conrad didn't know anything. He was my fear. He was trying to make me turn back, when I'd finally gotten close enough to rescue my brother. My madness was not going to sway me from my course, not now. Not when I'd promised Dean that I'd find out if I did possess the Weird, and Conrad—the real one—that I'd find him.

I walked in no particular direction, except away from Graystone. I didn't want to be around other people, to have to make pleasant conversation, because I had nothing to talk about. Either I had a gift that no one on the planet was supposed to possess, or I was crazy. One or the other.

It didn't make for an easy mind as I walked, and I wondered if I'd ever stop feeling fragile, like everything I'd managed to do since I left the Academy would shatter at any moment. Until I could regain my resolve, and the strength that I'd found when I ran across the Night Bridge with Dean and Cal, I would walk.

The fog was seductive, and it kissed my skin with cold and jeweled my untidy braid with droplets. It pulled me deeper into the orchard, until I lost sight of even the jagged weather vanes at the top of Graystone's spires. I felt that I could walk and wander until I found a new path, one that led away from the life of Aoife Grayson and into the land of mists, where, Nerissa had once said, lost souls wandered, wakeful and unclaimed.

The marching lines of apple trees dropped off, one by one, until I stood at the edge of the real forest, in a clearing of dead grass and toppled stones. An iron cider press, rusted to a standstill, and a chimney were the only things left of the cider house. Beyond, a stone well stood at the edge of the field. Frayed rope in want of a bucket flapped dismally in the wind.

I should turn back—Dean had said the woods around Arkham weren't safe, and the ghoul traps we'd seen last night proved it. Ghouls didn't need to live in bricked-over sewer tunnels. They could thrive nicely in bootleggers' caverns, I'd imagine.

Dean had told me to be sure. But I had no inkling of my potential Weird beyond the whispers inside my head whenever I got close to the secrets in Graystone. I had no sudden flash through the aether, no awakening moment.

The only thing I'd ever been certain of was machines. Machines and math made sense even when the world seemed to be burning down around me. Tinkering was the only comfort I'd had left when my mother went away. Machines put me in the School of Engines, where I had a chance to become something more than a stenographer or a nurse. But they couldn't help me now, and frustration welled up in me so sudden and strong that I gave the ground a kick, rotted apples and clods of earth flying.

Machines and engineering had staved off my madness, staved off the infection, but my father believed in something other, something invisible and intangible as the aether. He'd *used* his Weird. I couldn't even discern what mine might be. If he was telling the truth.

He might be. I wanted him to be. Otherwise, I was crazier than either Nerissa or Conrad and all I had to look forward to was a long life full of poking and prodding in a state-run madhouse.

That couldn't be my fate. Not when I'd come all this way.

Weary from the long walk, I sat on the foundation of the cider house, brushing my boots and stockings free of dew. A gust blew through the clearing, pulling strands of my hair free, and the temperature dropped, quickly enough to prickle against the back of my neck. The crows cried out as one, their cacophony ringing against the mountain and back, a chorus of discordant bells chiming a funerary toll.

I stood, pulling my cape tight around me. Aware for the first time of how utterly alone I was, I turned back toward Graystone. At this distance, Dean and Cal wouldn't hear me even if I screamed.

I hadn't taken three steps when the mist parted before my eyes, long fingers letting go their hold on the orchard. The soft tendrils curled in on themselves, caressing the ground, and formed a ring just a little wider than I was tall. It moved and flowed, weaving the air like fine dove velvet, and before I could move the ring encircled me. The crows continued to mourn.

"Dean!" I shouted sharply, so I wouldn't sound scared. I looked toward Graystone. "Cal! Bethina!"

I tried to move away from the ring, but it constricted, the fog closing in again, so I couldn't even be sure which way the house lay.

"Dean!" I cried. Real fear crawled in, beneath my unease. Something was here. Something that didn't belong.

"Aoife."

The voice came from all around, from the wind and the trees and the stone. It sat like a thorn in my mind.

"Aoife."

"This isn't funny!" I shouted, spinning in a wide circle, trying to penetrate the mist with my gaze. "Leave me alone!" The panic hadn't caught me yet, but it was snaking up my back and into my brain as surely as it did the day Conrad pulled his knife on me and I saw that the person looking out of his eyes was my brother no longer.

"Come away, human child. Worlds full of weeping. Come away, Aoife."

"I won't . . ." Hysteria bubbled in my chest and made itself known like a fist around my heart, the niggling whisper that I was just mad and this was all a product of my mind. "I'm not hearing voices. . . ."

The mist thickened until I swore I was blind. I couldn't see my own hands in front of me, not the cider house nor the forest nor anything but white.

"Don't fear us, child."

I was alone. Alone with the voice. I shut my eyes, like you did when a nightmare had hold of you and you couldn't wake up.

251

"Open your eyes, Aoife."

"No!" I shrieked. Silken fingers brushed over my cheek, across my hands and lips and neck, and I batted at them like spiders were raining down on my skin. This was not happening. This *could not* be happening. Just because I'd allowed the possibility of my father's magic didn't mean that I had to allow phantoms as well.

"You can't wish us away, Aoife." The voice became harsh, guttural and, most horrifyingly, real. "Open your eyes, child."

Shivering, standing stock-still to make myself less of a target, I managed to wrench my eyes open. I wouldn't bow my head. I would face the first vestiges of necrovirus infection, the hallucinations that ate a rational mind down to a nub.

"I'm not afraid," I whispered, but even to my ears it was a poor lie. I *was* afraid, so afraid I felt I might shake apart.

"No need to be." The fog was worse when I stared into it, writhing in every direction like a living thing. I swore I saw faces, shadows of tall, thin bodies just beyond my vision. Bethina's story of the pale men and my father's writings on the Kindly Folk came to terrible life in my memory, and I dropped to my knees, curling in on myself.

"You aren't real. You aren't . . ." My voice faded as the harshest gust of wind I'd felt ripped it away with icy fingers around my throat.

"You lie. You see us," the voice whispered. *"We are real. You just need to look closer."*

"Where am I?" I demanded. The ground had shifted under me, from fozen turf to a spongy marsh. The air smelled different, stiff with pine and deep wild forest

252

rather than the fermented sweetness of apples. And the voice . . . the voice echoed not against the mountains behind Graystone but across a vast open space.

The pale men had come for my father. I had to assume they'd been responsible for taking Conrad. Now they had taken me, and I strove to calm my hammering heart. If I panicked, I would never get home. I had to keep my head. Dean would keep his head. Dean . . . I'd shouted for his help and he hadn't come.

"Where am I?" I demanded again, louder. My voice didn't shake so much this time, and the small spark of anger grew into a font of fire. My father may have been at the mercy of the Kindly Folk, but they would get an altogether different story from me. I'd fight. It was all you could do if you wanted to survive. Fight was all I had left.

"You know where you are, Aoife."

"I can't see." Despite all of my efforts, cold sweat sprouted against my skin and with it cold panic, the kind that precluded a long trip to the Catacombs from which one never returned.

"Your eyes deceive you. Look again."

I pressed my trembling hands to my sides, closing them into fists. I looked, and didn't shy away from the twisted, skeletal faces living in the mist. I could be afraid, but I wouldn't let it show. That was the bargain I struck with myself as I stared, my eyes watering from the cold wind, into the dense blanket of white.

The mist was quicksilver, changeable with each breath of air, yet I looked not at the figures hidden in its chill embrace but past them, like glimpsing a faint star from the corner of the eye.

Bit by bit, I began to see eyes and faces, lips and teeth and skin in the mist. "I see you," I chattered. "Who are you? What do you want from me?"

"What are we, child. And who. Who do we want. If you so choose, step closer. See the answers."

The voice spoke as a ghost on my shoulder. It caressed me with a lilting accent, mercury sliding over glass.

"If I come to you," I said, watching the figures drift through the mist, "you'll let me out of this fog. Fair?" I didn't know if bargaining would be my final sentence or a sign that I wasn't some terrified, pliable girl, but it was what Dean and Conrad would do. "Either let me out or I'm going home," I stated. "I don't have all day."

Another gust whipped my hair and my skirt like flags at sea.

"So be it." The mist rolled back, quick and quiet as a velvet-footed animal fleeing a hunter. The figures and faces retreated with it, a rushing of leaves and the scent of briarwood smoke in their wake.

All around, the world came back into view. But it wasn't my world.

The grass was rust red, the color of rotten iron or old blood. The sky hung overhead, charcoal clouds scudding before a wind that brought a faint scent of night flowers and turned earth.

A line of humped black toadstools crookedly spread in a wide circle around my feet, as if cast by nature's hand.

"You can leave the *hexenring* now, child."

I shrieked as the owner of the voice appeared at my back. Spinning too fast, I tangled my feet and fell to the

254

ground. The spongy peat squashed and sighed like it was alive under me. Damp crept through my skirt and stockings, crawled over my skin and into my bones.

A form stepped into my sight, backlit by the faint white sunlight flashbulbing through the cloud layer. "Human child. Like a fawn. Fragile-limbed and limpid-eyed."

I swallowed hard, to push down the tangle of wordless screams in my throat. I couldn't run—he was right on top of me. I kept my face calm. I'd survived for fifteen years by learning how to make my face a blank slate, and I did so now. I kept my hands clamped in fists. It was either that or shake apart, and I wouldn't show weakness.

My companion, for his part, crouched and folded his hands over his knee. "You have no need to fear me, Aoife Grayson. Not at this precise moment, and not in this place."

"Are you . . ." I eased myself up and away from him, across the damp moss. "Are you reading my thoughts?"

"Hardly." The figure snorted. "It's written on your face, plain as ink on paper."

He leaned toward me, blocking the sun, and I beheld his face. It was thin, pale, with cheekbones and chin square as if they'd been cut from stone. Spidery gray fatigue lines crawled away from the corners of his eyes and a smile formed on his lips, amused and razor-thin. He wore a long green coat and heavy pants, a style decades or centuries out of date. His high boots were bound in brass, and when he moved his arm toward me, gauntlets made of the same caramel hide and sun-drenched metal creaked. "Get up, child. We've much to talk about."

I scooted farther away from him instead, feeling a few of the toadstools break under my hands. His smile lengthened and sharpened.

"Oh, I wouldn't do that. It's terrible bad luck, don't you know? To break a fairy ring."

"I wouldn't know anything about fairies. I'm an engineer." My voice came out high and childish, and I couldn't have sounded more cowed if I'd tried. The pale creature laughed—laughed until his face crinkled up and he could have passed for human.

"Is that so."

"It's the truth," I said hotly. "Fact." I got to my feet, still keeping my distance, and took my moment on the high ground to examine the stranger. His hair was the same shade of pale his skin held, the pale of a body too long underwater without breath or life. "You said I could leave," I reminded him, and this time I sounded stronger, more like I imagined Dean would. I glared at the pale man. "I want to leave *now*, please."

He stood as I did, and far exceeded my height. I wasn't petite, but I also wasn't large, even for a girl. The stranger was long and lank as a contrail left behind in the sky by a zeppelin, a pale column with powerful shoulders and hands that said they would catch and break me if I ran. "I said that you might leave the *hexenring*," he replied. "I said nothing about the manner in which you could do it."

Stiff all at once, I took a long, careful step away from the noxious-looking mushrooms. "Who are you? What have you done to me?"

The stranger leaned close, as if I were a small child who

256

needed a basic principle of physics explained to her. Silver-rimmed goggles with blue glass lenses dangled around his neck. The strap disappeared underneath his pale hair, long and straight as the rest of him. His hands were arrayed to the first knuckle with silver rings, and I saw the twitch of tattoo ink where his cuffs and bracers pulled back from his bony wrists. "I've already warned you, young lady, that 'who' is not the proper question." He stepped over the toadstools carefully, big boots flattening the grass. "But you may call me Tremaine. Seems rude and unbalanced, otherwise—I know so much about you." Whatever that meant. I had a feeling I was supposed to cower again and beg. He had another thing coming.

The pale man extended his hand, the rings giving off a dirty-water gleam in the clouded light. "Take my hand and you can leave the ring safe and sound."

"I don't want to touch you," I said frankly. Tremaine showed a crop of teeth, white and jagged as a shark's.

"And why is that, child?"

I kept my eye on his hand, the same way I'd watch a belly-crawling ghoul pup on the riverbank. "I don't trust you."

Tremaine's pale silver eyebrows quirked. "You're not as vacant as you appear at first blush, then." His long skeleton's fingers drifted across the back of my palm and I whipped my hand out of reach, burying it in my pocket. Tremaine's eyes narrowed.

"Listen well, Aoife Grayson. The *hexenring* is a place of great power; every second you spend in it, time passes on the outside tenfold. Here, in the Thorn Land, and in your

257

cold, sad little iron world as well. You've dawdled away a decade while you stand there quibbling with me over trust or the lack of it."

My stomach dropped like a stone. He must be lying. Must be. But I detected no lies in his marble face, no deceit in the set of his scornful mouth. I couldn't speak for a moment, and I thought, truly, that I would break down and lose all composure. "Ten years? I've been in this ring ten *minutes.*" A person could no more bend time than he could bend a spoon with his mind.

And yet my father reached out to me from a magic book and told me he could light viral creatures on fire with his mind.

"I don't believe you," I told Tremaine, and felt fairly sure that was the truth.

Tremaine laughed again; this time it sounded like knives sharpening. "It was a figure of speech, child. Perhaps ten years was hyperbole, but *know* that time is slow around vortices of enchantment just as it is around the vortices of your dead stars. Lift up your skinny fawn legs and come with me before we're both ancient. Time is what I simply don't have."

When I didn't move, Tremaine snapped, "Take my hand, girl!" His brows drew together and his visage was so fearful that I thought even Grey Draven and the Proctors would have recoiled. I certainly wasn't going to argue the point with him.

I took Tremaine's hand, and it was cold and bloodless—smooth. The pale stranger might have been constructed entirely of leather and brass, for all the life I felt pulsing through him.

258

He dragged me with him, and we cleared the toadstools as one. Tremaine dropped my hand the moment we were standing on the free soil, and brushed his own across his coat as if he had gotten grease on it.

I would have been offended, but I was too relieved to feel my panicky, frantic sickness ease, as if an invisible creature had removed its claws from my neck.

Tremaine smirked. "I trust it's more pleasant out here?"

My face went hot at having to admit he was right. "I thought you were tricking me," I murmured.

His smile vanished. "Not yet, child. Trickery comes when I make you a bargain you'll sore refuse."

I decided to let his rambling go for the moment. A more important question niggled at my mind. "Before . . . you called this the Thorn Land."

Tremaine spread his hands to indicate the rough red moor we stood upon. "And so it is."

Bethina's words, and my father's writing, rushed unbidden to my thoughts. The tall pale men. The Kindly Folk.

His encounters with the Land of Thorn.

"You're one of them," I blurted, truth making my own words tumble out too quick. "Kindly Folk. You knew my father." I kept the rest of my thoughts from rushing out—the Land of Thorn existed, the Kindly Folk existed, the magic that flowed through my Grayson blood existed.

There was no fairy story here. It was all real, all bleak as Nerissa's story of the princess abandoned in the high tower, never to be rescued because men no longer believed she existed. Magic, the Weird, the strange visits my father made to this land.

259

All of it was my secret now, because if I told anyone what I'd seen here, or that I believed it, they'd lock me away before I could say "blueprint."

"You knew him." I jabbed my finger at Tremaine. "You knew him and now he's gone. What did you do?"

Tremaine tilted his head, like he was listening to music on an aether frequency I couldn't discern. I was struck once again by his eyes. I'd seen the same eyes on madmen, sick with tuberculosis from the terrible drafty conditions of the madhouse. Their bodies were wasted and their minds shredded, but their life force blazed in their eyes like open flame. They were most dangerous then, because they had nothing left to lose by dying.

"I do indeed know Archibald Grayson," Tremaine agreed at length. "And now I know you. Anything else is beside the point." He turned his back on me and began to walk uphill, along a small deer trail that cut through the stubby brush growing on the moor. "Keep up, child. Like I said, we haven't much time."

I hastened to follow him, because it was follow Tremaine or be left behind. The Kindly Folk hadn't wanted to hurt my father. What they *did* wish of him, I had the sinking feeling I was about to find out. "Time for what?" I called to Tremaine's back.

"No ceaseless questions," he ordered. "Walk. I must have you back to the *hexenring* by sunset."

"You know, you shouldn't prohibit questions and then invite them with cryptic nonsense," I told him, annoyance overtaking caution. That was the counterweight to my practiced outer calm—my mouth was never steady and

260

never circumspect. The words rushed out, and the trouble followed.

Tremaine sucked in air through his awful teeth. "I do so wish the boy had come back. You, miss, are a frightful chatterbox."

Startled, I broke into a run to pull myself even with Tremaine's long strides. "Boy? Wait! What boy?"

Before Tremaine spoke, to reveal or deny some new information about my brother, he stopped walking, his eyes searching the sky. He checked a spinning dial in the brass of his bracers, fed by gears that were in turn attached to spikes that seemed to implant themselves directly into his wrists. The puncture sites, which I'd mistaken for tattoos, were blue and swollen. The gears began to tick, faster and faster, as cloudy blue liquid fed itself through a return system within the gauntlets. Tremaine grimaced as he examined the dial, worked in a crystal unlike any I'd ever seen. "Iron damn this day," he murmured. "I hope you've got a fast step to go with that quick tongue, child."

Instead of asking *what* and risk his ire again, I followed Tremaine's gaze skyward.

The mist thickened and curled around us, only this time it was stained yellow-green like an old bruise. The figures within returned also, but they were solid rather than slippery fragments, and I watched them turn as one and fix on us. I'd seen enough lanternreels about the exotic predators that roamed the West to know we were in bad trouble.

Tremaine took my arm. His grip was stronger than a machine vise. "Get back to the *hexenring.* Don't stop and don't

261

let the mist touch you. If you get caught up in it, they can find you."

"They?" I squeaked, partly from the pain in my arm and partly from alarm at the preternatural speed of the mist as it enveloped the meadow. I could no longer see the trees, the hills—even my footprints twenty feet behind were obscured.

"This part of Thorn is a borderland," Tremaine said. "It borders yours—the Iron Land—and it also borders places best left to the imagination. Do you understand?"

I nodded, while the same sharp odor of applewood and rot assailed my nose as when I'd passed through the *hexenring.* "I understand." There was no more fear beating its way out of my chest. There was only a cold determination not to fall prey to anything else that skulked on the borders of reality.

"Good." Tremaine nodded. "Now close your mouth and *run.*"

I obeyed his words and my own instincts, digging my toes into the springy peat and bearing for the gap in the mist that lead back to the ring. Behind and to the side and all around I heard a scattering of giggles and the flapping of wings. Gears ground in Tremaine's bracers as he brought up my heel, and a bronze-bladed knife popped free of its confines, nesting into his hand like it had grown there.

"Pay attention to your feet!" he grated when he saw me looking. I wanted to tell him that he needn't worry—if I couldn't fight off the bullies in Lovecraft, I could at least outrun them—but the mist was closing in, the corridor back to the ring growing more claustrophobic with every breath that ripped through my lungs.

262

I reached the *hexenring*, and Tremaine grabbed my shoulder and propelled me over the hump of toadstools. I stumbled and went down hard, scraping my knee on a rough patch of ground.

"Stand within the ring," Tremaine panted. "Don't move."

The mist was nearly upon us, and I felt something brush wet, sticky fingers through my hair.

Frantic to get the thing away from me, I grabbed air as I stood and swatted around my head.

"Don't move!" Tremaine ordered. "They'll see you!" He turned the dial in his bracers, but all I wanted was to make the mist stop touching me, to get the sticky miasma off of my skin and the stench out of my nose.

This time I twisted something in my knee as I dropped. My shoulder hit the earth, my hip and my ribs crying out, and I fell.

I fell and fell still, and kept falling. Sound ripped from my throat, sight from my eyes, my stomach twisting violently as if I were back in the crashing *Berkshire Belle*.

Just as I was about to black out, I landed. The air wuffed out of me, but when I rolled onto my back and sucked in a great gulp of cool moist oxygen, I saw the apple trees and the rosy morning sky of Massachusetts, welcoming as a warm fire after the flat gray sky of the Thorn Land.

Getting up was a difficulty, and I felt the dozen places where I'd have bruises later. I scrubbed off my cape and skirt as best I could, the red earth of the Land of Thorn falling away and mingling with the dead grass of the orchard.

I had been to the Land of Thorn, and I'd returned unharmed. But not by a large margin.

263

The fog still curled, but it had faded to lace, revealing the overgrown gardens and the spiky profile of Graystone in the distance.

"I'll come for you soon, Aoife." Tremaine's ghostly voice hissed at me once more before the ring vanished like the vapor it was and I was alone.

"We'll see about that," I muttered. There was no one to hear me, but it felt better to be defiant than to cower and wait for the next shock to my system.

Turning back toward the house, I limped as quickly as I could across the uneven ground and up the hill to the kitchen door.

My father knew how to deal with the Kindly Folk and the Land of Thorn. It was time that I learned, too.

20

The Mysteries of Thorn

Bethina looked up from the old-fashioned coal range when I banged through the door. "Miss. You're back."

"Yes, I . . ." I looked at the pots on the stove. "You're still cooking breakfast?"

Bethina shook her head, frowning at me. "Dinner, miss. Stew and potatoes. My mum's recipe."

"Dinner?" I sagged against the doorframe, recognizing the pink sky outside for what it was—sunset, not sunrise. "I'll be damned."

"Miss," Bethina scolded me, spooning out a bit of stew and smacking her lips against it. "A lady like you shouldn't use such language."

"I'm not a lady," I snapped. "I'm an engineer."

Bethina's face fell, and she turned her back on me and started slicing half-soggy tomatoes with short, choppy motions that telegraphed her irritation better than any words.

"I apologize," I told her sincerely. I didn't really want to

265

be that girl who snapped at the servants. "I got lost in the forest. I suppose I'm a little testy."

"I suppose you are," Bethina huffed, setting her knife aside. "Dean and Cal were both out looking for you. They've been searching all day."

The throbbing in all of my battered bits redoubled. Of course Cal and Dean would expect the worst. I'd lost an entire day in the Land of Thorn.

Even as I kicked off my dirty boots by the door and slung my cape over a hook, elation crept in. I felt terrible for worrying Cal, but I'd learned something. Tremaine had told the truth about the *hexenring*. Time did encroach around it, and my ten minutes inside had turned into ten hours.

One fact, but an important one. I resolved that before the night was out I'd learn another, and enough to discern what I was truly dealing with now that the responsibility of the Kindly Folk had come to me.

"Bethina," I said, "where are Cal and Dean?"

"Back parlor, I think. Mr. Cal said that he wanted to try and find the baseball game." She shook her head at the notion. She didn't know that Cal would crawl across an acre of glass to listen in on a baseball game.

"I'll go find them and let them know I'm all right," I said. "They must have been terribly worried."

"Dean was talking about calling up some friend of his with a dirigible and scouring the hills for you," Bethina said. "Pure foolishness. As if he really knows anyone licensed to fly an airship."

"Dean knows a lot of things," I murmured, though

266

I wouldn't debate her over whether Captain Harry was in actuality licensed to fly under the laws of Massachusetts.

"Supper's in half an hour. Don't you wander off again and let it get cold!" Bethina called over her shoulder.

I ignored her—she might try to sound like a mother, but she wasn't one, not even close—and went toward the sound of a scratchy play-by-play announcer in the back parlor.

"Come on, you bum!" Cal was shouting. "It's a fly ball, not a grenade!"

"Will you knock it off?" Dean demanded. "My noggin's had about all the yelling it can take for one day."

"You're the one who said we had to stop looking," Cal retorted. "I'd still be out calling for her if it wasn't for you."

"I told you," Dean sighed. "Woods ain't safe at night. You'd just get yourself drained by a nightjar or laid out by a ghoul if you stayed out after sunset." He shifted his weight restlessly on the settee, putting one booted foot on the parlor table.

"Listen to you," Cal scoffed. "You sound like you're scared of a few virals. I'm not scared of a thing out in those woods!"

Dean rubbed a hand across his forehead. "Thank stone Aoife has more sense than you. Being afraid keeps you from being eaten."

"So far, anyway," I said. Cal yelped and Dean jumped to his feet.

"Aoife!" He rushed to me and for a moment I thought he was going to sweep me into his arms, but he pulled

267

himself upright and put his hand under my chin, turning my face from side to side. "You look right as rain, princess. You all there?"

"I got lost," I said. "I'm sorry. Bethina says you went to a lot of trouble."

Cal practically knocked Dean out of the way and grabbed me by the arms. "Aoife, I thought you were dead. I thought you'd gotten snatched by something out there, or that you'd wandered off because you couldn't find your way home anymore—"

"Cal." I interrupted his red-faced slurry of words, dipping my head so that I could pretend not to notice the moisture in the corners of his eyes. My friend would do the same for me. "I'm fine. I promise."

Cal pressed me closer, against his bony frame, though I was startled to feel a bit of steel in his grip and a fullness in his chest that hadn't been there when we left the Academy. Being on the run had solidified Cal, firmed up his boyish edges. My wounded arm started to throb. I pulled away too fast, and felt a prick at the downturn his mouth took.

"Where were you?" he demanded. "We looked *everywhere*, over every inch of grounds. Even in the old cemetery . . . did you know there's a cemetery up here?"

"I just got lost," I repeated. Dean cleared his throat and cocked an eyebrow at me. I shook my head slightly, just once. Not here. Not where Cal could get an inkling. I couldn't go through another scene like the one in the library.

"You should get some rest," Cal said. "Bethina can draw you a bath and you need to have a long soak and forget all

268

about this day. What were you thinking, going into the woods like that?"

"I was thinking I wanted to be alone," I said, and it came out far sharper than I'd intended. Cal winced like I'd stuck him with an actual blade.

"You could have been hurt, or killed," he sniffed.

"Yes, but I wasn't." I could see the argument derailing the return of our good feeling and I put up my hands. "And you're right—I could use some rest." I caught Dean's eye and held it for a moment, and his lips twitched upward. Deceiving Cal sat badly in my stomach, like I'd eaten something too sour, but I consoled myself that it was for his own good. Until I could show him my Weird, something tangible, he'd just think I was nuts anyway.

"I can draw my own bath, but could Bethina bring up a plate for me?" I said. "I'm famished." That at least was the truth—I hadn't gotten any breakfast before Tremaine snatched me away.

Cal smiled and nodded, patting me on the shoulder as if I'd just agreed to take my medicine like a good girl.

"Of course. You run along and try not to tax yourself anymore."

"I will. Good night, Cal. Good night, Dean."

Cal was back at his baseball game before I'd stepped out of the parlor, but Dean gave me a smirk. "Good night, princess. Sweet dreams."

I pelted up the stairs, paying no mind to my bruises, and skidded into my bedroom. In the wash closet I spun the taps of the steam hob open and guided the water via valve

269

into the brass tub in the corner, leaving the drain open so I wouldn't cause a flood. When the hob was burbling away merrily, refilling itself with hot water, I stripped down to my slip and pulled a plain green cotton dress on, leaving my muddy clothes just outside the wash-closet door. Then I locked it from the inside and shut it from without. No one could get in without a skeleton key, and Bethina didn't appear to have custody of the house's key ring.

Then, stocking-footed, I crept back downstairs. Once I was in the shadow of the entry, I made a hard right turn into the library to avoid the sight line of the parlor, and pulled the doors shut behind me.

Dean would have to be disappointed tonight. I needed solitude, time with the books in the library above. I didn't quite trust Dean's faith to extend to some of the things in those books. *I* was still having a difficult time believing this wasn't all just a terribly long nightmare.

I lit one of the oil lamps on my father's writing desk and cycled open the trapdoor of the attic. I climbed, my slight weight silent on the ladder, and shut the door after me. I had at least a few hours undetected, until Bethina realized I hadn't touched my supper tray and Dean realized I'd never left the wash closet after my theoretical bath.

I couldn't claim to be one of those students who studies best when pressured. Cramming always made my head feel too small, as if facts were spilling out to make room for inconsequential chaff. But if all I had was a few hours to learn about the Land of Thorn, then by the Engine, I was going to do it. This wasn't a silly test, a fake schematic for a machine that would never be built. This was potentially

270

my life, and if I did poorly the lives of Dean, Cal and Bethina as well.

The truth was my passage to safety, and I had to find it before Tremaine found me again. Simply had to. Not to mention a way to avoid being snapped up by the Kindly Folk whenever the impulse took them. My father had some modicum of control. I needed it if Tremaine and his strange brass gauntlets were on the hunt for me.

I wasn't going to make the mistake of passivity with Tremaine again.

Settling myself in the same position on the floor opposite the arched window, I put the lamp on the shelf next to my head and dug into the pile of grimoires that I'd unearthed the previous day. Much as I wanted to peruse the *Machina* volume, I instead found a battered volume bound in purple velvet that had the word *Geographica* burned into the front cover. I rooted through every cranny of the map cabinet; at the bottom, shoved far back so that it gummed up the drawer, I found a book of charts. Armed with the book, the map, my father's journal and a fourth volume labeled *Animus* in the precise hand that I was coming to recognize as endemic to the Grayson men, I set to work.

The charts weren't useful—topographical maps that made no sense to me. Cal would know how to read them. He'd told me he'd been a Badger Scout before he came to the School. I hoped fervently that one day soon I could show him the charts and seek his wisdom, without him calling me crazy.

The *Geographica* book yielded more information. The

271

Grayson who'd set it down wasn't as precise or detailed as my father, but as I riffled the pages filled with delicate watercolors of mountain ranges, lakes and fields that could be found nowhere in the known world, I gleaned a few things.

The Land of Thorn, populated by the Kindly Folk, might seem at first an exotic and tempting land for exploration. Do not be fooled. For it is not the Kindly Folk alone who dwell within its nebulous and mist-ringed borders . . .

I turned pages, until I found one that I first took to be blotted with mildew. It was only another painting, however, this one of the noxious mist that had nearly snatched me away from Tremaine. The faces were different—elongated mouths with a horror of teeth as opposed to the frighteningly human visages I'd glimpsed, but the author of the grimoire and I had clearly glimpsed the same thing.

The transportive mist is a devilish companion. The Kindly Folk do not speak of where it originates and tell little of its incorporeal yet vicious denizens. Some of the Folk claim this foulness comes from a dark kingdom ruled by a dark king, but they will only whisper about this shadowland in the stories they tell at night, when they think no outsider can hear them.

Thinking of the sticky, grasping hand that had tangled itself in my hair, I shuddered. I never wanted to meet what lay beyond the borders of the Land of Thorn.

I swapped *Geographica* for *Animus* and paged through

272

description after description, detailed sketches accompanying each entry. Where the Grayson who'd assembled the book about the Land had been dreamy and slapdash, this Grayson had been compulsively detailed and immeasurably dry in his recounting of various species he'd encountered on the other side of the *hexenring*. I checked the endpaper of the grimoire: *Collected observations of Cornelius Hugo Grayson, compiled 1892.* I bet Cornelius was all the rage at parties.

His entry on the Kindly Folk was brief, but it made me cold, even though the snug library above never really got any cooler than the temperature of my skin.

Kindly Folk. Also called, in various languages such as Irish, Manx and Welsh, Seelie, Daoine Sidhe or elven. Their preferred term is Kindly Folk. They are susceptible to iron and to little else. They have mechanical aptitude, though they are backward compared with our advancements in steam and clockwork, and a command of what my compatriots in this venture call the Weird.

A few lines drifted by stained only by an inkblot, as if Cornelius were debating long and hard before he set the next line down on paper, where he couldn't erase it from prying eyes.

The Folk can be your greatest friend or most diabolical foe. They have motives that far surpass my understanding. I only pray that their eventual purpose for me is benign.

I cannot contemplate the alternative.

273

It was the last entry in the grimoire. I set it aside and turned down the lamp as it guttered. I was nearly out of wick.

The Kindly Folk weren't human, at least not like me or Dean or Cal. The Land of Thorn was real, and so was everything my father had written. Tremaine had sought me out, for what? I certainly wasn't my father. I didn't even have a Weird.

I was about to reach for the journal again when the lamp went out. It didn't flutter and die slowly for want of fuel or wick, it simply ceased to be. One moment there was light and the next I was plunged into blackness, a pale sliver of starlight the only hope I had to see.

"Shoot," I muttered. I'd left Dean's lighter in the pocket of my skirt, in my room.

I stood to feel my way to the trapdoor.

A heartbeat later, something smashed into the window.

I screamed, stumbling backward against the shelves. A rain of journals and paper came down from my impact, but I was focused upon the thing at the window.

Its great wings were outstretched, and its hooked beak smashed at the panes as its talons scrabbled for purchase on the windowsill.

An owl, but far larger than any I'd ever seen. It was so big it blocked out the light, covered up the glass, until the only illumination came from its glowing green eyes.

The owl reared back and smashed at the glass again. A spiderweb of cracks appeared, and the creature gave a shriek of triumph. Its wings beat louder than my heartbeat, and my panic wore off enough for me to realize that no owl would act in this manner.

274

This was something else.

I knew virals, perhaps too well, because of my mother. I knew the shandy-men and the shoggoth. This wasn't viral, wasn't from a lanternreel or Professor Swan's stupid pamphlets. This wasn't something that had once been human, twisted into a viral, or something purely a mutation that had come from this world.

The owl screeched as it splintered a pane, snowflakes of glass falling to mix with the debris on the library floor. Its feathers were a sick, watery bronze, and a few of them fluttered down along with the shards as it tried to wriggle through the hole.

It wasn't born from the necrovirus. It wasn't from anywhere this side of Tremaine's ring. And if it came through the window it was going to kill me.

These were the facts that unspooled through my mind, clinical and cool as the voice of Grey Draven through the aether tubes. Screaming for help didn't even occur to me. Cal and Dean were too far away, enveloped by the sound of their baseball game. They'd never get here in time and they wouldn't be able to help if they did.

I had to think. I had to be the girl who killed the beast, not the princess who became entranced by it and so trapped in its maze, forever.

I'd never liked the ending to that story, anyway.

The not-owl had one wing through the hole now, its greenish oily blood dribbling viscous on the library floor. I pressed myself as far back against the shelves as I could, trying to give myself a few precious seconds to think. *Think, Aoife. Thinking's what you're supposed to be aces at.*

The thing's hideous talons, twice again as long as a

275

flesh-and-blood owl's should be, left deep hash marks in the sill as it struggled toward me.

"*Child,*" it croaked, an obscene parody of a human voice. "*Little child . . .*"

I turned my face away from it, terror making me squeeze my eyes shut, dust and the corner of vellum pages tickling my nose. Graystone had defenses, even here in this most secret repository. But I was as far from the library panel below as I was from the moon.

If only I had some way to block off the window. If only I could spring a trap on the inhuman thing that hungered for my flesh and bones.

I felt it first in the very back of my head, a gentle ticking as the pendulum of my heartbeat counted off the seconds I had to live. It was a small pressure, like someone resting his hand on the back of my skull. The shoggoth's bite throbbed, as it had when I'd lain in a fever dream, listening to the house.

Listening to the voice of Graystone whisper. It crawled back to me, from the corners and crannies, the clockwork wheels and rods and gears that made the house.

The pressure built, flowing through me, into my chest and fingers and toes. I thought my skull was going to burst, but all at once my focus narrowed, to the window and the owl and the iron trap on the window waiting to snap shut.

My senses went razor sharp. Everything hurt. And then the pressure burst, my head filling with the voice of Graystone, and I felt iron in my blood and gears in my brain.

I was the house.

The house was me.

We were one.

276

The trap window smashed down, the spikes that locked the bars in place at the bottom cutting the owl nearly in half.

It gave a moan, hardly a sound at all, from its ruined throat. One wing fluttered spasmodically, and blood dribbled over the sill and ran down the plaster, staining whatever it touched.

Then it died, and the only sound was the wind through the shattered glass and my own heart throbbing in my ears. The fullness in my head was gone. The connection with Graystone was shut. My Weird had come and gone, and left me alone again.

21

The Lily Field

I STAYED IN the library above for a long time, staring at the trap and the thing caught in its jaws without blinking. I tried to raise the trap back up, to feel the fullness in my head again and the clean, sharp clarity of communing with Graystone.

A word like *weird* didn't do the feeling justice. I had felt like nothing else on earth. I wasn't simply Aoife when this foreign thing stirred in my mind. The Weird made me feel. The Weird made me alive.

But nothing happened. My head ached, behind my eyes, and my ears rang. The stench of the dead owl filled the small space, until I dislodged it from the trap and watched it fall to the ground four stories below. The blood got on my hands and I swiped them furiously on my dress, loose papers, anything to get the foul, oily blood off of my skin.

I went back to sitting, my knees tucked up under my chin, and stared at the window again. I concentrated

278

viciously, until I was sure my head would fragment into pieces from the pain of my headache.

Nothing stirred except the ends of my hair against my cheek as the wind picked up. Try as I might, I couldn't replicate the sweet, pure strangeness that had flowed through me when I'd been inches from the owl's talons. There were the things in the mist, things whose faces I hadn't seen. Something could have followed me home from the Land of Thorn.

I leaned my head back against a shelf, resting it on a soft pile of paper, and stared at the cobwebbed ceiling of the library. My father had made use of the Weird sound so simple. All I was finding was frustration and blood on my hands.

My eyes drifted shut. I told myself it was just for a moment, just until I could force my head to stop pounding, but when I opened my eyes the iron blue fingers of dawn had taken hold of the world.

I worked the cramps out of my neck and legs and went to the window. Surely Dean and Cal would be awake and have discovered the owl's body fallen to the front drive in mangled pieces.

Instead, I saw a lone figure standing on the drive, solitary in the glassy dawn light. The familiar ring of mist roiled at his feet.

Tremaine put up his finger and beckoned to me, and like my father before me, I went to him.

Tremaine stayed silent as we stepped through the *hexenring*, silent as he took my hand and helped me out. Once we stood on the red moor, he regarded me with his arms folded. His bracers gleamed. It was dawn in the Land of Thorn as well, a pinky-red dawn in a yellow sky. The scent of the air was foreign, and I shuddered as gooseflesh blossomed on my thinly clad arms.

Taking his blue velvet jacket from his shoulders, Tremaine wrapped it around mine.

"Thank you," I murmured. The jacket smelled like grass and roses, at once fresh and sick-sweet with decay.

"Don't," he said shortly. "I'm doing you no favors, child. I need your full attention." He regarded me, hunched inside his jacket. It was miles too large for me, and I swam inside the sleeves that flopped over my hands. "You are a frail little thing, aren't you?" he said, looking up at the ridge of mountains to our west. "Nothing like the others."

"I'm not frail," I snapped, chafing at the comparison, no doubt, to men like my father. Tremaine showed his teeth.

"We'll see." He beckoned to me and started up the same trail that we'd encountered the mist upon. This time we crested the moor and came down into a hollow, filled with a stone circle like a mouth of broken teeth. As we cleared the outer ring of stones I saw that they lay in a distinct pattern, a starburst like the ink stain the witch's alphabet had left on my palm.

"To stave off the no doubt interminable flood of talk," Tremaine said as we passed through the circle and started to climb again. "Those were corpse-drinkers in the mist. Before." He flourished his hand as if that explained everything. I was getting sick of his patronizing me, as if I were a very silly child who couldn't possibly understand.

"Can you at least tell me what those are?" I grumbled. "Or am I to guess?"

280

"Corpse-drinkers," Tremaine sighed, as if I were a hopelessly backward student. "Incorporeal beings searching for a vessel, a body. They possess corpses and drink of the living. They come from the other place. The Land of Mists."

Tremaine's explanation hadn't done anything to lessen my terror of the creeping mist, but I set my feelings aside. I was only interested in one thing the Kindly Folk had, and lore wasn't it. "My brother . . . ," I started. "Before, you said the boy—"

"If you spend any time in Thorn, with my people, you will come to understand the value and the beauty of bargain," said Tremaine. "You must do something for me, Aoife, before I'll grant favors for you, and—"

"I don't want a *favor*," I cut him off as he'd interrupted me, perhaps more viciously than was prudent. The Kindly Folk were not terribly kindly, and they were rude, too. "If something happened to Conrad, just tell me. *Please.*"

Tremaine stepped onto a set of steps carved into the downward slope of the moor, his green vest and trousers making him a living piece of the land. I followed, with far less grace.

"I said bargaining, not begging. Perhaps if you were a more sedate girl, who held her tongue before her betters, you'd have heard me."

I hated Tremaine, I realized all at once. I wanted to hit him in those shark teeth, swing for the fences like Cal's baseball players. "If you've just brought me here to riddle me, you might as well send me home," I gritted. "I didn't even know my father properly. I can't tell you where he's gone."

"But he *has* gone," Tremaine said. "He has not visited for three full moons. No inane tasks for our aid. No arcane

281

knowledge sought. I declare, I almost miss the old man. He was at least diverting. You are not." He walked, and I had the choice of following or being left alone on the moor. "So since you don't have a quick wit or a pleasant face, what *do* you have for me, Aoife?"

"Well, I haven't got anything except fifty dollars," I said primly. "And that's earmarked for someone else."

Tremaine threw back his head and cackled at the rapidly graying sky. "I don't want your money, child. I don't want any sort of tribute. You are not the Gateminder. Not like your father, and never will you be."

"All right." I dug my feet in. "You'd better tell me what you *do* want, or I'm not going another step." We had reached the edge of a pine forest, the sharp scent of the trees scraping the inside of my nose. Gravel paths wound away like ribbons, well groomed but eerily empty.

Tremaine stroked his tail of hair like it was a pet. "Do you see anyone else in this place, child, anyone to aid you? I could do you harm so easily. Your blood would stain the Winnowing Stone and the Stone would drink your offering down."

My father's book had talked about the Winnowing Stone. I had the distinct feeling I didn't want to meet it. Not yet, anyway.

"If you were going to kill me," I said, raising my chin so he had to meet my eyes, "you would have done it the first time I came through the *hexenring*. Or left me for the corpse-drinkers. Either way, you want me alive. For something."

I only hoped my fate wasn't worse than being consumed by one of those cackling, horrid things in the mist.

282

"So it is," Tremaine said, all traces of humor gone from his face. "You must think you're a clever girl, Aoife?"

My jaw set. "I do my best."

Tremaine's delicately hewn face rippled, just for a moment, with anger. It was the first emotion of any kind I'd seen pass over his features. "I despise clever girls," he spat. "Come along. I've something to show you."

When he got a few steps ahead of me and I stayed immobile, he threw up his hands. "It's the truth, you wretched human. I swear on silver. Now come along before I fetch you by that bird's nest you call hair."

I felt my eyes go wide. Even when I was just an orphan, not even an Academy student, people rarely spoke to me like that, either out of breeding or out of fear of my madness.

"Where are the other Folk?" I blurted. The question had been niggling me since the day before. "My father's writings speak of Folk. Not just one. And his chambermaid has seen scores of you." I put my hand on my hip, cocked it, doing my best imitation of Dean. He was the only person I could picture standing up to Tremaine.

The pale man scoffed, his nostrils flaring out like the sails of a weather ship. "So?"

"So," I returned, "what's happened to the rest?"

"You ask a lot of questions," Tremaine said quietly, his tone like a knife in the dark, "for someone who won't like the answers."

"Why did you bring me here?" I pressed on. "Why do you want me and not my father?"

"I *do* want your father!" Tremaine exploded. He closed on me, looming a head taller, his eyes ablaze.

I went cold and insensible all over, but I let the fear root

283

me to the spot rather than drive me on. I wasn't running from Tremaine. He'd enjoy it far too thoroughly.

"I would vastly prefer him," Tremaine amended through gritted teeth, his nostrils and body quivering with suppressed rage. "You think I want a simpering child when I could have a gifted future Gateminder? I do not. But you are all that is left, Aoife, and the sooner that you accept that, the better off you'll be."

"I want my brother." I could grit my teeth too.

"And I want the sky to open and rain down fine green absinthe," Tremaine returned. "Neither of us will be gratified today." His hand snapped out, quick as the traps of Graystone, and seized my arm. It was the first time he'd been overtly violent, but I can't say he surprised me. Tremaine jerked at me. "Now, are you going to come along, or do I have to drag you?"

I looked up, away, so I wouldn't have to meet those burning coal eyes any longer. If I stared Tremaine in the face, I'd lose my nerve. We'd come a distance—the sky was pure white now, clouds giving me a glimpse of a pink sunset—but only a glimpse. The air tasted cold and sharp. Winter seemed to hold sway, and I pulled Tremaine's jacket closer with my free arm.

"Tell me where the rest are," I whispered, "and I'll follow you."

Tremaine warred with himself a moment, shutting his eyes. His lashes were long and crystalline, and if I hadn't known what he was I'd have thought him beautiful beyond compare. As it was, he just reminded me of a wicked springheel jack—the creature with the beautiful face hiding a ravenous monster.

284

"The Land of Thorn is no longer a fruitful land," he finally bit out. "Many of the Folk have gone or fled, and many have simply wasted away. I am stronger, and I remain. That's all the answer your clever mind is getting." He snatched my arm again and growled through his pointed teeth. "Now, come."

Having no way of getting back to Graystone on my own, I had no choice but to follow.

"You do what I ask and I will answer you one question," Tremaine said as we cleared the pines and entered a low heath, heather scraping my legs. "That is the bargain. Say yes. Or say nay, and I'll return you to your home and never trouble you again."

I stayed quiet for a moment. What would Conrad or Dean do? They'd bite the bullet. They'd do what needed to be done. "I suppose I don't have any choice," I said, slogging on through the peat. Tremaine stopped striding and looked at me. He reached out a hand and put it on my shoulder. When we touched, I felt a deadening prickle down my arm, like I'd rolled over on it in my sleep.

"There is always a choice, Aoife. But often it is between the jaws of the beast and the doorway to death. This is fact, and I cannot change it."

It wasn't a debate for me, not really. I didn't even want to hesitate. Tremaine held the answer I'd sought so fervently. I was one simple indulgence away from finding my brother.

I sucked in a breath. "Fine. Show me what you have to show me."

"This way," Tremaine said. "Over the hilltop. They're not far."

285

Tremaine was a silent man, and his countenance forbade any effort to spark a conversation, so while we crossed the heath I busied myself with memorizing the details of my journey through the Land of Thorn.

Trees with blue leaves waved in the distance, a grove on the unbroken rolling hills of heather, pricked only by stone tors. The sky darkened slowly, like an oil lamp spending the last of its fuel. Everything smelled different, overpowering. The same mountains I'd seen from the *hexenring* loomed larger now, a bit like the Berkshires of my home, but they weren't. The Land of Thorn was as alien as the surface of the moon. You could taste it in the wind and see it in the bend of the horizon. It was beautiful, in a cold, frightening sort of way, like staring at a solar eclipse for just a split second too long, so that your eyes dazzled.

"Almost there," Tremaine told me, ending my plodding through the heather. "We're passing through a singing grove." He removed his goggles and handed them to me. "The agony trees sing the memories of those who've passed before and cloud your senses. Wear these."

"How can they do all that?" I demanded. "They're just trees."

"Aye, and the dryads who call the trees home exude a power that can sway you to their side for the rest of time. Would you like that, child? To put down roots here?"

I snatched the goggles and strapped them to my face. They were too large and pressed painfully against my cheekbones. But through the blue glass I saw things very differently.

The trees were alive, arms and hands reaching for me with a delicate hunger as we passed through. Even the

286

wind had a shape, and bore a laughing, dancing rivulet of tiny things with fangs.

"Blue is the color," Tremaine said. "The color of truth. Keep the goggles. Use them if you venture here on your own."

"Don't worry," I whispered. "I never will."

"So you say now," Tremaine murmured. The trees knotted and formed an archway, dying and overgrown with fungi and vines. The dryad who crawled headfirst down the trunk was emaciated, her barky body and vine-twisted hair dry and wilted.

"Everything is so bleak," I said softly, because it seemed as if speaking loudly would break the delicate balance of this grayed place.

Tremaine lifted a curtain of ivy and ushered me farther into the grove, as the agony trees moaned and sang around us. He looked just the same through the blue glass, his face pale and his teeth sharp as ever. Tremaine wasn't hiding himself from my gaze. He wasn't setting out a lure—the ice-sculpture beauty was his true face. That worried me far more than the sweet and seductive song of the trees. If Tremaine's cruel visage was his true one, I really did have reason to fear him.

The dryads watched with unblinking eyes like dark knots in their carved faces, claws digging into the bark of their tree. It was like listening to a funeral dirge come from far off, and I felt myself grow slow and sluggish even though I still saw the world through blue glass.

"Bleak indeed," Tremaine agreed. He steered me between the trees to the other side of the grove and the grasping limbs. "Come, Aoife," he said. "Observe the why

287

of Thorn's bleakness. Of the decline you see all around you."

I stepped through the branches and the crunching brown leaves, lifting the goggles away from my eyes and letting them dangle about my neck. I finally let out the shocked sound I'd been holding in, nearly gagging on the scent.

I stood at the edge of a field, contained by hills on every side. The field was filled with lilies, pure white, their faces upturned to the weak and dying sunlight. The funerary scent of them was overpowering, rotted and sweet enough to swallow.

The lilies went on unbroken but for two pyres raised in the center of the flowers. Gleaming with refracted light, they were so bright that I had to turn my face away. In the face of the vision of white and gleaming glass, my mother's voice whispered in my ear.

I went to the lily field. . . .

Unbidden, I started toward the pyres, crushing flowers under my feet, releasing more of their heady, witchy scent. I had to see for myself what dark shapes lay under the glass.

I drew close, and my feet stopped of their own accord as I stared not at geometric glass boxes containing formless shapes, but at a shape that was too familiar for comfort.

They were coffins. Coffins made from glass, seamless in their construction, sealed like diving bells floating on a sea of petals.

A girl lay in each coffin, one fair and one dark, their arms crossed over their chests. The fair one, closest to me, had a spun-sugar complexion and the dark one had hair like ebony and lips like wet blood.

No breath passed their flower-petal lips, and no blood

288

beat in their translucent veins, their skin flawless as marble.

"They sleep," Tremaine said, his voice startling me. He'd crept through the flowers silent as the mist. "As they have slept for a thousand days and will sleep for a thousand more."

I put my hand on the fair girl's coffin. "They're alive?"

"Of course they're alive," Tremaine snapped. "Alive and cursed." His shadow fell across the fair girl's snow-white face. "They walk between their life and the mists beyond, and they will walk until a cursebreaker lifts their burden."

"They look so young," I said. My hand still rested on the coffin of the fair girl. She was perfectly still, like a clockwork doll wound down. I couldn't stop looking at her unearthly face, her translucent eyelids. "Who are they?"

Tremaine stepped between the coffins. The flowers there were bent and bowed from someone's constant pacing. "Stacia," he said, placing his hand next to mine over the fair girl's face. "And Octavia." He bowed his head to the raven-haired girl. "The Queens of Summer and Winter."

"Queens?" I blinked. Neither of the girls looked a day older than myself.

"That's what I said." Tremaine, if it was possible, had become even more condescending when we entered the lily field. "Seelie and Unseelie. Kindly Folk and Twilight Folk. Call it what you will. Octavia and Stacia rule over the Land of Thorn. Or they did, until they fell asleep and the land began to die." Tremaine took his hand away. The look he gave to the dark girl was sorrowful, and then he brushed it off with a flick of his head and a twitch of his bracers.

"Who cursed them?" I asked. I couldn't look away from

289

the fair girl's face. It was beauteous. A more perfect face I'd never seen, but there was a flat waxy quality to it when I looked closer. Queen Stacia was a doll, a dead doll, and I backed away, crushing more flowers.

Tremaine still stared at the dark queen. Very slowly he reached out and laid the tips of his fingers, just for a moment, against the place on the glass where her cheek would be.

"Tremaine," I said sharply. "Who did this to them?"

"A traitor," said Tremaine. He dropped his hand from the coffin and strode over to me. I was unprepared when he grabbed me by the wrists, tugging me nearly against his broad chest. Metal clanked against my collarbone on the left side, some manner of brass plating under his shirt in the place of skin. He leaned down until I could feel his breath on my ear.

"I *will* be the one to awaken my lady Octavia and stop the slow blight on our lands, Aoife. I will return the wheel of Summer and Winter to the sky where it belongs and keep Thorn from withering on the vine."

"Let go of me," I said as his fingers dug into my shoulder painfully.

"You're the only one left now," he hissed. "You can play the fool with me, but I know what blood flows in your veins. Unsuitable or not, you *will* take up the mantle of Gateminder, and you *will* aid me."

Tremaine's face had changed—there wasn't anger or amusement there, just desperation, and that was more alarming than his quick, cold fury.

"I said"—I struggled against Tremaine's grasp, half

290

panicked and half indignant—"let *go* of me!" My shout rolled back from the gray hills. In the soft wind, the lilies worried their petals, whispering.

"We have a bargain, child," Tremaine reminded me with a snarl. "You do as I say. I answer your question."

"I don't want to do *this*!" I shouted. I was fighting in earnest now, and I felt the sleeve of my dress tear at the shoulder.

"Another hysteric." Tremaine shoved me from him in disgust and I fell back, landing in a bed of silky petals. "Just like that useless cow Nerissa."

"My mother . . ." I gulped down my tears and rubbed my shoulder where Tremaine had grabbed me. "How do you know her name? How?" That bastard. How dare he bring Nerissa into this!

"The same way I know yours," Tremaine growled. "Your father was the fourteenth Minder. He told me the truth when I asked. That is the duty of any man unfortunate enough to bear the Weird, if he wishes to remain free and healthy."

"My father hated you," I muttered, to counter his superior tone. "His diary said so."

"I have no doubt." Quick as Tremaine's ire rose, it receded, leaving his glacially beautiful face calm as before. "Archibald was a man of temper, but rest assured, mine is worse." He gestured to the coffins. "My world is dying every day they sleep, Aoife. My people are scattered to the winds. Do you really believe the blight will not reach the Iron Land once it has eaten Thorn to the bone?"

"Even if I would," I said, getting to my feet, "I can't.

I don't have any say over my Weird." My dress was stained with lily pollen, fragile fingers of yellow on the green cotton.

"Then I suggest you gain some," Tremaine told me. "Because you are the last Grayson in the line, and you must be the cursebreaker. Do it and I will tell you what happened to your brother. That's the last bargain I'm willing to give you."

I didn't care for the way Tremaine's eyes gleamed when he talked about me breaking the curse. "If my father wouldn't do such a thing, then I shouldn't. I trust his example in these matters."

I watched the tide of rage flow in again, and this time I dodged Tremaine's grasp. He backed me up against the fair girl's coffin, glass edges digging into my back. "Consider this, fragile little human fawn," Tremaine said. "I found you and stole you easily as a wolf brings down its prey. How easily might I find your Dean Harrison, or your strange friend Calvin Daulton? How might I savage them in my hunt, child? What would you, alone, do then?"

"They're not part of this," I whispered, feeling cold prickle all over me. It wasn't from the air. I realized my brashness had just pulled Cal and Dean into Tremaine's sights. I had to salvage this somehow. "Your quarrel is with me," I said softly. "Leave them alone."

"Go back to Graystone, get hold of your Weird and do your blood duty," said Tremaine. "And then I'll have no reason to make good my threat."

"I wouldn't know how to break your curse, I'm sure," I said lamely. The coffin was cold against my body, rigid and unforgiving.

292

Tremaine lowered his eyes. "You think me hard and unyielding. Frozen. I am a creature of Winter, it's true." He gently lifted my chin with his fingertip. "But I am not a hard master. Like opening your eyes to the sunlight for the first time, the Weird will point your way." He let go and stood aside. "Back to the ring, little fawn. And remember that this task is not one for failure. It is your duty now, whether it pleases you or not, to wake my queen."

I looked back at the dryad's grove and shuddered. "You won't escort me?"

"My place is here, with the queens," said Tremaine. "I guard their slumber."

The thought of the corpse-drinkers or the singing trees catching me alone was almost worse than being with Tremaine. He laughed, softly, at my expression. "The ring knows where to take you, child, and the dryads know your smell now. You'll find your way to Graystone unmolested."

"I guess I have no choice," I grumbled. I hated the fact that Tremaine had backed me into this crevice even more than I hated my inability to think my way out of taking up the mantle my father had abandoned. I didn't want to be like him, alone and lonely, troubled by the Kindly Folk.

"Indeed, you do not," Tremaine agreed. "I will return for you in one week. Use your days well." He raised his hand to me. "Fair luck, Aoife Grayson."

The worst bit was, I could tell that he was being sincere.

293

22

The Lore of the Weird

Morning had rolled around while I'd vanished into the Land of Thorn, and the apple orchard was painted with crooked light and shadows.

Blue light wound through the trees, along with Cal and Dean's voices.

"Aoife! Aoife Grayson!"

"Stop that racket," Dean said. "You want to bring down every ghoul living under the mountain?" His lighter snapped and smoke hissed into the morning air. "Aoife! Call out, kid."

"I'm here," I said. I was standing on the spot where the *hexenring* had snatched me, and I moved away from it with all haste, stuffing the goggles Tremaine had gifted me into my pocket. One less thing to try and explain. "I'm here!" My voice ripped out of me, echoing loud and earthly. My knees trembled with relief to be free of the Land of Thorn.

Aether lanterns bobbed around the corner of the house, from the orchard, and Cal came running. "Where in the

294

stars have you *been?*" he snapped. "You just ran off again. What am I supposed to think?"

Dean followed, slower, his cigarette ember trailing smoke spirits after him. "Got all your fingers and toes, princess?"

"I'm sorry," I said to Cal, folding my torn sleeve under so he wouldn't notice. The mornings had gotten colder since we'd been away from Lovecraft, and I could see my breath. "I was walking and I lost track of the time. My chronometer's in the library."

"You silly girl!" Cal's face contorted. "You could have ruined *everything.* What if a Proctor or someone from Arkham saw you?"

Cal's worrying would be endearing normally, but right now it just sparked irritation. "Ruined? Cal, this isn't anything to do with you." I was shivering, and I put my arms around myself, shrinking away from him. "I'm sorry I worried you," I said. "But it's all right. And stop calling me silly."

He tensed, fists curling, and then released, as if someone had cut his strings. "I thought I'd lost you, Aoife."

"Far be it from me to interrupt this little reunion," Dean coughed. "But it's freezing out here and I'd just as soon we were discussing this over a breakfast and a hot cuppa."

"He's right," I said in relief, stepping around Cal so I didn't have to look at his shattered face. "Let's all go inside. I'm starving."

We trooped back to Graystone, where Bethina waited in the doorway, twisting her striped apron between her hands. "Oh, miss!" she cried when I was close, and flung her arms around me.

"I . . ." I patted her back as well as I could, crushed between her plump arms. "It's all right, Bethina."

295

"When your bed hadn't been mussed and Dean hadn't seen you for hours, I knew you were lost for good this time, miss. Knew it." She sniffled deeply.

"It's good to know all of you have so much faith in me," I grumbled with a smile. No one returned it. I extricated myself gently from Bethina's grasp. "If you're up to it, I think we'd all like some breakfast."

"Of course," she said, dabbing at her eyes. "I've got some oatmeal and store-bought pancake mix. Should still be good. Pancakes and porridge all around."

While Bethina bustled in the kitchen I went to my room and changed into a pair of toreador pants and a silk blouse that I tied up around my waist. My hair was hopeless, but I managed to comb out the moss and leaves and lily petals.

Dean found me as I descended the stairs, stopping my path. "What's the word, kitten?"

"Exhausted," I said, glad he'd found me and not Cal right then. "Hungry. Pick one."

Dean tipped his head to the side. The light caught his eyes and turned them liquid silver. "You going to tell me what really happened after you went AWOL last night?"

I worried my lip. "I'm too cold to go up on the roof again."

"When the sun warms things up, then," he said. "We'll walk and you'll talk. Sound fair?"

Tremaine's words bubbled up in my thoughts, scornful and sharp. *That's the last bargain I'm to give you.*

"All right," I said. On an impulse, I grabbed Dean's hand and squeezed. He was warm, alive and solid and I clung longer than I needed to. "I'm glad you stayed."

Dean squeezed in return. "Right back at you."

"Breakfast!" Bethina's shout echoed from the kitchen. "Pancakes! Come and get 'em if you're able!"

Dean sighed and let go of my hand. "Stale johnnycakes and mushy oatmeal. The stuff dreams are made of."

"Dean . . . ," I started as he thumped down the stairs. He stopped at the bottom.

"Yeah, princess?"

I waved him off. Dean seemed willing to accept my flights of fancy about the Weird, but telling him I'd visited a land where the Folk watched their cursed queens sleep could only be asking for even more trouble than telling Cal about the library.

"Nothing," I said. "Forget it."

"I won't, but I'll be patient," Dean said. "Hungry enough to eat a nightjar raw."

I waited until he'd gone and then went to the library above and got my father's journal. I needed it near me. I needed to know that in shouldering the burden of Tremaine and his cursebreaker, I wasn't alone.

Cal shoved his third pancake into his mouth, rivulets of syrup coating his chin. "I don't understand why you read those musty things," he said, pointing at my father's book. "I'd kill for a copy of *Weird Tales.*"

"I like books," I said, tucking it under my elbow. "We always had books."

"That one doesn't even have a proper picture on the cover," Cal snorted. "Give it here, let's see what the fuss is about."

"*No.*" I jerked it away from his sticky fingers. Cal frowned.

"See, this is what happens when you read too much. You

297

get bad manners and bad habits. You'll need glasses before you know it."

"Nothing wrong with a pair of cat's-eyes," Dean said. "They can do favors for a pretty girl." He dropped me a wink while Cal's face pinked.

"We won't always be schoolkids, Aoife," Cal piped up. "What will a husband think of this bookworm habit?"

"Cal, why do you care?" I slammed down my plate, appetite gone after half a bowl of oatmeal.

"I'm helping," he muttered. "You—you don't have a mother to tell you these things."

I grabbed my father's book and shoved my chair back with a screech. I loved Cal like another brother, but right then I felt like I did when Conrad teased me once too often—like I wanted to slap him and tell him to go jump off a bridge. "Cal, unless you want the job, lay off. Stop being my fussy aunt and just be my friend."

"You're misunderstanding . . . ," he started, and then scrubbed at his chin with his napkin. "No, you're right. I shouldn't have spoken up."

"You shouldn't," I concurred. Cal's jaw twitched.

"Aoife, what's gotten into you? You're rude and short and you disappear for hours on end. Is there something you want to tell me?"

I tightened my grip on the journal. "Not a thing," I gritted and turned on my heel, storming into the library.

The orderly rows of books were soothing, familiar. After the alien landscape of Thorn, it was a larger relief than I'd imagined.

298

Alone after I'd climbed into the attic space, I felt a deep, fathomless cold envelop me. Tremaine had threatened Cal and Dean if I disobeyed him. He knew what had happened to Conrad and he would keep the secret eternally, I had no doubt, if I crossed him.

Even believing that there was more to my world than the School, the necrovirus and life with the stigma of madness was still difficult in the light of day.

To think that I now had the task of serving the Kindly Folk in my father's place made my chest tight, my heart beat too fast. I sat down, or rather folded over, and put my head on my knees. I breathed until it wasn't difficult anymore. I might not have known my father the way most children did theirs, but I was still his daughter. The truth was inescapable, after what Tremaine had shown me—my father and I shared a duty, and I would not let him down while our odd blood still flowed in my veins.

I opened his journal. The ink swam for a moment before it settled onto the page when I touched it. I paged through my father's more recent entries, but found nothing of much use.

I become more disconcerted each time the Strangers visit me,

my father wrote. Before my geas-bewitched eyes, he paced a vast bedroom, rain lashing the night beyond.

They conceal secrets beyond imagination about the Thorn Land, and I fear the dark shadow that belies their appearance a little more at each turning of the moon.

299

I heard glass shatter somewhere beyond my view, and my father's head whipped around, then he turned back and continued pacing.

Breathless, I read on to see what became of him.

Not very becoming of the line, to admit fear, but the Strangers are harbingers of the foe we both face in the Kindly Folk's secrets, and what that foe is, even nightmares could not conceive.

My father put his pen down quickly, then ran from his bedroom, and I rubbed my fingers over my eyelids. Sighing, I flipped to the most recent entry in the diary.

No further mention of Strangers leapt out at my eyes. They came in shadow, and shadow had taken Conrad.

Not for the first time, or even the hundredth, I wished that I'd known Archie sooner. If I'd grown up with a father who'd prepared me to take the reins of Minder, I would know where Conrad was already. I wouldn't owe Tremaine my end of the bargain.

"I could use some help," I told the diary. "Not that you appear to care one bit." I turned my eyes back to the ink.

2 September, 1955.

A few months before I'd gotten Conrad's letter. Such a small amount of time, when you put it on the vast line of the universe, yet so large when it was the gulf separating me from using my Weird and staving off the Folk from my friends.

I must be quick.

I paid full attention to the page for the first time that evening. My father was, if anything, as verbose as he was cryptic. His normally bell-clear handwriting was jagged, too, jumping all over the page and leaving behind a snowfall of ink drops from where he pressed down too hard with his fountain pen.

They are at my heels at last. I have refused their command, their mantle of cursebreaker, for the final time.

They are coming, and there is no help for it now. Not even the clockwork bones of my house can hold them back. I must flee. I must find the Bone Sepulchre and seek the shadowy aid of the mists, of the Strangers. I must, I must, I must, or perish on the Winnowing Stone surely as the chosen maiden at the harvest moon.

My throat was dry in the warm air of the attic and my fingers rattled the vellum paper as I turned the page.

Conrad, Aoife . . . my charge to you is to flee. Never visit the Land of Thorn. Never seek the truth that lies beyond the iron and steam of the Proctors' world. Let it die with me.

If you value your lives, let it die. Do not seek me. Do not find me.

Save yourselves.

The journal hit the floor with a muffled *thwack* as I pressed my hand over my mouth. Shivers racked me, the air suddenly icy. But not the air—just my skin. Chills crawled over me, digging in their thorny claws.

301

My father knew I'd come looking for him. He'd tried to warn me about the very thing I'd agreed to do for Tremaine.

What had I done?

A creak sounded at the foot of the ladder and I composed myself. "Cal . . . ," I sighed, turning to the hatch. "I just need to be alone for a bit, all right?"

"Not Cal, I'm afraid." Bethina's copper curls crested the ladder, eyes roving over the unruly shelves, the dust, my cross-legged seat on the floor. Anywhere, I noticed, but my face. "May I come up, miss?"

I composed myself, running a hand over my face to erase the anger and fatigue. "It's a free country," I said. "'Less you're a heretic." *Or a madwoman.*

"I don't talk so, you know." Bethina hoisted herself over the hatch, puffing. "The gals from Arkham—the nice ones—don't spit out whatever they're thinking."

"It'll be the bane of my imaginary husband's existence, I'm sure," I said bitterly.

"I like it, actually." Bethina ducked her head. "You're frank, miss. Like a boy."

I tucked the journal under my knee. I didn't want anyone reading it, especially not an ordinary girl like Bethina. She wouldn't understand and I didn't have the words to explain.

"Truth is the only constant thing we have," I said. "My mother used to say that." Like Nerissa would know a real truth if it bit her. There were the things my father wrote about, and then there were my mother's ramblings.

"She sounds like a whip-smart lady, miss," Bethina said.

"She's not." My curt tone made me even more disgusted

302

with myself. Useless to find my brother or my father, and now snooty on top.

"Mr. Cal speaks highly of her. He says that she did a fine job of raising you."

I worried the edges of the journal, surprised that he'd actually said that out loud after our fight, and to Bethina, of all people. Cal thought girls were a different species. "Cal's kind," I said aloud. "He . . . he prefers to see things as they might be."

"He's got a shine for you, miss," Bethina said. "And with the way you fight like cats and dogs, might I assume that it goes both ways?"

"You might not," I sniffed. "And you're being . . ." What was it the snooty characters in the lanterns said? "Entirely too familiar," I finished, with the requisite disapproving eyebrow.

"Apologies, miss," Bethina said, though she didn't seem sorry. "I didn't mean to jabber at you. I just wanted to give you this."

She reached under her apron and drew a battered notebook from her dress pocket. It was small, the type that would be carried in my uniform were I at school to work problems and jot down notes while I walked to and fro from classes.

"What is this?" I said. The book's black leather cover bore no marking.

"It was in Mr. Grayson's personal things after he went away," Bethina said. "I think he forgot to take it."

I took the book and thumbed the dog-eared, coffee-stained pages. Something new. Something that could help

303

me out of this mess. Bethina had actually come through. I tightened my grasp on the book. "I'm sorry I snapped at you," I said.

"Don't, miss." Bethina shrugged. "Most city girls with your breeding, they'd take me for a bumpkin and boss me about. You just talk to me. I appreciate it."

The notebook was nearly full, tight sentences almost too small to read. "Why not give it to Conrad?" I asked. "He was looking for the same things I was."

Bethina's smile fell away. "Mr. Conrad got taken before I could tell him any of this."

"I've been meaning to ask . . ." I paused, wondering if I really wanted to know. "How did he seem before he left? Archibald . . . my dad?" The last words of his witch's alphabet burned in my mind. *Do not seek me. Save yourselves.* Had he thought I might actually read those words, before he left? Had he thought of me ever, besides putting my name at the top of the entry?

"Like I told before, frantic," Bethina said. "Never seen him scared before that. He was a gentleman but he weren't no dandy, your pop." She put her chin on her fist. "It was like he'd done something wrong, you follow? Like he were a heretic and the whole Bureau of Heresy was coming for him."

"Worse," I muttered, thinking of Tremaine.

"Maybe that will help," Bethina said, tapping the notebook. "He were always scribbling in it, when he'd be up and about the house. I can't make hide nor hair of the coding he put his words into, but you're a bright one, miss. Good luck."

She started back to the hatch and I stole another look at

304

the notebook. The cramped writing swam before my eyes and became clearly legible. I blinked, and the type was gibberish again.

The notebook was enchanted like the witch's alphabet. "Thank you, Bethina," I said. "Really. I'd like to be alone with this, if you don't mind. To . . . er . . . think."

She bobbed her head. "Yes, miss. And if I may . . . I just know you're the kind of daughter Mr. Grayson'd hold his head up to have."

Well, that made one of us.

The ladder creaked, and she was gone. I shut the hatch, agonizing while it rolled its slow way into place, and then opened the notebook and stared at the writing while I waited for my father's memory to appear.

It didn't take long for the silvery images to fade the real world around me, graying my vision like rain and fog through window glass.

My father wasn't young in this memory, but his hair was still dark and he was sans spectacles. He sat thoughtfully in his armchair, tapping his fountain pen against his bottom lip. I did the same thing when I was stuck on a calculation or a persnickety mechanical problem.

After a moment, my father scribbled something in his notebook. *Conspirators? Who? Why?*

I'd stayed nearly motionless before, lest I disturb the enchantment and break up the reel of memory, but this time I spoke. My voice came out a papery whisper.

"Um . . . excuse me?"

My father continued to scribble, a lock of hair falling into his face. He hadn't shaved and he wasn't wearing a collar or a vest. Deep silver-gray crescents painted themselves under his eyes, and he scratched absently at the cleft in his chin.

"There isn't a lick of sense in this," he grumbled.

"Archibald," I said, louder, when his image didn't vanish. "Father?"

Memory-Archie's head snapped up. "You can see me?"

"Of course," I said, after a moment of silence at the shock of getting his attention. "I found your journal."

"The witch's alphabet?" Archie dropped his notebook and scrabbled for it. "Star and sun, do you have any idea how much danger you've put yourself in reading that thing?"

"I don't know how to say this," I began, deciding to keep on course even though his proclamations of danger threw me off balance. "But do you . . . do you know who I am?"

"Of course I do. You're my daughter. Aoife." My father rubbed a hand over his face. "I'll be honest—I'd hoped to never see you. But here you are."

"I . . ." My voice hitched without my accord at his disappointment in putting eyes on me. "I'm sorry—no, that's a lie. I'm not sorry. I need to know something."

My father sighed, his silvery image fluttering like a hand had passed through the lantern projector's light stream. "You want to know about the cursed queens. And why I didn't take Tremaine's infernal bargain."

I felt my eyes go wide, but composed myself even though a thousand questions were fighting for space in my mind. I bit down on them. "Yes," I said. "Tremaine says that I'm the cursebreaker, but . . . I don't know what to do. I don't know how to break the curse."

My father stood, tucking his notebook into the sagging

306

breast pocket of his jacket. "You look like your mother," he said. "I always imagined you'd take after me. Guess that's why I'm not a fortune-teller."

He did think about me. At least once. My stomach stopped flipping over. He did know who I was. I was still knotted up and terrified over my confrontation with Tremaine, but at that moment I could have sprouted clockwork wings and flown. "I have your eyes," I murmured. "At least, that's what Nerissa always says."

"Aoife." My father reached out, and his fingers brushed my shoulder and passed through me like a ghost in a beam of light. "You have to understand I didn't give you up willingly. It was for—"

"For my own good?" The words ripped from me and I jabbed my finger into the memory's face, all attempts to appear demure and well bred flying out the window at his words. "Do you have any idea what I've endured in the name of my own good? You made Conrad and me orphans, so please don't think I'm stupid enough to believe that you were being altruistic." I flung up my hands, my face heating and my voice rising. "*None* of this is for my own good, *Dad.*"

The memory held up its hands. "You'll believe what you'll believe, Aoife. Think me cruel if you want, but trust me when I say that the Folk are dangerous to a man, and that Tremaine is worse than most."

"Just tell me how to break the curse," I grumbled, "and I won't bother you any longer." I'd waited my entire life for this moment, and though I knew the enchantment wasn't my father in flesh, it was close enough. The crushing feeling on my chest was one I knew well enough that I wasn't

307

surprised by its presence, even in the wake of my elation. Nerissa had disappointed me innumerable times. I *had* been stupid to think that my father would be different.

"You can't break the curse," my father said impatiently. "No one can. The magic laid on the queens is like nothing else in either the Thorn Land or the Iron one." He slashed his hand across his chest. "I don't know Tremaine's motive for setting us the task, but it isn't anything good. Forget about trying. You'll only get hurt."

"Choice is a luxury I don't have," I said, holding myself straight as if I were being castigated by Professor Swan. "Conrad's missing and Tremaine knows where he is. So, *Father*, are you going to help me or not?"

He pressed a hand against his forehead and then paced away from me, like the library above was too small to contain even his memory. "No one among me and my kind knows who set the curse against the Folk. No one knows why and no one knows how. Even the Iron Codex has been no help, the pooling of all our knowledge for two hundred and fifty years. With that dearth of information, feel free to do your best with Tremaine's task. It's impossible. He's setting you up to fail, Aoife."

"Why?" I demanded with confusion. "He wants his queen awake—he told me."

"Tremaine would as soon have the Winter throne for himself," my father scoffed. "And to have a Gateminder in his pocket, when you inevitably can't fulfill your end of the bargain—he could travel in the Iron Land free as we do."

All of what he said made a certain, sickening sort of sense, but it didn't change the fact that I had to find

Conrad. Even though he'd begged me not to come after him, I couldn't leave my brother to the Folk. Knowing now how my father felt, Conrad was all I had.

"I'm doing it" was what I voiced.

"Aoife, dammit. There are things I can't explain to you, but know that the curse cannot be broken. To try is to fail." He reached for me again, but I backed away. My father's face fell. "Please, Aoife," he said softly. "Just go home."

I slapped the notebook shut, and the silver memory shattered into a million dancing motes before it vanished into the shadow of the library above.

"This is my home now," I whispered, but my father was gone.

I stayed where I was for a few moments, feeling sick with disappointment and confusion. My father wasn't going to help me. He didn't even want to speak with me.

There was a knocking on the ladder, and I swiped at my watering eyes and opened the hatch. Sniveling wasn't going to break Tremaine's curse or get Conrad back.

Dean stood at the foot of the ladder, rolling a cigarette between his forefinger and thumb. I shoved the notebook into my pocket and climbed down.

Dean examined me.

"You look upset." No pet names this time. No doubt he was sick to death of my antics and broody moods, just like Cal.

"I am upset," I ground shortly. "And no, I don't want to talk about it. I don't want to talk or think or do anything

309

but ball up my fist and hit something, but if I do that I'm unladylike, so I guess I'll just go try on some dresses or put up my hair until the urge passes."

Dean's eyebrows rose. "Let's you and me take a walk," he said.

"I don't want to walk," I snarled. "I don't need to be protected."

"No, you don't," Dean said. His calm was maddening when matched with my rage. "But I want to walk, and I want you to walk with me, so before you take my head off again, consider that you don't have to say a word." He flashed me his grin. "I hate mouthy broads, you know."

The tightness in my chest eased, a fraction. "You said you wanted to hear what really happened when I disappeared." I went to the panel and shut up the library above. "That still true?"

"So true it squeaks," Dean said. He put the cigarette in his mouth and tipped his head toward the door. "Come on. I've been listening to the cowboy smack over pancakes for the last half hour. I'd swear that kid was a rot-gut if I didn't know better."

I crinkled my nose. Rot-guts were gluttonous globs of used-to-be people who hid in dark damp places when the virus overtook them and ate anything they could. Tin, garbage, human flesh. It was all the same when the necrovirus was riding your bloodstream.

"No," I told Dean. "He's not. He just eats like one."

Dean nudged my elbow. "Come on. Walking. You and me."

I followed him outside, not wanting to admit how much I liked the sound of just Dean and me, together.

310

23

The Miskatonic Woods

"If it's a long story, we should go out on one of these woodland trails," Dean said after we reached the foot of the drive and he'd smoked his Lucky Strike down to the nub. "Get ourselves some privacy."

"What about the ghouls?" I said. "Isn't it dangerous?"

"Hey, now," Dean said. "You're with me, Dean Harrison. Finest guide east of the Mississippi and north of the Carolinas. And right now Dean Harrison wants to go somewhere where he doesn't have to listen to anyone talk about baseball or wonder if their shoes make their ankles look fat."

"You're terrible," I said. "Bethina's a good girl."

"Never was too interested in the good ones," Dean said. "The sinful ones are more fun."

"We'll go," I decided. I wouldn't have agreed even a day ago, but after the horrible scene with the notebook I was feeling downright impulsive. I had to get out of Graystone

311

before I screamed. It was my father's house, and I knew now that I wasn't welcome there.

The ever-present fog lay light, and I even caught a bar of sunlight as we walked down the narrow country road switchbacked into the side of the mountain before turning off onto a trail that snaked away into the bare-branched forest like any of the paths in Nerissa's tales.

The crows watched us from their perches in the naked trees, eyes like glass.

"They never leave," I said. "They just stay around the house. It's eerie."

"Corvids are smart birds," Dean said. "They stick where there's food and shelter and where nobody sprays buckshot at 'em. They watch and wait with the best."

"In Lovecraft, they use the ravens to spy and take you away," I said. "This is too similar. I don't like it."

"Crows don't take from you," Dean said. "They give your soul wings."

My mouth curled. "Well, who took you for a poet, Dean Harrison."

He ducked his head, his hair loose and falling in his eyes. "That book you had at breakfast." His boots scuffed the dirt of the path. "I take it that has something to do with this vanishing act you pull?"

I stopped walking, and swung in front of Dean so he had to stop too. "I trust you," I told him. "Implicitly. I barely know you, but I trust you with the truth. Am I wrong to do that?"

"Some cats would say 'undoubtedly'"—he grinned— "but I'm no blabbermouth, Aoife. If I were, Cal would have punched my lights out days ago. For my 'familiarity.'" He quoted the last word with his index fingers.

312

I ignored the gibe at Cal. "Day before last, I went exploring in that old orchard behind the grounds. I got lost in the fog and I . . ."

We walked again, picking our way over rocks and tree limbs, and it was a good twenty yards before I could get my courage up.

"I stepped through a fairy ring."

Glimpses of the old stone walls and a fallen-down farmhouse were visible through the mist, and I focused on them instead of panicking because Dean wasn't speaking.

The crows called to one another, inkblots against the mist, spattered across the tops of the trees ahead. They were definitely following us.

"Hold up," Dean said. "A fairy ring . . . you mean a *hexenring*? An enchantment circle?"

"You know that name?" Surprise negated my worry that Dean would finally decide I was too far-fetched for his taste.

"I've heard of them." He didn't look interested in my tale any longer. His mouth was set and the frown line had appeared between his eyes. Dean was angry, but with me or a secret something I couldn't tell.

"I got caught up in the ring and the mist," I continued. "And I swear, Dean . . . I wandered right into the Land of Thorn. A fairyland."

Dean whipped his gaze from left to right across the trail, into the trees on one side and the old farmhouse yard on the other. His hand went into his pocket, the right one, where he kept his switchblade.

A wind ruffled the hairs on the back of my neck, and the tree branches stirred, a clacking like hungry mouths as the branches scraped.

313

Dean snatched my arm. "We can't talk about this out in the open."

"What in the—" I started, as he dragged me down the lane toward the skeleton of the house. The roof had caved in and the floor gaped down to the root cellar. The crows increased their volume as Dean dragged me.

"Just walk," he murmured in my ear. "Try to look natural. We're just a boy and girl, out for a stroll." He let go his vise-tight grip on my arm and slipped his hand into mine instead.

I glanced at the trees again. The wind had ceased as quickly as it had been born, and the trees were still. The shadows under them looked longer, the bare branches sharper, and I felt the blurriness in my head that had overtaken me just before Tremaine's *hexenring* had spirited me to the Thorn Land.

"Just a boy and a girl," I agreed. My fingers locked tighter in his of their own accord, and I was reassured when Dean squeezed.

"Walk," he whispered, lips against my hair. "And don't look back until we're inside the house."

Soon enough we reached the doorway, devoid of a door, and ducked inside. An ancient, moldy table and chairs still stood in front of the fireplace, as if rot had overtaken the house at terrible speed, forcing the inhabitants to flee.

Dean let go of my hand, flexing his fingers. "You've got a grip, princess."

"I do when I'm nervous," I agreed. "You don't think I'm nutty for any of this? For saying I saw the Kindly Folk, and that—"

314

Dean pressed a finger to his lips. Around the house, I could still hear the crows, scrabbling and fussing in the trees.

"I know it sounds crazy." I lowered my voice so our conversation didn't reach outside. "But I met one of the Folk, talked to him. His name's Tremaine. He was awful." I shivered.

Dean nodded, as if he'd been listening for something. "The black birds are watching out. For now. As for this Folk, I suppose he wanted something."

"I . . . Why would you say that?" I blinked at him.

"The Folk always want something," Dean said. "It's the magpie nature. They see shine in someone or something and they have to steal it and keep it."

I decided I could pry how Dean knew so much about the Folk out of him later. For now, it was enough that he believed me.

"Well," I continued, "we made a bargain. He said he'd tell me where Conrad's gone if I used my Weird for his ends. I'm going to do it, and then I'm going to find Conrad. There doesn't have to be anything sinister about that."

"Aoife . . ." Dean took both my hands and sat in one of the chairs. The floor of the farmhouse creaked ominously. "You trusted me to tell this much and I'm going to give you the same trust now, right?" Dean peered outside again. "What I'm saying, Aoife, is that in all the stories I've ever heard, you can't trust the Folk. Treacherous, tricksy, terrible, every one."

"Those are stories," I said. "You've never met the Folk. I have. I don't really have a choice but to do what they say."

315

"*No one's* met the Folk and lived to tell," Dean argued. "Otherwise, there'd be more than stories. Break it off, Aoife. I'd say the same if you were dating a deadbeat."

"You'd say that if I were dating anyone." I smiled. Dean didn't return it.

"Listen, princess. No one's debating your smarts. Those, you've got in spades. But I maintain, you shouldn't deal with the Folk. Nothing I've ever heard tells they want to do you a good turn."

"I have no choice." My good mood dissolved like the sunlight as more mist rolled in over the farmhouse. "He threatened you, and Cal, and if I don't do as he asks, I'll never find Conrad."

Dean's jaw twitched. "I ain't afraid of virals and I sure as gears grind ain't afraid of some grody paleface who skulks in mist."

"I am," I said frankly. "I don't have a family, Dean, except for Conrad and I don't have any friends in Lovecraft if I go back, besides Cal and you. I'd never forgive myself if you ran afoul of the Folk on my account."

"Tremaine, that's his name?" Dean grumbled. "At least I know which one of those pasty bastards asked for a boot in his ass."

I'd thought I was alone for my entire life, and more so when I discovered the truth about my family and its Weird. But Dean's angry, twitchy insistence on hearing stories of the Folk and his accepting my words without a thought weighed on me.

I could fret about what his reaction would be to a suggestion that he was something more than a simple heretic,

316

or I could ask him his truth in return for mine. My throat tightened, but I stilled my hands and looked at my reflection in Dean's hard, silvery eyes. They were like hammered steel, steady and unwavering. You'd think twice about messing with a gaze like Dean's.

"Dean," I said, rushing out the words before I lost nerve. "I know that you're like me."

He raised an eyebrow. "Like you how, princess?"

"You can find lost things and you never get lost yourself," I said. "You can make lamps light without fire. You know about the Folk and you don't say boo to the idea that I might have powers every normal person in the world insists are impossible. You're uncanny, Dean. You see the world the way it really is, not like the Proctors tell us it is. You see it like my father did."

Dean shied away with a jerk, dropping my hands. "You don't know what you're talking about, Aoife."

"I do," I whispered, holding back the sharp jab that his pulling away gave me. "Dean, tell me the truth. Please tell me that I'm not alone."

"I want to say I can help you, princess," Dean told me. "But I can't. All I can say is turn back, forget this and go home. But you won't, because you're you."

"Do you have a Weird, Dean?" I'd had an inkling when he'd done the trick with the lamp, and his behavior since hadn't changed my suspicion, only strengthened it. The question hung between us, filled up by the sound of sirens and the yelling of the crowd. I wished he'd just answer me, even if he was furious—his quiet was agonizing.

"I have a knack, I guess," Dean said at last. "I know true

317

north wherever I am and when something's lost and needs finding it calls out to me. But tricks like what your old man has—no. I'm not a special kind of guy, Aoife."

Rain had started, stippling the floorboards of the old house and drumming on the half-ruined roof. "So you knew all this time the Weird and the Folk were real and you just stayed quiet and let me thrash around on my own. Some pal you are, Dean Harrison."

He rubbed his forehead with his first two fingers. "Listen. You can't force it out of the blood. Either it wakes up or it doesn't. You can wish and dream all you like but the Weird chooses you, not the other way around." Dean jammed another cigarette in his mouth and lit up. "If I'd've said something, you would have had Cal bash my face in as a heretic loony before we'd taken two steps outside Lovecraft."

My anger at Dean's withholding nearly made me smack him, but I restrained myself. Dean was right, even if he infuriated me. Before I'd found the journal, I would have thought him mad, as everyone said I was. "I suppose," I granted him, glaring. "But that doesn't make lying to me all fine and good."

"I was just trying to—" Dean started, but I hushed him with a gesture.

"Look, I know," I said. "I know and I understand. But promise me you won't ever do something like that again. Promise me you'll trust me to handle it."

Dean still didn't move, staring into my eyes as if he could see the secret origin of the universe in them.

"This world . . . ," he sighed finally. "It ain't a nice world, Aoife. It's not clean or easy or kind. In a lot of ways, it's worse than living with Proctors marching over you."

"My life wasn't so great before I came here," I muttered. "Trust me."

"You accept this, you can never go home," Dean said. "You can never work with those machines you love. You can never be anything but a heretic to all of those nice, rational folks back there in Lovecraft. Because trust me on this, princess: they will turn on you faster than ghouls fighting over a corpse. That something you're willing to give up?"

I drew back, feeling like he'd slapped me. But I knew, even as I felt my eyes get hot and wet, that he was telling the truth. I could never go back. The Proctors would arrest me. I'd be *lucky* to be locked up with Nerissa after what I'd found here in Arkham.

I couldn't be inside even half a house for another second. I bolted, out into the rain, nearly turning my ankle several times as I raced through the forest.

Dean caught me easily enough, his long strides carrying him along with the heavy thump of steel-toed boots. "Aoife, for the love of grease and gears, hold up. I'm sorry. I shouldn't have laid it out so bluntlike."

I slowed, reluctantly. "You're right, Dean. That's the whole problem. I wrecked my life over a fantasy." Just like everyone had always insisted I would. "I should just give up this ridiculous notion of the Weird and everything now before I get you and Cal executed in Banishment Square."

He frowned. "Giving up ain't like you."

"Dean, you've known me for a week. You don't know what I'm like," I said. "Cal's got family to bat for him—he can go back to the School of Engines with a slap on the wrist. Even you can fade back into the Rustworks—you're clever and wicked enough."

319

Dean rubbed the back of his neck. "What about you, kid?"

"I've got nothing," I said. "I'd have to turn myself in and pray to the Master Builder for mercy, like a proper Rationalist."

"Is that really what you want?" The trail looped and started back up the incline toward Graystone. It seemed much longer going up, and the fog welcomed us with open arms.

"No . . ." I kicked a stone. "Of course it isn't, Dean. I *want* to believe that I can do things a normal girl could never dream of. I want to rescue my brother like a heroine in a story. But stories aren't real. What's real are the Proctors, and they're going to find us eventually."

"Are you afraid of them?" Dean said quietly.

"Of course I am!" I threw up my hands. "Aren't you?"

"I think there's worse things than being locked up for heresy," Dean said. "Much worse. And one of them is being so scared of it that you just sit and wait for them to find you." He stopped and seized me by the shoulders. "You're the first person I've met who won't sit and wait, Aoife. Don't change on me now. Please."

The mist closed, and for a moment, Dean and I were alone. In that moment, it was easy to nod my head, to promise, so Dean's smile would come back to his lips.

Because I *did* believe my father. And I wanted, more than anything, to not need the life I'd abandoned in Lovecraft.

"I won't," I said to Dean, and gently moved his hands from me. "I won't give up. I promise you."

Even if not giving up meant sacrificing everything. I'd come too far now to look back.

24

The Graveyard Below

DEAN TOOK OFF to the parlor to fiddle with the hi-fi when we reached Graystone, and I went back to the library. I didn't have any desire to read more of the journals, or converse with my father, but I felt restless and itchy in my skin, and books always had the virtue of calming me. They promised an escape for a few hours if nothing else, a brief forgetfulness of what I'd agreed to do for the Folk.

If Tremaine didn't simply drag me into the Thorn Land and cause me to disappear surely as my father and Conrad had vanished when I, inevitably, failed to grasp control of my Weird.

"You look so sad."

I turned from my perusal of my father's history books to find Cal, hands shoved in his pockets and rumpled. He looked so usual I almost burst into tears. I'd lose all that, in a little less than a week. Whether from the Folk or the Proctors or the necrovirus when it came to life in my blood

321

at the turning of my year, it didn't matter. My life, the one that had Cal in it, was over.

"I'm fine." I tried a game smile. Cal shook his head.

"You're a good liar for a girl, but not that good. What's wrong?"

"Nothing anyone can fix." I pulled down one of the books. *A History of Rational Thought.* It had been heavily annotated, and rested in my hands as thick and weighty as my mind and body felt.

"Did Dean do something to make you this way? I'll pound his face in." Cal started for the door. "He may be big and carry that switchblade—"

"Cal, stop." I put the book down on the desk and went to him. "It's not Dean. It's me. I thought . . . I thought I'd found something special in the library above, and then you and I had that awful fight . . ." I pressed my fingers against my temples, dug in my nails. Used the pain to stave off tears. "Cal, I think I was wrong about coming here. You should go back to Lovecraft. You should get on with your life."

I expected another lecture on my relative madness, or for Cal to simply bolt like a dog freed from a kennel, back into the waiting arms of the School and the Proctors.

Instead, he nearly smothered me when he threw his arms around my frame. "I could never leave you," he said. "*Never.*"

I returned his embrace, tight and hard as I could. To touch someone else with no expectation of a result, or to worry about hiding my true nature, felt like all of my burdens, for just a moment, dropped off my shoulders.

I clung to Cal until he gently let go and smoothed my

322

ruffled hair behind my ears. "Now, it can't be all bad. Let's get out of this stuffy old room and you can tell me about it."

"I wish that it weren't," I sighed. "Truly."

"Come on." Cal punched me lightly on the shoulder. "Day's still young and there's lots of grounds to explore yet. We can be adventurers for an hour or two and I bet you forget all about what's bugging you."

Even after my walk with Dean, I felt relieved at something other than my father and brother and our fate as a family to occupy my thoughts. I got my cape and Cal his coat, and we took the kitchen door, but instead of turning to the orchard, Cal chose the boxwood path that curved around the west wing of the mansion. The maze was largely dead, the walls a phantom suggestion of the winding paths that once grew on the spot.

Beyond the boxwood there was a long lawn sloping down to a pond and a few tumbledown stone structures surrounded by an iron fence.

"That's the cemetery I told you about," Cal said. "It's boss. Want to see?"

"I suppose," I said. I didn't take the same delight that Cal did in boneyards. The dead didn't bother much. Live people were utterly worse.

"No iron rods in the ground that I saw," Cal said. "Hasn't been swept for ghouls and . . . you know. Walkers."

I rolled my eyes at him. "Cal, the necrovirus can't make corpses walk. That's a myth."

"You don't know that." He shuddered. "I've seen lots this past week that people back home call myths."

We crossed the lawn, agreement to visit the cemetery unspoken. "You know what Conrad used to say when

323

things went wrong?" I asked Cal. "I'd be sad or angry, and he'd pick out whatever was bothering me, and he'd fix all the broken pieces and say, 'There. All the stars in the sky where they're supposed to be.'"

"I wish that were still true." Cal stopped at the cemetery fence.

"Me too." But it wasn't, so I nudged him on the elbow because I was, all at once, fully sick of moping around. Conrad wouldn't give up and knuckle under to his fate with the Folk.

Conrad would master his Weird, and he'd fight. And I was his sister, and in his stead the least I could do was pick up the sword. "Come on," I told Cal. "Let's take a look at the dear departed Graysons."

The gate groaned when I pushed it open, and my feet sank into soft piles of rotted leaves that had gathered autumn upon countless autumn without disturbance.

I brushed the vegetation away from the nearest headstone. Wind and water had nearly obliterated the words carved into the bone-white limestone, and all I could see were the dates of birth and death, 1914–1932.

"Not much older than us," I said to Cal. I wondered if this Grayson had died of natural causes, or if something with teeth had come out of the mists. What was the life expectancy of my family? Not long, according to my father's book.

Cal rattled the door of the single mausoleum, tilted to one side like the earth was a deck of a ship, and peered through the gap.

"Cal, don't," I said. "That's grim."

"It's open," he said, sticking his head inside despite my

look of disapproval. "Oh, lighten up, Aoife. There's no pine boxes in here, just one of those whaddyacallits. The Greek things."

"Sarcophagus?" I rose and joined him at the narrow door.

"You always aced Greek," Cal said. "I don't understand what an engineer needs a dead language for."

"Archimedes was Greek," I pointed out. Cal ducked into the crypt and poked around behind the stone coffin. It was carved with mythological scenes, a weeping willow bending over a river, while a hooded figure poled the water. It looked similar to the Star Sister's illuminations of the path to R'lyeh, their eternal land in the stars, but there were no spaceways or starships, just the boatman, the river and his burden of souls.

The stony waves on the river rippled before my eyes, and a throb went through my forehead, through my bones, through the healing shoggoth bite in my shoulder. I felt as if I'd tilted along with the sarcophagus and was falling, my mind compressing like it had when the owl attacked me in the library. The warning that something had made the world not right.

Not here, I thought, my heartbeat turning frantic. *Not again.* An attack of the Weird I couldn't control wasn't worse than no Weird at all. Who knew what would happen in this crypt, what traps existed? I could bring the whole thing down on me and Cal.

"There are stairs back here!" Cal's shout yanked me back to the present, and the awful pressure on my bones and my brain faded away.

"Really?" I skirted the sarcophagus widely as I could,

325

brushing against the stones of the crypt and trying to act as if I were merely scared of ghosts.

"They go way down." Cal lowered himself into the small passageway. "Looks like the bootlegger tunnels, maybe. This could be where they stored the hooch."

"They'd bury it in coffins during Prohibition," I agreed. "But we shouldn't, Cal." The tomb felt too close, too cold. It reminded me too much of a madhouse cell.

"Oh, don't be a goose," he said, wriggling into the passage. "It's daytime." His head disappeared, and I looked back at the daylight in the door, which seemed impossibly far.

"Not underground, it's not."

Cal's shout echoed from somewhere that sounded miles below. "Come on! It's crazy down here, just like *The Mummy* or something!"

I huffed out a sigh. Cal was such a boy—show him something shiny, ancient or hidden and all rational thought flew out of his head. "Now who's being a goose? Cal, come back here!"

No reply floated back to me, and I could hear Cal scuffling away in the passage below, lost to my shouting range.

I sat down and scooted until I could crouch and stand, descending the stairs after him. The passage was narrow, but light trickled in from somewhere above, and air breathed over my face as I wound deeper, down into the earth.

"Cal!" I caught up with him at a turn in the passage, where the earthen tunnel met a stone main, some long-forgotten artery for water running from the north, where the cider house sat, to the south, where at one time a dairy or barn would have had a cistern.

326

The water was gone now and only dust and the skeletons of rats and unlucky birds remained. I rubbed my arms, my gooseflesh not born from the cold air.

"This is great!" Cal's face was flushed even in the low light. All of the lumpy planes of his face stood out in sharp relief, and his long slumped frame filled the low space of the tunnel. Cal cupped his hands and bellowed down the passage. "Hello!"

"This isn't great, it's silly," I groused. Making Cal think the tunnel wasn't a grand adventure was the quickest way to get him back aboveground. "There's nothing down here and it's filthy and it smells funny. It's just an old hole."

"You have no imagination," said Cal. "It could be bootlegger tunnels, or smugglers. . . ." He took another twitchy, excited step and jerked his head at me. "Just come! I want to see where this goes."

"Cal, no," I said. "All of Graystone is rigged to its clockwork. You don't know what we could be walking into . . ."

Before I could finish, Cal's foot depressed an iron plate concealed by a gap in the stone flags that made up the floor. A great hand rattled the ground under our feet, tired gears shrieked and at the far end of the tunnel, where shadows congregated, an iron gate rolled back.

". . . down here," I finished, half expecting iron teeth to flash from some hidden place and finish us off. My heartbeat redoubled.

"Neat," Cal breathed. "Did you see that? It's a secret tunnel!"

"It was aces," I said, copying Dean's most drawn-out drawl of boredom so Cal wouldn't hear my voice shake. "You found a hole inside a bigger hole. You're my hero."

327

"You know, Aoife, that Dean has given you a regular snippy mouth," Cal grumbled. "Time was you'd have thought this was fantastic."

"Dean didn't need to say a thing to make me not want to be crammed under the ground," I snapped. "I don't like it down here, Cal. It could be dangerous."

"I'll protect you," he dismissed me, pulling back his lips so that his teeth gleamed in a bony smile. "Don't be scared, Aoife."

"Dean says—" I started, but before I could finish telling Cal that fear kept people alive, my shoulder began to throb anew. After my experience with the thing at the window I knew what was coming. From the dark of the newly opened tunnel, I heard the scrabble of clawed feet over rock. The snuffle of nostrils taking the air. The grind of teeth on bone.

"Cal?" My voice came out high and paper thin, with good reason I thought. Those sounds were from something alive. "Am I hearing things, or is there something in there?"

Cal's expression had gone from delight to terror in the space of a candle flame flickering. "I think we should go," he said finally, foot jostling foot as he tried to back away and succeeded only in stumbling. "Right now."

I tried to move with him, but hot steam pain from the bite in my shoulder seared through all parts of me. This was worse than the owl. This was worse than anything.

Cal grabbed for my hand, and his touch was like plunging my fingers into liquid nitrogen. I screamed and doubled over, bruising my knees on the tunnel floor as I batted him away frantically, only wanting the pain to cease.

From my vantage I watched pieces of the darkness

ahead break free from the tunnel mouth and crawl along the walls, growing limbs and teeth and tails. Hides gleamed like oil-stained water and high-pitched cackling like nails on glass filled the air.

I knew that sound. And nothing I knew about it was going to help us stay alive.

"Aoife!" Cal had me up and moving away from the shadow hounds, like a puppet on a string, and then his foot caught in a crack and we both went down again.

I landed hard on my wounded shoulder and screamed, and the cry that answered me ripped from no human throat. It echoed off the tunnel, a howl of hunger and delight.

The howling was younger than what Dean and I had heard on the roof, but the things coming for us were ghouls just the same. Pups, a flock of them, trapped and starved by Graystone's defenses.

We weren't getting out of the tunnel in less than a dozen pieces.

"I'm sorry," Cal choked. "Aoife, I'm so sorry, I should have known. . . ."

Dizzy with agony, my skull pulsing like it would burst, all I could do was watch as the ghouls bounded toward us, clinging to the stones of the ceiling as easily as if it were the floor. They were the size of hunting dogs and bore whiplash tails, teeth like straight razors hanging over bloody cut lips, and blue tongues lolling with black spittle. Their eyes glowed yellow, like the Proctor's ravens, but aether and gears wasn't powering these devils. Only hunger drove them, and only flesh would sate it.

Cal was screaming, yelling something over and over, but

329

through the agony that my body had been consumed by, I couldn't understand his pleadings.

The leader of the ghouls landed in front of me, dropping from the tunnel roof, twisting his horrible glistening body in midair. He was stocky, with a smushed face like a Chinese dog, and stood on his hind legs while he scented, deep and drafty. His mouth opened in a grin and he gibbered to his fellows.

"This one tastes like fresh meat. Whiter'n a dead thing, her skin."

I choked in terror, tears of pain dribbling down my face. The ghoul's speech sounded like that of the drunkards on the last jitney to Uptown in the evenings, but to hear speech coming from that razor-tipped mouth stirred a bleak horror in me greater than any viral creature I'd yet witnessed. The ghouls weren't mindless, like the shoggoth. I knew from endless lanternreels and lectures that they were intelligent pack hunters, and they'd brought us to bay.

"Let me taste her, Tanner." A thin one with a spotty hide slid forward. *"Been so long in a cage. So long since we had anything live."*

"Get off, you." The one named Tanner swatted at the upstart with a paw the size of a dinner plate. *"You can have the chitterlings that smell like death. The soft one's meat is for me."*

I couldn't hold my vision steady any longer, and I ground the heel of my palm into my forehead in an attempt to drive out the pain. Beyond the scraping of the ghoul's guttural snarls there was something in my head, something cold and swelling to bursting. Black whirlpools formed in front of my eyes and my breath caught.

330

Perhaps I would faint, and wake up with the wandering things in the mists, the corpse-drinkers. Perhaps I'd wake up in the star-home of R'lyeh, with the Great Old Ones.

Either way, the cold knowledge that I was about to perish cut through the pain in my head, and on its heels came the desperate thrashing desire to stay alive.

I heard a slow ticking, the clockwork of my heartbeat. It quickened even as everything around me went fuzzy, loose and slow from pain and panic.

Tick. Tick. Tick. Tock.

Everything went very still, hard and cold inside of me. This wasn't like the owl in the library, a sudden burst of Weird ripped free by the root, leaving a bleeding hole. I died for a split second, and in that time something living in me silently until that moment uncoiled, wrapped itself around my mind and squeezed.

My Weird blossomed again and I allowed it to spread all through me like molten ore. I felt the iron of the gate mesh with the iron in my blood, the clockwork of the mechanism turning wheels and gears inside my head. It didn't feel like madness or pain, or anything like the necrovirus that had gripped me after the shoggoth bite.

It felt like I had put on clockwork wings and learned how to make them fly.

And then I could see again. My breath scraped in and out, my lungs burning like I'd dunked my head in a swimming pool. The pain was gone and in its place was a pinpoint of cold, tingling sensation that I recognized from stepping through the *hexenring*. Enchantment was riding my blood, and my Weird was demanding to be set free.

331

The ghouls snarled at me, their hungry mouths inches from my flesh.

I was freezing, and under my fingertips I felt iron, even though I wasn't touching anything but air. I breathed in and out, and I could feel the parts of Graystone protecting the tunnel respond.

The gate snapped shut behind the ghouls, rusted mechanism shrieking protest at the speed.

Tanner, the enormous ghoul, levered his heavy head around like a wrecking ball. *What's going on? My blood's burning!"*

It wasn't enough. The creatures were still in the tunnel with me and Cal and could still harm us. I reached out, pushing the spear of the Weird out from my mind, and found gear wheels and metal teeth lying in wait all around us. I tugged at them, feeling the resultant stab of agony through my chest and heart. With a rumble and a groan, Graystone's majestic machine woke from its slumber.

A spring snapped, and the echo filled my skull.

I was the machine. The machine was me.

Rusted spikes shot from the floor and walls, in and out, random grids covered in old blood but still sharp.

Tanner's foot exploded as iron bored a hole in his flesh. The ghouls howled and screamed, as their blue blood spattered the stones and coated the spikes.

"What's happening?" Cal shouted, covering his ears as a ghoul fell, screaming, between us. Cal watched it convulse in horror, his mouth hanging open and his face ashen.

The machine was in my blood, its gears turning brilliant in my brain. My fear had vanished, and all that fed my impulses was the Weird.

332

I could feel all of Graystone, a great pulsing, shuddering, breathing thing with its heart of steam. I knew that what I asked of it, the house would give.

I demanded the death of the ghouls, and the house gifted me with a sacrifice. I didn't move, didn't let go of Cal, until the last howl of despair had ceased and the last droplet of brackish blood had spattered the stones.

Cal and I managed to get to our feet. He was quaking like he was made of paper, but I pulled him to me and together we limped back to the stairway to the light. My knees were skinned and bleeding, and my shoulder, where the shoggoth bit me, was an agony of flame, but I felt light. Free. Floating. The Weird whispered, curled and fell back to sleep inside me, leaving me wrung out, as if I'd just run until exhaustion.

"Why are you smiling?" Cal demanded. He'd clearly been too panicked to suss what was really going on, and for that I was relieved. I didn't properly understand it yet. I'd be hopeless at explaining.

Cal panted as we stumbled up the stairs and into the crisp autumn air. "We could have died, you realize." Elated as I felt, Cal looked proportionately haggard. His skin almost seemed to droop over the bones of his face and he was sweating through his coat, damp wool under my hand as I leaned on him for support.

"We didn't," I said. "They didn't get us, Cal. We're alive." A small laugh escaped me, pure adrenaline given voice. I'd survived. I'd saved myself and Cal. "I did it, Cal," I whispered. "I found it."

"Alive. Great," Cal said flatly. "What are you on about?"

"Cheer up, Cal!" I demanded, punching him in the

333

shoulder. "Not even a pack of hungry ghouls can stop me! Think of what you'll have to tell the guys now."

"Crazy girl," Cal said, but without malice. He slumped against the sarcophagus, breathing heavily, shaking. I rubbed his back and patted his neck with my handkerchief until he stopped sweating and quivering. After a moment, color began to return to his face and he lost the morbid walking-corpse pallor, the dark veins no longer standing out under his sagging skin. Once he looked like my friend again, I got us up.

"Let's go back to the house. I don't know about you, but I feel like my head might wobble off." The overwhelming sensory push of the Weird was wearing off, and I could feel my hands and knees beginning to shake like they hadn't before. It seemed the harder I pushed, the more of a toll it took. But I could figure it out. I could figure all of it out, because I was alive.

"You don't look so hot," Cal agreed. "Come on. Let me help you before you fall down."

"I'm not crazy yet," I said, and breathed deep of the day. I had found my Weird. I had Cal back. I wasn't crazy and I might not *turn* crazy, either. For just a moment, as Cal and I walked arm in arm to Graystone, it was enough.

25

The Arcane Payment

BACK IN GRAYSTONE, in my room, I slept away the pain and creeping fatigue that overtook me on the walk from the graveyard.

When I woke, I found myself covered and with plumped pillows behind my head. My ceiling was stained with the same alien world map, the blankets were the same itchy wool. My shoes were missing, but otherwise I was just as I'd been before the ghouls.

"Cal?" I'd had dreams, dark and dripping blood. The ghouls could hurt Cal. If I wasn't there, wasn't able to pull him free from their jaws, they'd take him to their nest, consume him, turn his face into the twisted snarling things that snapped at me from the dark. . . .

The door to my room swung open of its own volition, with a rifle crack. A simple hinge assembling, connected to rods and wheels in the hollow walls of the mansion, they ran through the place like a cold-blooded nervous system.

I hissed and pressed a hand against my forehead. The Weird appeared to come out when I lost control of myself, got upset or panicked, like when I'd stopped the library clock. I needed to rein it in before something other than a ghoul stepped into its path and I hurt someone. My father didn't run about setting people on fire—I'd have to get better at using my talent.

Dean's face appeared in the frame, and he looked at the door askance. "I think your castle needs a tune-up, princess."

"That's not all it needs," I said. "Have you seen Cal?" My door swung back with another rifle shot, and Dean flinched.

"He's downstairs blabbing Bethina to death about his grand adventure in the zombie's tomb, or whatever did happen when you two went off." Dean sat next to me and the dubious bedsprings bowed under his weight. "You've been sleeping like you pricked your finger on a spindle, kid."

I rubbed my shoulder, but the shoggoth's bite had gone back to being just a sore patch, shallow cuts and bruising.

"I guess I fainted?"

"More like passed out cold," Dean said. "You came back from your jaunt looking pale and walleyed, babbled something about blood underground and staggered up here. By the time I got after you, you'd fallen asleep and all the rockets both sides dropped in the war couldn't have stirred you."

My head felt hollowed out and I was fatigued as if I'd run for miles. The Weird whispered, scratching at my senses, begging to be let free. I shut my eyes. The talent in

336

my blood had wrung me out and I felt in my bones that if I let the Weird go now I'd never get control of it again.

"There were ghouls down there," I said. "Down under the ground. Cal wanted to explore the crypt in the cemetery, and he opened the ghoul trap by accident and let them out."

"Sounds like our cowboy," said Dean with a toothy grimace. "You all in one piece? Or did they get a bite?"

"No . . . I killed them." I looked up at Dean. "I got the trap working again, and the house . . . it killed them. I was the house. My Weird . . ."

My hands were still frozen and blue-veined and I shoved them under the blanket. "I can feel it, walking around in my head. The machines and the house. My Weird can speak to them and I hear them now. Whispering."

The sensation when I'd been lying there, a handbreadth away from bloody scraps for ghoul pups to fight over, of a vast and sleeping consciousness sharing my head, came back with a rush and I grabbed Dean's arm. It was bare, exposed by the short sleeves of his white T-shirt, and I blushed at the feel of his skin.

"Cripes, Aoife." He rubbed my hand between his palms. "You're freezing."

"I think it's a side effect," I said. "I got so cold when I used my Weird in the tunnel, I thought I could never move again."

"You know what they say." Dean tucked the blanket around me and edged closer. "Cold hands, warm heart."

"My mother used to say that," I murmured without thinking.

337

"You don't mention the old lady much," Dean said. "What's her story?"

Dean Harrison knew more about me than anyone but Nerissa herself. He knew, and he hadn't spilled a word to anyone.

"My mother is in a madhouse back in Lovecraft."

It came in a rush, once I'd decided to break the dam on my worst secret. "She contracted the necrovirus before Conrad and I were born and she started to lose her grip when she was pregnant with me, I mean really lose it. She could still fake sane when Conrad was a baby, I guess. They say everyone in our family goes mad, usually at sixteen—it's our strain, our particular virus—so, you see, it doesn't matter that I've found out all this about the Folk and the Weird. In no time at all, I won't remember you or myself or any of this." I gestured at the faded grandeur of my bedroom. Tremaine could threaten me, but he'd never frighten me as much as the thought of losing who I was to the virus, leaving Cal and now Dean behind and becoming just another deluded madwoman locked in a cell.

I could do as Tremaine asked, but I was still afraid, if I were honest, that I wouldn't be around to see the result. I'd just have to help him and his queens and pray my effort kept my friends safe.

"I had no idea," Dean whispered.

I scrubbed the heel of my hand across my eyes. I'd cried over the situation enough. "Yes, well, it's not a tidbit I go spreading around."

Dean shifted, leaning down on his elbow so we were roughly perpendicular. "Cal know?"

I nodded, a small gesture because the memory still

338

strangled me when it broke to the forefront. "He was there when my brother tried to kill me. On Conrad's birthday."

Cal held up his hands. Big and ungainly, like puppy paws. "Conrad, don't hurt your sister. She's all you have."

Dean whistled. "So Conrad gave you that scar."

I didn't have to confirm his suspicions. Dean knew. "The virus incubated and it came out as madness," I said. "He didn't know what he was doing, Dean. He's still my brother."

Dean shook his head slowly. "That's a hell of a thing, Aoife."

"It's your payment, Dean." I smiled even though I felt more like screaming. The door hinges tensed, but I bit down hard on the inside of my cheeks, balled the Weird up inside my chest and kept it small. The door stayed where it was.

Rubbing his face with both hands, Dean shut his eyes. "I don't want it. This is the kind of secret that never stops bleeding."

"I can't keep hiding from everyone in the world," I said softly. "It's becoming everything I am. Like a shadow that falls only on you even though the sun is out." The stone of madness dogged my ankles even as I felt the Weird spurring me to fly, as it had in the cemetery tunnel.

"I don't want it," Dean said again. "You didn't have to tell me this, even for payment. I . . ." But he trailed off, shoving a hand through his hair, so it fell every which way.

"I expect you'll be leaving, then," I said. "And I thank you for all of your help. Truly. I won't inconvenience you any longer." I felt the thickness of tears behind my eyes, and despised it. Some Gateminder I was, crying over a boy.

339

Dean stood up and went to the door, wiggling it experimentally as if it might decide to slam shut on his knuckles. "I get that you've had a lot of running out in your life, princess. A lot of empty rooms and doors slammed in your face. But you paid me fair and square, even if it's not what I wanted, so dig this when I say it: I'm not leaving you alone. I don't run out."

For the first time that day, I managed a real, if wan, smile. I believed Dean when he made his promises, and I wanted to kiss him for it. Stone it, I wanted to kiss Dean Harrison for any old reason at all, but I settled for saying, "You're one of the good ones, Dean."

"I'm about as far from good as you can get without running into it again," he said. "But I keep my bargains and my word is my bond." He flashed me a smile that was far from his usual killer grin—no, he looked like any boy trying to find a way to ask a girl on a date without stumbling over his feet, his words, or both. I wondered if Dean had ever been that Dean, before he went to the heretics and started guiding in the Rustworks.

He came back and tousled the hair on top of my head, fingers spreading a little static electricity between us. "Rest, princess. It's been a very long day."

"Yes, it has indeed," I said, but instead of obeying Dean I swung my legs over the bed and found my boots. "Could you get Bethina to make me some coffee?" The Weird had exhausted me, and I contemplated that if this was what I had to look forward to every time I tapped the enchantment in my blood, I was going to go through a lot of hot beverages.

"That's pretty much the opposite of resting your bones,"

340

Dean said. "But I don't think we need to bother Bethina over a cuppa. I learned to brew a pretty good pot when my old man had the third shift at the foundry."

"Good," I said. "Because if I'm going to break Tremaine's curse, I'm going to need all the help I can scrounge."

26

The Bottomless Room

AFTER DEAN HAD made a pot of strong coffee, he poured me a mug and followed me into the library. "Feel like an assist, princess?"

"I'd like that," I said as he helped me onto the ladder. Apparently, we weren't speaking about what I'd shared with him upstairs, and that suited me just fine.

Dean sneezed when he came through the hatch into the library above. "Dusty as old bones up here."

"Look for anything about the Folk," I told him. "Tremaine knows everything about me and I know nothing about them, except that they like to play tricks."

"And I could have told you that." Dean flashed me a grin and reached for a book. He stopped, hand fluttering in front of the shelves on the far side of the attic.

I joined him, staring at the gap between the journals and papers, which revealed nothing to my eye except water-stained plaster. "What's wrong?"

Dean's eyebrows drew together. "You know there's another room back here, right?"

I snapped my gaze to his. "What?"

"Another room," Dean said. "I feel it. Open space, hidden space." He shook his head, like someone had slapped him. "A place that got lost. I found it."

Hidden rooms in hidden rooms. Perhaps this room held what I needed to fulfill my bargain with Tremaine.

"There's got to be a locking lever and a switch here somewhere," I said. I put my hand on the wood near Dean's trembling palm. I let my own Weird unfurl, ever so delicately, like letting just a few grains from a handful of sand slip through your fingertips. The switch twitched against my mind, the lock and the wheels all clicking into place with that pressing fullness.

It wasn't nearly as torturous as when the ghouls had found Cal and me, but it hurt more than enough. After a moment the entire section of wall swung away, ponderous under the weight of its volumes.

"Our own little hideaway," Dean said. "I think I might like this."

"Behave yourself," I said. Abruptly my feet were as unsteady as if we were at sea. I couldn't be distracted by Dean and what he did to me, even if I wanted to be for the first time ever, with anyone.

Dean's lighter snapped and the dancing flame sent slivers of bright into the corners of the dingy space beyond. He sucked in a breath, focusing the blue flame on my face. "You're leaking, doll."

I felt under my nose with the back of my hand, saw the skin streaked crimson black. "Dammit," I said, swiping at the blood.

343

Dean held out his bandanna with his free hand. "Put your head forward until it stops."

I did as he bade, and he watched me with a calculating eye. "This happen every time?" he said quietly.

I shrugged as best I could with a blood-soaked rag on my face. "I'll let you know once I've used it more than twice," I told him, muffled. The trickle of red from my nose eventually ceased, and I laid the rag aside. Taking a moment to compose myself, I nodded at Dean.

"Let's take a look at this hideaway of yours, shall we?" I was relieved that I kept the quiver out of my voice. If this was the result of using the Weird to open a door, what would happen if I tried to stop a jitney or manipulate Graystone's clockwork in earnest? I didn't particularly care to think of it at the moment.

"This is something else," Dean said, as the lighter's flickering flame caressed the hidden room with fingers of shadow and light.

I spied a worktable, covered with bundles of plants and bell jars of long-dead animal specimens, a ruin of gears and machine parts alongside all the trappings of witchcraft that we'd been warned of by the Proctors—chalk, candles, red string and black, petrified frogs and eyeballs of unknown origin. Enough evidence to earn the owner a stint in the Catacombs that only ended when he was carried out dead. Claiming to believe in this stuff was bad enough. Actually practicing it, even though the Proctors repeated over and over and over that magic was fake and witches were only charlatans, was a death sentence back home.

And it might be here too, though for very different reasons.

344

"This is some workshop," Dean said. "I don't know what your old man was up to, but this isn't something I'd let get around."

"I think my life's complicated enough," I agreed. I investigated the curio cases and devices scattered about the perimeter of the room. A few I'd seen before, in lantern-reels or in my textbooks. A bell-shaped diving helmet with a pair of air filters attached to the front; a hand telescope with a plethora of extra lenses, attached to a pair of goggles and a headband; and a gun-shaped device with a glass bulb soldered to the end. Aether swished back and forth gently inside the barrel, blossoming and folding within the glass.

I started for the cabinet, but Dean curled his fingers around my shoulder. "Could be dangerous."

"I'll take my chances," I said. I picked up the goggles and slipped them over my eyes. The lens in place at the moment was blue, and the room jumped into sharp black-and-white relief. I rotated the brass dial on the rim of the hand telescope, and a wavering green-blue lens that picked up Dean as an outline of crimson body heat moved into place, followed by a lens that outlined all of the witchcraft paraphernalia in the workshop in bilious green, wavering like seaweed in a current. My vision bulged as if I were looking through a fish's eye, throwing me off balance and roiling my stomach until I removed the set from my eyes. The effect wasn't as bad as the one caused by the goggles Tremaine had given me, but these goggles were definitely something of my father's design. I'd never seen anything like them.

I smoothed my hair. "These things are incredible," I said, pulse quickening. Devices, machines—this sort of thing was familiar, and yet exciting, because I had never seen

345

machines like these in Lovecraft. "Want to try?" I asked Dean.

He shook his head with a smile. "Not much scares you, does it, Aoife?"

"Plenty," I said. "Plenty scares me. But not the dark and what *might* be in there. I've plenty of facts that frighten me more than shadows and spooks."

"Spooks are spooks for a reason," Dean said. "I've seen a few things that'd straighten your hair."

I started to tell Dean that the specter of encroaching madness, the ever-present Proctors and knowing that your life had a chronometer attached to it was worse than any ghost tale, but before I could, the world fell away.

The twisting, churning, falling sensation was worse this time, my being stretched thin across too many universes. Dean's hand slipped from mine, and I heard the flutter of a thousand wings before I landed, upright, in a room lit only by firelight.

"There, now," Tremaine said. "I did tell you we'd speak again."

"'S not been a week yet," I panted. "I have more time."

Dean, mercifully, was with me when I glanced over. He went down on a knee and clutched at his forehead. "What in the frozen starry hell is all this?"

"Dean," I sighed, "this is Tremaine."

Tremaine stepped forward and held out his hand to me. "My dear. You may leave the *hexenring*." His cold pale eyes locked on Dean. "Your companion, however, stays where he is. He has the sheen of clever wickedness about him."

346

"Get bent, paleface," Dean gritted. His face was bereft of color except for two spots of flame in his cheeks, and sweat marked all the hollows of his face.

"Breathe," I told him, trying to let him know with my eyes we'd be all right. "It gets better."

"Hurry along, child," Tremaine said. "Decades are running through the boy's fingers while you dawdle. You don't want to have an old, gray steed in place of a fine yearling when we're through, do you?"

"I'm not ready to help you," I insisted. "I'm still learning how to use the Weird."

"Aoife, I did not bring you to chastise you." Tremaine let go of my hand as soon as I'd crossed the *hexenring*. The floor of the room was earthen and white mushrooms sprouted in every corner, phosphorescent in the dim light. It was a haunted place, all shadow and glow. The walls were composed of rushes, sprouting moss that swayed overhead like the sighing of lost souls. The fire itself was purple-tinged and ghostly. The only solid, dead thing in the room was a stone table, with deep grooves in the sides and a depression at one end.

Tremaine passed his fingers against the hollowed spot and gave me a smile so sharp I felt it against my throat. "This is where the head rests during the full moon, you know. There is a hole in the ceiling and in their final moment, one may view the cold fire of our stars."

"Dreadful machines," I murmured, my stomach turning over. "That seems to be your hallmark."

Tremaine's smile dropped off. "You weren't defiant last time we spoke. I prefer that."

"This is what you get," I said, sticking out my chin. It

347

had started as Dean's gesture, but I'd adopted it as my own. "You can like it or not. If you hadn't lied about how much time I had, I might be more inclined to behave."

Tremaine moved around the table, his image blinking in and out like a faulty lanternreel. One moment he was feet from me, the next he loomed up in my vision and his knuckles connected with my face, a sharp backhand slap that echoed inside the domed room.

I stumbled, felt my head ring from the blow and couldn't believe Tremaine had actually hit me. Dean rushed at Tremaine, but the Folk held up a pale beringed hand.

"You step over that line, boy, and you will disintegrate like so much dust in a storm. Think before you do it, greaseblood. Think very hard."

Dean pulled his boot back from the line of toadstools. "All right," he gritted. "But don't think I won't pay you in full for hitting her."

Tremaine turned his back on Dean like he was no more than a mumbling hobo on a Lovecraft street and pulled me up from my hunched position. "Now that I've knocked you sensible, Aoife, you need to listen." He gripped me hard, hard enough to grind my wrist bones. "Come along. There's a good girl."

"Dean . . . ," I said as Tremaine jerked me toward the long grass-woven curtains that served as the door of the dome. I couldn't leave Dean. Not here.

"This is not for his ears," Tremaine said. We passed through the curtain and I gasped to find myself back in the lily field.

Under the cold steel moon, the coffins of the queens glowed. The light writhed and caressed the sleeping visage of the Folk girls, an unearthly borealis that turned the flowers and the faces of the queens into something spectral and transparent, an illusion that flickered and flamed and danced.

"Don't think I enjoyed that," Tremaine said. "I do not take pleasure in pain."

My face throbbed, and I could taste a little blood where my cheek scraped my teeth. I swallowed it and didn't say anything, just glared and hoped Tremaine would melt under my gaze.

"You've used the Weird," Tremaine said. "But you don't understand it. I tell you now, what you need for my task can't be found in the shortsighted journal of a foolish man."

"My father isn't foolish," I said. Cold, yes. Unloving, maybe. But never foolish. Tremaine folded his arms.

"Aoife, with respect: you don't know the man."

"Well, either way, I can't do what you ask," I muttered stubbornly, even though he was right. "You may as well end me now," I said, and then outright lied. "I don't even know if I have a Weird."

"You do, and it is prodigious," Tremaine said. "Your gift for lying, less so. I've seen your Weird."

"How . . ." I liked to think that I'd know when Tremaine was spying on me. With his powdery skin and skeleton-white hair, he wasn't exactly blending into the landscape.

But perhaps he didn't need to see me to watch me. I didn't know the full power of the Folk. I shivered, and rubbed my hands together, tucking them up in my sleeves.

"My eyes venture far," Tremaine murmured. "Even if my body cannot. In both Thorn and Iron. They are all colors, all shapes. Silent eyes on silent wing." He was smirking at me,

349

and all at once the memory of shattering window glass and the shriek of the ghouls rushed back.

"You sent that *thing* after me!" I cried. "In the library. And again in the cemetery!"

Tremaine nodded mildly, polishing one of his bracers with his opposite sleeve. "I did send the strix owl, as incentive to defend yourself with your Weird. I don't know of any cemetery."

"You almost killed me," I snarled. "I could have—"

"The poisoned queens sleep eternal." Tremaine cut through my words with the sharpness of his tone. "In the old times, the shining times, we would gather at the Winnowing Stone and harness its great bounty to awaken the sleepers from their curse. But now no magic borne of the Thorn Land can wake them. This is the truth. This is the curse." He turned his gaze from the lilies and the coffins. "It falls to you, Aoife, you and your Weird, to find a way."

I swallowed hard, trying to keep up the toughness I had started with. "I don't know what you expect me to—"

He reached out and put a hand on my face, cupping the cheek that he had struck. "There was once a great spark in the races of your world, Aoife. But it has extinguished, gone to ash, all but the barest ember. From the ashes of magic has risen the phoenix of the machine. That is what I seek."

His fingers tightened on my cheek, diamond chips of nails digging against my skin. "My world is dying, Aoife, and by symbiosis yours is as well. Ours is a sudden and violent cataclysm, and yours is a death spiral into the entropy of reason." Tremaine's nails drew blood from my cheek. "You are something never seen before, in the history of your

350

bloodline," he whispered. "You will rekindle the flame. You will cleanse this insidious plague of science by fire."

I struggled, but he held fast with the desperate grip of a drowning man. "You will awaken the queens, Aoife. And to free my lands from the shackles of so-called enlightenment, I will do what I must." He leaned in so that our faces nearly touched. "Forcing a stubborn child to do her chores is the least of my reach, Aoife. Continue to defy me and see what else I can send to find you."

"You're hurting me," I whispered. What Tremaine was asking me to do was impossible—my father had said so—but I had a feeling that objections would just get me slapped again. And Tremaine seemed sincere, even his anger born more from the desperation in his eyes than any deceit that I could see.

Releasing his grip, Tremaine wiped the blood away from my skin with the tips of his fingers. "Don't force me to hurt you worse to convince you of your importance to me, Aoife. Break the curse. Bring light back to both of our worlds."

"I can't . . ." Tears started, stinging the cuts and mingling with my blood. *Have you ever seen blood under starlight, Aoife? When it's black?* "I can barely control it," I said, thinking of the great pressure on my head when I'd slain the ghouls, the pain and cold that had nearly stopped my heart. How was I supposed to break a curse? I didn't even know how to make my Weird respond unless I was about to be eaten or clawed to death.

"Aoife," Tremaine sighed. "You have spirit and a certain fey quality that reminds me of my own daughters, may they travel through the Mists unharmed. But these are the

351

darkest hours of my people. If you confound me, you will not appreciate the consequences."

I was trembling all over, from cold and from plain-faced, ugly fear, but I managed to keep my voice steady, because I was keeping my vow to not show weakness to Tremaine. "And if I do, and still refuse?"

"Why, then," Tremaine said softly, "the terms still stand: I will come to Graystone and forfeit the lives of Dean and dear Cal. And you will never know Conrad's fate, and both of us will live to see the end of our species' existence."

I looked back at the hut, imagining Dean aging by the year inside the *hexenring*. Imagining him or Cal lying dead on the library floor by Tremaine's hand. Of never seeing Conrad again and only having an inkling of his fate through my madness dreams. I shook my head to clear the images.

"Well?" the pale man purred.

I nodded, unable to look into his stone-sculpted face for one more moment. "I'll do it."

Tremaine smiled again. I didn't want to see it, but I could sense it—his thin lips pulled taut, his razor teeth exposed in victory, like a wolf's.

"I knew you would," he said. He reached into his coat and drew out a brass bell, muting the clapper with his thumb. "Use this when you've done as I asked. Until then . . . I hope we do not have to meet again. I grow weary of scolding you."

Tremaine took my shoulder and led me back to the hut and the *hexenring* where Dean waited. He pushed me over the ring of toadstools and I shoved the brass bell into my pocket. The last thing I saw before the ring closed was Tremaine watching me, the wolf's smile still on his face.

27

The Enchantment's End

MY FATHER'S ATTIC room appeared around me again by degrees, as the enchantment of the *hexenring* slipped away. Dean grabbed me by the shoulders. "Aoife. Aoife, what did he do to you?"

I blinked at him. "Nothing. He did . . ." I breathed deep to compose myself. "It's nothing I can't handle."

"Did he hurt you?" Dean gave me a shake. I winced as he grazed the shoggoth bite.

"Not any worse than you are right this moment." I shrugged Dean's hands off. They were too heavy, too hot. The spot where Tremaine had touched my face was cold—felt brittle, as if it could break.

"Doll, you look like something chewed you up and spat you out the other end." Dean moved my hair out of my face, his fingers rougher than Tremaine's, warmer and livelier.

"I think I want to go downstairs," I muttered. I wasn't

up to reassuring Dean I was all right. *I* wasn't sure I was all right.

Dean opened the hatch and gave me his hand to help me down the ladder. "Are you sure nothing's wrong?"

"Honestly?" I paused on the bottom rung. "I'm more concerned with you. You were trapped in that ring. . . . I thought you might have lost years when he took me out. . . ."

Dean put his hands on my waist and lifted me the last foot to the floor. "I told you they lie, Aoife. Besides, it takes more than the Folk flashing magic to stir me up."

"Still." I smoothed a speck of dirt from the Thorn Land off Dean's shirt, his skin beneath warming my fingers. "I'm sorry you had to see that." I didn't want Dean to see the ugly consequences of my Weird. If he did he'd give me a wide berth, and I didn't want Dean to be gone. I needed him there.

Dean nudged me. "Forget about that. Come with me."

He took me to the back parlor and stood me in the center of the room while he flipped the switch on the hi-fi to start the aether warming up. I regarded him suspiciously. After what Tremaine had threatened me with, I wasn't in the mood to switch back to cheerful.

"I tinkered with it while you were gone," Dean told me. "The hi-fi. You can get a little more than static and the Miskatonic U station now."

"Cal will be thrilled," I said. "But what's it to do with me?"

"Listen," Dean said, "I know that what happened is twisting you up. Twisted me up, and I'm fairly sure I've seen a lot more oddness in my life than you have."

He turned the hi-fi's dial until a wax record scratched

354

and dropped over the aether, burbling pop music. "You're not gonna think straight until you calm down. So will you trust me for a few minutes? I want to help."

The song continued, and Dean held out his hand. "Now or never, princess."

"Never," I said, darting out of Dean's reach. His mouth turned down, but I held firm. "I don't dance."

"And I aim to rectify that situation," Dean said. "Please, Aoife. Trust me."

I hesitated. Tremaine had shaken me terribly. I was getting better at not showing it, but my stomach was churning and I couldn't stop thinking about his last words.

Dean was right. I wasn't going to figure anything out in my state.

I jumped as Dean slipped his arm around my waist. "Here we go," he said. "Put your other hand on my shoulder."

"Dean," I said as we swung in a wide, parabolic circle. "This is ridiculous."

"Listen," Dean said. "Close your eyes and listen. Let yourself move."

My steps smoothed out as I obeyed him, though I still kept a death grip on his hand and shoulder. And just like a switch flipping over, we were dancing in time, moving by turns around the parlor. It was easier to focus on my feet than the storm inside me. I felt a tiny bit less terrible.

"It's, well . . . not so bad," I conceded.

"And?" Dean gave me a small smile.

"I might like it," I admitted. "A little."

Dean spun me out and back. "Course you do. I'm hoping you'll grow to like me, too." He winked. "A little."

I didn't answer, I just danced until the song ended and static hissed along the empty aether. "Too forward?" Dean said, lowering our hands so they were pressed together between us. The shine faded from his eyes.

"It's not that." I didn't let go of Dean and he didn't let go of me. "But this won't last. Me, and the Weird, and the Folk—"

"Aoife," Dean interrupted, bending his head toward mine. "I don't care about lasting. I just want right now."

We swayed together on the spot, bonded by hand and hip, my breath and heartbeat trapped in Dean's starlight gaze.

"Dean?" I whispered.

"Yeah, princess?"

I stood on tiptoe to close the distance between us. "I want right now too."

When I kissed Dean I shut my eyes as if I were dancing again, and shut out everything except his scent, and his skin, and the music whispering in my ears.

Dean let out a soft sound when I pressed my lips to his and then pulled me tight and flush against his chest. His hand on my waist was warm, and I could feel every finger pressing into my ribs. His other slid across my neck, the tips of his fingers catching my hair.

"Aoife," Dean said huskily, when we finally pulled apart.

I opened my eyes, slowly, afraid that he'd become nothing more than smoke if I looked at him.

"Yes, Dean?"

His eyes were stormy, darker than I'd ever seen them. Dean's hand moved from my neck to cup my cheek, the spot where Tremaine had slapped me. When he touched

356

me, my skin was finally warm. "I don't want to let go of you."

"Me either," I whispered. My stomach was light and my head was full of vertigo, like the floor was falling away beneath me, and yet I knew Dean would anchor me, keep me close.

Dean pressed his forehead against mine. "So let's just stay like this a while."

"Aoife!" The new voice slammed me back down to earth.

Dean and I turned as one, his hands still on me. "Cal?" I gasped. How much had he seen? His expression told me that he'd seen far too much for me to have any hope of explaining.

Cal stood in the doorway, a plate of chocolate chip cookies and a glass of milk slack in his hands. "I heard music. I brought you some . . . ," he started, eyes darting between Dean and me. "Bethina got some groceries in this afternoon and made them. . . ." He shook his head, lips peeling back to show all of his teeth in a grotesque echo of Tremaine. "Really, Aoife? Him? *Him*?"

"Cal, it's not . . . ," I started. His face went stone, and his expression was ugly. He wasn't my Cal in that moment, and I didn't want to know the new person who was staring at me with unabridged contempt. Cal looked like every student who'd stared down at me—Marcos, Cecelia, every one.

"It *is*, Aoife. He's not our kind. You'll have to choose, and you'll leave me behind." He slammed down the plate and glass, so that milk sloshed all over the parlor table. "I hope you're happy."

357

"Cal . . ." I extricated myself from Dean's grip, anything but happy. I'd never seen Cal so angry. "Cal, wait!" But my friend had stormed out, and the frightful foreign expression hadn't left his face.

"You should go talk to him," Dean said.

I pressed my hands over my face, feeling a hot tangle of anger and sadness, but not shame. I wasn't embarrassed about what Dean and I had done. I'd wanted to kiss him since our first day in Arkham, and after what had happened since that day, I was through being ashamed of wanting things. "It won't do any good," I said. "Cal's . . . fragile. He'll think that I lied to him."

"I don't mean salve his dashed notions of romance. I mean calm him down." Dean shoved his hair off his forehead. "If he throws a rod and goes back to the city spouting stories, he could hurt you, Aoife. And then I'd have to beat the crap out of him, and that'd be a real shame."

"Cal wouldn't . . ." My stomach flipped over, dizzy and unsettled. I realized I didn't know Cal as well as I had the night we left Lovecraft. "Would he?" I realized I didn't know the Cal who'd run out of the parlor at all. He might.

"I once spent six hours in freezing rain outside the flat of a girl I was crushing hard for," Dean said. "And when her boyfriend came around I got myself a night in lockup over the scene I caused." He took my chin between his fingers and kissed my forehead, softly. "A guy does a lot of things he doesn't think too hard about when he's got it bad for a girl."

"Was she pretty?" I said, a tinge of sharpness I hadn't intended in the question. "The girl you went to jail over."

"Pretty enough," he said. "Gold hair, blue eyes. The

358

usual." He let go of me and winked. "She was sure no you." He tried a cookie, crumbs lingering on his chin. "That Bethina's got a real trick for the hearth." He licked his fingers. "With my kind of people, you might almost call her a witch."

I cocked my head. "And what would you call me?"

He considered. "Dangerous. What you have, and your old man—the knack for elemental enchantment, messing with fire and iron—that ain't usual, and we heretic types know not to cross what's unusual. No future in it."

I looked at my hands. Even here in the parlor, where there was no clockwork to speak of beyond the door hinges and the shutters, I could feel the Weird under my fingers, resonating with the iron that ran in my blood. For the first time my hands were terribly alien to me, the hands of a stranger who commanded eldritch, unearthly forces.

"I suppose I better go put things right with Cal before he takes a runner," I muttered. The thought that I had to talk my best friend out of betraying us galled me.

"I'll go out for a smoke," Dean said. "I'll be within hollering distance if he gets sassy."

He kissed me on the top of my head before he went out and I tried not to feel guilty at the magnetic pull as my Weird responded to his touch.

"Cal?" I went from parlor to billiard room to kitchen, finding not hide nor hair. "Cal, where are you?" If he'd already gone, I'd have to go after him, and I didn't relish that scene.

"He went out for a walk," Bethina said. She had her

sleeves rolled up and was working a white lump of bread dough on a butcher board. "Said he needed air. Looked fit to pop."

"That's my fault," I sighed. Rational or not, I'd upset Cal, and that, I did feel terrible about.

Bethina stopped kneading and brushed her hands. She left ghostly prints down her apron front. "Can I ask you something, miss? And expect honesty in return?"

"As honest as I can be," I said, wondering what fresh hell I was in for. I went to the icebox and opened it, picking out nothing. My stomach was far too troubled for hunger, and there was nothing edible inside anyway.

"Do you fancy Cal?"

I lost my grip on the chrome handle in my surprise, and the icebox slammed shut. "Do I . . ." It was a fair question. Cal was noble, true and innocent. Dean wasn't any of those things. But Cal saw the worst in me, and I couldn't go back to what he thought I should be. Not now that I had opened the way to a world I'd thought was only my mother's stories with the Weird and with the Folk.

"Miss?" Bethina stood very still, as if she were waiting for a slap. "I'd like an answer. Please."

"No. Not that way," I said. "Not in the way that he wants."

"He's your friend, though, miss," Bethina insisted. "He's loyal to you, and he thinks you're pretty. He said."

I threw up my hands. I'd figured Cal might have a crush, but I'd been careful not to give him hope. "It doesn't work that way in real life, Bethina. I know what he wants and I don't want the same. I'm sorry."

Bethina's face fell. "Well, I—I do care for Cal. In the way he wants. He's just like Sir Percival, in the King Arthur tales."

"And I thought *I* read too many books," I murmured. I'd never thought like Bethina and normal girls did. Boys didn't look at me and I had no time for them. Dean was the first one to talk to me like I wasn't beneath him or just stupid. Even Cal talked down to me at times. He'd been raised to, in a respectable household with respectable people. Dean was the only boy I'd met who was like me.

Bethina folded, like someone had cut her strings. "You don't think someone like me is worth him."

"No," I said, "I don't think anything of the sort." Bethina would be good for Cal. She was steady and sweet and practical and she'd keep him with his feet on the ground. "Just tell him," I said to Bethina. "We don't get much time as it is, and we waste too much of it wondering."

"You're smart, miss," Bethina said. "So much it's spooky."

"I frighten even myself," I assured her, and went out the kitchen door to find Cal.

Cal wasn't hard to track—he'd gone directly to the cemetery and was sitting on the gate, letting it swing back and forth while he perched on the top bar, his heels hooked in the scrollwork.

"Aren't you worried more ghouls might come?" I said when I was a few feet away—just speaking distance. I'd never felt awkward in front of Cal before, and it sat as a stone in my throat.

"They wouldn't want me," Cal grumbled. "I'm not a big side of beef like your friend in there. I'm only scraps."

I had been prepared to be contrite, but my annoyance came back at his complaining tone. "Listen to yourself, Cal!" I snapped. "I'm sorry that you thought we were something we're not. I'm *sorry*. You're my friend and I never wanted to hurt you."

"Maybe not," Cal said. "But you did it." The gate swung under his weight, imitating the voices of the circling crows.

"What's that supposed to mean?" I sat on a pile of leaves against the fence and tucked my skirt under my knees. We both looked at the pond and the slowly dying season. I didn't want to meet Cal's eyes in that moment and see his answer.

He propped his chin in his hands. "You're not who I thought you were, Aoife. I got a lot of guff for being friendly with a girl who carries the necrovirus. And when Conrad went mad in front of everyone—"

"I'm not responsible for Conrad's madness," I said. It stung that he'd use that against me after all. "But neither was he. I won't abandon my brother, Cal. Blood is blood and friendship is friendship. It doesn't have to end just because we've changed."

"You're not the Aoife Grayson I met on the first day of classes," Cal said. "She asked to borrow my pen. She helped me pass calculus. She was a good girl, a proper girl. You're not her."

A long moment passed while we watched leaves fall and float on the glassy surface of the pond beyond the cemetery walls.

"No," I agreed. "I'm not." I looked at Cal again. "I'm scared to tell you how much I'm not, Cal. I want to, but I'm scared of what you'll do."

"Scared?" He swiped his hands through his hair. "Aoife, you have nothing to be scared of from me. That Dean, he's the problem. He'll lead you astray and you'll never find your way back."

"Cal," I said quietly, knowing there was only one thing I could say to stem his anger. "I don't like what's gone between us, and if I tell you something to make things right, you have to promise me that you'll stop ripping on Dean and really listen."

"Fine," he said after a long time. "But don't expect me to like it."

He was hurt, that much was evident, and I tried not to let his hard tone and hard eyes sting too much. "My father used enchantments," I said. "Not fakery and sleight of hand. Real power that science can't explain. He communicated with creatures from beyond this world. I can do the same thing."

"That's the necrovirus talking for you," Cal said, too quickly. The words put a blade in me, low down, in the stomach, and started a fury that, after my encounters with Tremaine, was becoming familiar.

"Dammit. I'm not crazy, Cal, and I'll prove it to you." I held out my hand. "You have anything mechanical on you?"

He shrugged. "Just my portable aether tube and my multitool."

"The tube," I said. "Give it to me."

"Aoife, don't embarrass yourself," he said. "The virus has made you see things. Enchantment isn't possible. All of the great minds have proved that. The Proctors tell us—"

"You don't really believe I'm only infected," I cut him off, folding my arms. "Or you wouldn't still be here. I think you want to believe, Cal." Just like Nerissa wanted to believe there was something beyond the dreary horror of the madhouse. Just like I wanted to believe our family wasn't doomed and like all of the so-called heretics the Proctors chased wanted to believe in something beyond cold, hard rational thought, prison bars and raven spies.

I took the tube, the bits of copper and glass and aether that I'd taken for granted a week ago, with its enamel dial and thin tuning wires running along the inside of the glass, where the cloudy aether swirled, breathing like a sleeping animal.

I could feel the machine slither under my skin. The copper and the dial and the wire binding everything together. The aether prickled my Weird, like static electricity when I touched metal in the cold of winter.

My eyes fluttered closed. I saw all the components in my mind, the switch that sparked the aether to life with a static charge, the wires that reached out into the fathomless distances of the fabric of the universe to receive the signal beamed from one tube to another.

I knew the pressure now, the fullness. The machine coming into my mind, my Weird sliding out to the machine.

The tube came to life in my hands, and a sportscaster broke the afternoon quiet. "It's the windup . . . the pitch . . . strike one for Susce, in a surprising performance."

"Maybe this is the year for the Sox," I said. "The curse can't last forever."

Cal stared at the tube, at me. "How'd you do that?"

"I told you, Cal," I said. I pushed at the tuner, the small black slide on the side of the device. The station changed, big band music, the NBC comedy hour, back to baseball. "Take it," I said, handing it to him. "See that I'm not just doing one of Conrad's tricks."

He accepted the tube with stiff fingers, and when it was in his grasp I pushed the static away from my mind, sending it back into the switch.

The tube shut off. Cal started. "Aoife. This is . . ."

"Unbelievable?" I offered. "Yeah. But there it is."

"So back there, in the tunnel?" He dropped the tube into the leaves like it was a vial full of necrotic blood.

"Me," I said quietly.

"The airship crash?"

"Cal, don't be stupid. The Proctors caused that by blowing big holes in the *Belle*." I picked up one of the leaves, a perfect skeleton, and stared at the pond through it.

Cal moved from the gate, standing between me and the water, twitching like I'd just covered him in ants. "This is . . . this is bad, Aoife."

I crushed the leaf between my palms. "It's me, Cal. You wanted to know."

The gate creaked, and long shadows crept from beneath the trees and the headstones before Cal spoke again. "You're my only friend, you know. Those guys back at the School aren't my friends. I can't tell them anything the way I do you. After Conrad . . . you're it."

365

"I still want to be it," I said. "I wouldn't have got on at the Academy without you, Cal. Without someone to talk to, a friend . . ." I stood up and brushed myself off. "I know you're angry, but I'm afraid that's all I can offer. You can stay and we can try it, or you can go home and turn me in."

"Jeez, Aoife," Cal sighed. "I'd never turn you in. Not to the Proctors."

For all of his moods, Cal was honest to a fault. He wouldn't turn me in. I reached for his hand, but he tugged it away. "Thank you," I said, and meant it, even though my hand was hanging in midair like a fool's. My face went warm again, Tremaine's bruises turning rosy.

Cal shrugged. "It's nothing. But I have something to say, if we're still friends. That Dean . . . he's bad news, Aoife. Conrad would slap sense into you if he saw what I saw."

"I'm going inside," I said, holding up a hand to end the diatribe I sensed in my future. "It's cold and I have a lot of practice to do."

Cal climbed back onto the gate as I walked away. The hinges spoke in the gathering dark, a dirge for something that we'd both lost.

28

The Cursebreaker

DEAN WAS STANDING in the shadow of the kitchen door when I returned, squinting into the sunset as he blew smoke into bird shapes that flew up and away around his head.

"Everything square?" he asked, flicking his ember into the damp grass.

"I don't know about square," I said, the look Cal had given me in the parlor still chafing. "But he's not running to the Proctors."

Dean nodded once. "Good."

I reached forward and pushed the locks of hair from his eyes, smoothing them back into place. Dean leaned into the touch like a cat. "You've got soft hands, princess. Soft clever hands."

"You'd get a lot further if you complimented my brains," I teased. Dean straightened up from the wall and followed me inside.

367

"Oh, I plan to. I'm just taking my time so I can compliment everything the way it deserves." Dean's grin grew wider at my flush.

I'd never had that much male attention before, aside from stares and whispers, and I shied away from Dean's searching gaze. "I need to not think about Cal for a while," I told him.

"You and me both, princess." Dean trailed me into the library. I knew where I needed to go before I put my hand on the switch, knew the only thing that could truly erase a rotten scene with someone I cared for.

"What do you say we take a look at that stuff we found in the workshop?" I asked.

A portable aether lantern threw more light on the workshop, and I set it on the dusty worktable while I perused the shelves.

Dean put on the goggles, tested them out by staring at the dead specimens under the glass. "This is boss. You know you can see through cloth with these lenses?"

I flipped a hand at him as he turned his gaze on me and waggled his eyebrows. "Stop teasing. You cannot."

Dean pointed at the gun-shaped thing I'd examined before Tremaine had taken us into the Thorn Land. "Think it's a disintegrator ray? Heard the Crimson Guard have them. Maybe we can aim it at that pale bastard Tremaine and solve all of our problems."

I picked it up, feeling the heft of brass and mahogany in the stock. I looked down the silver sight at the end, behind the aether bulb on the tip. "I think this is an invigorator,"

I said to Dean. "I've seen them in the Engine, when we'd study there." This one was homemade, nothing like the square, blunt steel tools that the Engine workers used. Still, I'd never had the chance to use one and I ran my hands over it slowly, memorizing the machine.

"Yeah?" Dean said. "What's it invigorate?"

"It's for cutting steel and brass and things," I said. "It can freeze or melt—the barrel vibrates the aether at such a frequency that it can go through all sorts of things." I'd always wanted to use one, but girls weren't allowed.

"Neat," Dean approved. With the goggles, he looked back toward the dim library. "These things can even see in the dark."

I set the invigorator gently back on the shelf. No use in cutting a me-sized hole in the side of Graystone if my finger slipped. "Too bad I can't see Tremaine and his cursed *hexenring* sneaking up on me with them," I muttered. I examined the diving helmet—it was attached to a bulbous bladder that leaked air when I squeezed it. The scrubbers attached at the front would recirculate the air for as long as the bladder fed it fresh oxygen. A dial on the side of the bladder went from zero to one hour. How I wished for time to explore the workshop at my leisure, but I knew I had none. It was a vast disappointment—exploring the workshop was my idea of a perfect afternoon. Machines made sense when nothing else did.

"It's a real shame," Dean said, "that you ever had to meet him. This right here"—he brandished the goggles—"this is magic. Machines, what you can do with them. That's the truth of it."

"Tremaine doesn't feel the same as you," I said, feeling

369

the weight of the enchanted blue glass he'd given me in my pocket. I hadn't wanted to leave it anywhere Bethina might snoop. "He thinks I'm so magic I can break a curse all the Folk can't."

In the old times, the shining times, Tremaine's remembered voice whispered in my ear, *we would gather at the Winnowing Stone and harness its great bounty to awaken the sleepers from their curse.*

"But no magic born of Thorn can break the enchantment," I whispered in answer.

Dean frowned at me. "You talking to me, princess?"

"No, I . . ." I pointed at the goggles in his hand. "What you just said."

"It's the plain truth, kid. Forget all of the Folk's hand waving. You've got a gift with your Weird, for machines." Dean shoved the goggles back onto his forehead. I could see his eyes once again.

"Tremaine said that no magic in the Thorn Land could break the curse," I said. Which made me wonder what sort of thing had set it in the first place. I decided it was better not to think about. "They use stones and enchantments, but they don't have this." I set the helmet on the worktable with a crash. "They don't live in the Iron Land. They don't have our machines. Tremaine said my Weird could break the curse. *My* Weird."

"Aoife," Dean started, "what are you—"

"Machines," I said as my idea took form, gained speed. Machines were my only true affinity, for as long as I could remember. The thing the Folk didn't have, the thing only the Iron Land, my world, did. "Tremaine said nothing in Thorn could break the curse. What does Thorn not have?"

370

"Sense of humor?" Dean said.

"Engines," I whispered. "It doesn't have a power like the Engines."

Of course, I could be wrong. Machines could have nothing to do with breaking the curse. But it was all I had, all I'd ever had. Just my mind and clever hands and an instinct for what made things work.

If I could repair a chronometer, I might be able to break a curse the same way.

"Aoife, I don't like this," Dean said. "What if it doesn't work?"

I pulled the brass bell from my pocket and held it in my palm for a moment, feeling my pulse beat against it. If it didn't work, I wouldn't have any more mundane concerns like staying alive. That was certain. "Don't worry," I lied to Dean. "I know what I'm doing."

When the world settled around me again, Tremaine was standing before me. We were in the same spot near the lily field, in the same night I'd left, or a different one. I was learning time held little meaning in the Thorn Land.

I didn't wait for Tremaine's invitation this time, merely grabbed hold of his cool, papery hand and stepped through the *hexenring.*

"Look at you, so spirited." Tremaine straightened his collar and sleeves. "I take that to mean you have good news for me."

"I've found your cursebreaker," I lied, but I knew by now I could do it convincingly enough. Tremaine nodded encouragement.

371

"No need to build to it. Spit out your plan, child."

My hands were trembling so violently I thought that I might break my fingers, but I curled up my fists and looked Tremaine in his fathomless, soulless eyes. "Before that, I need something from you. Right this moment."

Tremaine's lips twitched in irritation. "Very well. Say it."

I exhaled, my breath steaming in the chill air. All at once, I didn't want to know. But I pressed on. "Tell me about my brother."

Tremaine looked away from me, sighing. "All the secrets of the Folk at your fingertips and you're still harping about that boy."

"Either you hold up your end of the bargain, or I'm going to walk," I said. "And your queen will sleep forever, until the world rots away around her." I folded my arms. "My brother. Where is he?"

"I told you, I find this new attitude of yours distasteful," Tremaine said. "But the Folk keep their bargains." He folded his arms, bracers clanking dully like coffin lids. "Your brother is dead, Aoife."

My heart stopped. "No . . ." The word slid out past the wire that strung itself around my throat. I couldn't breathe, couldn't speak except to blurt out, "That's a lie."

"He fell to the Proctors in Arkham Village," Tremaine said, placing a hand on the back of my neck. "I sent him back, as I sent you, so that he might help me release my queen and the Summer Queen by consulting your father's library. He was not as adept at evasion as you appear to be."

"He can't be." I felt as if everything inside of me had frozen. Conrad. Dead. I thought of the last time I'd seen him.

I'd never imagined it would truly be the end. "He can't . . . ,"
I tried again. "Bethina said shadows took him away. . . ."

"The chambermaid? The blithering girl who can't
see the end of her own nose, who fears the sight of us so
much that she makes up stories about ghosts in moonlight?
You trust her word above mine?"

"Tell me . . ." I shut my eyes, unable to stand the sight of
Tremaine's sharp diamond face for another moment. "Tell
me how he died."

"You don't need to know that, child," Tremaine sighed.
"You don't need more nightmares."

"Tell me!" My shout echoed off the glass coffins and the
hills beyond, like a faraway bell.

"He was shot in the back running down a village street,"
Tremaine said. "My strix owls couldn't stay long. Arkham is
bound in iron and we do not know where they took his
body. A pauper's funeral, I imagine, and then the crema-
tory furnace to burn off any memory of their crime. Is that
good enough for you, Aoife?"

The world slid sideways. "You're lying." He had to be
lying. Conrad's end couldn't be so simple.

Conrad had to be alive.

"You know that I would not," Tremaine said. "You know
that's what happened, child, because you know your
brother. I wish he had survived, truly. He was an intelligent
and respectful boy. Very much not like you."

I couldn't speak, couldn't move. I didn't want to believe
that Conrad was gone, but there wasn't a hard certainty,
just soft, slithering doubt taking up residence in my heart.

"I've given you a task," Tremaine said. "Now you give me
your half."

When I didn't speak, he clapped his hands in my face. Once, sharp. Like the gunshot that had taken Conrad away from me.

"Aoife," Tremaine growled. "Focus. What will break my curse?"

"I think . . . ," I started, and then couldn't continue.

Tremaine's lip curled, and he placed his hands on my shoulders. "Don't think, child. Know. Thinking won't help me."

"The Engine," I said numbly. "The Lovecraft Engine. Thorn doesn't have Engines or anything like them, you said it yourself. I can use my Weird. Send the power that the Lovecraft Engine generates into Thorn. Use it to wake up your precious queens." My will to defy Tremaine had run out. I felt as hollow as one of the Proctors' ravens, just a mess of gears and metal on the inside. No feeling. No will.

Tremaine, for his part, patted my cheek. "Good child. I knew you'd be the one. Of course, I'll be far more excited when you succeed." He took my elbow and guided me back into the *hexenring*. "May you have fair weather and a following sea in your task, Aoife Grayson. You know what will happen if you fail me. Your brother may be gone, but Dean and Cal are still alive, I take it? They will still bleed if you force me to find them?"

I just shrugged. It didn't matter any longer. Nothing did. Conrad was dead.

"And there's your mother," Tremaine mused as the *hexenring* took me. "So alone, in that madhouse. So many other screams to cover hers up . . ."

I tried belatedly to reach for Tremaine again, to demand that he leave Nerissa and Dean and Cal alone, that I'd do his work even though he'd tricked me, had known Conrad was dead. Had known from the moment he took me in the orchard.

Too slow, I touched nothing. A sob wrenched from my throat.

"Aoife." Dean's face blurred back into view, lines at his mouth and eyes. "Dammit, I hate it when you just blink out like that." He examined me more closely and his jaw set. "You look awful. What'd he do to you?"

I tried to speak, but all that came out was a soft, broken sound. I fell against Dean and he wrapped his arms around me to save me from falling. My tears were silent, but they soaked my face and the fabric of Dean's shirt. All I saw was white as I clung to Dean, and all I felt was a widening black pit where my insides used to be.

29

The Flight of the Crow

"My brother's dead," I whispered after twenty heartbeats. "The Proctors shot him in the back."

Once the words flew from my lips, the truth slammed into me, a weight I could never shake off. I fell to my knees, grit and old dirt digging in through my stockings, and I shook, wrapping my arms around myself.

"Oh, princess." Dean knelt and hugged me again. I sobbed, wretched sounds ripping from my throat, as a knife of memory twisted deep in my stomach. I would never see Conrad again. Never tell him that I knew he wasn't mad. Never tell him that I understood why he'd run away.

I could never tell him I forgave him.

I had wasted my time on the Weird, on Dean, on relishing my own freedom. I had let Conrad fall and I hadn't been there to hold out my hand.

"Bethina said he was alive last she saw him," Dean

whispered. "That those shadow folk took him. Nothing about being shot. The Folk lie, Aoife. They're already a lie to most rational people, so why shouldn't they lie to you?"

"I don't . . . ," I managed. "I don't think he was lying."

"You don't know that for certain," Dean said. "Nothing in this life is ever certain, doll."

I had lost my tears, and my eyes stung, swollen and gritty. "It doesn't matter, anyhow," I muttered. "Doesn't matter that he lied to start. I made my bargain. I have to go back to the city, Dean." Before Tremaine could unleash his particular brand of sadism on everyone else I cared for. Even if I'd lost Conrad already, I could still lose Dean and Cal. And then I couldn't go on.

Dean helped me to my feet, gently. I was fragile now, a thing that needed to be cosseted. I despised myself in that moment.

"That's a dangerous proposition. You saw what the Proctors do to heretics who fly across their radar." Dean rubbed out my tears, tried to clean my face off, but I couldn't stop more tears from coming.

"I have to," I repeated. "I have to go back." Words had lost their weight, their usefulness. Words hadn't kept Conrad from a bullet in his back, alone on a cold stone street.

"All right," Dean said. "All right. We'll work it out. We can talk about it."

I let him lead me down the ladder and out of the library, feeling adrift as if I were floating in a vast new sea, a sea of sorrow. I had no anchor and no weight. I could float forever.

*   *   *

377

Bethina and Cal sat at the kitchen table, cards arrayed between them. Bethina slapped her hand down, victory in her grin. "Gin."

Cal sighed and threw his cards down. "This isn't normal. You're some kind of cardsharp, missy. You belong back in the old days in Dodge City."

"Kid," Dean said. Cal turned and saw me, and his eyes widened.

"What did you do to her?"

"Shut your trap. She's had a bad shock," Dean said. "Bethina, you have any hot tea?"

She pushed back, scattering their rummy game. "Sure enough. Just brewed a pot."

"With something stronger, if you have it," Dean said. "For a chaser."

Bethina pumped water into the chipped enamel kettle and hung it on a hook over the fireplace. "Mr. Grayson kept some whiskey in his desk in the library."

Dean sat me in a chair and left. He had a half-full bottle of amber when he returned. I couldn't muster the words to say anything, to do anything except sit and stare.

Cal watched us with a sharp frown. "Aoife, what in the Builder's name happened? You look like someone walked over your grave."

"Conrad's dead," I whispered. It wasn't any easier to say, but if possible, the words tasted more bitter.

Cal slumped, like a scarecrow with all of its stuffing pulled out. "How?"

Dean accepted the cup of tea Bethina handed him, added a jigger from the bottle and put it in my hands. "Drink," he said. "It'll keep you upright."

378

"I'm not sure she should be drinking at a time like this," Cal said.

Dean sat with the bottle in his hands. "Cowboy, if this isn't the time for drinking, there ain't no time at all."

"We have to go back to Lovecraft," I said. "We have to go today."

"Aoife, that's suicide," Cal told me. "You said so yourself."

"That was before," I said. The tea was terrible, bitter black tea leaves and whiskey combined to burn my throat and tongue, but it calmed the constant waves of vertigo. "Before I made the deal with the Folk."

"What are you talking about?" Cal edged his chair back. "Are you feeling all right?"

"Dammit, Cal!" I slapped my hand against the table. The playing cards jumped. "This is not the time! And I'm not crazy! Your life and Bethina's and Dean's too . . . they're all in this balance, so for once, Cal, *listen* to me."

"All right, fine." Cal made a gesture of surrender. "I'm listening."

I told Dean, Cal and Bethina about Tremaine, my first visit to the Thorn Land, the task he'd set upon me. I told him about how I intended to go home, to the Engine, and try to awaken the queens with my Weird.

I did not tell them how my Weird reacted to even the slightest touch. To feel the Engine flowing through me, the vast and breathless power of its pistons and gears . . . what would that power do?

I didn't think about it, and I didn't say it. I kept my tale short and sparse, because talking about the Folk left a foul taste on my tongue.

379

When I was finished, Dean gave a low whistle. "That's a burden to lay on you, Aoife. True enough."

"It's . . . unbelievable," Cal said. "And impossible."

"Impossible just means they ain't thought of a name for it yet," Dean answered. "What it is, is dangerous."

"I'm going back," I told them. "With or without all of you." I was decided. I had never been so decided before.

"I'm just telling it like it is," Dean said. "Think on the danger before you go running back into the iron jaws of that place, will you? For me?"

"You saw what can happen," I said. "Tremaine isn't a good person, but I made a bargain. My family has a history with the Folk, and I have the Weird, and it means I have the history now. The duty."

I stood up. The tea had flushed me, warmed me, and dulled the ache of losing Conrad. I had to move now, before I became a cripple again.

"You can help me or you can stay here. I won't blame you either way. But I'm going back to Lovecraft."

The Peter Pan jitney depot on the outskirts of Arkham was pockmarked with rust, chrome rubbed off, glass shattered. No one else sat on the damp bench inside the shelter. I was the only one, the old carpetbag I'd found in the wardrobe stuffed with my school clothes and my father's journal, plus the invigorator and Tremaine's goggles.

I hadn't taken much. I wore the sturdy boots and woolen coat and the red dress. I didn't need anything else.

In the end, I'd elected to leave early in the morning,

380

silent and alone. Cal and Dean needn't be part of this. It was my bargain to uphold and my burden to bear.

I'd slept not at all. I kept thinking of Conrad, of how it was all gone now—the smile, the sound of his voice, the feel of his hand on my shoulder. His simple tricks, the last, anguished glimpse of him before he dropped the knife and ran from my dormitory room.

I had to pack it away and move on because I wasn't a simple schoolgirl any longer, one who had the luxury of flinging herself across her bed and crying.

I had a duty. My father had lost his brother too. He hadn't let it stop him. I wouldn't be the weak link in the Grayson bloodline.

The crows flapped overhead, one alighting on the shelter's roof. It cocked its head, danced to the left, stared at me with its glass bead eyes.

"Why don't you go fly back to Tremaine and tell him I'm doing as he asks?" I snapped at it.

"She wouldn't." Dean's voice startled me, his appearance out of the ever-present fog like a camera lens clicking.

I kicked at the carpetbag with my toe. It was indescribably ugly, great orange cabbage roses on a hunter green background. "How can you know?"

"The crows don't serve the Folk." Dean sat next to me and performed the ritual of tapping and lighting a Lucky. He clicked his lighter shut and nodded to the crow. "They're psychopomps. Guardians protecting the ways between the lands. Iron, Mist and Thorn, they all got doorways."

"I don't see why they're always bothering me," I said. "I'm not going anywhere."

Dean took a drag. "Then why are you at the jitney stop, sweetheart?"

I shot him a glare. "You know that's not what I meant."

He picked up my hand and pressed his lips against the back, the briefest of touches, but it shattered the fragile dam I'd built around the events of the previous day. I moved into his arms silently, and let his body warm mine while the fog swirled.

"You're alone?" I said.

"Nah." Dean exhaled. Tobacco smoke made a halo around our heads. "The kid's coming too. I left him with time to say goodbye to Bethina."

"Good. I hope he goes back to her when this is over." I checked the schedule for the dozenth time. There were still quarters of hours yet before any jitney would come, but my stomach was throbbing with nerves.

"I know you're not scared, not you." Dean's heartbeat was steady, steady as a clock. "So what are you? I know something's up after that scene about your brother."

"I'm angry," I said. "I'm angry that I know nothing about my family and that those Proctor bastards shot Conrad, and I'm angry there's nothing I can do about any of it except take orders from that pale bastard." I crumpled the schedule and tossed it into the road. "That's all my life's been, Dean. Doing what I'm told."

Dean dropped his cigarette and crushed it with his boot. "I made you something."

"Oh really?" I grumbled, not in the mood to be cheered up. "Have you taken up knitting in all of your spare time?"

Dean pressed a folded scrap of vellum into my hand. "That's what folks in my part of the underworld call a geas."

382

The scrap was folded on itself eight times, inked with a circle and a cross. "Dean . . ." I flinched as it prickled on my palm. "Dean, did you go snooping in the witch's alphabet? You *used* it?"

"No!" Dean exclaimed forcefully. "I told you, I can't do that sort of thing."

"Then how?" I demanded, fed up with his denials. I wasn't dumb. "You said you didn't have a Weird, just a knack. Either you're lying or snooping."

Dean heaved a sigh. "Those the only two options you can come up with, eh? I'm either a liar or a spy?"

"Or both," I shot back. "Dean Harrison, tell me what is going on this instant. And take this." I thrust the paper at him. I wasn't prepared to bear any more secrets for anyone else.

"A geas is a powerful enchantment," Dean said. "It can steal your free will and your breath in the same moment. You shouldn't give it back lightly."

"I expect fibbing from Cal," I said, getting angry he'd try to flummox me with a silly trick. "But I'd think you, at least, would be straight with me."

"I am being straight with you!" Dean shouted. All around us, the crows took flight. "I made that. Made it for you, and nobody but. I didn't need a musty book to tell me how, either."

"You said you didn't have a gift," I gritted. "So either you lied, or you didn't trust me."

Dean jumped up as well and met me, our gazes inches apart. "You're right, okay?" His face bore two spots of red and his chest was heaving with angry breaths. "I'm not like you, but I do have something. Did it occur to you that

383

maybe I'm not as thrilled about it as you are? That maybe it's more trouble than it's worth?"

That put the damper on the flaming spout of anger boiling in me. "Dean . . . I didn't mean it like that."

"For your edification, *princess*, my mother taught me that geas," he said, voice rough as sandpaper. "She stuck around just long enough to teach me to find north. Find lost things. Bind the truth. Nothing like your great *gift*"—the way he said it was like a slap—"but enough so that I could get by with one foot in Iron and the other foot somewhere else."

"I didn't know your mother taught you," I said, suddenly feeling very small. Dean thought I found him common. I was just as bad as the horrid Uptown brats in Lovecraft. "Was she . . . a witch, like?"

"She wasn't a damn witch," Dean snarled. "A witch is a faker who gets hunted down and burned alive by Proctors. She was better than that."

"I'm sorry," I said, too quiet because I was embarrassed. "I was wrong to accuse you."

"Aoife," Dean said, and the pain in his voice broke me from my own moment of shame, "I'm not mad at you. But . . . I ain't told you the truth. And I owe you that."

"Don't worry," I said, even though I desperately wanted to know Dean's secret. "I didn't expect to get your life story when I hired you."

"It's different now," Dean said. He stepped forward, cupped my chin and kissed me softly. I cocked my head.

"What was that for?"

"Because when I've said my tale, I might not get the chance again." His gaze darted from me to the road and the

384

trees and back. I'd never seen Dean nervous before now, never mind scared. I wasn't sure I liked it.

I reached out and smoothed down the lapel of his leather jacket. "Just tell me."

"You weren't wrong," Dean said. "My mother wasn't a child of men, Aoife. She was something else."

I pulled back, suddenly mindful of Tremaine's tales of places outside the Thorn Land, places that spawned things like the mist, the corpse-drinkers. "I don't understand."

"She was an Erlkin," Dean said. "No word for it in English. The People of the Mists, they're called, ruled by the Wytch King. The shadow-mirror of the Folk."

In the new light of his words, Dean's elfin ways and his peculiar skills with direction and finding, his miles-deep eyes came together, and when I looked again, the boy I'd hired in the Rustworks stared back at me, changed into something otherworldly. He didn't frighten me, though. If anything, I wanted to kiss him again even more badly.

"Please, Aoife," he whispered. "Don't you bolt on me. When my old man kicked, I decided I'd rather be a heretic than a—a half-breed. And I've been living underground ever since. You're the first person I've told."

"Are there many of you?" I said. It was the only question that came to mind. "Have the Folk been coming here all this time and having children like you?"

"I am *not* from the Thorn Land," Dean snarled. "The Folk enslaved the Erlkin at the start of everything. We may have bowed to them, but we ain't broken."

"Tremaine called you something," I remembered. "'Greaseblood.'"

"That's their word." Dean's eyes were darker than I'd

385

ever seen them, thunderheads and lightning in his gaze. "Not ours. It's what they call us when we work in their silver mines and their foundries. I'm an Erlkin, and I'm not shamed by it."

He stood with his fists curled, like he expected someone to challenge him on the point. I waited for a horrid transformation, for the noxious mist to curl in around us and steal me away, but Dean just stayed where he was, looking like he wanted to pick a fight with the shadows.

"I wish you'd told me," I said. "At least after we saw Tremaine. He made me think that everything outside the Thorn Land, in the mist, was vile, and I"—I swallowed down the lump of shame—"I was scared of you for a moment."

"I guess I handled that like a rat," Dean said. "And I'm sorry. You and me . . . we're new. The truth is new."

"I guess you won't be coming back with me," I said. "Seeing how you feel about the Folk, and me being bound with them."

Dean started to speak, but I held up a hand. "I understand, Dean. It's too much to ask." I got my carpetbag and stepped out of the shelter. The fog was ready to welcome me, as it always was.

"Aoife." Dean ran to catch up with me. "You really think after what I just told you, I'm going to walk away?"

"I would," I admitted, "if I were you. I wouldn't do a thing for the people that hurt my mother. She's my mother. I have to look out for her."

"Our mothers are real different, then," Dean muttered. "Mine was no prize. I'm proud to be Erlkin, but I ain't proud to be her son. No"—he shook his head—"I'm going

386

with you, because I know that you can never trust the Folk. A bargain with them is a glove full of thorns. No way you go alone."

"And the geas?" I was still holding the knot of paper. It still prickled and crackled in my palm.

"That geas binds the recipient to the truth," Dean said. "I was thinking you could use it on Tremaine." He folded my fingers around the enchantment. "He'll call you back after the bargain is done. Probably to gloat. Set a flame to that slip of paper, and a lie couldn't crawl past his lips if it had turbines and a tailwind."

"I know you think it's a bad idea," I said, secreting the geas in my coat pocket, "but honestly, the Folk haven't had a good turn either. Someone cursed them, killed their entire world."

"You're sure?" Dean's mouth flattened to a thin line of skepticism. "The Folk have a slippery grip on the truth, at best. I wouldn't be sorry if their whole land of oak, ash and thorn crumbled up into nothing and blew away."

I patted the journal, inside the carpetbag. "I'm sure." Even as I half-lied, my father's words came back to me. But maybe he hadn't listened to the truth. My father was hard and certain of everything. And he used the Folk as much as they used him. His Weird wasn't mine, and I had Cal to consider as well.

A rumble grew from the mist, and twin lanterns pierced the fog like the great eyes of the Old Ones.

The jitney hissed to a stop, steam escaping the vents and tracks chewing up the gravel road. The driver cranked the door open.

"The cowboy better get a move on," Dean said as he helped me up the steps. "Otherwise he'll be waiting for the next jitney with no one but ghouls for company."

"I'm here!" Cal came flapping down the shoulder of the road, hauling his schoolbag in his wake like a ferry towing a rowboat. "I'm coming!"

The driver looked at all of us. "Where are your parents, girlie?" he demanded.

"Back in the city," I answered without skipping a beat. "My mother will be waiting for us."

"I don't like your look," the driver told Dean. "No trouble on the bus. I'll toss you off and I've got a nightstick to do it with."

"I'll behave like I'm in the Builder's chapel," Dean said. The driver glared.

"And I don't like your smart mouth. Go to the back, sit down and shut up."

He stopped me with an arm. "That'll be three-fifty apiece, girlie. For my good nature."

"Three *dollars*?" I looked up at the posted fares: LOVECRAFT—$1, POINTS SOUTH—$2.50, NEW AMSTERDAM PORT AUTHORITY—$3.

"Or I could always call the truant officer up here in Arkham," he said with a grin that dripped venom. "Have him speak to the Proctors about three kids running around the country when they should be in school."

"You shyster . . ." Cal started for the driver, but I got between them.

"Cal, it's fine." I pulled out eleven dollars from my money roll and shoved it into the fare slot. "He'll get what's

388

coming to him." To the driver I said, "Keep the change, pal," with a sneer worthy of Dean. He punched my tickets and handed them over, still grinning.

"You're cute when you're mad, girlie. You should sit up front by me."

I darted away from his grasp and followed Dean to the last row of seats. "Why are normal people such scum?" I growled.

"Because scum floats," Dean answered. He slouched, his hair in his eyes, and glared at any passenger who stared too long at our trio. Cal fussed himself into the seat ahead of me, nearly too tall for the space under the luggage rack.

"Plain highway robbery. I should report him to the jitney company."

The driver put his fat hands on the levers and spun the steam dial to full, and the coach lurched forward, rattling over the road. I listened to the thrum of the gears and they soothed my Weird, speaking to it and warming it in steam. It still sat uneasy inside my head, but it no longer felt as if it would split my skull.

"We have more important things to worry about," I said.

"Like what?" Cal demanded, still in high dudgeon. I wiped condensation away from the window and made a small pane to watch the country pass. I would do as Tremaine asked and then I would be free, and I could avenge Conrad, find my father and give him back the job of Gateminder.

I looked back at Cal. "Like how we're going to gain entrance to the Engineworks."

We sat in silence until the jitney came off the mountain

389

and was rolling along the broader road through the valley, all conversation of the other passengers drowned in the hiss of steam and the clank of the track.

I'd let the idea grow and germinate in my mind while I'd lain awake the night before. It was a welcome relief from the niggling fear that Tremaine's lie about Conrad had been only the first of many.

I laid out my plan for Dean and Cal.

"There are plenty of vents under the city," I said. "And some go out to the river." I rattled the devices secreted inside my carpetbag. "We can wait until low tide and we can use this to go down to the vent. We can use the invigorator to get through the guard lattice and then we'll be in the Engineworks."

"Aoife, the river's got to be near freezing," Cal said.

I'd also thought of the contingency plan. "We'll go to the Academy first. The Expedition Club has cold-water diving suits." Marcos Langostrian was president of the club, and I'd take a distinct pleasure in using his silly diving suit to infiltrate the Engine.

"That might work," Cal said slowly. Dean shook his head.

"Dangerous. Just like I said before."

"It will work." I pressed my forehead against the glass and watched the mountains turn to hills and the hills turn to frozen fields. "It has to."

30

The Secret of the Steam

LOVECRAFT APPEARED OUT of the dark and mist-wrapped day like the skeleton of a great beast, resting on the riverside, phantom breath rising from the foundry chimneys.

Though it had been little more than a week since I'd left, seeing the familiar spires and rooftops was like returning after a journey of immeasurable distance and time.

As we bumped through the streets, I saw lamps flicker to life and steam vent from far below into the cold, ghost dragons dancing on the wind. The Engine was power, and its great heart turned day and night, creating the steam that powered the aether generators, the jitney lines and everything else in the city.

From our class visits to the Engine, I knew that it was guarded, by Proctors no less. Unless a worker possessed of identification came to the gates, visitors would be turned away at best or shot at worst. The Engine was buried

391

hundreds of feet below the streets, and the vent tunnels to the surface were welded shut and patrolled regularly.

All of this I'd learned in Civil Engineering. No one tampered with the Engine. It was the heart of the city.

And I was going to rip it out.

The jitney ground into the depot on lower Miskatonic Avenue, stabling itself next to a dozen similar steel-and-steam bodies. The driver didn't spring the doors, though, and I peered out the window. Dean joined me, hand on my shoulder. "Something's wrong," he murmured.

"Sorry, folks." The driver's slimy voice oozed out of the phono above my head. "Official security alert. We gotta stay put for an inspection before I can let you off."

Groans and complaints sounded, but after grumbling, the passengers settled and went back to their magazines and newspapers. A girl a few seats ahead of me took out a compact and started to fix her lipstick. How in the frozen hell could she be so calm?

Because she wasn't a fugitive, I realized. She was normal. I had never wanted to be normal so badly.

"Inspection?" Cal cracked his knuckles one after the other, a tic he didn't seem to notice. "That's bad news, Aoife. These aren't podunk Proctor recruits like they've got in Arkham."

The bus door hissed open and Dean growled, "Cool it. They're here."

From the outside, I caught the wail of Klaxons and the scent of acrid smoke from grinding gears. That wasn't normal, unless there was a riot. My stomach knotted. A riot was all we needed.

Two Proctors in black tunics and black caps stepped

onto the jitney, their gold wings gleaming on their breasts like shields.

"Everyone keep your seat," the Proctor in the lead shouted. "Keep quiet, and produce your identification when asked."

"Is it heretics?" the girl with the compact said. "Are they in the city? Are we *safe*?"

"What did I just tell you?" the Proctor snarled. He stomped down the center aisle, jackboots shaking the entire jitney, and held out a hand. "Identification."

The Proctor was tall and thin, the sleeves of his tunic flapping, much like the ravens his agency employed. His nose even hooked, beaklike, below small pinched eyes.

Muttering, the girl fished through her purse. "Don't have to treat a person surly just because some crazies lit a few jitneys on fire." She had a drawl, and enough brunette curls to give a reel starlet a run for her money. I imagined she'd been going to New Amsterdam to give Broadway a try and somehow ended up in the grim iron claws of Lovecraft.

"This isn't a joke!" the Proctor barked. "Give me your papers!"

It wasn't normal, even for a Proctor, to behave so. Something was wrong in Lovecraft.

Tears sprang to the girl's eyes as she rummaged frantically through her ditty bag for her identification.

"There's a lot of them out there," Dean said, nudging me to look out the bubble window. The Proctors were arrayed in a loose ring around the jitney depot, more of them than I'd ever seen in one place except for Banishment Square.

The smoke and the wailing Klaxons came into place for me. From burning buildings, from a riot started by Dean's

393

people in the Rustworks, or for one of a thousand other reasons that people had to hate the Proctors.

Like someone whose brother had been shot by them.

I knew then that there was no chance we were getting off this jitney. Cal's and my papers were only good as students of the School, within city limits. And if Dean had ever had papers, he didn't have them now.

We weren't going back to the Academy to steal Marcos's diving suit. We weren't getting into the Engineworks. The only place any of our trio was going was the castigator if they caught us out when we tried to run.

Heretics didn't receive mercy. Only those who turned themselves in had a chance to have their case heard before a tribunal of Proctors. It was a joke, but it was better than the alternatives presented.

I stood up. Dean grabbed my wrist. "The hell are you doing?"

"Aoife!" Cal hissed. "Sit down!"

I looked them both in the eye. "You need to trust me," I told Dean. "And I'm so very sorry."

The Proctor was staring at me when I looked back into his hooded face. I steadied my shaking legs and stepped forward, holding out my wrists. "My name is Aoife Grayson," I said to him. "I think you're looking for me."

The handcuffs rubbing my wrists were heavy, hand-forged bands with skeleton locks. I tried to slip my thumb under the cuff to scratch my opposite arm, but they were clamped tight.

"Stop that," said the Proctor sitting across from me. The

394

windowless jitney bounced up Northern Avenue. I'd turned us in to avoid a chase, to avoid being caught. To save Cal and Dean the worst of what the Proctors could offer—at least, I hoped so. The jitney slowed as we approached the end of the street. The Ave terminated at Banishment Square, and above the bricks, Ravenhouse lurked.

The Catacombs lived beneath. I was at the end of the line.

"What happened to my friends?" I said. "The boys I was with?"

"Be quiet," said the Proctor. "No speaking until interrogation."

The jitney rattled to a stop and the doors cranked open. The Proctor gripped my arm, not hard, but firm. He knew and I knew who was in charge here. "Out. Watch your head."

The officers who worked in Ravenhouse wore plain black suits, not the double-buttoned uniform tunic of street agents. One checked a booking sheet while the other, a woman in a sharp jacket and pencil skirt, patted me down. The Proctor who'd arrested me at the depot tossed them the carpetbag.

"She had that with her."

"Search it," the officer said to her mate. "File it."

"Hang on," said the one reading the sheet. "You need to see this." He held out the clipboard. "She's been flagged. Grayson, Aoife."

I knew I should be truly terrified—if I was flagged, I was on par with the worst Crimson Guard fugitive—but a tiny thrill went through me. The Proctors thought I was dangerous. Maybe I could turn that to my favor.

395

The trio bowed their heads over the paper, and then one fixed me with bright eyes. "She's a person of highest interest." He shoved the clipboard at the female officer. "We need to get her up to Mr. Draven's office."

I started. Grey Draven was Head of the City. His picture was in all of the Academy's classrooms. He oversaw the Proctors. He might as well be the Master Builder himself.

"Walk." The officer's grip wasn't just firm this time. It hurt, and it would leave bruises come tomorrow.

31

An Audience with Draven

INSIDE THE WORKINGS of Ravenhouse, I was buzzed through a series of gates, from the plain tile entrance with the booking clerk sitting underneath a spitting aether lamp reading *True Confessions* magazine, to cement stairwells, higher and higher with just the Proctor's breathing and my own heartbeat for accompaniment.

Grey Draven. The Head of the City. Equaled only by the other three City Heads, of New Amsterdam and San Francisco and Chicago. We'd all seen the picture in the newspaper of Draven with the President. All the Proctors in Lovecraft reported to him. He wasn't just powerful in the city—Draven was an offshoot of the immutable will of the Bureau of Heresy, which his father, Rupert Draven, had helped found.

If I was being taken to him, I couldn't imagine what might have happened since I ran away. I wondered what

397

sins I'd been accused of and what my fellow students were saying about me.

When I stepped through the innermost doors of Ravenhouse everything had changed. Walls were solid metal, held in place with rivets the size of my fist. Doors were submarine hatches, fully airlocked. Even the aether globes were constrained by mesh cages, useless to any prisoner wily enough to break them. My already leaden stomach sank further.

"Here," the officer grunted finally. "Stand still and straight until the door opens."

"I don't understand why Mr. Draven wants to see me," I said, trying one last ploy for innocence. "I'm just a student."

"Shut up," the Proctor told me. "I don't want to listen to you yap, and I don't have to."

The door we stopped at was a real door, bound in brass, polished wood reflecting my pale face and sleepless eyes back at me. The Proctor pressed the call button on the phonovox next to it, not without hesitation.

"Yes." The voice was high, thin, smooth like glass. It chilled me as if I'd stepped into an icebox.

"Mr. Draven. One of your flagged fugitives, sir. She surrendered to us at the jitney depot a few hours ago."

There was a wait, while the Proctor stared at me and I stared at my reflection. Trying to stay calm was just making things worse.

"Bring her in." The gears at the top of the door turned, releasing lock bars, and the door swung inward.

Draven's office was enormous, a long room that took up

398

the entire back of Ravenhouse. It was also largely empty, floors and shelves bare, windows covered by metal shutters like a war shelter. A desk and two chairs sat at one end of the vast space, underneath a mural on the ceiling of a man in a chariot pulled by a light horse and a dark one traveling above the map of the world, constellations glowing softly in the light of the aether lamps.

"Miss Grayson. Sit." Draven rose and pulled out a chair. The Proctor shoved me, none too gently. I let out a small squeak as the hard chair impacted with my spine.

Draven narrowed his eyes at the Proctor. "Leave, please."

The Proctor got out of the office so quickly that he left a wake of air. I kept my eyes on Draven as he walked with measured tread back to the seat behind his desk. He was tall, thin-faced, hair cropped so one could see the scalp underneath. Younger than I had imagined him by at least a decade, lines were beginning around his eyes, but his gaze still cut straight through me. They were frightening eyes, absolutely flat and yet alive. Predatory, was how I would classify Draven's gaze, and I felt a dull chill work its way over my skin, like I'd pressed against a cold sheet of iron.

Draven took a black cigarette from a silver case and offered me one.

I shook my head. "I don't."

"Good girl." Draven lit his from a tubular jet lighter and exhaled toward the ceiling. "I noticed you looking at the mural."

"It's very . . . detailed," I said gamely. Anything but talking about why I was really here. Any amount of time for Cal and Dean to escape.

399

"That, my dear, is Apollo, chasing the night across the face of the world. It is a blasphemous and heretical depiction of a dead religion, practiced by a fearful, craven civilization that the Master Builder ground under his heel."

I looked at my hands rather than make eye contact as he lectured. The shackles were beginning to burn as they chafed my skin.

Draven let out a low chuff of laughter. "Don't look so scared. I didn't paint it over—it's important to remember our history."

"Those who ignore history are doomed to repeat it," I quoted. I felt tremors all over, and terribly cold, almost like I had a touch of influenza.

Draven's mouth curved up. When he smiled, all of his graveness disappeared and he looked like a boy at the School. One who'd delight in playing cruel pranks on girls like me.

"Aren't you a little straight A?" he said. "I bet you make the boys in your classes furious. The bell curve wasn't made for clever girls." Draven smirked and I forced myself to keep my face neutral. Good thing that was far from the most insulting thing someone had said about me.

"I get along with everyone," I lied. "A ward can't afford to be snobbish."

"No." Draven stubbed out his cigarette. "But I suppose it's difficult to keep that vapid smile on your face. Mad mother, mad brother, the bastard child of a rich man. How the barbs must fly."

"How did you know about my father?" I said, my surprise genuine. I tugged against the shackles. They were as immobile as the other ten times I'd tested them.

400

"Come on now, Aoife," Draven said. "Aoife Eileen Grayson. We Proctors are the eyes, ears and wings of the entire nation. There's nothing we don't know."

There was at least one thing about all this I was pretty sure Draven didn't know, but I kept that to myself.

A knock on the door cut off Draven's smug smile. "Yes?"

"Superintendent Draven." A uniformed Proctor stepped in with my carpetbag. "The girl's effects."

"Put them on the desk, Officer Quinn."

"Yes, sir." Quinn set down the bag and stepped back. Draven lifted one eyebrow.

"Something else, Officer?"

"One of the boys is giving us trouble," Quinn said. "The skinny one."

"Cal—" I bit back a further cry when Draven's eyes crinkled in amusement. At least I knew Cal was alive.

"Take him to a separate interrogation room and do whatever it takes," he ordered. "I want information from him about what he and the girl have been doing out there in Arkham. He'll give it quickly if he knows what's good for him."

"No!" I shouted as Quinn saluted and backed out. "No, Cal had nothing to do with this!" I started up, to lunge for the door, to do *something* to prevent them from hurting him.

"*Sit.*" Draven pinned me across the desk, his finger hovering in front of my face. "I am not going to humor your lies, Aoife. Not when I know what you are."

"I'm not anything," I whispered, although I had the horrible feeling Draven knew my secret. "I ran away, I admit." Maybe if I confessed to what the Proctors expected, I could buy Cal leniency. I started again. "I consorted with heretics

401

and I've got a latent necrovirus infection, and you can do whatever you want with me, but I swear that Cal hasn't done anything wrong."

"You're so sure of your good friend Cal? That's nice," Draven said, standing and going to the single window that wasn't closed off by a shutter. His view looked down the hill, to the river, the bridge, the foundry. "I want you to think, Aoife. Think about the day your mother was committed. A young girl and her brother would go to a state orphanage, girls and boys in different institutions. You would never see your brother again. You knew this. You perhaps shed a few tears right there in the courtroom."

He turned back, arms folded. "Where did you go, Aoife?"

"To . . . to a group home," I said, wondering where this was leading. The house I'd gone to had been close, noisy, full of other children, who pulled my hair and taunted me with jokes until Conrad chased them off.

"With your brother." Draven ticked off on his fingers, backlit against the windows by the endless gray of the sky. "You stayed with your brother. Your needs were met. You both went to the finest school and you both gained entrance to the Lovecraft Academy." He looked at his fingers. "If one were a heretic, one might almost say you had a guardian angel, Aoife. But of course we know the real reason, don't we?"

"I want to see my friends *now*," I snapped. "What does this have to do with them?"

"Don't pretend you don't know," Draven said. "Archibald Grayson may have fathered bastards, but he made sure they'd be as smart as him. He had his clever little ways of ensuring they were taken care of."

402

"My . . . my father?" I blinked at Draven, genuinely confused as to why he thought my childhood was so important. To my mind, it had been nothing but misery from the day Nerissa was committed.

Draven slammed his fist against the window sash. "*Don't pretend you don't know!* Archibald Grayson is a heretic and a traitor to the Iron World and you are going to be the honey that brings him home." Draven leaned in and sucked a deep breath through his nose. "And what sweet honey it is."

I cringed away from him. *The Iron World.* How did he know that term? "I never knew my father. He doesn't give one whit about me. I can't make him come anywhere." That, at least as far as I knew, was the absolute truth.

Draven shook his head and laughed. I saw something else in his hard, beautiful face, a marring and a blurring. "You didn't know him, Aoife, it's true. But I do. And I know exactly what he thought of his filthy-blooded brood."

I felt tears starting and shut my eyes briefly to hold them back. "My father never even spoke to me in person. All I have are his eyes and his blood."

Draven's lips pulled back and he gave a wordless snarl. "You think Archie's little band of conjurers are the only things in this world that have magic beating in the blood? You think the Graysons stood alone after the Storm and the erecting of the Gates?"

I was lost as to what he meant, but the rambling and the abrupt anger—that I'd seen before. I gave voice to what I'd recognized in his eyes. "You're insane, Mr. Draven." Not because he'd admitted he believed in magic as easily as he breathed—that was merely surprising. The insanity wasn't apparent in photos and lanternreels, but up close, to a

403

person who'd seen madness every week for nearly a dozen years, it was clear as day.

"What I am is possessed of the truth, Aoife, and being called things like insane is the price I pay. And here's the truth of that pitiful spark inside you that gives you a pitiful little piece of power: it will only get you killed."

Undoubtedly, that would be easier. If I confessed to heresy as the Proctors defined it, I'd be spared burning. But I didn't want to be easy. Not after everything I'd endured trying to prove I wasn't going mad. I met Draven's eyes. "I'll never renounce the Weird. It's real. I know it and you know it. So burn me. Get it over with."

Draven reached his hand back and cracked me across the face, faster than a snake striking. The spot where Tremaine had hit me began to bleed again and I cried out in shock.

"You walked through iron to come here," Draven snarled. "This room may look like the lair of a soft man, but there are bones of steel running through these walls, bones charged with enchantment that will bleed something like you from the eyes. *Do not* force me to use it."

"Now who's speaking heresy?" I grumbled, too confused and enraged to worry about whether he'd hit me again. "A City Head using enchantments. Honestly. Tell me another."

"The world was much younger when the Storm came." Draven's eyes went soft. "There have been many names for what came into our world that day since—witchcraft, Spiritualism, necrovirus. Many explanations to sate the public and make it feel safe. But they are all poison, all a filthy, otherworldly plague. And they have the gall to call it magic." He sneered, then reached out and tucked a stray

404

piece of hair behind my ear. "Archibald Grayson thinks differently. He believes these forces are his to use. He consorts with the Folk and endangers every human being on earth each time he passes through the Gates. He thinks the Bureau of Heresy extremists, but I *know* he is a traitor to everyone like me, who only want to keep the Lands separated, keep the infection Archibald calls magic at bay. That is why I *will* have him here in Ravenhouse, and assure myself he can do no more harm."

I reeled. The avalanche of information was making my head hurt. I picked out the most shocking fact of the bunch. "You . . . you know of the Folk?"

"Of course I know," Draven scoffed. "The Folk, the Weird, the Mists . . . all of those portentous names humans before the Storm gave such things."

"But . . . no one believes in the Weird . . . no one in Lovecraft, no one rational. . . ." I was sure I was going to toss my last meal onto Draven's elegant carpet. He was telling me he knew all about the Folk, all about magic. And it was clear this wasn't new information to him.

"People do not have the capacity, Aoife," Draven said, as if I were a very small and stupid child. "Something called the necrovirus, something that has a specific cause and perhaps some day a cure, they can control. They can guard against infection. The Folk, magic—the truth, that 'virals' are really creatures crawled up from a world that only exists in their nightmares? That lands exist beside our own and some human's very blood causes them madness or greatness, depending on a flip of a coin?" He sniffed. "If the world knew the truth, it would burn within the week. It nearly did, until a few of us took action, after the Storm."

Draven sighed. "I'm not one for telling tales, but in brief: in 1880 there was a man named Nikola Tesla. He was like Edison, but Tesla had a weakness of spirit. He saw things beyond this world, beyond reason. He created a machine, a machine that could tear the very fabric of the universe asunder. And he turned it on."

Draven passed a hand over his forehead. "It was terrible, terrible what happened. My father was only a boy, but he spoke of the magical cataclysms, the strange creatures that flowed unencumbered through the gateway Tesla ripped open. They called it the Storm. And a brotherhood stepped forward, composed of sorcerers and scientists and madmen. They beat back the Storm. They created the gates with magic and the wonder of Tesla's technology. But they were not good men."

I stayed silent, not giving Draven the reaction he clearly wanted, even though my brain was racing to assimilate his version of history. His nostrils flared as he inhaled sharply. "They did not see that the only way was to cleanse the world of *all* supernatural corruption. We did. And so we called them heretics. We erased magic from all the corners of the earth, and only a few times has it reared its head since. But we'll burn them out. Have no fear. And magic will always be a lie, be no more substantial than a shadow, as long as people believe it's really only the necrovirus."

He stepped to his desk and pressed his buzzer as I watched him, insensible.

The necrovirus wasn't real.

Magic was.

Draven had known all along. He'd let it go on, the burnings and the lockdowns and people like my mother being

406

shoved into madhouses. Why, I didn't know, and it didn't matter.

Everything about Lovecraft was a lie. Everything about this modern, scientific world, the ghoul traps and the madhouses and the worship of reason, was wrong.

Before I could scream, Quinn and another officer appeared. Draven jerked his chin. "Take her to interrogation and test her blood for the usual panel of infection. She's been outside the city limits. She's a contamination risk."

"Let me go!" I screamed as they dragged me along. I lost one of my shoes on the thick carpet, skinned my knees as I thrashed and the Proctors wrestled me along. The truth was sinking in, and as Draven had warned, it was terrible. My head spun and I thrashed like I was a spastic in my mother's asylum. "Let me go! I'm not contaminated! There *is* no necrovirus! He's a liar!"

As Quinn and the other officer dragged me away, Draven placed his hand on my carpetbag, on my father's journal and the goggles and the invigorator, as if they belonged to him, and then he met my eyes and tipped me a wink.

Draven and I. United in the awful, world-burning truth.

The door of Draven's office slammed shut and then only my own voice echoed down Ravenhouse's long iron halls.

The interrogation room was bleak and bare, entirely different from Draven's office. There were no bones of finery here, just concrete and one-way glass.

Cal would have loved it, I thought. It was just like his novels and Saturday matinees. Sweat the villains and make them talk.

407

"Doctor's coming in," Quinn said. "Don't you make a move, kid."

My lip had stopped bleeding. Now it just felt swollen and sticky, like I'd let candy melt and linger on my tongue.

I counted stains on the acoustic tiles of the ceiling until the door buzzed and admitted a man in a white coat with a black leather bag. He had a cotton surgery mask over the lower half of his face, but he was taller than Quinn, rangier.

"This is her?" He reeled himself to a quick stop inside the door.

"What?" Quinn said. "You were expecting Al Capone?"

"She doesn't look contaminated." The doctor took an identical mask from his bag and handed it to Quinn. "But all the same, I need to ask you to put this on and leave the room."

Quinn blanched. "I might be exposed?"

It'd serve him right, I thought. Every one of them, if they did contract something nasty from Thorn. Get devoured by a nightjar, or see what really lurked in the Mists. Every last stinking Proctor on earth fed to a corpse-drinker. That would be a start.

"Necrovirus is not transmitted through the air," the doctor said. "As far as we know. But there are procedures the public health office must follow. Now please, for your own safety. Wait outside until I've drawn her blood."

The Proctor scuttled out of the room, and the door slammed and locked.

"Oh yes," I said loudly, to the door. "Watch out for the big, bad necrovirus." Draven and the Proctors had lied to everyone. I couldn't even begin to contemplate what their lie meant for me. For my madness. For my family. If there was no necrovirus, then . . . what? What made my mother believe dreams and visions over reality, even if some of them had come true? Because she certainly wasn't normal. What had made Conrad transform, at least for a moment, into someone who'd spill my blood?

And when my birthday turned over, what in all of cold space would happen to *me*?

The doctor gave me a smile from behind his mask, seemingly impervious to my shouting panic. "Pretty grim in here, isn't it?"

"It's not a vacation to Cape Cod, that's for sure," I grumbled. The doctor chuckled.

"Keeping your sense of humor. That's important." He took out a rubber cord and a syringe. "I'm going to roll up your sleeve, since you're shackled. Is that all right?"

"There is no necrovirus," I insisted. "I'm not infected. Draven lied. . . ." I realized that my frantic denials at least *sounded* crazy to somebody who was a doctor, a man of science. I had to try to convince him and not sound like a lunatic. "I haven't contacted any . . . any virals," I amended. The word sounded so trite now. If there was no virus, there could be no virals.

My shoggoth bite still throbbed when I moved too quickly.

What was a shoggoth really? A monster? A thing from beyond the stars, fallen to earth? A creature that had oozed into our land from Thorn?

"I know," the doctor said. He tied the cord around my arm and slapped the inside of my elbow with two fingers. I blinked at him, not understanding.

"You do?"

409

"I do." The doctor picked up his syringe and laid it against the blue vein crawling up my arm.

"How do you know?" I pulled away as much as the shackles would allow. *What* did he know?

"Listen to me very carefully," the doctor said. His eyes bored into mine, stony green as if they'd been mined from some dark, secret cave. "In fifteen seconds, the aether and vox feed for the interrogation rooms will be interrupted. Look around the room. What do you see?"

"I . . ." I tried not to gape. I might have a week ago, but now I just darted my gaze from the mirrored glass to the tired blue aether lamp bolted into the ceiling to the scuff marks, slimy and concentric, in the cement from a poor job of mopping.

"You're going to have less than thirty seconds in the dark," said the doctor, jamming the needle into my arm and filling the long glass tube with blood, ignoring me when I gasped and jerked. "Go through the vent. Go quickly."

"Who *are* you?" I said. I might not be surprised any longer but I was just as bewildered.

The doctor snapped the band off my arm and zipped his bag closed. "You know who I am, Aoife."

He backed away from me and pressed the door buzzer. I jumped from my seat, feeling like I was moving through a molten river, but I couldn't let him leave before I'd seen his face.

I wasn't quick enough. The doctor stepped through the door, vanishing like he was a vision borne by madness.

A half second later, the aether lamp went out.

Darkness closed over my head like a drowning pool, and

410

I moved forward on instinct. I fetched my shin against the metal leg of the table and bit back a curse.

Go through the vent. Go quickly. Doctor's words echoing in my mind, I closed the distance to the far wall and reached up with my shackled hands to grasp the vent cover. It was coated with dust and grease, but it fell away easily enough.

Climbing in with my hands bound was nearly impossible, but the doctor hadn't gifted me with a key or a leg up. Just the darkness.

Outside the room, there was shouting, and the door buzzed. Quinn was coming back, coming to see that his prisoner was still in her rightful place and to administer pain if she wasn't.

I jumped and landed half in, half out of the vent, bashing my forehead on the top and my stomach on the lip.

Pain was tertiary. I could feel it later, for any length of time it desired. Now I felt as if there were a furnace inside me, a steam engine pressurized to bursting. I crawled for my life, using my elbows, my knees, bruising and skinning all of the sharp edges of myself.

I was perhaps fifteen meters down the vent when the lights came back on. A junction presented itself and I curled up in a ball, rolling to the left just as a hand lantern's light sliced the spot where I'd been.

"Foul the gears! She's in the ventilation!" Quinn's nasal voice, made sharper by bouncing off metal, followed me. "Lock down Ravenhouse. Get officers at all the exits. Alert the raven mechanics to have a flight ready to sweep the city."

I kept crawling, his exhortations to his fellows growing

411

fainter and fainter. I passed over grates, saw Proctors running to and fro like insects in a man-sized ant farm.

When I felt like I had stripped every last shred of skin from my knees, I stopped, panting, above a grate that covered me in bars of light.

The door in the room below swung open and I heard the clank of shackles. "Get in and stay put!" a Proctor shouted.

"Up your vents!" the prisoner snapped back. I froze in place, curling my fingers over the vent. I knew the voice, the tall silhouette and the dark hair.

Dean.

32

The Proctor's Truth

"Dean!" I hissed. He cast about for a moment and then looked up.

"Aoife?" His mouth slackened. "What the hell are you doing up there?"

"Long story," I said. "I promise, when we've gotten away from here I'll explain in full." I shoved on the vent until it gave, then swung myself down, wincing as I landed. I had knocked myself around but good getting out of the interrogation room.

Dean helped me up as best he could with his hands shackled, pressing his forehead against mine. "I can't believe you're here. I thought I'd never clap eyes on you again."

I breathed in for a moment, letting his scent of leather and cigarettes and boy calm my ragged breathing. "They tried," I whispered. "But it'll take a little more to get rid of me for good." I held out my hands. "I think I can slip the

413

door, but these shackles are another matter." The skeleton lock, complex and virtually without moving parts, gave not a whisper to my Weird.

"Leave that to me," Dean said. "Got a hairpin, princess?"

I reached up and snatched one from my bun, which had become just another one of my wild nests of hair in the face of Proctor force.

"I met Grey Draven," I said as Dean went to work on my shackles. Even with his hands tied, he was quick and smooth as a cardsharp shuffling a deck.

"No kidding." Dean stuck the tip of his tongue between his teeth as he worked the lock. "Always gave me the creeps in the lanternreels. He has those dead-man eyes, like he sees everything at once."

"He told me some things," I said very quietly. "Some really terrible things, Dean. About me, about my father—"

"Got it!" he said as my handcuffs snapped open. He handed me the pin. "I'll talk you through it—get mine off and we're gone, baby, gone."

"There is no necrovirus," I said as I went to work on Dean's shackles. "They made it up. Draven knows about the Folk. He told me how the gateways between Iron and Thorn used to be open. How people like my father have been trying to keep the balance while the Proctors just lie. Draven knows everything about me."

"That's . . ." Dean shook his head. There was a long time where the only sound was the scrape of the pin against the lock. "Aoife, I don't know what you want me to say to make that all right," he said at last.

"Nothing," I said as I wiggled the pin in his locks. "Don't say anything. I just had to tell someone before I exploded."

414

"So if there's no virus"—Dean gave a long breath of relief as his shackles came loose, and rubbed his raw wrists—"what's wrong with your old lady and your brother?"

I turned to the door, laying my cheek against the metal, caressing the lock and the handle with my Weird. "I don't know," I told Dean. "But something is making us mad, and I aim to find out what." I had always known that Nerissa's behavior and her hallucinations and my dreams weren't normal, never mind my own brother coming at me with a knife. There was still something in our blood. But now, at least, there might be a real cure.

The lock popped and the door swung open before me. The Weird was quiet in this place encased in iron, easier to control. I flinched as my nose began to leak blood again. My vision slurred left and right as I stumbled along the wall with Dean.

"We need to find Cal," I gasped. "Draven said . . . he said for the Proctors to torture him. . . ."

I became aware that Dean was no longer behind me.

"I don't think we're going to get far on that plan, princess," he said, and I turned to watch him put up his hands. My stomach plummeted. We'd been so close.

"Nice to see you again." Quinn was flanked by two other Proctors, and they were all armed. He shouldered his weapon and snatched me by the arm. "Be a good little girl this time," he whispered. He dragged me away from Dean and down flights of stairs, until dripping water and mold told me I was deep beneath the earth. We spilled into a hallway containing a row of iron doors lit only by a series of aether lanterns hung from crossbeams.

"We're below the riverbed," Quinn told me as he

415

unlocked the nearest door. "Unless you've got gills, you're ours for good."

He tossed me into the cell and the door shut behind me. I shouted and screamed and pounded on the door, but it did no good. Once more, I was alone in the dark.

33

Escape from Ravenhouse

I LAY IN the dark for a long time, on cold stone, listening to water drip and things slither in the dark. Rats scuttled in and out of my view, through a drain in the floor trickling filthy water from the cell into the new sewers. I wondered if this blackness and the foul, eldritch caress of damp river air would be the last things I saw and felt before I was executed or lost to madness.

I thought about what Draven had said, that he meant to use me to lure my father back to Lovecraft. I thought about the fact that nearly the entire world believed the most elaborate of lies.

I wondered how many other heretics had gone to the castigator knowing what I knew.

At last, when I couldn't be alone with my thoughts for another moment, a second door rolled back from a nether part of the cell, letting in light and sound and two more

417

forms, both of whom hit the floor with a thump and a curse from the Proctor herding them.

"Who's there?" A man's voice, from the corner. I curled myself up, putting my back to a wall, trying to get as far away from the invisible rasp as possible. Who'd been dumped in here with me? I had a feeling they might be worse than the Proctors.

"Who are *you*?" Something ran over my foot and I kicked at it.

"Aoife?"

I squinted into the dimness of the cell. "*Dean?*"

A hand reached out and felt for mine, and I grabbed it. "Oh, Dean. You're all right." I had never been more glad of anything in my life. Alone, I might make it out alive, but knowing that Dean's life rested with me as well redoubled my resolve.

"Of course I am, kid," he whispered. "You never doubted me, did you?"

"Did they hurt you?" I demanded. "I can't see you." I reached out and felt for Dean's face, and he caught my hands and pressed them against his cheek.

"I'm in one piece, at least," he murmured. "It's going to be all right, Aoife."

"Cal," I said, seized with panic again. "Where's Cal?"

Dean went quiet. I stood up, slowly, feeling my way along the wall. "Dean. Where's Cal?"

"You can't get marginal on me, Aoife," he said. "But they brought us in at the same time. He's in here." There was a shuffle and a click, and Dean's lighter flamed to life.

The light illuminated Cal's body, and I let out a small

418

cry, which I trapped with my hands. My empty stomach rebelled for the hundredth time that day and I choked, the sight before me grotesque and unbearable.

Dean leaned forward, cupping the flame with his hands. "Looked pretty rough when they brought us in here. He didn't say anything."

Cal's face was a welter of bruises, his right eye swollen shut and his lower lip split. Bruises on his wrists mapped where he'd been tied with something sharp and elastic, and his shirt had blood on it.

"Oh, please no . . . ," I whispered. "Cal, Cal, Cal." I shook his shoulder, but he didn't move except to roll away from me, toward the wall.

"Why would they do that?" I said. I wanted to hit something, and I banged my fists against the cell door, over and over, wishing it were the Proctor who'd beaten my friend. Dean grabbed my hands, pinned them at my side.

"I don't know why, Aoife, and there doesn't have to be a reason. The situation is, they beat him bad and he's going to kick off if we don't do something."

Dean had bruises too, when I looked closer. I touched the cut on his cheekbone, twin lines of red. He flinched. "It's nothing. Just standard heavy work. Letting me know they weren't fooling around."

"Cal's not a criminal," I said. "They had no reason . . . Draven just needs *me*."

"These people don't need much of a reason for anything, Aoife," Dean said. "They need you, sure. Us, they'll keep here until they need more bodies for the castigator. Then . . . we'll be broiled beef."

419

"Stop saying that," I ordered, my last reserve of will close to snapping. I could put on a brave face, but sooner or later my true one would show and I'd be in a heap. "I almost got out of here, and there will be another chance."

"Not to piss on the parade," Dean said, "but all the Rustworks knows: you end up in Ravenhouse, you end, full stop." He held the lighter over me while I felt Cal's pulse and checked his eyes, the basic first aid all engineers had to know in case of an accident on the job.

I never imagined using it like this.

"You can't give up on me," I said to Dean. I was scared, so scared my fingers were vibrating, but more than that I was angry. Angrier than I'd ever been. Draven's lies were the reason we were down here, not through any fault of ours. "If you give up," I told Dean, "then I'm going to break into a million pieces."

Dean frowned as the lighter flickered, flame lowering. "Bad news, kid. We're going to be in the dark for the rest of this party." He shut the lid of the lighter. "But I'm here, Aoife. I'll give you everything I've got."

"Thank you," I said softly. "I need you, Dean."

He nodded, squeezing my shoulder in the dimness. "Figure I need you too. You are the brains of the operation, after all."

I rolled Cal onto his back and felt him over. He groaned when I touched his ribs, his chest. "He might have gotten something crushed internally," I said. "He needs a doctor."

"And I need a drink," Dean said. "I figure Cal and I have the same chance at both. We should wrap his ribs, at least for comfort. I busted one during a pit fight in Jamestown and it hurt like knives."

420

"Pit fighting?" I was talking so that my mind wouldn't run away, chattering like I was at one of Mrs. Fortune's inane tea parties, to keep from the ugly reality of my situation. "Who would have guessed an upstanding boy like you would enjoy such a pastime?"

"Never tell an Irishman three sheets to the wind that he's got a pretty sister," Dean said. "Sound advice."

"I'll keep it in mind," I murmured as I ripped open Cal's shirt, buttons flying, and extricated his long arms from the too-short sleeves. "Dammit. He never gets anything tailored." Tears welled up, the pressure too much.

"Give it here," Dean said. "I'll make bandages. Get him talking—if they whammed his noggin, he shouldn't fall asleep."

"Cal." I shook him, gently as I could. "Cal, say something."

"Aoife." My name on his lips was thickened with blood and delirium. "They brought you back."

"I was trying to get out," I said. "I got caught."

"I . . ." Cal coughed, and dark blood appeared on his chin like inky raindrops. "I gotta tell you something, Aoife."

"No," I said, smoothing a hand over his forehead. "Save it. There's time yet."

Linen shredded as Dean ripped up Cal's school shirt. Cal grabbed for me. His palm was slick, with blood or sweat, I couldn't tell. "Can't wait. I can't wait."

"All right, all right," I said. "You have to stay still, Cal. Tell me what's wrong."

"I lied to you. . . ." Cal's voice went dreamy, and his pulse under my fingers slipped away like a drop of mercury on glass.

421

"It doesn't matter," I said. "Whatever you did, I forgive you."

"You shouldn't," he said. "I'm so far away, Aoife . . . so far away from home. . . ."

My shoulder began to throb, and I clamped my free hand over the bite. "Dean, he's not making any sense."

"He lost a lot of his juice," Dean said. "Probably needs a transfusion."

"Cal." Shaking wasn't working anymore, so I slapped him across the face, trying to avoid the worst of his bruises. "Don't you die on me, Cal Daulton. I'll get you blood. Just *please* hang on."

"I don't need blood," he wheezed after a moment. "I need . . ." Another coughing fit, more blood droplets scattering across the stones and my hands.

"What?" I said. "Tell me, Cal."

"I need meat," he rasped. "Fresh meat. Something live."

I gaped at him. "Why in the stars would you need that?" The pain in my shoulder where the shoggoth had bitten intensified and I groaned. I'd be seeing double if I could see at all. The last time it had hurt this much was when I'd been close to eldritch creatures, as if, in a peculiar way, the shoggoth's venom had given me an early warning. . . .

"Meat," Cal whined, in a voice that echoed off the high parts of the cell. "I want to eat. . . ."

"Aoife." Dean grabbed my shoulder and I yelped. His touch burned the shoggoth's bite. "Get away from him. Now."

"He's in shock," I said. "He's hallucinating."

Cal gave another groan like bones creaking, and then he sat up, as if someone had jammed a rod into his back.

422

The spot on his face I'd touched was beginning to peel back, skin hanging in loose ribbons. I stared, unable to think of moving, or anything but the sloughing flesh on the face that had formerly been Cal's.

My stomach lurched as the pain crested, and Dean yanked me out of Cal's reach as he swiped at me. His hands were huge, and tipped with black claws that flexed and retracted.

"He's not hallucinating," Dean whispered in my ear. "He's a ghoul."

Trapped in the half-dark, I clung to Dean while Cal convulsed on the cell floor. "Cal . . ." I reached out an experimental hand, and Cal snapped at me. His teeth had multiplied and lengthened, and his bones protruded from under his skin like a mountain range.

I jerked my hand back. Cal wasn't Cal any longer. He snarled at me, and I flinched as if I'd been slapped. How could I have not seen this? Cal had fooled me, more than even Draven.

"Keep away from him, princess," Dean said. "Ain't anything more we can do."

"No," I said, wriggling free of Dean's grasp. "He's still Cal." I was mostly talking to talk myself into believing the thing on the floor was still my friend. I couldn't deny he had changed. There was precious little of him left to the naked eye. Just the thing I'd been told my entire life was the embodiment of terror. Only the fact that I couldn't see much in the dark kept me from screaming.

Keeping myself clear of his claws and jaws, I crawled

423

over to Cal and forced myself to touch the clammy, loose skin hanging from his newly hollow ribs. "How could you not tell me?" I demanded. My voice rose, anger echoing off the cell walls. "How *could* you?"

Cal hacked and trembled, and reached for me. His claws put furrows in my wrist. "I had to. I *had* to. He came down and he found me and he told me that if I didn't follow you, he'd burn us out of our home."

"What?" I said. "Someone made you spy on me and pretend to be my *friend*?"

"Aoife, you should get away from him *now*," Dean said. "If he's changing, that means he's going to feed."

"Don't tell me what to do!" I shouted at Dean. "I want to know why my best friend in the world's been lying to me!"

"It was Draven," Cal croaked. "He found me two years ago. The Proctors would have burned me out, but I had something he wanted. I can take human skin, and he said . . . he said if I went to the Academy, watched you . . . I had to keep you under my eye."

"Cal, *why*?" I gripped his shoulders, shaking him. I could feel bone and gristle, the foreign physiognomy of a ghoul instead of Cal's skinny frame, and it made my skin crawl. I held on, anger overriding disgust. "Why did you pretend to be my friend?" I whispered.

"Because of what you are," Cal said. His voice wasn't Cal's voice anymore. It was guttural, a growl of hunger rather than the person I knew speaking. "Draven told me that if you ever found out who you really are . . . what you can do . . . it would be . . . a disaster."

"You've been bird-dogging us," Dean said. "The ravens

424

on the bridge. Alouette calling in the Proctors on the airship. Every bit of bad luck since we met." He curled a fist, flexed it like you'd pull back the hammer of a gun. "I should smash your ugly face in. Do you realize what you've done? It's *your* thrice-damned fault we're in here."

"No more." Cal's breathing was shallow and rapid, his limbs jittering and twitching of their own accord as his nerves played their last notes. "You found your Weird, Aoife. In the crypt, when my brothers tried to stop you. I played dumb because I hoped I could still salvage this and make you go home, but I failed. Two years watching you, pushing you away from the truth, two years being the most horrid, intolerant, party-line-spouting excuse for a human being I could be to keep you in check, and I failed." He let out a shuddering gasp, a wheeze bubbling from his lungs that sounded dire. "Draven put me in here to kill you, I expect, when he gets what he wants from your pop. And then rot away from hunger myself."

I sat back on my heels. My only friend, the gawkish boy who loved *The Inexplicables* and *Gunsmoke*, who helped me with engineering assignments tirelessly, was a monster.

In my chest, a cold ball of iron formed and expanded and turned into resolve. I would pay Grey Draven back for what he'd done to me. If I had to die to do it, I was going to expose the Bureau of Heresy's lie.

"I won't hurt you," Cal managed. "I . . . won't. You don't deserve this."

"You're damn right I don't," I said. Cal shied away from my voice.

"Understand," he begged. "It was this, or watch my nest

425

burn alive. My whole family. You, with Conrad . . . you'd do the same, wouldn't you?"

"There's a difference." I hadn't known my voice could hold so many ice crystals. "I wouldn't have betrayed you over Conrad, Cal."

"Doesn't matter, anyway," he said. "They'll use you to bring your father out of hiding, and interrogate both of you until you forget all about me. And I'll die, and the world will go on."

"Star and stone, Cal," I said. The anger trickled out, replaced by the solid ingot of defeat. "You're just giving up. The Cal Daulton I knew wouldn't give up."

"The Cal you knew is fiction," Dean said. "Just like his trashy magazines."

"He's not." I kept my eyes on Cal. "He was my friend, my best friend, and he wouldn't just curl up and die. He'd help me, because he'd know we aren't getting out of here any other way."

Cal let out a long, shuddering sigh. "You changed my mind about humans, Aoife. You showed me they're not all roaches. But we're not getting out of here."

"You'd better hope we are," I said. "Because Draven needs me alive for now. He gave the order to beat you senseless himself. You're expendable." I scooted closer to him, implored him with my gaze. "We need each other, Cal. No matter what you really think of me, if you want to keep breathing, we have to run before they come back. Now, you've been here at least once before. What can you tell me about Ravenhouse?" Below the water table as we were, trapped in the bowels with layers of Proctors above us, my

426

little trick of opening doors wouldn't do any good. I needed variables, options, a plan.

I heard Cal's tongue flick out, tasting the blood on his lips. I tried to ignore his small, starved groan. "There's a sewer main under the cell block," he said. "Old main. Before the Army Corps dug the new underground. I used to hunt there . . . with my brothers."

"Boss," Dean said. "And we're locked above it in a concrete cell with an iron door and two hundred Proctors who want us fried on the other side."

"Give me meat," Cal harshed, "and I can get us out."

Dean looked at me. "You really want to help this critter get stronger?"

"He knows he's just cannon fodder to Draven," I insisted. "And he has as much to lose as we do staying here."

Dean whistled through his teeth. "I just hope this plan is better than your last one."

I gave him a dirty look even though he couldn't see it. "Why don't you find him something to eat?" I could tell by sound that there were many more living things in the cell than Dean, Cal and me. I held Cal's head cradled in my lap, stroking the few strands of hair left on his lumpy skull to keep him awake, trying not to pull away from the feel of his clammy new skin. Dean felt along the floor of the cell and came up with a squealing, thrashing rat. "Just what the doctor ordered."

I shied away. "Don't make me touch that."

Dean crouched next to Cal. "Fresh meat, buddy. Open your trap."

Cal reached up feebly and grabbed for the rat. It

427

screeched, and disappeared into his gullet in two bites. I had thought my gag reflex was exhausted, but it clamped again at the sight of the wriggling tail between Cal's lips.

After a moment of chewing, Cal sat up shakily. He opened his mouth, unhinging his jaw by degrees, and dug his clawed hands into the floor. "You feel it, Erlkin?" he growled at Dean. "Below our feet?"

Dean's brow quirked, and he placed his hand against the cell block floor. "He's right. Something's down there."

Cal lay down, his cheek against the floor. He let out a low wail, notes spiraling and twisting. The dirge changed, lilting and high, then moaning and low. Cal sang, and my shoulder began to hurt, a twinge I was beginning to recognize as the shoggoth venom responding to its fellow monsters.

It was a beautiful song, the ghoul's song, full of pain and loss and hope.

When Cal finished, my eyes were hot with tears. Dean coughed once. "That helps us how, exactly?"

"Just wait . . . ," Cal cooed. "My blood will answer me. . . ."

A rumble came from below, a thud, and the drain in the floor lifted out of its seat. Cal scrabbled at it with his claws. "Help me!"

A ghoul paw burst from below, and Cal grabbed it.

"*Carver.*" The throaty voice was like Tanner's back in the crypt, but lacked the cruel edge of starvation. *"Is that really you?"*

"Me, Toby," Cal said, as the floor around the drain collapsed with a rumble of stone and mortar, splashing into the water below where an old sewer main laid bare. "It's really me."

428

Outside the cell, a guard shouted.

"Go," Cal rasped at Dean and me, gesturing to the hole. "Run for your lives."

I snatched at his bare arm. His skin was loose now, papery like that of a man decades older, and his face was hollow-eyed and grim. A rictus grin showed off his teeth. Not the Cal I knew. Except in the eyes. His eyes were still Cal's.

"You're coming with us. You have to."

"Get your cute little rear down that hole!" Dean shouted. "More Proctors are coming!"

Cal stared back at the door. It rattled as the guard struggled to cycle the hatch. "He smells like fear."

"If you kill him," I said, "Draven will be right. You'll just be an animal on his leash. Come with us, Cal. Forget Draven."

The longest seconds of my life went by while Cal crouched at the edge of the hole in the floor, staring hungrily between me and the door.

Then he jumped into the hole next to me, and Dean followed him. "Move, Aoife! That guard will shoot you in one more second!"

"Wait!" I cried, realizing that I was missing something. "The book! The witch's alphabet and the tools are still back there with Draven!"

"No time!" Dean jerked me farther into the sewer. I thrashed, fighting in earnest against him.

"I have to get the book!"

Dean met my eyes. "It's too *late*, Aoife. We have to run. *Now.*"

Sick at my failure, I followed him down the tunnel.

429

Wood and brick dust dropped into the slowly trickling water below.

Behind us a Proctor bellowed for us to halt, in the name of reason. Dean squeezed my hand. "I'm right behind you."

I ran into the dark without looking back.

34

The City Under the World

THE SEWER MAIN was ancient and close, cold running water up to my shins. Dean caught me and held me up when I turned my ankle on the jagged bricks that hid beneath the fetid water.

Cal and the other ghoul loped ahead of us, panting. "This way," Cal growled. "Two lefts, then a right."

I followed his bobbing head until the sounds of the pursuing Proctors faded, and then climbed out of the slough and huddled against the wall. It was too much. Cal, his true face, this escape with more of the same monsters who had tried to devour me in Arkham—I had to stop and regain my equilibrium before I lost it for good.

I felt the madness, stronger than ever, scraping at the back of my brain. No math could will it away now. Especially since I knew it wasn't infection, but something I couldn't name or control.

Cal stopped as well, and kicked off his shoes and socks.

431

His toes curled under, and he climbed out of the slough using claw and nail. He slithered rather than walked, and I scooted away.

"We have to keep moving," Cal said. Even his voice was foreign, and I tried to look nowhere but his eyes.

"Not until you tell me where we're headed."

Cal lowered his lumpy head and gave a snarl of frustration, but I didn't back away. Cal-the-ghoul wasn't the worst thing I'd seen today.

"The lady's got a point," Dean said. His breathing was ragged, and he felt his pockets for a cigarette but produced only a squashed, empty pack. "You planning on adding us to your ghoul buffet, cowboy?"

Cal scritched behind his ear. His hair was the same autumn straw but thinner, longer, wilder and spattered with dirty water. "I'm taking you home. My home."

The second ghoul came loping back from his position in the rear. *"Men in the tunnel. Men with lights. Got to move."*

"Aoife, Dean," Cal said. "This is October. My nest mate."

"You call it brothers," October said. *"Are we ditching the meat or taking it along?"*

"Don't," Cal warned him. "They saved my life back there."

"Bah." Toby flicked his tongue out, tasted the air. *"No intruders in the hearth. We don't make friends with meatsacks, we eat them."*

"Toby," Cal growled. *"Enough."*

The tall, blue-skinned ghoul grunted. *"Enough when I say it's enough."* With that, he loped down the tunnel ahead of

432

us. I hung back, not sure that I wouldn't be turned into supper if I followed Cal's brother. Cal shook his head sadly.

"I apologize for him. Not all of us can take the skin—look human—and he's not used to people."

"No need to apologize for your brother not being a rat-fink liar like you, Calvin," Dean said cheerfully. "Or, not Calvin—it's Carver, right? Fits a slimy, ground-dwelling nasty like you."

Cal bared his teeth, but he brought up the rear as we hurried away from the underside of Ravenhouse and the Proctors and their shouts.

I gave Dean a look, one he answered with a shrug. I didn't really blame him. I was furious and frightened, but most of all I just couldn't believe Cal had deceived me so thoroughly. That I hadn't seen, in all his toothy grins and odd habits, the ghoul within. I was supposed to be smarter than that.

The slog through the sewers and forgotten places of Lovecraft was arduous and wore on endlessly.

Eventually, we reached an abandoned metro station, a subterranean jitney car still sitting on its tracks. The windows were smashed, the station number in the glass above the driver's seat was obscured by decades of dirt, and bright round eyes watched us from the shadows under the seats.

Lovecraft had shut down the Metrocar after the ghouls came into the underground, nearly fifty years ago by my count. The station was as it must have been the day the Proctors bolted steel plates over the entry stairs and cut the

433

aether feed. The sign worked into the tile of the wall read DERLETH STREET STATION, and the long, echoing drip of water all around confirmed we were close to the river.

"You feeling all right, doll?" Dean said as we crossed the tracks and ducked into a hole broken through the scarred, sooty tiles of the jitney tunnel.

"My shoulder hurts," I said. The Proctors hadn't lied about the ghoul infestation. Just about everything else.

"This is a terrible idea." Toby clambered up the wall and walked along the ceiling, suspended overhead like a great spider. *"They've both got blood in the wind. They're food, Carver."*

I flinched at the hunger underlying Toby's words. Everything I knew about ghouls screamed at me to run before I was in six pieces, but everything I knew came from the Academy. They'd lied about the necrovirus . . . what else had they been wrong about?

Cal sighed. "Toby, shut up. I told you, I owe Aoife a debt, one of blood, and she'll be safe in the nest." He fixed his brother with a glare. "One way or another."

Eventually the tunnel became brick, older than the Metrocar line, and mud sluiced around my ankles. Toby dropped back to the floor, his way across the ceiling blocked by glowing stalactites of fungus.

"Carver paid a heavy price for your skin, girl. He's still paying it."

I instinctively flinched away from his humped form and gravel-grinding voice, then felt myself flush. Whatever he was, whatever he thought of me, Toby had saved our lives.

"I—I had no idea about Draven and his assignment,"

I said. "Cal told me he had a family, but obviously I didn't know his . . . situation."

"His situation is that he's bringing humans to the nest," Toby snarled. *"In case you're dumb as you look, that doesn't happen. Not with live ones, anyway."*

"Toby, I know that Cal had to do what he did," I said gently. "But he helped us escape and I bear him . . . you . . . no ill will." I hoped he couldn't tell I was only marginally sure he wouldn't eat me.

"How about you?" Toby jerked his pointed chin at Dean. *"You smell like the wind and wet. You're no more human than we are . . . you going to be trouble?"*

"You know, you can keep walking down that road, friend, but you sure as hell aren't going to like where it ends," Dean told him. " 'We ain't got a quarrel unless you're fixing to start one." He glanced behind us, back down the tunnel.

"The Proctors won't follow us beyond Derleth Street," Toby said. *"The tunnels beyond aren't clear."* He grinned at me, and it was like looking at a basketful of razors. *"The tunnels north of Derleth Street belong to us. The people of* ghul.*"*

I turned away from his grim smile and fell back to walk with Cal. I forced myself to look at his face—his new face—and his hunched body with his plate-shaped hands and black razor claws. What could a girl possibly talk about with a ghoul?

"Have you . . ." My voice was rough and squeaky, and I abhorred Cal thinking I was frightened of him, even though he unsettled me. I cleared my throat behind my hand. "Have you always been able to turn into a human?"

"It's called taking the skin." Cal's tongue darted out and

435

over his lips. "It's shape-shifting. I'm not human. Isn't that what you're trying to say?"

I tossed up my hands. "Hell, Cal. You're a monster that mothers threaten children with and you're still touchy as an ugly girl in a pretty dress."

After a moment, I heard a gentle snorting in the dark. The snorting turned into chuckling, Cal's laughter, familiar and safe.

I joined, unable to keep a most unladylike giggle from rising to the surface.

"Do you remember when we hid an aethervox under Marcos's bed and convinced him his room was haunted?" Cal asked finally, gasping for breath.

I nodded, clapping a hand over my mouth. "He was ready to take orders for the Master Builder's seminary to make it stop."

"You know," Cal said abruptly, "I have plenty of hearth mates in my nest. We grew together, we learned to hunt together—hunt *humans* together—and Toby is my twin." He lowered his head. "But I never had a friend until I met you."

The fear ebbed. That was Cal talking, even if his face was strange.

"I didn't even have that," I said after a moment. "I grew up in group homes. Conrad and I . . ." I trailed off, hoping he'd understand.

"Survival doesn't make for fast friendships," Cal agreed. "The goddess Hecate teaches us that any one of us might die on any hunt. Her faces are the Huntress and the Hunger. She forbids frivolity. Friendship and love make the *ghul* weak."

436

"People, too," I said. Cal reached for me, then realized there was no way we could clasp hands with his elongated digits, and pulled his paw away.

"Don't say that, Aoife. You showed me yourself it isn't always true."

We came to a junction in the tunnel. Toby stood on his hind legs and scented the air, making himself a head taller than I was. I backed up.

"We're alone," Toby said. *"We can head for home. If you still insist on bringing the meat."*

"I do! And stop calling them meat," Cal growled.

Toby gave a wet sniff. *"Whatever you say. They're your problem."*

He scampered down the left-hand tunnel, and Cal padded after him, mumbling under his breath. I followed, glad that I was bringing up the rear with Dean, where nothing could surprise me.

The tunnel widened into a disused water main. Old clay crumbled under my feet. I watched my tread, and nearly plowed into Cal when he stopped abruptly.

Cal pointed to a glow in the distance, where three massive mains made a junction half collapsed from age and disuse. "Up there. It's home."

437

35

The Gift of the Ghouls

The GHOUL NEST crouched under the junction like a giant spider, the long fibrous ribbons of the nest tunnels clinging to the ancient drainage main that swept debris from old Lovecraft south and out to the river.

"Go slow," Cal said. "Let them smell you and see that you're not hostile."

I had no desire to rush into the heart of the city's worst nightmare, and I stopped a few yards from the waist-high hole that was the nest's entrance.

The ghoul nest was woven from snatches of metal and leather, canvas and fabric, humped tents clustered around a central hub wafting gentle smoke that smelled of char and something richer and darker. An old, old memory, of a madhouse surgery after my mother broke her mirror into a knifelike shard, called back to me. I was smelling blood.

An ancient jitney, so old it still bore the seal of the Massachusetts Transit Authority rather than the City seal, contained a horde of ghoul pups, all jockeying for position at the windows. They bared their teeth, pocketknives instead of wicked blades, but still sharp enough to eat me.

"Ever feel like an entrée?" Dean muttered. "All we need is a little drawn butter."

"Mother!" Toby called, dropping onto all four limbs so he could pass easily into the nest. *"We're home. We're all home!"*

"Your mother lives in there?" I said, then realized I sounded as spoiled as any typical Uptown princess. "I mean, of course she does."

Cal looked to me. "This is what Draven said he'd come and burn to ashes." His eyes begged me to understand.

A female ghoul half my height came forth, an ivory-handled walking stick in her grasp. Though she limped on two legs, her hair was only half silver, and twisted into gypsy braids, and her arms and legs were banded with iron muscle. There was a scar across her smushed nose, and unlike Cal, nothing human glinted in her gaze. *"We?"* she demanded. *"I sent you out for a simple errand, October, and you return with—"*

Cal lifted one paw. "It's me, Mother. I came back."

The woman's walking stick clattered out of her grasp, and she let out a sound that was half shriek and half sob. *"Carver!"* she gasped. *"I thought we'd next see you in the hunting halls beyond. . . ."*

They met halfway between the nest and where I stood, and I couldn't help but feel a stab close to my heart when Cal threw his arms around his mother.

I wouldn't get the chance to do the same with Nerissa. I wouldn't ever see Conrad again.

The pups bounded forward from the doors and windows

439

of the jitney, chattering to Cal and Toby and, thankfully, ignoring Dean and me.

Toby laid his hands on the heads of the two smallest and growled gently, shaking them by their scruffs. The rest mobbed Cal, climbing up his legs and into his arms, demanding to know where he'd been and if he'd brought them presents from aboveground.

Cal and Toby's mother turned her eyes on Dean and me while Cal roughhoused with the pups.

"Does some kind soul wish to tell me why there is live meat at my door?"

Dean stepped forward and extended his hand. "Dean Harrison, ma'am."

Cal's mother snarled at his fingers, and Dean snapped his hand out of range. I felt my eyes widen at the sight and size of her teeth.

"Erlkin," she snarled. *"We'll have none of your trickery here."*

"No, ma'am," Dean assured her, eyes the size of quarters. The crone humphed, and picked up her stick once more, jabbing it at me.

"A female, young . . . you're the bag of bones my boy was taken and tortured over."

My knees knocked at her cut-glass gaze. Her eyes were the same color as Cal's but sharper, tempered with anger and more sights of the hard world. "Yes," I said quietly. "I suppose I am. My name's Aoife Grayson."

"I don't give a tinker's damn what your name is, meat," she croaked, reaching up to pinch my arm. Her claws dug into my skin. *"You're barely fit for a cook pot, never mind my boy's life."*

440

"Mother . . ." Cal shifted in place.

"I'm sorry that Draven took Cal away from you," I said. "But we've helped each other get free of him, and I don't have anywhere else to go." I stiffened my spine against the next words, which I could hardly believe flew out in the face of something that could tear me limb from limb. "If you don't like it, I suggest you ask your son about me."

"Carver, what foolishness is she spouting?" Cal's mother demanded, jabbing one clawed finger at me. There was something dark and crusted at the end of her talon.

"The Proctors want to burn me," I elucidated. "The Kindly Folk have threatened to kill me, and I may or may not be going mad inside of a week. So if it pleases you . . ." I paused and waited for her name.

"Reason." She spat it at me, with a hiss on the end.

"If it pleases you, Reason, I'm here to fulfill my duty to my father and my friends and then accept whatever fate is mine, and being called names and threatened is, frankly, nothing new."

Cal's mother looked me up and down, a pale white tongue flicking over her spotted lips. I didn't know if she was about to slap me or eat me, but I stood fast.

"You're still meat," she said at last, and then tapped Cal on the leg with her cane. *"But for the life of my son, you gain yours."* She put her teeth away, her grimace becoming something marginally less terrifying. *"Bring them inside, Carver. Who taught you manners?"*

"You did," Cal shot back. Reason gave him a quick box on the ear, and when Cal hissed in pain her smile vanished.

"You're hurt," she exclaimed.

"It's my fault," I piped up. "The Proctors said they

441

wanted information. But I really think Draven just paid him back for not stopping me soon enough."

Reason glared at me over the top of Cal's head. *"You think that you're special, little girl? You have something extra the other meatbags don't?"*

"I have a task," I said quietly. "And I'm sorry that Cal got caught up in it, but he was protecting me. You can be proud of him for that."

Reason put her arm around Cal and drew him away from me. *"I don't need to hear from human meat that my boy is a good boy. I know it."*

They disappeared into the nest, and Toby followed them. *"You can wait with me,"* he grumbled. *"Cal's the baby of our litter. Mother fusses, but he'll be fine soon enough."*

I ducked my head to fit into the door of the nest, the scent of burnt meat and wood smoke filling my nostrils. My eyes watered from the close, hot atmosphere, but the nest was clean and dry, and soon enough we came through the woven tunnel to a center point.

Toby flopped down on his haunches with a sigh. *"This is our hearth. Never had any humans sitting at it before."*

"First time for everything," Dean said, sitting cross-legged next to Toby. Dean's shoulders were tight, but he took pains to settle himself close enough to Toby that the ghoul could have leaned over and bitten him in the throat.

I sat on Toby's other side, showing the same trust. Beds of shredded rags and hay and small coal fires dotted the ground of the central nest. The air was close and heavy but not spoiled, laden with spice and tang. The hearth itself was a brick chimney built around a heat source drifting up from below the brick. The rotten-egg scent of a pipe fire was

442

missing, but the chimney exuded warmth, and I curled against the outer wall.

Presently, Cal and Reason returned, Cal's bruises and cuts faded to weeks old rather than hours. Cal crouched next to me, and I brushed a finger over his temple. His skin as a ghoul had a velvet cast, nothing like the slimy, clammy hide I'd first touched when he'd changed.

"You're all fixed," I said. "Good as if I fixed you myself."

Cal grinned at me. I still wasn't able to reconcile his teeth with the boy I'd known, but it was getting easier to look at him. "I'm not sorry about what happened in Ravenhouse."

I smiled. "Me either."

He pointed down a tunnel off the hearth. "I'm going to sleep. You and Dean can stay by the hearth. None of the others will bother you there, but don't wander around. You smell pretty tasty."

"Just what every girl wants to hear," I told him. "We won't go anywhere."

"Don't," he said. "Not all of us feel the same way about humans." He crawled off down the tunnel, and after a time Toby took his leave as well.

I poked in corners of the hearth room a bit, while Dean dozed with one eye open against the warm brick. "You need a pillow, princess, I've got an arm," he said.

"I'm not tired," I told him, fingering a dog-eared, year-old copy of *Amazing Stories*. I smiled to myself. Knowing that Cal's love for trashy pulps, at least, hadn't been a lie eased the wound his true face had left.

Dean drifted to sleep while I examined the detritus that the ghouls had collected—broken china, collections of

443

gears that came from a hundred different machines, a single red patent-leather pump. Shards of glass and metal hung on red string from the ceiling, refracting the gentle light from the gaps in the hearth chimney. Broken dolls were nailed in rows along the walls of the nest, their empty eyes staring down at me. At the apex of the roof, glass globes from old lamps had been arranged on wire to reflect our solar system. A ghoul had made a miniature universe above my head, stars and planets spinning slowly in their orbit.

Even here, ghouls saw the same stars I did, though not in the same way. They saw broken, fractured, fragile glass, while I saw the only constant in the world. The sky was the sky, no matter where I stood.

Except, it appeared, under the ground.

To distract myself from the cold knowledge of where I'd ended up in my mad plan to awaken the queens, I tried to discern how the hearth chimney worked. A small cooking door sat nestled into the hand-laid brick, and I turned the wheel to crank it open. Heat pinked my face as I squinted into the depths of the hearth. A steam pipe sat in the center of the brick, puffing fragrant warmth into the open air. My Weird prickled as I realized what I was seeing. I gasped and then shouted for Dean.

He came upright with a start, and Cal and Toby appeared from the nest tunnels.

"What's wrong, Aoife?" Dean demanded. "You find trouble?"

"No," I said. "Just the opposite." I pointed to the gear and sickle stamped into the pipe casing, just above where it had snapped and left itself open to the ghouls.

444

"You're gonna have to explain this one," Dean said. "I'm not seeing the excitement in a grody old pipe."

I beamed, feeling sweat trickle down my spine from the proximity to the steam. "You will, Dean." I pointed at the pipe, at its route down and back, toward the heart of the city. "This is how we're going to get into the Engineworks."

The ghouls had collected a vast store of lost things, and Toby showed me the nest where most of it was kept. *"It's all here,"* he said. *"Meat keep the strangest things, and they throw even stranger things away."*

I beckoned to Dean. "We need to find some climbing gear. Something to make a harness and crampons from."

Dean cocked an eyebrow. "I know you're not talking about climbing down that thing, kid. You'll roast."

"Not if we can vent this chimney," I said. "Ventors work in the pipes every day. I can certainly make one trip."

Dean uncovered a length of sturdy rope, and I found a pair of golf shoes roughly the same age as I was. "These'll do," I said.

"Well, find a pair for me, too," Dean said. I blinked at him, already pulling the spikes off the bottom of the shoes.

"Whatever for?"

"If you think you're going down there alone all on the spur of the moment, you're cracked," Dean said. "We've already gotten sucked into a ghoul nest—I'd hate to see what else is down here."

I gave Dean a small smile. Him coming with me meant I'd come back. Dean could always find his way back. I clung

445

to the sentiment as I found a toolkit with most of the tools missing. A few minute's work had fashioned the golf spikes and some wire into a serviceable pair of crampons, which I strapped to new shoes I found amid the mess.

I took a deep breath. I couldn't turn around now.

My only adventure into a steam pipe had come the previous year, when the chief ventor of the Engineworks took us into the bowels of the Engine, one by one. I'd never forgotten the roar, the oppressive heat and the weight of the water in the air as we journeyed as close as an unprotected person could come. As I lowered myself down the side of the steam pipe, the heat stippling my skin with moisture, I thanked every ventor I'd known at the School for their wisdom.

"You all right down there?" Dean shouted.

My foot found the bottom of the pipe's junction, and I tugged on the rope. "Yes! Come down."

Dean lowered himself until he landed next to me, panting. We'd both stripped down to our bottom layer: I to my dress and stockings, Dean to his white T-shirt. His hair hung lank, while mine became like a thundercloud in the humidity.

"If the Proctors are wrong, and there is a heaven . . . this is definitely hell," he said, swiping his hand over his face.

"The Proctors are wrong," I said, sure of that if nothing else. "So very, very wrong about so much."

We crouched to make our way down the pipe, until it widened, and a grate blocked our path. The sign hanging from the mesh had nearly rusted away, but the flared symbol, like a blooming flower, was familiar from our first-year safety lectures.

446

I snatched Dean's arm. "Get back."

"Why—" he started, but was drowned out by a great rumbling. A moment later a jet of concentrated steam shot along the pipe, heating the mesh so that it glowed.

"It vents up," I said. "Direct from the Engine to aboveground."

Dean whistled. "Well, we sure aren't getting in that way."

"If we can't go in through the river then we have no choice," I said. "This is the only way into the Engineworks besides the front gate, and we're sure as hell not getting in that way." I tugged at Dean's hand. "Let's go back. I need to ask Cal exactly where we are relative to the Engine and make some sketches." And get out of the heat before I collapsed into a puddle. I never would have made it as a ventor.

The climb back into the ghoul nest was far harder than the climb out, now that I was tired and wrung of moisture. Dean had to pull me out and onto the soft floor of the nest. Cal hovered where he'd obviously been waiting since we'd gone, claws flexing in and out. "Stop breathing so hard!" he ordered me. "You sound like prey!"

I concentrated on bringing my heartbeat and breath back under control. Dean found a scrap of burlap and blotted some of the sweat and grit from my face.

"That's better," Cal said at last, as a few of his skulking brethren who'd been watching me from the tunnel entrance retreated. "Did you find anything?"

I nodded and tried to smooth down my hair in a token effort to look human. "Where are we, exactly?"

"Near the riverwalk," Cal said. "Close to where we met the nightjar, below Old Town."

447

I shrugged back into my jumper, chilled now that my sweat had beaded and cooled on my skin. "I need a pen and some paper."

I settled in one of the hammocks in the hearth room, and presently Dean brought me what I'd asked for.

"Won't be easy," Dean said as I sketched.

"No," I said. "It won't be." I thought of my goggles and the invigorator, back in some cold evidence locker at Ravenhouse.

Damn Grey Draven three times over. Him and his lies, and his peculiar fascination with my father.

The paper was the back side of an ancient Metrocar schedule, and the pen was barely more than a nub dipped in cheap, grainy ink, but working from remembered diagrams and lectures and the rough coordinates Cal had provided, I soon had a rudimentary sketch of the vent tunnels into the Engine. I handed it to Dean.

"Some of it is from memory, but I think we can use it to get in."

"Not bad," Dean said, examining the sketch. "Of course, there's the small matter of getting out again."

For once, I was on sure footing and had an answer for him. After weeks of drifting anchorless, it made me a bit giddy. "We can trip the pressure alarms in the Engineworks," I said. "There will be an evacuation. It happened once when I was doing field study. People scrambling everywhere, no order. Nobody will notice us." A pressure vent could fling shards of Engine, gears and rods at hundreds of PSI in every direction. Another way a ventor could die. Anyone caught in the line of fire looked like they'd been in the path of a war Engine. If I went to the heart of the

Engine, I'd be going the opposite way from everyone else and could be unobserved, hopefully for as long as I needed to use my Weird. If I could do what I'd claimed to Tremaine. Right now it was a theory, and I knew I could be very, very wrong. But I couldn't be scared. Cal's and Dean's futures and my own were riding on me being strong, stronger than even my father.

I could be. I had to be.

"I can get a message to Captain Harry to get us out of the city once we go topside," Dean said, "but up until then . . . it's up to you to make this work, princess."

"Don't worry." I elbowed him. "I'm the brains of the operation, remember?"

Dean leaned down and kissed me, and I still wasn't used to the weightlessness it brought on. He helped me fly for a moment, and I slid my hands under his jacket, so I could touch cotton and skin. "That's not what I meant. If this goes badly . . . ," he said.

I touched my finger to his lips. "If it goes badly . . . I'm glad I met you, Dean."

We sat quietly after that, watching the ghoul pups play with a doll among the piles of junk in the corners of the nest, stalking and killing the crude human shape over and over. It didn't get darker or lighter under the city, but when night closed in, I curled in my hammock and dreamed, of a burning city and falling stars.

I woke, frantic and alone. My mother stood over me, in her nightgown, a man's cardigan and bare feet. Her expression twisted up, the one that came when she wanted me so

449

badly to believe her and knew I wouldn't, because she was crazy.

"You shouldn't have walked in the lily field, Aoife."

"You're not real," I said. My mother reached out and slapped me. It stung.

"I warned you! I warned you, daughter. The dead girls dance on the ashes of the world and we will all weep for what they do."

I held my cheek where it stung. "You are mad, Mother."

"And what do you think seeing me makes you?"

When I came awake into actuality, where the world was real and solid, I was screaming. Dean grabbed me, caught me as I fell from the hammock.

"Aoife, what is it?"

"I saw . . ." My teeth chattered so hard they stole my speech and my thoughts were racing faster than my tongue could form words anyway. "My mother," I managed. "She was here."

"There's no one here," Dean said gently. "No one but me."

Cal crept in from the nests. The fires were low and I knew that this was what passed for night under the earth. Cal's face fell. "It's the madness dream? You're still having it."

"At least you're not saying *necrovirus* any longer." I half-smiled.

"No need." Cal's tongue flicked in and out. "All a lie, isn't it? You don't know how it stuck in my craw pretending to be scared of the Proctor's fable. *Ghul* weren't made by any virus. We've always been here, under the skin of your world."

450

"It's no comfort, the lie," I said. "My family does go mad, no matter what causes it. I feel like there's an abyss in front of me, and a wind at my back. . . ."

"Aoife." Cal wrapped his long, skeletal arms around himself. "No matter what happens, you'll be Aoife. I'll come visit you in the madhouse, if that's what it takes, but I won't desert you. I'll learn a new boy-shape. Draven will never catch me."

"Why can't I just go back?" I whispered, ignoring his attempts at comfort. "Erase all of this and go be a student whose biggest problem was a schematic she couldn't draw?"

"Because," Dean said, "then you'd lose everything you've gained since. Truth, magic. Even the real face of your obnoxious little friend here."

"You're calling *me* obnoxious," Cal huffed. "If you could only hear yourself."

I managed a laugh. "At least some things haven't changed."

"I'm still the Cal you knew," he said. "I know you don't trust me, but underneath I'm the same. I'll go to the Engineworks with you. If I don't make it, or the Proctors grab me again—"

"Don't talk like that," I said, moving away from Dean and straightening up. "You won't be coming."

Cal sighed. "I'm not working for Draven anymore. I swear it."

"I mean," I said, "we need someone to meet the airship. To come for us if Dean and I get caught again." I gave Cal a smile, a whole one, even though it was purely meant to make him cooperate. I guessed I had learned a thing or two from Dean. "I can't think of anyone I'd rather have looking

451

out for me." And if Cal did decide that his loyalties lay elsewhere, at least we wouldn't be together in the Engine when he did.

Dean stayed when Cal crept back to his nest. "I can stay," he said. "If you want me."

I moved and made room for him in the hammock. I wanted Dean to stay, badly. I never, I realized, wanted him to leave again. "Please."

Dean slipped out of his leather jacket and his heavy boots and settled next to me, letting me sink back into the comfort of his chest, wrapping his arm around my waist and resting his chin on the top of my head. His breath ruffled my hair. I stayed still, afraid I might break our comfortable silence like a soap bubble.

Dean spoke, eventually. "Dreams, huh?" he whispered in my ear. "Bad ones?"

"The worst imaginable," I said. "Ever since I was a little girl."

"Well," Dean said softly. "I'm here now. Any bad's going to have to get through me." He ran his fingers down my cheek, over my neck and arm, and then kissed the back of my neck before settling his head onto the pillow. "Sweet dreams, princess."

I knew that no one, not even Dean, could keep the dreams at bay, but I allowed myself to think he might, until I fell back into a fitful, smoke-tinged sleep.

I woke alone, shivering in the chill of a dead fire. Ashes blew softly across the hearth, as if subterranean snow had fallen while I slept.

452

"Dean?" I whispered, scrubbing vision back into my eyes. I was stiff and sore from sleeping in the crook of the hammock, but I had slept soundly and long. Light fell from somewhere far above, in bars and crosses across the rough earthen floor.

"He went to smoke a cigarette," Toby's guttural voice piped from the corner of the hearth. *"I don't understand why you breathe the smoke in willingly. Your city is covered in it."*

"We all have our vices," I said. Toby grinned at me, his bluish fur almost silver in the early light.

"I said I'd watch you so you didn't turn into breakfast. Although I am hungry."

I swung myself down from the hammock, planting my feet with a thud. "We both know you're not going to do anything of the kind as long as Cal's around, so why don't you shove a sock in it?"

Toby laughed. I was beginning to see subtle differences in the ghouls—Cal was slight and skinny no matter what shape he was in, while Toby was larger, darker. Tanner's voice had been nightmarish, but Toby's and Cal's were strange in a way that made me want to listen.

"I sorta see why Carver decided to protect his meat friend," he said. *"You're not like a human. You're more like one of us."*

"I wish that were true," I said, and meant it. If I could fight and hunt, if I were something to be afraid of, none of this misfortune would have happened.

Toby drew something out from behind his back, awkward as any human boy. *"Carver said you lost your kit in Ravenhouse. I know humans need things. Even though they*

453

just clank and clack, hanging from your bones." He shoved the object into my hand.

I gasped when I saw Tremaine's blue goggles. "Where did you get these?"

Toby grinned at me. *"Those men following you and Carver and the Erlkin. Some of us went back, went hunting. The fat one had them on his belt."*

Quinn. I'd be lying if I said I was sorry.

I slid them over my eyes and looked at the nest. Toby appeared wavy and insubstantial, only his bones showing clearly. His ghoul spine with its cruel curve that made him able to spring and twist in midair, the long jaw full of teeth, and the knifelike claws.

All around me, the underworld revealed itself, disused pipe and tunnel running off in every direction, a drain that dribbled overhead directly to the river, and the broken, branching chimney that vented the ghoul's hearth.

Toby panted, itching behind his blunt ear with one long claw as I slid the goggles onto my forehead. *"So it's a fair bargain, yes? For saving Carver's life?"*

"Yes, Toby," I said. "More than fair. Thank you." I tried Tremaine's goggles again. "Now I know what it's like to be Dean—to see everything that's hidden."

Dean poked his head from the nest tunnel to the outside. "I hear my name?"

"Dean!" I waved the goggles at him. "Look what Toby found."

He took a glance through the lenses and just as quickly jerked the mask off. "That's Folk trickery. Splits my head in two."

454

"I'm sorry," I said. "But they'll help us get down the vent tunnel. I can watch for the steam, and time it."

"Assuming we get through that grate," Dean said.

Toby extended his claws with the sound of daggers being drawn. *"Leave that to us."*

36

In the Engineworks

Cal and Toby went into the hearth pipe in the lead, Toby loping easily on all fours and Cal in his boy skin, walking upright. Dean stayed with me. I was relieved that Cal seemed to have stopped sniping at Dean. It was clear in hindsight why—Dean represented everything Draven was trying to keep me from.

Cal's clothes now were rags, an old Engineworks jersey and pants tattered about the hem. His feet stayed bare.

"I figured this might make it a little easier for you," he told me.

"Don't worry about sparing me," I said. "Toby's already laboring under the impression he owes me something for saving your life."

"You did," Cal said shortly. "Not in Ravenhouse, but before. You made me realize I didn't have to be afraid of Draven."

"Cal . . ." I'd never find someone as loyal as Cal again. That I knew, in an immutable bone-deep sense.

"I'll let you into the vent, and we'll be even." Cal flashed me a smile, and I saw that he hadn't bothered to hide his ghoul teeth.

"If she comes back, you two can skip merrily over the ground. If not, someone will have a fine supper." Toby chuckled to himself and climbed up to walk on the ceiling.

I took the pedestrian route, sticking near Dean and Cal. Tremaine's goggles dangled from my hand, and across my back I'd strapped a small pack that bore the partially chewed-away logo of the Lovecraft Academy Expedition Club circa 1933, clearly a year where they didn't teach student members not to go wandering around old sewer mains.

I'd taken only tools and a little water, for rehydrating after Dean and I had gone through the steam. No books, no pens, no paper. Only Dean's geas, tucked up tight under the wrist of my jumper.

"You haven't said much since last night," Dean said.

I shrugged. "Not much to say." The dream of my mother lingered, like a corpse's touch against my skin, a spot of chill that no amount of steam heat could erase. *You shouldn't have walked in the lily field.*

"How long do you have?" Dean said.

"Six days. I was born at four a.m. Six days and four hours."

Dean fingered a Lucky but didn't light it. "You might be spared, you know."

"I won't be," I said shortly. "Because life's not fair." On this point, I was sure.

Dean spread his hands. "I don't—"

457

"We find out there is no necrovirus and my family is still mad," I said. "So clearly, I will be too. And now I'm even further from knowing why."

Dean took me by the shoulders and turned me to face him. "I ain't good at words, Aoife. I made my living with my blood and my boots and my fists, and I'm not a poet."

His hands gripped more tightly, but I didn't try to wriggle away even though he was hurting me a little. He was the only thing in the tunnel that was really solid.

"I'm not running," he said simply. "I've seen what can happen and I'm not scared. You may be mad and you may not be, Aoife, but you're stuck with me. I ain't run from a problem yet and I'm not about to start with you."

He released me, and walked on. I wished I could be as brave as Dean. I wished I could be as loyal as Cal. But I was only me, and that was going to have to be enough for what was ahead.

"Dean." I caught up with him, my feet echoing in the empty pipes. "I know," I told him. "I know that you won't leave."

He nodded, some of the knots slipping from his posture. "Good," he said. "Then we're square. You've paid your part of the bargain and I've held up mine."

"No more bargains," I said as we reached the guard grate and came to a halt. "Just Aoife and Dean from now on, all right?"

He smiled, brushing a thumb down my cheek. "I like the sound of that."

Toby tugged at the grate ineffectually, his claws shrieking over the rusted iron. *"Carver, don't just stand there catching flies. Give me a hand."*

I slipped on the blue glass goggles while Cal crouched. His skin rippled, bones with it, like his skin was sand and his insides were the ocean, pushing and re-forming it. He grunted as he became ghoul, the only hint of the pain that must rack him whenever he twisted his bones and skin into the shape of what he despised.

I wondered how long Cal had been passing as a human, how often he'd ventured over ground to find medicine or food.

How long Draven had tortured him the first time, until he agreed to spy on me.

Someday, I vowed, as I searched the vent and its connected discharge pipes for a hint of the next jet of steam, I would see Grey Draven again. And I would take back my father's book and make him answer for all that he'd done to those I cared about.

The vent fell away with a clang, and Toby stuck his finger in his mouth. *"I broke one of my claws clean off."*

"Now who's the baby?" Cal asked him.

"Quiet!" I snapped. I could see the steam, moving like a phantom through the discharge pipes, gathering speed like a spectral hurricane. "It's coming," I whispered.

"What's that mean for us?" Dean said.

I grabbed his hand and squeezed it tight. "It means we have to run. Now."

"Aoife!" Cal shouted as we ducked through the opening the ghouls had made. His voice was lost in the roar of the gathering vent jet, but I think he was telling me to be careful.

* * *

459

Dean and I ran through steam, and it took me back to running through the mist with Tremaine. Just as it had been then, I risked being stolen away, not by the corpse-drinkers or the other things that lingered in the fog but by the molten jets of steam from the Engine that even now throbbed under my feet.

The goggles showed me the encroaching vent, the access hatch we needed to reach before the heat exploded into the tunnel.

It was so very far away. My breath jabbed in and out of my chest like a pickax, and my heart throbbed in time with the Engine. Dean's damp, hot hand was the only thing I felt besides the blinding pain of sprinting.

"Hatch!" I managed to gasp. "Open it and get through before . . . before . . ."

Dean grasped my meaning and caught the hatch wheel with his full weight, attempting and failing to spin it open. "It's rusted shut!" he shouted.

The floor shook in earnest now, and my hair started to curl up as the humidity and heat rose. Every pipe I could see through the goggles was full, dancing with the ghosts of steam.

I grabbed the wheel, my hands over Dean's, but it was impossible to budge.

"Open it! I know you can!" Dean screamed above the whine of venting steam. This time, I didn't argue with him about the Weird. I pressed my forehead against the hatch, focused on the wheel, the machine within. Light exploded in front of my eyes like a sulfur bulb on a camera, and then I fell.

460

For an awful moment, I thought I was back in the Thorn Land, but the floor was hard steel and there was shrieking steam just outside the hatch as we tumbled through.

I watched Dean give the wheel a hard twist, shutting us off from the vent pipe. He was panting, sopping wet with sweat running down his face like tears. "Let's never have a close one like that again."

My breath didn't want to come back, my throat fighting it with the tightness of near death. "I . . . no. Let's not . . . ," I managed.

Dean cast around the small iron room. "Where in the cold starry hell are we?"

I lifted the goggles from my eyes and examined our surroundings. Heavy treated-canvas suits hung in orderly rows, along with hoods that were a grim and greasy parody of the Proctors' uniforms. The opposite wall held axes and pressure scissors, the large blades used to free a man crushed under the sort of metal wreckage that happened when rods threw and boilers exploded.

"It's the fire room," I said. "The accident brigade can suit up in here. It's completely iron like a submersible—if there's a fire or an explosion they can still go rescue the survivors."

Dean lifted one of the fire suits from its hook and held it to his chest experimentally. "Whatcha think? About my size?"

I could breathe a bit easier, so I joined him, taking down the smallest suit. I still swam in it when I pulled it on, but now I appeared as a short, squat, genderless Engine worker rather than a slight and out-of-place teenage girl.

461

The goggles back over my eyes and the hood over my head caused Aoife Grayson to cease. I was anonymous, the very thing I'd wished for most of my life.

"I'll go first," I told Dean. "Just follow me. If someone stops us, say we're doing a routine safety inspection."

"And they'll buy that?" Dean frowned.

"Dean, when you work at a job as miserable as a steam ventor's, routine safety is the only thing keeping you from boiling alive," I said. "Trust me. This will work."

There is a sound to an Engine, the particular hiss and clank of steam and gears that is like no other sound on earth. It's a heartbeat more than a machine, and it pulsed and thrummed through my feet, so that I felt it from my toes to the top of my head.

The Engine was alive, and my Weird snaked out, reached into the vast and complex chambers of its heart, nearly burned up in the great mechanical organ that gave aether, steam and life to Lovecraft.

I gasped and Dean gripped my arm. "Keep it straight, doll. You went all funny."

Day workers passing gave us a curious glance, but no more. The entire outer Engineworks was a hive, full of engineers and control operators and foremen, entrances and exits guarded by bored Proctors who yawned or stared into space.

Only the best mechanics were allowed into the works themselves. A steel hatch manned by a Proctor saw to that.

Under all of my fear and anxiety, all of the chatter

around me, the Engine sang. It was a siren song, and I felt my focus slipping again.

"Aoife!" Dean gave me a sharp shake, and I knew I'd begun to wander not just in mind. "You have the plan, girl. Tell me where we need to go."

"Main ventilation," I said. "There." The man-sized vent was in plain sight of the Proctor, but the goggles showed me the clear path to the inner workings of the Engine. I chewed my lip. "Hang it. We need a distraction."

"In that case," Dean said, "allow the master of misdirection to thrill and astound you once again."

He grabbed hold of a passing worker. "Hey, buddy, what's the word?"

"Huh?" The worker tried to back away, but Dean balled up his fist. "I saw you looking at my girl last night at Donnelly's! She's high-class, friend! She goes to the Academy! Grease monkeys like you got no business eyeballing that!"

The worker, young as Cal or me, swung his tin lunch box at Dean. "Screw off, chucklehead!" The lunch box connected with the side of Dean's head, and even though it was protected by his fire hood he doubled over, selling the effect.

Attracted by the noise, the Proctor left his post. I turned around and put my hand against the vent lock, asking my Weird for one last favor.

After a stab against the inside of my forehead, the lock clicked, and I pulled the hatch open and stepped in. A small platform for my feet preceded a ladder and a long, black drop.

463

I started down, and after a moment a shadow flashed. Dean appeared, and mounted the ladder after me.

"Are you all right?" I whispered.

"Clocked me," he said. "Bleeding a little. Going to have a scar. Should make me look dangerous."

"As if you need any help with that," I murmured, relieved he was all right.

We climbed down in the dark, quiet. I wanted to enjoy these last minutes with Dean.

At the bottom, I pulled the plan I had sketched from under my fire suit. "Light?" I said. Dean handed me his lighter. I checked the route, for the hundredth or thousandth time, I couldn't be sure.

I checked what I'd drawn against the goggles. Only one hatch here, in the depths of the Engineworks, was shielded with lead sheeting, just a black blank patch in the gaze of the schema goggles. I pointed at it, flipping them onto my forehead. "There."

We opened the hatch, and I went first once again, bracing myself to find Proctors, arrest, Grey Draven himself waiting for me on the other side.

Instead, we were alone, the mechanics and the chief engineer absent from their posts. I decided to count it as luck. I had no sense of time—they could all be having a birthday party or simply a lunch break for all I knew. I was just glad I didn't have to trip the pressure alarm and fight my way through chaos after all.

The four-chambered heart of the Engine hummed just out of view around the iron blasting walls, and I mounted the spiraling iron steps that rose from the venting floor to concentric walkways about the heart of the works. And looking down, into the center of them . . .

The Engine was the most beautiful thing I had ever seen. The great gears turned on their planetary assembly, and the aether within the Engine's four glass hearts burned, creating the heat that drove the city. My Weird thudded violently at contact with the only kind of machine on earth that could harness steam and aether together to create a power that could crack the world in half.

Only the four great Engines held that power.

And I was about to steal it.

37

The Kindly Folk's Bargain

I LOOKED BACK to Dean as we crested the highest cat-walk. I needed his calm face and storm cloud eyes, even hidden behind a hood. The Engine sang to me slowly, and I drew its enchantment around me, warm and close and humming with so much power my head went light.

When I looked away from Dean, Tremaine was there instead.

"Aoife. You have arrived at the heart of all things."

The Engine sound faded around me, the foreign air of another time reaching me through my mask, and I saw only a frail, rust-bitten skeleton where my feet should be resting on solid metal. The Engine itself groaned and shuddered, in death throes of grinding gears and pistons. The aether in its four gigantic globes was a sickly violet. Above and far away, air-raid Klaxons wailed. This wasn't happening—I was being shown something, something I'd only glimpsed in the shoggoth's dream before now.

466

"Where are we?" I said, my stomach dropping in concert with the shaking walkway. This wasn't right. Wasn't real. Something was dreadfully out of prime with the world Tremaine and I stood in. My Weird curdled, retreating into my mind like it had been burned.

"The end," Tremaine said simply. "I cannot pass through the Iron Land, and you cannot yet venture alone into Thorn. As iron poisons the Folk, this is the intersection of time and tide upon which we must meet while you linger in that infernal Engine." He spread his arms to encompass the ruined Engine. "You've seen it before, Aoife. In your dreams, perhaps? The end of all things, if you do not break the curse?"

He pointed at the Engine, now a shuddering wreck of metal, now perfectly fine and whole. My mind was playing tricks on me, my madness digging its claws tighter into my brain. "Harness that power vaster than any in Thorn. Wake the queens, Aoife. Even now that foul machine sings its desire in your blood."

The Engine gave another clank and rattle in this time-crossed vision I was seeing. Toxic smoke and gas poured from its ruptured core, and it begged me, in the language of machines, to set it free, to channel its great death-blast away from the innocents of Lovecraft and across the lands of Thorn instead, to the queens, who would soak it up and save my city from immolation.

I could feel the Engine in my blood. All I had to do was turn the channel toward Tremaine and his queens. The Weird was my blood, my legacy. The last thing I could do before I, a small and insignificant girl, went mad and lost the gift that my lineage had granted me. I could save Dean, Cal and the Folk. That had to be enough.

467

Dean's voice came to me from far away. "Aoife, wake up!"

"Why, child," Tremaine said, stronger and more present as I hesitated for just a moment, Dean's voice tugging at me. "Surely you are not afraid?"

The power at my fingertips gibbered and whispered seductively. It begged to be grasped, and it burned when I did. I felt I could disintegrate on the tide of power from the Engine.

"I'm not," I told Tremaine, knotting my fists. "But I'd feel better if you stood with me." Everything except the Weird—Dean's voice, the real Engineworks, even the vision—was fading like a spotty aether connection. The combination of the Weird and the hallucination had crossed the wires in my mind.

Tremaine came to me, the knifelike smile playing about his face. "Of course I will stand with you, child."

I pulled the lighter and the paper knot free of my suit and, with a flick of my thumb, touched the flame to the paper. The geas, at least, was something I was certain I wanted to send at Tremaine. Dead certain.

"And while you stand with me, I'd like it if you told the truth," I said to Tremaine as the paper hung suspended in the air, pulling in the flame, turning into a prism of fire. The enchantment of the thing tickled and bedeviled my Weird, as if I'd sat on my hand and gotten pins and needles all up and down my arm.

"What is this?" Tremaine bellowed.

"This is human," I told him with no small satisfaction. "You'll give me a straight answer, Tremaine. One way or another."

Tremaine's throat worked. "You think an Erlkin geas

468

holds a member of the Folk? A member of the *courts*? You *presume?*"

I drew back from him, for he looked terribly angry and I didn't want to get a blade in the gut before I'd asked him my questions. "I do." I snapped the lighter closed. The geas continued to burn between us.

"My mother," I said. "You knew her. How?"

Tremaine twitched, but he spoke in a slurred rush. "Your mother was born with a foot in and a foot out of Thorn. There are a lot of names for Folk who have a little human blood, who can cross the gates, but the one in those infernal human storybooks she loved so much is 'changeling.' In her younger days, Nerissa traveled freely between her true world and the Iron one. Until she met *him*."

I felt my eyes go wide, of their own accord. "My father?"

Tremaine sneered. "He only discovered her nature when she had already begotten your brother. And then it was too late. He knew the fate changelings face in the Iron World."

When my lips parted to deny it, Tremaine let out a laugh, cruel and throaty as the crows'. "You mean you haven't figured it out? One bred of the blood and the iron, that's a changeling for you. But iron poisons your blood just as it poisons mine. Slower, but just as surely. Usually womanhood speeds the poison. It's your fate, for belonging to neither side. In the Thorn Land, we drown your kind. Though you and Conrad both escaped that fate, your brother was smarter than you. He escaped me entirely."

I nearly lunged forward and socked Tremaine in the jaw at that last, but I kept the geas between us. The flame began to flicker from the draft. "You told me he was shot," I snarled.

469

"I lied," Tremaine said. "I do so, from time to time. Oh, did your mother tell you the pretty fairies couldn't lie? Her mind must be rotten enough from iron poisoning by now to believe that."

"Why?" I cried, wanting to strangle him bare-handed. "All it did was nearly make me give up and die. I wasn't going to help you."

"I am pragmatic," Tremaine said. "A useful trait of men. If you thought that sot of a brother was alive, you would be loyal to the Graysons, not the Folk. You'd try to find him. To *rescue* him. You could be diverted from your mission. But revenge against the Proctors by awakening the Folk? That cause made you quite able."

"I hope I fail and your queens sleep forever," I spat. "You're vile." I felt as if I were seeing Tremaine for the first time, and that even with his sculpted face and haunted eyes, he was indescribably ugly.

"I am the Regent of Winter!" Tremaine growled. "And the Thorn Land is mine to command whether my queen lives or dies!" He breathed and gained control over his trembling visage. I could tell the geas—and the truth it drew out like venom—was straining him.

"If this little tale has put you off your purpose," Tremaine said, "consider that I could still simply kill your brother, your ghoul friend and your besotted Erlkin. Slowly, and in that order. Would that be sufficient motivation?"

The geas gave off the scent of rowan wood as it began to sputter and go out. "I'm not your subject," I said softly, looking Tremaine in the eye so he'd know that he might have me cornered, but he didn't frighten me anymore.

"And don't ever make the mistake of thinking I'm loyal to anything that comes from that foul place you call a kingdom."

"I think you'll change your tune in . . . six days, was it?" Tremaine folded his hands with the satisfied expression of a predator that had just brought down a lame deer.

"My father may have understood you," I snarled. "But I don't."

"Your *father?*" Tremaine spat. "Grayson was my adversary, Aoife. He sought to keep Thorn and Iron locked in their old ways, old traditions. He and those foul mistling Erlkin."

I started when he mentioned Dean's people in the same breath as my father, but I kept my composure. "I knew Dean hated you, but it's nice to know why."

"The Gateminder and the Folk need one another for many reasons, Aoife, but need does not equate to love," Tremaine said. "Someday, you'll learn that. Archibald Grayson was not the human who favored the Folk. He sought to learn our secrets of sorcery and craftsmanship with his foul Brotherhood of Iron, and I, for one, am glad he's gotten himself good and lost."

Before I could retort, the geas went out with a crackle and a snap. Tremaine lunged for me, and in my shock I let him take hold of my throat. "Open yourself to the Engine," Tremaine ordered. "Allow your Weird to right the wrongs visited on my people." His nails dug half-moons from my flesh. "I had to threaten you, but I'd rather you understand. Whether you approve or not, there is a natural order and the Folk have a place in it. With their queen ruling and

471

their lands alive. Otherwise, we'll both suffer. The natural order. That's all I want."

"Do you really?" I demanded, thinking of Conrad's voice in my dream. "Do you really want your queen awakened, or do you want Winter for yourself?"

Tremaine's lips peeled back in a sinister grimace. "Politics of the Folk aren't your concern, Aoife. The safety of yourself and your friends is."

Tremaine hadn't answered my question, but it ceased to matter—I couldn't hold back the Engine any longer, the power I'd drawn already breaking through my last barriers. My Weird flamed in my mind and I saw the lily field, the coffins wreathed in their poison sleep. Far from being noxious and foreign, the curse wreathing the coffins was familiar. I'd felt the enchantment before, when I'd stared into a pair of cold eyes.

Human eyes.

Grey Draven's eyes.

What I'd mistaken for insanity had really been power. Draven had a Weird too, a terrible and poisonous one.

He wanted to destroy the Folk, all memory of magic. He'd cursed the queens so Thorn would wither and die.

But if I listened to Tremaine, it would destroy the Iron Land as well. Did Draven not know, or did he not care?

And then, it didn't matter. My Weird had taken over.

The Engine sang in me, sweeping like a wind across the lily field. I saw the energy I commanded with my Weird swoop and cut across the pure white of the flowers like a flock of ravens. Real ravens, not the clockwork obscenities of the Proctors. It met Draven's curse—Draven knew of the Thorn Land, like my father. Draven had cursed the queens.

But none of it mattered as the surge I'd taken from the Engine and harnessed to my Weird met the curse of iron and, like a hammer on a cold morning, shattered it, scattering its flimsy, glass-shimmer pieces to the four corners of Thorn.

Grey Draven had cursed the queens, but the enchantment broke, snapped, shattered into a thousand gleaming fragments before the power of the Engine, driven by the impetus of my Weird. I could wonder at his true motives another day.

Now I was stronger than Draven. In that moment I was stronger than anything in the world. I was fire and ice, cleansing and calming, opening the bonds that held the queens in eternal sleep.

I was the Engine. The Engine was me.

And then Tremaine let me go and the connection with the Engine broke and I was nothing but Aoife again. I fell, feeling the catwalk dig into my legs. "You have done the right thing, child," he said. "Perhaps more than one human will take our side in the coming war."

I blinked at him, dumbly. "War?"

In their coffins, the queens stirred.

In my mind, something pale and terrible raised its head and woke. It was larger than the Weird, sharper, and it blew through me like the aetheric fire of Oppenheimer's war Engine.

Magic.

The Winter Queen opened her eyes and stared into mine. My shoulder flamed with pain and my vision blacked out.

"The Iron Land has dreamed a great dream," Tremaine whispered in my ear as I writhed under the onslaught of

473

power pouring back into the Thorn Land. "Peace from all but a few escapees of Thorn, exceptions that you explained with a virus. Peace from ensnarement and enchantment, as it was in the old days. But no longer." He touched my forehead.

"Your father and your brother and Draven all played their parts," Tremaine whispered. "In their furor to do what they felt was the true and righteous thing for Thorn and Iron. And now you've played yours. And now a new storm is coming, Aoife. If I were you"—Tremaine's lips brushed mine, so soft and close was his whisper—"I'd run and hide."

New pain erupted from my palm, sharp, thin silver pain, and my eyes flew open.

38

The Iron World

Mᴄ ᴘᴀʟᴍ ᴡᴀꜱ crosscut, bleeding freely into the heart of the Engine where I'd reached out my hand to touch the glowing star-fire blue of the aetheric chamber.

"You wouldn't wake up." Dean knelt by me where I lay. His voice shook. "I cut you. You wouldn't wake up." His switchblade was dark with blood.

The Engine gave a rumble, a death spasm, and a girder dropped in a graceful parabola, narrowly missing us and falling into the gears, fouling a set the size of cottages.

"It's overload," I murmured, because I'd seen the lanternreel. *What to Do in Case of Overload.* "We have to . . . get down . . . under our desks. . . ."

"Desks, hell," Dean said. "We're blowing this joint. Up you come."

I managed to get up, with his help. "Yes . . . run." The Engine was giving off smoke now and pressure alarms were screaming from every control set.

475

The end of that lanternreel showed a burning, cratered city. A great wound on the earth, burned from the inside out.

I had only meant to divert the Engine's power, just for a moment. I hadn't meant to cause overload.

I hadn't meant to unleash Tremaine and his Folk on the Iron Land.

What had I meant to do? What had I *done*?

Dean grabbed my good hand and together we joined the stream of evacuating workers, up staircase after staircase as the earth shuddered and convulsed beneath us.

Up and up, into the free, fresh air. It tasted like nothing except metal and death to my tongue. Tremaine said the iron drove me mad. Drove *changelings* mad. He'd said so many things.

Tremaine had done the thing my father had sought to deter his entire life. *The Gateminder and the Folk need one another.* To maintain a balance, to hunt down things that crossed from one to the other, to keep the gates between Thorn and Iron shut.

And I'd opened them. I'd let magic into a world that called it a lie, that couldn't absorb it. That was what I'd done.

"Move, kid!" Dean bellowed in my ear. "This monster is gonna blow!"

The Engineworks had vents, all over the city, and they were sending out jets of steam that were melting the stone and iron around them as we crested the ground. Manhole covers flew off like bullets and Klaxons screamed in the air.

The grounds of the Engineworks were chaos, workers running headlong for the fences, piling up at the gate, screaming at the Proctors, who were themselves running for their lives.

In the city itself I could see the steam gathering over the tall spires of Uptown like a pair of vast wings, stretching to engulf everything that the Proctors and the Rationalists held dear.

The screaming wasn't just sirens, I realized. There was a drone in the air, of human voices that rose and fell with the air-raid Klaxons. Outside the fences of the Engineworks, black shapes darted and hissed at the people inside. Nightjars, in the daytime. They were freed from the gates at last—every Proctor in the city was occupied, and the population was theirs for the picking.

Thorn's children would feast.

"It's horrible . . . ," I whispered. "I am so sorry. I didn't want this. . . ."

"Enough," Dean said. He ripped off his fire suit and helped me do the same. "We have to go, doll."

The mob of workers were breaking the fences, only to be set upon by a cluster of nightjars and springheel jacks still wearing vestiges of their human faces. New screams joined the faint ones rolling back from the hills of Uptown.

Dean turned away from the carnage at the gates and ran for the river, dragging me with him. The icy black rushed up at us, and before I could protest or balk we went over the edge, off the pier.

In midair, a great hand snatched me and pulled me away from Dean, a crackle like a thousand rifle shots and then a boom and a loss of air.

A great emptiness opened up where my Weird sang.

477

I plunged into the dead winter water of the Erebus River knowing that the Lovecraft Engine was no more.

The cold kept me from fainting at the great bodily shock the overload of the Engine caused. It seized my lungs and forced me to kick for the surface. I scraped my palms on floating chunks of ice, but when I broke free of its grasp I sucked down air and tried to kick against the current.

From my vantage on the water, I watched Lovecraft burn. Crimson smoke from the Engineworks blanketed the sky like a red tide, and screams floated over the water. Clockwork ravens swirled aimlessly overhead, flummoxed by the devastation.

By the shore, black shapes crawled, coming out of sewer drains and shadows and the air itself. I couldn't discern which screams came from the Engine and which from the crawling remnants of the Folk.

"Dean!" I shouted. My voice was gone, stolen by ice and smoke. "Dean!"

"Aoife!" His shout came from a piling on the bridge, toward which I rapidly swept. "Hold on! I'll catch you."

I caught his hand, nearly lost it again, grabbed on to his leather and clutched. Dean hauled me onto the piling next to him, only half out of the water, but half was better than none. "Thought I lost you, kid."

"I'm n-not . . ." As soon as I hit the air, I began to shiver again. "I'm not that easy . . . t-to lose."

"I'd drink to that, if I still had my flask," Dean said. He squinted across the river. "It's all gone. The Engine. The city. Lovecraft is eating itself."

I looked away. I didn't want to see my old home, the cold streets and Ravenhouse and my mother's asylum.

My mother . . .

"My *mother*!" I shrieked at Dean. "She's still there . . . I have to go back!"

Dean snatched me before I fell into the river again, but his arms couldn't contain the swell of fear. Nerissa and I did not behave like mother and daughter, had never behaved that way, but she was my only mother and she was trapped in a dying city where the Folk were running free. I had to find her, had to take her somewhere the Iron Land engendered couldn't touch her.

"We'll come back for her," Dean said, rocking me. "We'll come back. She's locked down in a madhouse; she'll be all right. You have my word."

I didn't have the strength to fight his arms any longer, and I collapsed back against the pilings.

"It's all gone wrong," I rasped. My throat was raw from the water and the smoke that even now filled my nose.

I pulled my legs up to my chest, keeping myself as dry as I could, even though the wind meant that hypothermia would already be setting in. I'd escaped the Engine and Tremaine only to die under a bridge.

"The awful thing," I said, "is that I was starting to feel bad for Tremaine. His dying world. His poor, subjugated people. His cursed queen."

"I'm not going to say that I told you not to trust the Folk," Dean said. "I think you've learned it by heart."

"It's not easy to be ground under a heel your entire existence," I said. "That, I understood."

I was starting to shake, to lose feeling in my hands. My head was floating and I gave a light giggle. "I understood. How stupid am I, Dean?"

479

"Shit," he said, rubbing my arms and back. "You're sliding under. Stay with me."

"That feels nice," I said. I knew that I was detaching, my mind like a dirigible drifting away.

"Aoife . . . ," Dean started, and then stripped off his jacket, wrapping it around me. "Dammit, Aoife, don't you check out now."

A rumble and a roar penetrated the warm, buzzing world I'd found myself in, and I looked up, irritated that yet another disaster was going to overtake me. "What now? Hasn't the city been thoroughly destroyed yet?"

"Harry!" Dean bellowed. "You swamp rat! Where've you been?"

I shaded my eyes to watch the oblong shape of the *Berkshire Belle*, much patched and welded where she'd plowed into the ground, swing low over the river and come to rest above the waves.

The hatch slid up, and Cal peered out, extending his hand. "Climb aboard! Make it fast—there are ravens everywhere!"

Dean handed me up, and when the warmth of the cabin hit me I collapsed on the nearest bench, shivering uncontrollably. Dean hopped into the hatch and pointed at Cal. "Blankets and a hot water bottle if you have it. She's in a bad way."

The *Belle* lurched and Harry shouted from the cockpit. "Where to, *mes amis*?"

I turned my back on the wreckage of Lovecraft, looking west, toward Arkham, and curled inside the blanket Cal draped over my shoulders. "I want to go home."

39

The Fate of Graystone

Dean slept on the flight back to Graystone, but the rocking motion of the *Belle* failed to soothe me. Instead, I got out of my seat and made my shaky way to the cockpit, to stare over Harry's and Jean-Marc's shoulders at the landscape below.

"You all right, mademoiselle?" Harry demanded. I tried to smile at him but it hurt.

"I suppose I'll live." I'd stopped shivering and mostly dried out, but the ache of falling into the freezing water was prodigious. My head still rang from the Weird, and I'd watched my nose stop and start bleeding three times since Harry had snatched us from the jaws of the river.

"Coming up on the village, Captain," Jean-Marc said. "And it's a pitiful sight."

The ship passed small fires burning like ghoul eyes in the fading light, over wrecked jitneys in the street and prone bodies lying facedown on the cobbles.

"What's happened?" Cal said, coming to stand next to me. "The whole town's blazing."

I felt an awful premonition creep along my spine and into my twinging shoggoth bite, and turned to Captain Harry. "Can we go faster?"

"We are at the mercy of the winds now, *petite,*" Captain Harry said. "And the ill wind, she's blowing over your valley."

As we crossed the empty field and drifted up against the mountain, I saw more and more signs of carnage. Blood smearing the cut cornstalks of the fields. Dead crows circled by worrying, cawing live ones. Dark shapes that darted from shadow to shadow, like liquid.

The rising moon overhead was swollen and yellow, nearly full. Ghoul howls echoed from the mountain, and the only respite I saw was that Graystone was not blazing like Arkham.

"Set it down. Set it down!" I shouted at Harry, already scrabbling for the hatch. It was my fault the Folk's monsters were lose, my fault that bodies were littering Arkham's streets. Tremaine had played me, and it had worked. The barriers between Thorn and Iron were no more.

Harry lowered the dirigible only long enough for me, Dean and Cal to jump off. He hollered at us from the cockpit, "Good hunting, *chère!*" and then with a whirr of fans the *Belle* was gone.

40

The Enemy of Thorn

IN THE SILENCE, I heard the hiss of a nightjar from the garden.

Cal's nostrils flared and Dean's switchblade came out. "We got some uninvited guests," he said.

"They're everywhere," Cal said. "All over the garden. Under the porch . . ." His eyes went round and milky in the twilight. "Bethina."

Cal shifted into ghoul on the fly and took off at a four-legged run for the house. I thought that poor Bethina was about to get the shock of her life, if she hadn't already.

"He had the right idea, doll," Dean said. "About making tracks for inside, I mean."

A nightjar crawled away through the apple orchard, and from the roof tiles, a springheel jack snarled at us before leaping from cupola to ground in one fluid motion.

"Definitely the right idea," Dean said, and we ran.

The creatures were everywhere, crawling over the house itself. "Why are there so many of them?" I shouted to Dean, though I had an idea. Maybe there had always been this many horrors lurking in the shadows of Thorn.

"Figure it out later!" Dean shouted, and that also was a good point. We slammed and locked the kitchen door behind us as something ran into the other side, scrabbling and chittering and making the hinges bow from the impact and the assault of its claws.

I braced the door while Dean grabbed a kitchen chair and stuck it under the knob. When I let go, I nearly fell into the arms of a ghoul.

He didn't look anything like Cal, Toby or their mother—this was one of the cemetery ghouls, wild matted hair, wilder eyes, and a stench that could fell a war Engine. He snarled at me.

"You murdered Tanner."

I reeled away from him, until I realized I was backed into a corner. I heard soft whimpering behind me and turned slightly to find Bethina occupying the same space. "Are you all right?" I asked.

She shook her head, eyes wide and pupils vibrating with shock. Cal stood behind her, hand on her shoulder. Thankfully, he'd made himself look human again. We'd have a discussion about his deceiving Bethina, but this was most certainly not the time.

"Don't worry," I told her. "I've got it under control."

"How," Bethina gasped, "in *hell* can you have this under control, miss?"

More ghouls crept into the kitchen, and in the dim light they appeared all eyes and teeth.

484

I looked at Dean. He was watching each ghoul in turn, an expression I hoped to never see again on his face. Dean looked as hungry for a fight as they did, and his switchblade flicked open. "Who wants the first taste?" He grinned at the ghoul's leader. "It's silver-coated. I hear you puppy dogs don't much care for that."

Graystone whispered to me frantically, pleaded with me to rid it of its interlopers. The Weird wanted to open itself up, wanted it so badly it made my heart beat out of time.

The Weird had unleashed the ghouls in the first place, brought every awful thing to bear on the Iron Land.

I supposed it was time my Weird did something good. I touched Dean on the arm. "I think you'd be better served by giving us some light, please."

He looked at me for a long moment and then nodded. "I dig you, princess."

To Bethina, I murmured, "Cover your eyes."

Dean gave the kitchen aether globes a nudge, just a shove, with the wicked bit of wild magic that always wrapped around him. A globe cracked, then another, and then in a brilliant flash the aether exploded, contacting the air and sending the scent of burning parchment running through the hallways of the house.

I reached out to every trap and trigger in Graystone with my Weird, brought them to bear on the ghouls as they howled and clawed at their faces, their night-blackened eyes dazzled by the blue fire of the aether.

The house responded to me, with a vengeance. I could hear the howls and cries resounding from top to bottom as the clockwork fed on its Folk intruders, and the ghouls

485

broke for the kitchen doors and windows, fleeing before they became like Tanner.

It was dark again in two and a half seconds, the aether burned out as quickly as one blows out a candle. My dazzled eyes couldn't see a thing, but Dean found me. "We got them," he said. "Traps all sprung. Not a living thing in this house besides you and me and Bethina and, er, . . . the kid."

Cal held up a sobbing Bethina. "She needs to sit down."

"Take her to the library," I said faintly. The Weird hadn't overwhelmed me this time, hadn't tried to swallow me alive. Cold comfort after what I'd done.

"Library's a good idea for all of us," Dean said. "It's safe there."

"At least from the Folk," I muttered. I wasn't sure, as I trailed after Dean, about myself.

The danger inside the house was dead, but as we hurried into the library and barred the doors, the howling outside did not cease.

"Something's stirred my brothers," Cal said softly so Bethina couldn't hear. "Stirred everyone. There's a Wild Hunt. First I've ever seen. Thought such things went the way of horse-drawn jitneys."

Bethina and Cal huddled together while Dean lit the fire in the library grate. I wondered if Cal would ever tell her, or if, like me, he would carry a secret to the grave.

"The queens are awake," I said. "And I think . . . I *know* I'm responsible for all of this."

486

Dean blew out his lighter and put it back in his leather. "We're safe for now. They can't get past the clockwork."

"Did you not hear me?" I demanded. "I did it, Dean. Magic is walking the world. The gates are down. I did that."

"Aoife." Dean came and wrapped my fingers with his. "Don't think of that."

"What am I supposed to think of?" I demanded. "How Draven wanted to ensnare me to ensnare my father? How Tremaine wanted to burn me to ash? If I think of anything besides what *I* did I really *will* go mad."

I jerked away from him and paced to the window, looking down at the ghouls and springheel jacks roaming through the orchard and the garden.

"I've never seen ghouls like this," Cal said again. "It's like a war zone out there."

"That's what Tremaine said," I murmured, pressing my forehead against the glass. "He said it was a war. He wanted this to happen."

"Waking up the queens must've sent out some waves," Dean said. "But wouldn't they take the throne and have done? I would."

"The queens have to be awake," I said. "To keep Thorn alive. But they aren't in charge. Tremaine is the Regent and he makes the rules. He made that very clear." The nightjars in my view were turning on one another, having decimated every other living thing in the garden.

A mortal curse in the Folk's lands. Cast by Draven, who either had been tricked into thinking his campaign against the Folk had just reached its greatest success or was in league with Tremaine.

487

I didn't care. What mattered was that I was just as gullible. I'd done exactly as Tremaine had planned for me to do. Conrad and my father had held out, had refused to play into the Folk's hands. Whereas pliant little Aoife had fallen in line with Tremaine because she felt sorry for him.

The memories unspooled like a needle under the skin. My first encounter with Tremaine. Draven's smirk. The doctor who'd stared at me with his mossy eyes. The same eyes that looked back at me from the rippled glass now.

"You know who I am, Aoife."

It was my father. My father had saved my life. I felt a flutter in my chest. He hadn't left me in the end, hadn't believed I shouldn't have had anything to do with my birthright. He'd helped me as much as he could.

And I'd betrayed him. I'd betrayed every one of the Graysons, Conrad, even Nerissa. Draven had the witch's alphabet. Tremaine had his queens, his open gateway, his place ruling the Thorn Land, which was no longer dying, but was awake and hungry after hibernation.

All I had left was my Weird, but I was not bowed. I had Dean, and Cal. I had my wits, and I still had my mind.

I could stay away from the cities. I could find a way to stave off the iron madness, and I could get the witch's alphabet back.

I would find my father and the truth.

As the first sliver of hope in a very long time slid back into view, every light in Graystone went out.

Bethina screamed, and her tea mug shattered on the library hearth.

"Stay calm!" Dean shouted. "Find Aoife."

"She's there," said Cal, his eyes like lanterns in the full dark. "By the window."

Outside, a blue flash lit the garden for just a moment, a streak of heat lightning in the coldest part of the year.

My shoulder twinged and my Weird rubbed against new magic in the room. In the blue, witchly light I saw three figures: two short and one tall, two crook-backed and elfin-faced and one with shaggy black hair, a tattered tweed blazer and a face that mimicked my own.

My heart twitched, stopping my breath for just a moment before I flew to the tallest figure and threw my arms around him. "Conrad!"

"Hey, little sister," he whispered. "I'm home."

I pressed my face into him, memorizing his warmth and his scent, the bony rib cage I thought I'd never embrace again. "I thought you were dead. He told me you were dead." Even after Tremaine had admitted he'd lied, I'd thought I'd never see Conrad again.

"I know," Conrad said. "I know you did, and I'm sorry."

"How did you . . . where have you . . ." My questions tumbled over one another, tangled and fell.

"All I can say at this moment is that we have to leave," Conrad told me. "The Winter Folk are coming for all four of you—their scouts are in the garden."

Another flash of lightning, another glimpse of the creatures skittering through the shadows. They were taller than nightjars now. Paler. With more teeth. Folk.

"Where can we possibly go?" I asked Conrad.

"There's one place where they can never find us," Conrad said. "The Land of Mists."

"No," Dean said instantly. "That's bad business."

489

"You don't get a choice, Erlkin." One of the two figures hunched behind Conrad spoke. It was little more than a shadow, its silver teeth the only solid thing. Bethina's shadow-people who'd come for Conrad. "The Wytch King commands it. You and the daughter and the ghoul and the mortal. To the Mists, now."

"Aoife, please," Conrad said. "I know I don't deserve your trust after what happened but I've changed. I've healed. The madness doesn't follow us into the Mists, and once you're away from the cities and the worst of the iron. We can stay sane if we stay out of the Iron Land."

Cal lifted his head, flaring his nostrils. "I smell silver and hawthorn trees. Cold blue blood."

"That's Tremaine and his Winter men," Conrad said. "We're out of time." He snapped his fingers at the Erlkin behind him. "We have to go back to the Mists. Now."

In the reflection on the window glass, a black shape grew and gathered, until our reflected images became a bottomless door, a swirling vortex in the flat of the windowpane.

"Come with me," Conrad said. "I promise, everything will be explained."

"In Lovecraft," I said. "In Ravenhouse. I saw our father."

"Impossible," Conrad said. "Archibald's been missing for months."

"I saw him," I insisted. "He got me out of there."

"Aoife," Dean said as glass shattered and gears shrieked in the bowels of the house. The traps whirred to life against an overwhelming attack. "We should go with him, much as I hate to say it."

490

I looked from Conrad to Dean, to Cal and Bethina, who clutched his sleeve.

"All right," I told Conrad. "But only for now. You better believe you're going to explain this to me when we're safe."

"Say it," Conrad said. "Or the gate doesn't work. Say that you trust me." He held out his hand, but I grabbed Dean's instead.

"I trust you, Conrad." I still did, in spite of everything. My brother was still my brother, and when he'd asked for my help those weeks ago he hadn't lied to me.

Conrad turned his eyes on Dean. "And how about you, halfkin?"

Dean's lip pulled back to show his teeth. "Only because I don't got a choice, friend."

"Anywhere has to be better than here right now," Cal agreed. "C'mon, Bethina."

"You have nothing to fear," Conrad said. "Not from me. Fear the events you've set in motion, and the ripples from this world to the worlds beyond." He held out his hand to the doorway. "Aoife. You first."

I shook my head, still holding on to Dean. "We go together."

"Together," Dean agreed. "Or not at all."

"Fine!" Conrad snapped. "Whatever you like, just *go.*"

He sounded more like my brother then, and a little of my trepidation vanished.

Dean and I stepped into the Mists as one, and blackness gripped me. Not the sick vertigo of Tremaine's *hexenring,* but a vast and windy emptiness that seemed to stretch on forever. I saw visions of Lovecraft, burning and forsaken.

I saw the lily field, trampled, and the glass coffins, shattered. I saw the stars and the eyes of the Great Old Ones, burning up space as they flew onward, infinite.

I was falling toward a place made of smoke and shadow, a darkness I had only seen in nightmares, but Dean was with me and Cal, Bethina and Conrad were behind.

I fell into the Mists, passing worlds beyond number as I did, while above me, the stars turned out of time, in a vast and darkening sky.

ACKNOWLEDGMENTS

Writing a novel is oftentimes a solitary and maddening pursuit, and I'd like to thank everyone who's aided or influenced me individually, but that would run on for pages, so I'll try my best here: My mother, Pamela Kittredge, who gave me a love of books and who never minded that I only wanted to read the scary stuff. My amazing literary agent, Rachel Vater, who took the Iron Codex from an odd idea to full-blown, contracted series of novels. Krista Marino, my endlessly patient editor, and the entire team of copy editors, publicists, marketing staff and designers at Random House for their unending support of Aoife and her story. The book would never have been finished without the encouragement of my fellow authors and friends: Mark Henry, Richelle Mead, Kat Richardson and Tiffany Trent. Special thanks belong to Cherie Priest, Sara McDonald and Stacia Kane for the literal hours they endured of my assuring them the book would never be finished and that I was going to be forced to go join a shady circus to make ends meet, because I was just no good at this writing thing. They kept telling me I could finish, and I did. And I'm not cut out for circus life, anyway. Any number of fabulous fellow writers influenced this story with their work, but I owe particular thanks to Mike Mignola, Holly Black, Ed Brubaker, Warren Ellis and Joe Hill. Joe, I'm sorry I inadvertently stole the name of your city. Feel free to steal it back. Finally, I want to thank everyone who introduced me to the finer and funner aspects of the steampunk community in Seattle and beyond—it's a brave new world, and I'm thrilled to be part of it, goggles, dirigibles and all.

ABOUT THE AUTHOR

CAITLIN KITTREDGE is a history and horror movie enthusiast who writes novels wherein bad things usually happen to perfectly nice characters. But that's all right—the ones who aren't so nice have always been her favorites. Caitlin lives in western Massachusetts in a crumbling Victorian mansion with her two cats, her cameras, and several miles of books. When she's not writing, she spends her time taking photos, concocting alternate histories, and trying new and alarming colors of hair dye. Caitlin is the author of two bestselling series for adults, Nocturne City and the Black London adventures. *The Iron Thorn* is her first book for young readers. You can visit her at caitlinkittredge.com.